I0831299

Eagle Rising

by

Shelly Greenhalgh-Davis

ISBN: 978-0-9821766-0-3

This book is printed on acid-free paper.

Timber Fork Publishing - rev. 11/06/2008

Prologue
Nebraska Territory
Autumn, 1870

The twilight foray on the rancher's cabin had lasted no more than a few minutes. One brave had thrown a blanket over the chimney, smoking the rancher out into the open where he was mercilessly exposed to those he had angered by his presence on their sacred land. Now he lay dead in the waning crimson light, pierced by seven Cheyenne arrows, blood dripping onto the cold ground.

Gray Wolf patiently waited while the others pillaged the cabin. He'd accomplished all he had come to do; he wanted nothing more. His companions returned, disappointed with their minimal spoils. Gray Wolf hardly looked at the grisly scene as he and the others turned to leave. An imposing brave with over forty winters behind him, he had long since stopped caring about having to mete out such justice to the invading enemy. That more would come was certain, but he would give them the same.

He thought again about the man he'd been longing to meet, the one he'd heard of so often but never seen. Just last night he'd had the dream again about him. The dream came more frequently now, and he knew their paths must cross. Gray Wolf had distanced himself on purpose till now, allowing the dust of past contentions to settle and wounds to heal. But enough time had gone by. He felt the season nearing when he might finally know the man who had become unwittingly entangled with his people but who, in the end, had shown his loyalty. That he could still show any degree of allegiance despite all that had happened meant everything to Gray Wolf, a sign that there was still hope for his family and an ally to be made. He wanted to question the man, to see how true and loyal his young heart was. But he dared not go to where the man lived, where he would be alone amongst the enemy. So he began praying the man would come to him. In his urgency, he had asked Chief Red Feather about it. Red Feather said the one he sought would probably come in the Moon When the Ponies Shed, bringing horses to their people. Red Feather asked no questions, for he alone understood Gray Wolf's compulsion.

Gray Wolf could bide his time a little longer. He interpreted the dreams to mean that his opportunity would come soon. The white men, the greedy and despicable white men, knew the man by another name, but Gray Wolf knew him only by the noble Cheyenne name he'd deftly earned for himself......Eagle Shadow.

Chapter 1
Fort Mason, Montana Territory
Spring, 1871

Major Joshua Blaine, his brown hair and mustache combed, uniform pressed, every brass button polished, sat straight and attentive in a chair across from the new commander. Lieutenant-Colonel David Gunning McHenry, "Ol' Gun" as his troops called him outside of his hearing, was a man whose gritty, no-nonsense reputation had preceded him to this frontier outpost defended by a garrison of three hundred men. Fort Mason was not a place officers requested as a post; it was a place to which they were assigned. Except in the case of Colonel McHenry. He had lunged at the opportunity to take over this garrison on what many believed to be the edge of the known world. He had scores to settle, and distance from interrogating superiors suited him.

Major Blaine's hat and gloves rested on his crossed legs as he sized up the large, gray-haired man before him with a meticulously trimmed beard.

"Colonel Estep told me I could count on you for anything," said Colonel McHenry's deep, throaty voice. "Said you're one hell of a soldier."

"Well, Colonel Estep was always generous with his compliments," Major Blaine modestly replied.

"I understand you had a hand in some negotiations with the Northern Cheyenne four years ago," the colonel continued. He referred to a paper in front of him and guided his index finger down the page till it landed on the line he wanted. "And you got a colonel demoted and reassigned to some guard duty position back East." He chuckled, and when there was no response, he looked up to see the major's reaction. "Is that true?"

"I was deposed, and I laid out the truth. I don't know what happened after that."

The colonel set the paper aside. "It doesn't matter. Have you spoken with leaders of the Cheyenne since then?"

"No, sir."

"They haven't come to you? They haven't told you anything?"

"Why would they?" Major Blaine could see that Colonel McHenry was waiting for more. "I'm not sure I know what you're getting at, sir."

"Unfortunately, it seems the treaty's been broken."

The major furrowed his brows. "By which side?"

"Ours, I'm afraid. There's some prime grazing land southeast of here a piece, right where these Indians bunk, and ranchers have begun staking claims there, about half a dozen of them, ignoring any legal papers, or maybe just not knowing any better. There's been an Indian attack on one of them already."

Major Blaine opened his mouth to speak, but Colonel McHenry cut him off. "Yes, I know they're breaking the law, Major. But there's not a lot we can do about it. We can't just force them to abandon their ranches."

"Why not?" queried the major.

Colonel McHenry raised an eyebrow and smiled. "I think you know more about soldiering than practical dealings with cattlemen. Anyway, the Cheyenne have been pushed up further into Montana. They're getting restless. Since this post was involved in setting forth the terms of the treaty, I fear they'll hold us directly responsible."

"Regardless of what I don't know about cattlemen, I believe we are responsible, Colonel."

"That's open to discussion." Colonel McHenry didn't like Major Blaine's assessment of a situation that seemed clear to him. He started to use his hands to make a point, but he quickly abandoned the thought and forged ahead with his original purpose. "We'll have to work with the Cheyenne, make a deal with them on that land."

Major Blaine shifted uneasily in his chair. Colonel McHenry hadn't dealt with the Cheyenne before. Granted, he was an intelligent man. He had graduated from West Point with honors, built an impeccable record of service in the War Between the States in which he'd risen to the rank of major-general, and was a personal friend of President Ulysses S. Grant. When the end of the war had left a flood of officers while enlisted men returned home to their families, he'd accepted the rank of lieutenant-colonel while still being allowed to wear his previous insignia. But he hadn't been in the Territory when the Battle of Mount Defiance had taken place in '66, or the confrontations that followed. He knew no more about the Cheyenne than the outgoing commander had told him. But he brought his pride and confidence to the position with him, and the combination seemed overbearing enough to worry Major Blaine.

"Do you have some kind of compensation in mind for the Indians?" asked Major Blaine.

"Oh, sure," the colonel readily replied. "We would naturally provide them with acceptable land in exchange. What I need is time to look the situation over carefully and see what I can do. You can help me by encouraging the Indians to be patient. You surely must know the influential figures among the tribe. Arrange to meet with them and explain our intentions."

Major Blaine chuckled. "I'm afraid I can't help you at all in that way. But I know who can."

"And who is that?"

"Someone who is on much better terms with the Cheyenne than I. I have a weekend furlough coming up. I'll be taking my family to Timber Fork for a wedding. I'll speak to him then."

"I leave that to you then. And give my regards to your lovely wife."

"Will do."

Chapter 2

It had turned out to be a clear day for the outdoor wedding of Jared Sinclair and Rebecca Madison of St. Paul, Minnesota. A solitary old oak provided a grand backdrop for the couple taking their vows. A soft, cool breeze fanned the faces of the dozens of guests that included a good number of the population of Timber Fork, Montana Territory and the immediate outlying areas. Here in one place for a day were ranchers, a cavalry officer, merchants who counted themselves among the business competition for the young groom and his father, their wives who insisted they attend, mischievous sons, dreamy-eyed daughters. Many were dressed very fine; some appeared to have scraped together what appropriate clothing they could manage. The noonday sun shone equally on all of them and fended off the April chill.

It would be a fine day for a funeral as well as a wedding, thought the black-haired, piercing-eyed Nate Hunter as he listened to the minister's voice drone on. When it came to dressing up and wearing the dreaded tie, one seemed just as unpleasant as the other to Nate. He couldn't wait to jump back into his buckskin leathers and moccasin boots. His Cheyenne beads remained tied snugly about his neck, hidden by the white collar and tie. He rarely removed those, and certainly not for a long-winded minister. The gunbelt holding his Colt .45 was strapped about his hip. He wouldn't give that up for the occasion either. The thirteen notches on the burnished oak grip were worn but still visible, an impulse of his youth.

Out of the corner of his eye, he glimpsed his wife Tara sitting beside him with proud and elegant posture in her dark green taffeta dress, a cascade of lace gracing her collar, her thick, light brown hair swept up and held in place with tortoise shell combs. She'd been named for the Hill of Tara, the legendary seat of power in her Irish grandmother's homeland. The name was every bit fitting. She carried herself like a queen exiled to a far frontier, a land she'd grown to love in the eleven years she'd been here.

She smiled broadly as she watched the ceremony, and Nate felt guilty. This was a big moment for her. Her little brother was getting married, and she had been so excited to help plan the first wedding ever held on the Broken Bow, their hundred-and-fifty-thousand-acre cattle spread that was just beginning to turn a decent profit after four years of sweat and hard work.

Nate's eyes scanned across the guests, many of whom he had known for a decade. What had changed in that time was their estimation of him. As the owner of the Broken Bow, he occupied a position no one would have expected of a one-time poor, unassuming ranch hand. But he had slipped right into the position with ease, and it was the confidence and assertion of his demeanor that had won the respect of the people of Timber Fork, a settlement now twice as big as when he had arrived with his parents and sister from the Platte River in Nebraska ten years before.

There were nine steady ranch hands in his employ; the number swelled by four or five during roundups and cattle drives. He was Mr. Hunter to all of them, but since many a day he worked alongside them, he had considered requiring less formality from them. It was Tara who had discouraged him from allowing it, saying that less familiarity and more distance would keep them in line and more willing to work hard. She ought to know, he figured. She was of the Sinclair family, still the most esteemed name in Montana Territory as well as Chicago.

Nate glanced over at the section where the numerous Chicago relatives were seated. Why on earth, he wondered, would they have been so eager to travel so far for such a long, drawn-out event as this? He couldn't understand it, but it didn't matter. Although he had little or nothing in common with any of them, he appreciated how willingly they had accepted him into the family. Tara had taken a big chance in marrying someone of his blood and background, but it was her family's backing that had swiftly put down any attempts to mar her good name. Regardless of the few who didn't like Nate, she was able to move among people comfortably—still, as always, a dignified lady.

She was also an astute businesswoman. While Nate had thrown himself wholeheartedly into the physical workings of the ranch, her administrative abilities were equally responsible for their success. When the cavalry at Fort Mason wanted to contract to buy beef from the Broken Bow, they were surprised when Nate sent Tara and he himself never even showed up to the meeting. She had charmed them all, even while she rewrote the contract they had prepared and negotiated them well over their proposed budget. How he had whooped and hollered when she showed him the paper. An errant colonel had once threatened to hang him, and now he had a government contract worth hundreds of dollars.

Nate craned his neck to see how Buck was doing, his three-year-old son who was standing beside the bride and groom and holding a small pillow with Rebecca's wedding band resting on it. The dark-haired, brown-eyed tyke had been named after Nate's Cheyenne father, and he was already displaying the independence and determination of his namesake, eliciting Nate's good humor and often Tara's frustration.

The boy was becoming awfully fidgety. His eyes met Nate's, the pained look on his little face begging to know how much longer he must stand there. Nate felt for him. As a half-Cheyenne, Nate could track a mosquito through the brush, and he had acquired skills sufficient to build the four-room cedar home in which they comfortably lived, and to boss all the ranch hands, yet he was utterly powerless to rescue his son from this harrowing experience. He offered Buck a smile and a wink which he figured would pacify him for at least a half minute or so.

At last the bride and groom had kissed and begun laughingly making their way up the aisle through the sea of chairs of assorted shapes and sizes that had been lent for this occasion by several families in town. Tara looked up at Nate with sparkling eyes. "Wasn't that beautiful?"

He squeezed her hand. "Yeah, it was nice."

***

The new couple was still shaking hands with guests on the porch when Tara seated herself on a chair on the lawn to sip her lemonade. The neat rows of chairs were beginning to be scattered across the lawn as guests found those with whom they were most comfortable and arranged their own circles for visiting. She caught sight of her best friend Julie Blaine and waved her over to sit beside her.

"So, another Sinclair getting out from underfoot, huh?" said Julie, smiling broadly, a few blond curls peeking out from her straw bonnet that protected her fair complexion.

"Not exactly. Jared will still run the store with Papa and live in the house. For Rebecca it only means moving across the street from her parents' home."

"And do you like your new sister-in-law?"

"Oh, yes. I think she'll be good for Jared. She's very fun-loving, and he's so serious, you know. Did you know that she is Ward Taylor's cousin?"

"Yes, I think I remember hearing that somewhere. She's from St. Paul too, isn't she?"

Tara nodded. "I believe it was around '64 when the Madisons moved here. You were in Oregon. They were like your family and wanted to see the frontier. That reminds me, what do you hear from your family?"

"They're still doing very well and living in the same place. I guess Pa figures he's moved as far as he can go since an ocean stopped him."

"Well, don't they have ships there?" asked Tara, drawing Julie's laughter.

Tara looked over to where Buck was playing with a sandy-haired, freckled-faced boy about his own size beneath the oak trees. "Your Mark has grown a bit since we last saw each other."

Julie raised her head proudly. "He's Josh's boy, that's for certain. He says he wants to be a soldier when he grows up. I need to get him away from the fort more so he can see there's more to life than what his father does."

"Good luck," answered Tara skeptically. It was so good to see Julie again and hear her familiar and contagious laugh. Tara always appreciated any moments she had with her childhood friend and continually worried that at any time she may move far away because of her husband's profession.

***

Nate was never pleased when Major Blaine wanted to have private words with him, for it was never good news. So when the two of them broke away from the wedding guests and settled into a corner of the parlor in the Hunter home, Nate made sure he had a glass of brandy in hand. He wondered if it would be enough. He should've brought the bottle, he concluded.

The parlor was simply but smartly furnished with a wine and tan rug with a flower and scroll pattern, a deep red upholstered sofa and a matching wingback chair. In one corner was an oak writing desk, and next to the sofa, in front of the window, was a small, round marble-topped table on which sat a lamp with elongated crystal prisms dangling from the etched glass globe. Some of the items had been wedding gifts from Tara's family and Nate's sister and brother-in-law Lena and Ward Taylor, belated gifts that had had to wait until there was a home sufficient to house them. Some items Tara had ordered herself from Chicago. She always wanted to make a good showing for the occasional business meetings held in this room.

As for Buck, he always liked to jingle the prisms on the lamp and watch the sunset light that streamed through the western window shoot through them and make glittering sparkles on the opposite wall. Nate could never figure out how in the world the top-heavy lamp had survived as long as it had without suffering a collision with Buck and being smashed into pieces.

The focal point of the room was the oil painting of the late Jerome Sinclair, the founder of the Broken Bow. It was a portrait done in his younger years, before Nate had known him. It had resided with a family member in Chicago who had shipped it out to Montana when the house was finished, as a housewarming gift. Although Nate had very much liked Jerome, he wasn't particularly fond of this likeness of him. It did not capture the kindness for which Nate remembered him. Instead, his stately, chiseled features stared out solemnly from the wall, constantly reminding Nate of the ideal he had to live up to. One of Jerome's hands was concealed inside his jacket, the American Napoleon, Nate called it, to Tara's amusement. The painting hung just above the chair where Major Blaine now sat, both of them watching Nate intently. He was outnumbered.

"So how many new calves you branding this year?" began Major Blaine.

"Let's cut through the chaff. How are you going to ruin my brother-in-law's wedding day for me, Major?"

Major Blaine burst into laughter. "Don't give me that, Hunter. If I know you, you can't wait for this day to be over with."

Nate bowed his head, smiling. Major Blaine did know him well.

The major looked up at the ceiling and thought for a moment. "I guess there's just one way to say this. The new commander says the treaty's been broken."

Nate stiffened. "And by white men, I'm assuming?"

"I'm afraid so. The Cheyenne are being pushed out by cattlemen. Some Indians are here in the Territory. I found out your bunch is with Red Feather about fifty miles southeast of here, camping on the Sun River. Colonel McHenry's afraid they're gonna cause trouble for us."

"For you," Nate corrected him.

"Yes, I told him you were on good terms with them."

Nate started to take a drink but then lowered his glass. "What do you want from me?"

"Colonel McHenry wants the Indians calmed down. I would like you to talk to them."

"And tell them what?"

"Just head 'em off from any more trouble till we can sort this out." Major Blaine could tell Nate's help would not come readily, and he began to talk faster. "The colonel is going to straighten this out, Nate. He's a good man, very experienced. He will make sure the Indians are given land and—"

"But not their ancestral land."

"Well, no, that's quite impossible by now."

"Oh, I don't think impossible is the word for it. What I think is that your Colonel McHenry wouldn't hesitate to make war on Indians who were taking over white men's lands, but when whites move onto lands belonging, by law, to Indians, he's not so troubled about that."

"Nate, you must understand our position. Our hands really are tied. We can't just drive out white settlers by force."

Nate narrowed his eyes and flashed a taunting smile. "What's the matter, Major? They give you a promotion and put a little gold decoration on your shoulder and you have to come and ask help from me to do your job?"

"Because I know you can help." Major Blaine took a quick glance through the doorway to be sure they were alone and lowered his voice. "I know you have your own agreement with the Cheyenne. You gave them horses once before, and you're planning to send another string this year. Now I didn't tell the colonel about that, but I think you ought to reconsider that, at least for the time being. I mean, helping out the Indians like that..." He hesitated, hating even to broach the subject with Nate. "It just doesn't look good, Nate."

Nate stood and slowly walked to the window and leaned against the wall beside the glass. Outside, he saw Buck playing with the major's son under the trees, chasing each other about, so innocent, so unaware of any weightier matters. He watched as Buck jumped on the major's son and wrestled him to the ground with hardly any effort, and he tried to conceal his proud smile. He downed his shot of brandy in one swig and turned to face the major with new and hardened resolve. "I'm not gonna tell the Indians one damn thing for you, Major. I've upheld my end of the bargain. I have no obligation to the cavalry except for a beef contract. Other than that, I don't exactly feel like doing something for them out of the goodness of my heart."

"Nate, please, I'm asking you—"

"No. It is your job, Major, to see that everyone abides by the terms of the treaty as written." He started to leave but stopped to point a finger in Major Blaine's face. "And my shipment of horses to the Cheyenne will still go through this summer."

Nate was finished with this conversation and left the frustrated major alone in the parlor. That Major Blaine had some nerve, thought Nate, grabbing his first opportunity to dump bad news on him in the middle of a party. Not one 'Hello, how've you been?' or 'Could we meet and talk, say, tomorrow at supper, or the next day? Or even next week better yet.' Nate was still shaking his head in wonder when he showed up at the outdoor table where Lena and Ward were dipping lemonade for guests from a cut-glass punch bowl.

Nate thought his sister pretty in her best flowered calico dress and her long black locks swirled up into a bun with some sort of butterfly hairpin on one side, but he guessed that she just might, almost, be as uncomfortable as he was. She had become cultured during a stay in Minnesota where she'd met Ward, although Nate preferred to think it was forced on her, but she'd been back on the frontier long enough to prevent certain ruination by city ways. She was a mother to two little girls who were being raised on a ranch as their mother had been, and doing just fine because of it.

Lena's husband, on the other hand, fit right in with such occasions as this, even owned several ties, but lucky for him, his curly brown hair never seemed to need combing.

"Lemonade?" asked Ward. He lowered his voice. "Or if you prefer, I have a secret bottle of brandy down here behind the table."

"It's no secret," replied Nate. "I found it an hour ago. But I'll have some more now."

"You don't even care for brandy," Lena reminded him.

Nate tugged at his tie in an effort to loosen it, but it wouldn't go any further."Well, it's a celebration, isn't it?"

"Yes," said Ward. "Try not to look so unhappy about it."

Nate looked over at the new couple standing nearby—Jared Sinclair, a tall, lean young man with straight blond hair, spectacles, and very storekeeper looks, and Rebecca, his beautiful bride of seventeen with her thick and curly auburn hair shining like a horse's mane against her cream white dress. "Your cousin looks positively stunning, Ward," he said, raising his fresh glass of brandy towards the couple in a silent toast.

"I fixed her hair," Lena proudly announced. "What do you think of it?"

Nate wasn't listening. He was eyeing Ward, knowing it wasn't the right time to break the news but not being able to hold it in any longer. "Major Blaine says the treaty's been broken," he blurted out suddenly.

"The treaty?" Ward looked blank for a moment, then his eyes lit up with sudden recognition. "Ah, yes, the treaty, the one I helped negotiate."

Nate was always amused by how Ward honestly thought he was a most integral part of the negotiations of four years before. "Yes, that one. But it looks like you should've shot for stronger wording of the part about what would happen to either side that broke the treaty."

"Oh, come on. I'd never done that before. How was I to know that…" It dawned on Ward that he was being teased. "Okay, fine. Why are you bothering to tell me about it?"

Nate shrugged and looked to Lena. "Blaine wants me to talk to the Indians, to make sure they won't try anything."

"What did you tell him?" asked Lena.

"I told him no." His eyes gleamed. "Ward can do it."

***

The party was finally winding down. Most of the guests had begun making their way to their wagons and carriages so they could return to Timber Fork before dark. Several young boys were picking up chairs and carrying them to the older men who were tying them to the wagons. The women and girls were collecting the many wedding gifts and arranging them in the wagon bound for the Sinclair home.

Tara headed for the kitchen with a tray of dirty glasses. The nervousness and excitement she'd experienced all day were now being replaced by a sense of accomplishment that the biggest gathering she'd hosted had gone well. Inside the house, she was met by the new Rebecca Sinclair.

"Could I talk to you privately, Tara?" asked Rebecca in her whisper-soft voice.

Her tone puzzled Tara. Rebecca had always looked up to her, like an older sister. More than once she'd confided in Tara and sought her advice, but Tara couldn't imagine what the new bride would want to discuss with her now. "Certainly," she replied. She deposited the glasses on a table and led Rebecca to her bedroom where she closed the door behind them and gestured to Rebecca to sit on the bed beside her. "What is it?"

Rebecca cast her cocoa brown eyes downward and began idly fingering her white lace handkerchief. "I don't know what to do, Tara."

Tara waited for her to complete what she was sure was an incomplete thought, but Rebecca remained silent. Confused, Tara shook her head. "You don't know what to do about what?"

"Tonight, in bed."

Tara's eyebrows raised in sudden revelation. "Ah, I see." She stared at Rebecca, not having the faintest idea how to reply.

"Well?" prompted Rebecca.

Tara squeezed Rebecca's shoulder. "It will be a wonderful experience I assure you. Why, you and Jared are so much in love and—"

"But I don't know what to do. I mean, I'm sure you remember your wedding night so I thought I'd ask you."

Rebecca had never put her on the spot quite like this, and Tara felt rushed to end this conversation. "Oh, Rebecca, I wouldn't want to spoil it for you with any preconceived notions. Jared ought to know—oh, my goodness—yes, I'm sure Jared will know exactly what to do. Now go to him. He's waiting for you." She stood up, placing a hand on Rebecca's arm as she did so, to urge her to come along. "Just relax. It'll be fine, I promise."

Rebecca appeared comforted, barely, but sufficient to bravely go and face her new life.

Alone in the room, Tara sat back down on the bed and stared at the wall. Yes, she did indeed remember her wedding night. There'd been a very simple wedding in the parlor of the Sinclair home with just her family, Lena, Ward, and Julie in attendance. It had been planned only the day before. Tara was sure Nate had planned it that way on purpose to avoid the Chicago relatives and the pomp that would accompany their visit, but she did get him to wear a black string tie borrowed from her brother. Her mother, Margaret Sinclair, had surprised her by presenting her with Tara's grandmother's wedding ring. Julie lent her the wedding dress she had made for her own wedding that had not yet happened. Margaret worried that there might be some kind of bad luck associated with the sharing of the dress, for either Tara or Julie. But Tara had assured her that if she wore her hair comb studded with blue sapphires, she'd have something old, something new, something borrowed, and something blue, and that should take care of any problems with luck. She'd then pass the hair comb on to Julie so she'd have good fortune as well.

Then there was the matter of the minister. He was feeling ill that day, but his wife, eager to see the long-awaited Hunter-Sinclair wedding, had drug him from his bed and helped him dress to go and perform the ceremony. Nate had suggested they come to the minister's house to spare him a trip down the street, but his wife insisted that he was just fine, so the poor man had to make do with a smile and sympathetic look from Nate and a pot of chicken soup brought over by Margaret the following day.

Having no home of their own yet, they spent that first night in a dugout on Elkhorn Creek on the north section of the Broken Bow. Nate had stayed there before, but Tara felt like a prairie dog. Nate went hunting and insisted on cooking her a special wilderness supper, the likes of which she had never tasted before. She reminded him she'd eaten pheasant, rabbit, deer, elk, even bear before; he couldn't surprise her. He went ahead anyway and wouldn't even let her watch him cook, but after she devoured a plate of his succulent stew, he declared that he was happy to see that she liked rattlesnake so much. Tara immediately ran into the bushes and vomited, then she laid into him with all the fury she could muster in her weakened state. He'd had to do a lot of talking before he was allowed to get in bed with her that night. But once the odd, chicken-like taste of the snake had worked itself out of her mouth, she couldn't stay angry. After all, only the day before she had wondered if he was even still alive.

The next day they worked together to put up a very small cabin and chinked it between the logs with mud. They lived there comfortably and happily through a harsh Montana winter and the following spring till Nate finished their house, just in time for the birth of their son Buck. The cabin still stood near the bunkhouse and was the abode of their foreman, Clay Tatum.

"What's that smile for?" asked Nate, who had slipped unnoticed into the room behind her.

Snapping out of her trance, her smile became a chuckle. "I was just thinking of when we were married, and of the stew you fixed that day."

"Oh, that," he sighed. "You would've been fine if I hadn't told you what it was." He collapsed onto the bed and closed his eyes. "I've had too much to drink, and I have a headache. Tell Lena and Ward goodbye for me."

Tara noticed that he looked exhausted. She was well aware that it had been a long day for him, but she was surprised at his drinking. It wasn't his nature. He appeared to have already drifted off to sleep, so she quietly slipped from the room to continue the cleanup.

***

As dusk gathered, Tara stood on the front porch, arms folded, and leaning against a cedar pillar, watching Jared and Rebecca's carriage grow smaller in the distance on the road that wound eastward towards Timber Fork. A cloudless cobalt sky arched over the carriage, portending a promising future for them. Tara basked in the feeling of successful completion of her part. She had started them out right. The rest was up to them.

Their carriage dipped out of sight below a swell in the waving grasses, and Tara's eyes were drawn to the old oak beside which they had been wed earlier. It was silhouetted against a blazing pink orange horizon now, counting down another sunset in its long life. Tara wondered at the stories the tree could tell as it witnessed seasons passing by, people now gone who had spent a moment or two in the shade of its branches. It now boasted a thick rope swing on which Buck loved to play.

She wanted to linger, but there was still much to do. She started to go inside the house but stopped when she saw a solitary figure walking toward her from the bunkhouse. "Hello," she called to Elijah Medley, a Broken Bow ranch hand and a good, steady worker.

"Howdy, Mrs. Hunter," replied Elijah as he arrived at the porch steps. He immediately removed his hat. His tousled blond hair swayed to one side in the breeze, and he was sporting the beginnings of a mustache. "Did you have a good time at your shindig today?"

"Yes, thank you."

"Clay had an errand to run up in town. He asked me to report the day's work to Mr. Hunter."

"Mr. Hunter is not feeling...well, he's asleep. You'd better report to me."

"All righty. Well, the good news is, we rounded up all those cattle out in Medicine Creek Canyon, and they look to have wintered pretty well. We branded eighteen calves there. The bad news is, we lost another calf last night in the north section."

"Oh no, not again," sighed Tara.

"It's those wolves, ma'am. They're gettin' more brave and venturin' further in each night."

"Put someone on a nightwatch out there, someone with good eyes and good trigger aim."

"Yes, ma'am." He stood still, looking up at her on the porch, almost admiringly.

Unfazed, Tara asked, "Is that all?"

Elijah quickly donned his hat. "Yes, ma'am." He turned to walk away, then halted. "Oh yeah, I meant to tell you, I'm almost done reading that book you lent me. I like it a lot."

"Good." Tara smiled. "When you're finished, I have another book I think you'll like, Alfred Lord Tennyson."

Tara watched him saunter back to the bunkhouse. These cowboys were all alike. They were respectful and polite, but they all watched her, not in an ogling sort of way, just sneaking glances when they thought she wasn't looking, like they didn't think she had peripheral vision. But they only spoke when spoken to, so that suited Tara just fine.

But this one was different. Elijah Medley had always been a drifter. Tara didn't know where he was from originally, just that he was "up from Denver," but she could detect the mere tracings of a genteel Southern accent. He didn't seem inclined to talk about where he was from, so Tara didn't ask. Nate had met him in town one day just as Elijah was preparing to leave for Nebraska. Nate offered him a job, and along with Clay Tatum, Elijah had proven to be invaluable to the struggling, new ranch. He was especially good with horses. Of his own accord and on his own time, he had begun rounding up and breaking in mustangs. There never was a horse he couldn't train, so Nate had expanded their business to selling trained mounts and made Elijah top wrangler. Nate had always been grateful for

Elijah because he figured the drifter would not stick around for more than one or two seasons, but now Elijah was beginning his fourth season on the Broken Bow, and he seemed content.

Elijah was one of the only hands who could read, and he especially loved poetry, so Tara was happy to lend him books since he didn't have any of his own. He was handsome and intelligent, and Tara wondered why he had not married by now. She had introduced him to eligible young women friends of hers in town on a few occasions, including Rebecca before she became involved with Jared. Although he was friendly and minded his manners, he never seemed very interested in them, unlike Clay Tatum who was always on an "errand in town" to court various women. Elijah's light clear blue eyes maintained their melancholy expression, and Tara imagined that in another life he could've been a brooding poet. But whatever was behind those eyes was still a mystery to everyone.

Back inside the house, Tara settled herself at her writing desk in the parlor and began the week's work on the payroll book. Nate had become a very able ranch boss, much like Tara's uncle, Jerome, but he detested paperwork. That he left to Tara, whose experience had been gained in her father's mercantile business.

She didn't hear Nate steal into the room until he pulled up a chair and sat beside her, resting his whole upper body on the desk where she worked. He looked drained but recovering.

"Buck's already asleep," he said.

Tara smiled. "He played hard today." She stopped working and looked up at him. "Why didn't you tell me the treaty was broken?"

Nate's eyes widened. "Don't tell me Blaine dumped this on you too. I bet that scoundrel asked you to talk to me to change my mind. I can just hear him now—"

"Lena and Ward told me before they left."

"Oh." He scratched his chin and contemplated for a few moments. "Do you think I should do as he wanted and go talk to the Indians?"

"Nonsense. That's the cavalry's responsibility. Besides, I don't recall the cavalry giving you any sort of reward for negotiating the treaty in the first place."

"Reward? Of course, there was a reward. I didn't get hung."

Tara disliked being reminded of that episode. "I mean the positive kind of reward."

"Well, there is the beef contract."

"That was a completely separate business arrangement and had nothing to do with the treaty."

Nate leaned back in his chair and smiled his admiration. It was the kind of statement he'd come to expect from the ever-business-minded Tara.

Tara hesitated a moment, then asked. "Nate, what do you think the Indians will do?" It was more than a mere question. There were memories, painful ones of past actions of the Indians. They remained buried for the most part, overshadowed by the passing of time and by the everyday concerns of running a ranch and raising a family, waiting for a day such as this to be aroused from their deep slumber.

Nate's demeanor turned serious. "I don't know."

"Do we have anything to worry about?"

"No, not us."

Chapter 3

Any attention on Indians was soon diverted, for shortly after the wedding, a fearsome, deadly evil slithered its way into the town and outlying areas. Probably borne across the plains by wagon teamsters, its source was, nevertheless, unidentifiable. And so it seemed to spring up from within and manifested itself as a debilitating sickness, exhibiting first by achiness and weakness, and continuing on through fever, nausea, delirium, and a suffocating cough. An influenza epidemic of this depth and magnitude had not been seen in Timber Fork before, and when many victims' illnesses progressed to pneumonia, and death seemed almost a surety, panic set in. In one month's time, over sixty settlers took sick, and two dozen died. The town's lone doctor, himself only superficially educated in medicine, was helpless in the throes of this epidemic and appealed to Fort Mason for help.

No such help had arrived when Nate visited the Split Timber Ranch where Lena and Ward Taylor's oldest daughter Laura lay weak and incoherent. Nate took one look at the child and knew that nothing short of a miracle would save her. It tore at his heart to watch his sister tirelessly caring for Laura, who by now was completely unresponsive.

"I know she can pull through this, Nate," said Lena, wiping the sweat from Laura's pale brow and pushing the girl's wet black hair off of her forehead. "She's strong. You know she is."

"Yeah, she is," whispered Nate. He couldn't watch any longer. He quietly slipped from the room and found Ward in the parlor, rocking his youngest daughter Sarah, who lay asleep against his shoulder. Nate slumped into a chair beside him and listened as Ward talked softly, as if to himself.

"Lena's stronger than I am. She never gives up." He stroked Sarah's brown curls, and his voice began to crack. "She's only three years old, Nate. I feel so helpless. What am I to do?"

Nate hated feeling helpless, hated putting up with circumstances beyond his control. It frustrated him to the core. There must always be a solution for everything, one more thing to try, no matter how futile. He sat up straight and furrowed his brow in concentration. "There is one thing we could do."

"What's that?" asked Ward skeptically.

"There's supposed to be a couple wagonloads of quinine coming out from Fort Mason. They should have left by now. If you and I ride to meet them, we could each load up as much as we can on our saddles and get it back a lot faster to treat the most sick people."

Ward's listless eyes brightened at the suggestion. He was immediately agreeable.

Without a moment to lose, Nate located Tara at the Sinclair store where she was helping to care for her sick father, Edward Sinclair, and informed her of his plan. In less than two hours, he and Ward were packed and ready to leave.

"Take care of my little angel," Ward said to Lena in the front doorway.

"I will." She gave Ward a hug and reached to squeeze Nate's shoulder. "Please hurry. We're all depending on you."

It seemed far easier to Nate to have a whole town depending on him than to sit and watch a little girl die. He was most eager to get going.

***

Nate and Ward simultaneously caught sight of two wagons far in the distance, tiny dots near the horizon, and halted their horses. "There they are," Nate announced.

Ward tilted his head back and closed his eyes. "Thank you," he whispered in a silent prayer. He viewed this as the moment that made the difference of life or death for his daughter.

It was the second morning of their trip. They had traveled fast, ate little, and slept less. Now as they whipped their horses into a run and raced side by side, the dots of the wagons grew steadily larger. In one instant, Nate's excitement turned stone cold. He jerked his horse to a stop so fast it almost sat down and signaled Ward to stop as well. He pulled his Colt .45 revolver and held it poised and ready as he stood in the stirrups.

Ward noticed Nate's eyes darting to and fro, not missing a single detail, and he was afraid to breathe. "What's wrong?" he whispered, not sure if he really wanted an answer or not.

Nate couldn't put a finger on it, but he knew something was terribly wrong. Three specks punctuated the sky above the wagons. "You see those buzzards circling?" he asked Ward.

"Yes," Ward quietly answered.

Nate could see no animals near the wagons, and none were hobbled nearby. He could see no person, and to Nate, who depended on his keen senses for everything, the silence was deafening. Waving his gun, he motioned to Ward to proceed with caution. They eased their horses forward at a walk while Nate stayed alert for signs of trouble. As they drew closer, a deathly stench permeated the air and made it obvious to Ward and Nate that no living thing had been here for a while. Closer yet and they could make out the forms of dead mules, still in harness, lying crumpled on the ground in front of the two wagons.

As they approached the gruesome sight, Nate dismounted with gun still in hand, still on his guard. Flies buzzed over the mule carcasses, rotting in the sun. The smell was sickening, and Nate put a hand over his mouth and nose. The only movement visible was the wagon canvasses, which hugged the bows loosely and flapped in the breeze, making a particularly lonely sound. Ward joined Nate on foot, and they began a frantic search of the area for the wagon drivers. They knew what they would find, but still, it was a shock to see the scalped bodies of the two men lying side by side in a shallow ravine. They hiked down into the ravine, and Nate solemnly knelt by the first man and inspected the arrows protruding from his shoulder and chest. His blue pants with a gold stripe down the side identified him as a cavalry teamster, but his boots, hat, and gun were missing.

"Indians!" It was a struggle for Ward to get the word out. He turned away and scrambled out of the ravine.

Nate's mind was clouded with shock, rage, and confusion. This was obviously the work of Indians, but he resisted the thought of Chief Red Feather's band being involved in this. It was not what he expected of them, despite anything Major Blaine had told him. A rogue faction maybe? Why would they have struck here, and now?

But for now, he must curb his scattered emotions. Personal matters were more pressing. He could already hear Ward rummaging through the wagons, and he knew Ward's only thought was of his daughter. He joined Ward at the wagons where they searched through chopped-up wooden crates, broken glass bottles, and straw padding. Nate was filled with dread as he crawled across the floor of one wagon, rifling through loose boards and straw, not caring that his hands were bleeding from cuts from glass. He was sure that if he willed it to happen, he could find at least one bottle of quinine intact. But after searching both wagons and the ground around them with no success, he pounded a bloody hand against a wagon box in frustration while Ward looked on, pale and distraught.

They had been told by the town doctor that this quinine might not even do much good for the sickest of the people, but it had been the only hope. Now that hope had vanished into thin air.

Nate surveyed the grisly scene once more. This work had been done a couple of days before. Where had the killers disappeared to since then? Was this the beginning of a rampage? A new urgency seized Nate's heart. "Ward, get on your horse and head for home."

"What are you gonna do?"

"I'll bury these men, then I'll go on to Fort Mason and report this."

"I'll help you bury them," offered Ward.

"No, go home to your family now!"

The sternness of his command was not lost on Ward. Without another word, he retrieved his horse, mounted up, and raced off into the direction from which they'd come.

***

Nate sat stiffly in a chair across the desk from Major Blaine, who had just learned of the massacre from him.

Blaine rubbed his forehead in exasperation. "And you're certain it was Cheyenne?"

"Most likely," Nate heard himself saying. He still could feel no certainty, no matter how obvious it seemed. Was he blinding himself to the truth, he wondered, just because he didn't want to believe it?

"I'll form a detail to go clean up the mess and try to track those Indians," said the major.

"You won't get far. The trail's already cold."

"But you could track them. I know you could."

Nate stood. "I have to get back to Timber Fork."

Major Blaine's expression turned incredulous, and his voice rose. "Come on, Nate, even now you're refusing to help me? What is the matter with you? How can you be so complacent?"

He had touched a raw nerve, and Nate was incensed. "You expect way too much of your supposed friendship with me, Major. I owe you nothing, and don't you presume to draw me into your problems!" He headed for the door.

"Nate!" shouted the major. "You can't hide from this! If you're not going to help, won't you at least talk to Colonel McHenry and advise him?" His voice softened, hoping to tempt Nate with a different approach. "Maybe you could ask for leniency for the Indians. Don't you want that?"

Nate returned to the desk. He had never wanted so badly to punch the major. Instead he slammed a fist on the desk, his eyes blazing. "My father-in-law is very sick, and I don't even know if my niece is still alive as we speak. I am going where I am most needed right now." The major tried to talk, but Nate's voice rose to a crescendo and drowned him out. "I don't have time to play politics with you people!" Again he turned away, but he stopped at the door. "Is there any more quinine I can take back with me?"

"Those two wagonloads were all we had. We won't get more in till next week."

Nate nodded in acceptance. It was just one more outrage in a string of them. "I saw the new Gatling gun outside. Bet you had no problem getting *that* here." He left before Blaine could reply.

Chapter 4

Laura Taylor hung on for one more day after Nate's return to Timber Fork. She died clutching a rag doll, her favorite toy, and surrounded by her parents and Nate and Tara. A grief-stricken Lena shut herself in her room for a whole day and would not speak to anyone. When she did, she insisted that Laura not be buried in the town cemetery but on the Split Timber in a spot near the house under a large pine tree where she had loved to play.

The day after Laura's burial found Nate and Tara at the bedside of Tara's father, Edward Sinclair. Edward's wife Margaret had tirelessly cared for him, and now she sat on the edge of the bed, holding his weak, shaky hand.

He had put up a valiant fight, reminding Nate of an old war horse that was tough to put down. Nate and Tara had had great hope that he would emerge the victor, but now, with his peaked face gaunt with days of sickness, his strength was played out. In just days, he seemed to have aged many years.

Edward endured a wheezing coughing spell, then he struggled for a breath and whispered Nate's name.

Nate leaned closer to the white-haired figure in the bed. "Yes, sir."

"You're worried about trouble with the Indians?"

Nate had not wanted to cause him any concern, but as he looked into Edward's knowing eyes, he knew he couldn't fool him, even now. "Yes, sir."

"I know you'll do the right thing. You always have."

Nate tried to reply, but no words would come out.

"Always," Edward continued. "When you went to make the peace four years ago and I didn't think you could, I was wrong, and you were right." He swallowed and struggled for a breath. "When you told me you could build up the Broken Bow again, you were right."

Truly humbled, Nate felt the need to place credit where it was due. "Everything I learned, I learned from you and your brother Jerome."

Edward managed a smile of appreciation for the compliment. "I have no fear in leaving my daughter and grandson in your care."

Nate pursed his lips, trying to prevent the lump in his throat. He wasn't ready to say goodbye to Edward.

Edward mustered all of his strength to say one more thing. "I've been proud to call you my son."

Nate's composure caved, his eyes clouded with tears, and he quickly looked away. He heard Tara's muffled sobs next to him. She knew how much that statement meant to him. Ever since he had married Edward's beautiful and treasured daughter, next to her and their little boy's safety and happiness, earning

Edward's full respect was what had always meant the most to him.

Jared and Rebecca and Tara's younger sister Rachel were called into the room. Within the hour, Edward had passed away. As Tara reached for Nate and cried in his arms, he knew he must be strong for her, but no one knew how much he would miss Edward. Nothing had come so close to when he had lost his own parents.

***

On the day of Edward Sinclair's funeral, over a hundred and fifty mourners gathered in the town cemetery to say goodbye to an honored citizen and businessman. One of the first settlers of Timber Fork, Edward had been a man of powerful influence across the Territory. Whether in business dealings or relations with the Indians or with the cavalry at Fort Mason, his was the opinion that swayed the local populace. He was laid to rest next to his brother Jerome. Together they had come from Chicago eleven years before, and between the success of Edward's store and Jerome's Broken Bow Ranch, they had made a mark that would last for years after they were gone.

To Nate, it seemed like part of Timber Fork was being buried. The Broken Bow was what had brought Nate's family from the Nebraska Territory when he was just fourteen years old. Over the next four years, he had honed his cattle ranching skills, but unlike other hands, he had also silently watched Jerome Sinclair from afar, eagerly absorbing snippets of information about the work of an expert rancher. He would never forget the day he had approached Edward about buying the Broken Bow. He had no money or collateral, but Edward had been willing to give his future son-in-law a fair shake. Nate had promised to restore the ranch to the greatness it enjoyed before the massacre of '65, and Edward had trusted him to do it. Nate truly believed that no one else in the world would have given him such an opportunity at that time, and he had bent over backwards to make his annual payments to Edward in full and on time. Now as he held Buck and stood beside Tara at the graveside, he was at least grateful that Edward had lived long enough to see the growing ranch being successful.

Tara faltered and leaned on Nate, and he grabbed her arm to steady her. He looked into her face and was alarmed by her pallor. "Are you all right?" he whispered.

She blinked a couple of times and nodded but still clung to his arm tightly. He did not hear any more of the service.

Chapter 5

Elijah Medley felt terrible about Tara losing her father. He hadn't known Edward very well personally, but he knew this was hard on Tara, and thus it was hard on him too. He stewed for hours over how to express his sympathy to her, subtly enough for his shyness to allow and within the bounds of propriety. He finally settled on just asking her how she was coming along and leaving the way open for her to respond however she wanted. He took along a poetry book of hers that he intended to return, and on his dinner break, he approached the front door of the Hunter home and knocked. He turned and looked out at the range while he waited. Everything seemed so quiet. All the cow hands were across the valley in Medicine Creek Canyon. Only he and a partner had spent the morning at the corrals breaking in some new saddle broncs. The house was even unusually quiet, and he wondered if Tara was in town at her mother's home.

Just as Elijah's hand was raised to knock again, he heard the doorknob turn, and the door slowly creaked open. Tara's face appeared around the edge of the door, as if she did not want to be fully seen. Elijah was shocked by her appearance. Her skin was ashen, and her usually bright blue eyes were listless and distant. It seemed to have been a major effort for her to open the door, and she now leaned against it for support.

"Oh, Mr. Medley, I'm glad you're here," she said, rubbing her forehead. "Where's Mr. Hunter?"

"He's been up in Medicine Creek Canyon all morning, ma'am."

"Please find him and tell him to come home. Buck's real sick, and I'm so worried."

"Mrs. Hunter, you don't look so good yourself. Can I get you…"

As he spoke, her eyes rolled upwards, and she began to slide down against the door. The poetry book fell to the floor of the porch as he bolted through the doorway and caught her as she crumpled into his arms. He knelt holding her for a moment as his heart pounded and he wondered what to do with her. He looked into the house behind her and saw two doors at the back, one on either side of the fireplace. He rose to his feet with Tara in his arms and carried her across the room. He picked the door on the left, turned his back to it, and pushed his way through. By the window was a neatly made double bed on which he laid her.

For just a fleeting moment, it occurred to him—this was her bed, where she slept every night. He immediately banished the thought, ashamed of himself and angry for wasting precious time.

"No, I can't lie down," Tara suddenly said, startling him. "I've got to take care of Buck." She tried to rise, but Elijah's strong arm stopped her.

"I'll look in on him for you. You just rest, okay?"

She seemed to accept the offer and relax more, so Elijah pulled the blue and green quilt over from the other side of the bed and carefully tucked it close around her. Giving her one last, concerned look, he exited the room and headed for the door on the other side of the fireplace. In that room, he found the little boy asleep with a thick blanket drawn up to his neck, his wan face visible above it, centered angelically on a white goose down pillow.

Elijah slowly backed up the way he had come and stepped carefully towards the front door to keep his boots and spurs as quiet as possible. When he had made it outside again and eased the door softly shut behind him, he bounded down the porch steps and ran for the stable. He was much relieved when his horse cooperated when he slipped the bridle on its face and mounted it bareback. He kicked into a gallop for Medicine Creek Canyon.

Soon after, in the rocky confines of the canyon, he followed the sound of lowing cattle till he met up with the small herd being driven in his direction. He found Nate riding point and halted in front of him.

"Mr. Hunter, you gotta get home right away."

Nate pulled up his reins. "What is it, Elijah?"

"Mrs. Hunter and Buck are real sick."

Nate's brows furrowed. "You've seen them?"

Elijah nodded. "I just now came from the house."

Nate's momentary stare hid the uncommon fear that seized his heart. Without a word, he turned his own horse and raced toward the mouth of the canyon.

Elijah didn't like leaving behind the situation up at the house, but he knew what was expected of him. He fell right in, taking Nate's place riding point.

***

Arriving at the house in near-panic, Nate caught sight of the poetry book lying on the front porch. Any other day he would've paused to smile to himself about that—*there she goes again, trying to introduce some culture to the hired hands.* But today he snatched up the book, dropped it on a table inside the house, and went first to his and Tara's room. He knew what influenza looked like; he'd seen his share of it in the past few weeks, but still, he couldn't possibly prepare himself for seeing Tara so ill.

Next he stole quietly to Buck's room, felt the boy's burning forehead, and his heart sank. This had all happened so quickly. He'd seen them looking well only a few short hours before. He gently gathered the blankets around Buck, picked him up, and carried him into the main bedroom where he laid him on the bed beside Tara to better care for both of them.

He took a deep breath, trying to calm himself and gather his scattered, confused thoughts. He must first try to bring their fevers down. He fetched a couple clean cloths and a bucket of cool water from the well outside the back door. Sitting on the edge of the bed, he stroked their foreheads, cheeks, and necks with the wet cloths.

The coolness roused Tara from slumber, and she seemed relieved to see Nate beside her. "Thank goodness you're here, Nate. How is Buck?"

"He's going to be fine. He's lying beside you. I'm going to take care of you both."

"I'll throw this off, Nate. I'll be okay. It's Bucky I'm worried about. He's so young."

"But he's a tough boy."

"I don't want you to get sick, Nate."

"I won't," he answered confidently. It was the first thing he'd said of which he felt absolutely sure. He'd had a slight fever a couple of days before, but he'd fought it off without even slowing his pace. It was his wife and son who concerned him, and he wasn't sure what to do. He'd seen the doctor in town bleed Laura Taylor and Edward, but he knew better than that. All that had done was weaken them. He didn't even feel inclined to call on the doctor now. He wasn't about to turn over his family's care to someone else, someone who couldn't possibly care about them as much as he.

He urged them to sleep when they could while he spent the afternoon sponging them and giving them water to drink. By nightfall both were markedly worse, and Buck had developed a severe cough. Nate felt helpless as all he could do was hold Buck and comfort him till each coughing spell passed.

Tara was inconsolable. "Nate," she cried, "he's getting worse so fast. What are we gonna do?"

"He's gonna pull through this same as you," Nate firmly insisted.

He sat up the whole night with them. In between caring for them and while they fitfully slept, he sat by the window and looked out at the ghostly silhouettes of trees in the yard and, above them, at the hundreds of stars that formed a celestial umbrella over the Broken Bow. Somewhere in a faraway valley beside a crystal clear river, those same stars shone down on a group of Cheyenne tepees. Nate suddenly missed Chief Red Feather and wished he could talk with him now. He didn't know why. He wasn't particularly close to the chief. But he had gained a great deal of respect for him during the peace negotiations of '67. Red Feather had never seen little Buck, and Nate wanted very much to show him his pride and joy. He had determined that as soon as Buck was big enough, he would take him along on a horse drive to the Indians.

Buck's coughing shook him from his reverie. He clasped the boy's hands and contemplated. He was beginning to latch onto an idea, one which seemed desperate and crazy at first, but which took on a more realistic air towards morning. He didn't trust the town doctor, but neither could he do this himself. He was going to need help. By daybreak he was hurriedly packing his poke and readying blankets and canteens. He was a little apprehensive about this decision, but inaction could only be worse, he told himself.

When the knock came at the door, Nate had no time to stop and answer it. "Come in!" he called. He looked up in surprise when Lena entered.

"I saw Clay Tatum up in town last night, and he told me about Tara and Buck," said Lena. "How are they?"

Nate shook his head. "It's bad, Lena."

"I came to help out."

"I appreciate that, but I won't be needing you. I'm taking them to the Cheyenne."

Lena's mouth dropped open. "You're what?"

Nate couldn't make eye contact with her, and he busily went about filling a canteen from the water bucket on the tabletop.

Lena moved closer to him. "You would entrust your family to those Indians after what they did to Laura?"

"They'll know what to do for Tara and Buck. They have cures the white man doesn't even know about."

Lena's eyes blazed. "They murdered my daughter when they destroyed the medicine in those wagons."

Nate looked squarely at her. "They did not murder Laura! She was very sick. The quinine might not have helped her. If I'd thought of it in time, maybe the Indians could've done something for her."

Her voice softened. "We'll never know, will we?"

Her sorrow tugged at Nate's heart. He couldn't expect her to understand, but he tried anyway. "Lena, I knew you wouldn't approve of this. But there's nothing else for me to do."

"You can wait for more quinine to come and pray like the rest of us."

"They don't have that long," he replied, struggling to keep his voice steady. "I'm desperate, Lena."

"The Indians who killed my little girl have no mercy on anybody. What makes you think they care about Tara and Buck? What makes you think they have any secret miracle cure?"

Nate slammed his fist on the table, causing water to splash from the bucket. "I don't know! Maybe they don't! I don't know anything! But I sure as hell can't sit here and watch them die while I wonder if there's something I could've done."

"You are killing them by taking them there, Nate!"

He resumed his preparations. "You still have a daughter, Lena. Go home to Sarah."

Lena was taken aback. "You're pushing me away, just like that, when I came to help?"

"Lena, please..."

She vehemently shook her head. "If you do this thing, I will never speak to you again."

"I know you don't mean that. You're still grieving over Laura. It's too soon—"

"I do mean it. This is an outright betrayal to me, Nate."

"I have never in my life been disloyal to you, Lena. And there's no reason I would start now. Don't you dare try to make me choose between you and them," he said with a nod towards the bedroom.

Lena stared, crestfallen, for a long moment. "All right. You do as you please." She started for the door.

"Lena, I'm sorry. Please don't leave like this."

"You go to hell!" And she was gone.

He still watched the door, even after she was gone, pained into silence for a moment, a bundle of confusion and mixed emotions. This whole situation had hit him unexpectedly, and he wasn't sure what the final result was going to be. Lena had never withheld her support from Nate for anything, and it hurt him fiercely. He was afraid that Laura's death would change her forever and that what he was doing now would cause irreparable damage to their relationship.

The awareness of time hit him, and he disciplined his mind to focus on the task at hand. After this confrontation with Lena, the whole trip would seem harder, but he felt that everything hinged on him putting it out of his mind for now.

Another knock came at the door. Hoping it was Lena returning, he rushed to open it. It was Elijah.

"Clay and I made the travois just like you said, sir. I hitched it up to the Appaloosa."

Again Nate struggled to calm his thoughts and focus. "Good, thanks. Now would you load up these supplies on the horse while I see to Tara and Buck?"

"Yes, sir."

Nate caressed Tara's cheek and whispered her name until she awoke and looked at him. "I'm taking you and Bucky to the Cheyenne."

"Oh, no, Nate, please. I don't wanna go there." She couldn't bare the thought of leaving her bed.

"It's all right, really. They will make you better. I've got a travois for you to ride on. I'll make you as comfortable as I can. This will work. I know it will."

She hadn't the strength to object. She dutifully pulled herself to a sitting position.

"No, I'll carry you," he offered. He gathered her up in the blankets, carried her outside and to the travois, and strapped her down snugly. Next he laid Buck beside her, and Tara cradled the boy close.

As Elijah handed the reins of the bay-colored Appaloosa to Nate, he asked hopefully, "Do you really think the Indians will make 'em all right, sir?"

"I hope, if I get 'em there in time. They're strong. That will help." He addressed himself more than Elijah. Remaining positive would be a key factor during this trip. He mounted his horse. "Will you do me a favor, Elijah? Will you go into town and tell Mrs. Sinclair what I'm doing? And tell her not to worry. She's probably on her way here right now."

"Sure, I'll go right away."

"I trust you and Clay to run things while I'm gone."

"You betcha. Good luck, sir."

Nate's arduous journey began. He was not certain where Red Feather's band was camped, but Major Blaine had heard they were near the Sun River. Nate's plan was simply to locate the river and follow it east. He expected to find signs of them in a couple of days.

Late in the afternoon, they skirted a small lake. Nate was disappointed that they hadn't gone far. His impatience was intense, but he could proceed no faster than a walk, and even then he could feel Tara and Buck's discomfort as they were jostled over rough terrain on the travois. He'd had Elijah thickly pad the travois with saddle blankets in hopes of affording some comfort and ease of travel, and he talked often to Tara and Buck, though not knowing if they could hear him.

This was a new experience for his horse, but the Appaloosa behaved well. The horse had once been owned by the Arapaho, but Nate had trained him to polished perfection as a cow horse. A subtle flick of the rein and the horse always knew what he wanted. Nate had never had a horse matched to him so well, and now, when the long day afforded him time to think, he found it odd that he had never given the horse a name.

The first night Nate sat leaned against a tree by the Sun River, holding Buck's shivering body, listening to his weak whimpers, and stoking the fire at intervals. Close to the fire lay Tara, covered in blankets and so still except for her shallow breathing. The night stretched on, lonely and endless, broken frequently by Tara and Buck's rasping coughs. Nate hadn't slept in nearly forty-eight hours, yet still sleep would not come. His tired mind was tortured with horrifying thoughts, and it took every ounce of mental resolve to push out the unpleasant possibilities of what the next day might bring. That resolve weakened as the time cruelly inched toward morning. Finally, close to dawn, his exhausted body gave in. He dozed off, and the thoughts melded into dreams of frustration. He awoke in less than an hour, feeling less rested than before.

He successfully urged Tara and Buck to eat a little bread before strapping them back down on the travois. The dread in Tara's eyes at facing another day of slow, bumpy riding pained him. "Don't worry, sweetheart," he whispered. "We'll get there soon. They'll take good care of you."

Nate gave her one last pat before walking to the Appaloosa and taking hold of the saddle horn. As he put one foot in the stirrup, he happened to glance behind him at the valley in which they had camped. He looked back at the saddle, then his eyes shot back to the valley again. Two and a half, maybe three miles away, he spied one thin stream of smoke rising to the sky, very faint, but unmistakable. He had not seen anyone on the journey so far, and he wondered who had camped so close. He afforded no more attention to the curiosity as he mounted and commenced his day's travel.

It was a full hour before he thought of the mysterious camp again, and something made him twist around in the saddle to look behind him. Against the horizon, now lit by full sunlight, he could make out a tiny dot, which he could tell by size and movement was a person on horseback. He was undoubtedly being followed. But he could not stop to look into it now; he must press on.

As he rode, his mind worked non-stop. It had to be someone from the ranch, he thought. Instantly he thought of Elijah, the one most concerned about Tara and Buck. But then why was he hanging back, Nate wondered. Certainly Nate was traveling slowly enough that the follower could easily catch up to him. Somehow he knew that the follower was aware of his predicament and that Nate wasn't going to take the time to check him out. A tinge of hope stirred him when it occurred to him that perhaps Lena was following and, in her own discreet way, was looking out for him and making sure all went well. His hope soon subsided. Lena would know that Nate was aware of someone's presence behind him and that she wasn't hiding from anything. Still, he found himself hoping that it really was her.

The second long day passed. Again he talked to Tara and Buck, about the landscape, the Cheyenne, any anecdote he thought of. He told them about their follower and wondered aloud who it was. Later in the afternoon, his weary mind drifted to the past, and he told what he remembered about the day he and Tara first met. He recounted the wonderful, happy days they'd spent in the tiny cabin the first winter of their marriage, planning their ranch, riding horses through the snow during the day and mapping out where the house and the outbuildings would go, talking in front of the fire in the evenings. He talked about the funny things little Buck had done. He knew Tara always liked to hear about that, especially the time that, after being overly concerned because Buck was slow learning to walk, she'd had to chase him down when he suddenly broke into a run towards the barn to "see the horseys." From that day on, he caused messes faster than she could clean them.

Nate rode until after the sun had set before allowing himself to search for a place to camp. Locating a suitable spot by the river, he dismounted and went first to the travois. As he knelt beside it and undid the straps, Tara struggled to rise.

"The payroll," she sputtered. "I've got to do the payroll."

"The payroll's fine," replied Nate as he reached for her. "It's all taken care of. You're having a dream."

His touch set her off, thrashing wildly against his grip, drawing on some deep reservoir of strength. The lack of recognition in her eyes frightened him. She was obviously seeing a stranger and the source of her fevered torment. He weathered a barrage of fists from her till he was able to get hold of her arms and grasp them firmly against her breasts. She moaned in frustration with her limited freedom, until finally, panting heavily, she went limp in his arms.

Nate sat holding her with one hand on her sweaty forehead. He discovered he was trembling, and he took a deep breath and tried to relax. After laying her down, he moved to Buck's side of the travois. Buck's eyes were open, but they would not focus on Nate when Nate said his name. Nate put a hand to Buck's lips. The boy was breathing but had not the strength left to even whimper.

In a confused daze Nate walked back to the Appaloosa and began to remove his gear from the saddle. The irrational nature of his actions suddenly hit him with the force of a brick. His family was nearly dead and he was about to set up camp. He figured Tara could still last a day or so, but the boy would likely be gone by morning. Nate was aware of the quiet around him, broken only by the soft roll of the river. It was too quiet here, too lonely. Mental images of a tiny grave here by this river so far from home numbed him. He could feel his heart breaking, his world caving in on him. He laid his forehead against the saddle and closed his eyes. "Dear God," he weakly stammered, "please help me. I cannot bear this."

He replaced his gear on the saddle, tied the straps on the travois, and remounted. He would ride through the night with the river as his guide. Through endless hours of darkness, a cold wind whipping his hair and filling his ears with a lonely sound, the Appaloosa steadily plodded while Nate battled the stubborn fatigue that dulled his senses. As always, he carried a hunting knife on the left side of his waist, a Colt .45 on his right hip, and a Henry .44 lever-action repeating rifle in a sheath on the saddle. He was proficient enough with all of them to nearly use them in his sleep. Still, he worried that they were left more susceptible to any danger which may lie in wait. He would nod off and be jolted awake when he began to slide off the saddle, then he would straighten himself up, only to repeat the cycle within moments.

Hour after hour his awakenings were greeted with blackness and wind. He knew nothing of what was more than a few feet ahead of him. But finally, he noticed the surroundings looking lighter. He looked to the east and saw pink appearing above the horizon. A sense of relief flooded him. Another milestone had been reached; he had made it till the morning, and so had his precious load. Once it appeared, the sun rose quickly and, in another hour or so, burned off the coolness of the night and stilled the wind.

Morning brought still no sign of an Indian camp, but Nate determinedly pressed on, certain that if there was a camp to be found, he would happen upon it soon. Later in the morning, he stopped by the river for a drink, filled the canteen, and splashed some water on his face. When he stood up and looked back, he spied the familiar dot on the horizon. After camping overnight, his follower had spent the morning catching up but was still not going to ride in and make himself known.

Punished by exhaustion, Nate muttered irritably, "So stay back there, you damn fool. See if I care."

Next he checked on Buck, found him breathing shallow but steady, and felt grateful to have such a tough little boy. He untied the straps, lifted Buck from the travois, and carried him to the Appaloosa. As he mounted and started the horse at a walk, he clutched Buck against his chest and talked incessantly, partly to keep Buck hanging on and partly to keep himself awake and aware.

The scenery changed little. Trees, bushes, and rocks slowly passed through his vision, and always the river flowed east, traveling faster than he was. He stopped checking the position of the sun; it moved ever so slowly and depressed him.

After a long while and another stop for water, Nate's head lowered as he rode until his chin rested on his chest just above Buck's head. He felt it safe to rest his eyes. The horse knew enough by now to follow the river on its own; his follower wasn't coming closer; and in over two days, they had not come upon any danger.

He had lost all track of time, but when he lifted his head again, he was met with a sight he was certain was a mirage perpetrated by his beaten, exhausted mind. Spread out in a little riverside meadow before him were about two dozen tepees and next to them a herd of horses grazing the luscious grass found there in the moist riverbottoms. Smoke curled from the tops of some of the tepees and quickly dissipated in the blue sky, and he could hear distant voices. The solitary cry of an infant and a dog's playful bark greeted Nate's ears, and never had he appreciated a sound so much. He urged the Appaloosa to quicken its pace.

He picked out Chief Red Feather's tepee right away. There was a new one each year, but the chief always decorated it with the same markings. On former visits, Nate had seen the distinctive drawings of arrows and spears commemorating Red Feather's many exploits in battle. He always wondered which drawing stood for the massacre that had killed his parents, and the thought flashed through his mind once again now. But, ever focused on his objective, he never broke the Appaloosa's stride till he halted in front of the tepee and carefully climbed down with Buck in his arms. Almost instantly the chief appeared outside the open tent flap. His two long braids were grayer than the last time Nate had seen him, and the battle scar on the left side of his chin was becoming lost among a few more wrinkles.

At first Red Feather seemed pleased at this unexpected visit from Nate, till he saw the look on Nate's face and the limp child in his arms. "You have trouble, Eagle Shadow?"

"I've come here for your help," Nate began. "The influenza has devastated Timber Fork, and there's no medicine. My wife and son are dying. Please help us."

Red Feather glanced at the travois bearing a still body wrapped in blankets. "You know that we are having trouble with the white man now. The new white chief does not honor our agreement."

"I don't care about any of that," replied Nate evenly. "I've just ridden straight for two days and a night to get here."

"What I mean to say is, the whites will surely know you've brought your family to us and will cause trouble, not for us, for you."

"I don't care," Nate breathed. "They can't do any worse to me than what's done already. Your medicine man can work miracles." He fought to keep his voice steady. "My wife and son need a miracle." He was driven to his knees, whether from desperation or exhaustion he wasn't sure. He looked down into the calm face of his unconscious son, and the lump rose in his throat. "I'm not too proud to beg this of you," he whispered.

Nate was aware that several of the people had gathered around, but he did not look at them. He only watched Red Feather's buckskin-clad legs advancing toward him, and quickly warned, "Don't come any closer. I don't want to bring sickness among you. Just please allow me to take them to your medicine man." He held his breath, not daring to look into the chief's face. He heard Red Feather speak to someone nearby.

"Tosa'e Ve'ho'Hotoa'e?"

As the chief's wife nodded and rushed away, Nate looked questioningly at Red Feather. The chief was smiling down at him.

"White Buffalo will come. He has healed this sickness before."

A brave walked to the Appaloosa, took the rein, and began to lead him away with the travois. Soon after, the chief's wife returned with White Buffalo, a gray-haired brave with a kind-looking face. He reached strong, leathery arms underneath the boy, and Nate willingly gave him up. Nate closed his eyes as an overwhelming sense of relief washed over him, seeming to relax every tense muscle in his body from his head to his toes. *"Nea'eše,"* he whispered. "Thank you ever so much."

"You pray to Heammiwihio for their lives," said Red Feather. "That is all you can do. And then you rest. My wife will bring you food."

Nate felt like he could just lie down where he was and sleep, and he thought about doing just that, but instead he summoned every ounce of strength and slowly rose to his feet. He walked alone to the river and found a quiet, soft spot in the grass to lie down. He didn't remember any more.

Chapter 6

In the midst of sleep, Nate was briefly aware when the chief's wife was covering him with his blankets, setting his possessions around him, and watering his horse. When next he was aroused from slumber, it was dark and the song of crickets floated across the night air. He slept on, hour after hour, waking only for short moments occasionally. He felt safe here among the Indians, although he was a short distance from the tepees. Always, whether awake or asleep, his concern for Tara and Buck was paramount, but he knew someone would come to him if there was anything to report.

At last daylight came to his camp by the river, and the sun's warm rays began working to bring him back to full awareness, a slow process following such a long, though fitful, sleep. But in those foggy moments between sleep and consciousness, that time when a cloud of half-dreaming lingers in the mind, he had the distinct feeling of someone watching him. Alertness came with a sobering rush now, and he sat bolt upright. His eyes were drawn to the top of a butte across the river from him. He saw nothing out of the ordinary, and he wondered if he'd been experiencing the end of a dream. He tried to recall what his eyes might have seen that would have given him that feeling, but it was already gone, vanished with the last of the mind fog.

A nearby beating flutter of wings startled him. From a ledge on the side of the butte, a bald eagle took flight, its powerful wings singing through the air till it gained enough lift, then it glided gracefully away in search of its breakfast. Nate shook his head, amused at himself. He'd been alarmed because of an eagle watching him.

He looked now to fully take in his surroundings for the first time. A rolling mist hovered ghostlike over the river and the grasses beyond. The butte was a monolithic, granite formation, rising skyward out of the mist as if suspended in the air. Its smooth gray face shone in the sun and brightened the whole atmosphere. Nate's eyes trailed up the face to the top of the butte where a thin scattering of junipers was silhouetted against a cloudless blue sky. What must this Indian camp look like from up there, he wondered. He had always been awestruck and humbled by the insignificance of his own life against the massive wonders of an untamed wilderness, yet the wilderness was often the only place he felt entirely safe from life's ills. Deep in the wilderness, civilization's arguments mattered little, and money and possessions were worthless. Young Buck would likely grow up with some of both, but Nate had determined from the time his son was born, that Buck should be acquainted with the earth as his ancestors knew it. He felt a towering responsibility not to let Buck stray far from his heritage.

But he reminded himself that those lessons would be for another day. Right now he must go to them, see how they fared during the night, and give them will and strength to carry on. Casting one last glance toward the butte and the dissipating mist at its base, he left his camp by the river, climbed the embankment, and walked among the tepees.

He figured he'd slept possibly fifteen hours and mused that that was the first time in his life he had ever done that. The normal daily activities of the people seemed to be well underway, breakfast done, cleaned up, and the work of the day begun. Apparently many of the braves had gone hunting. There were mostly women in camp, busily scraping and tanning deer hides, for not many buffalo had been seen lately. He saw one young girl sewing beads on a sheath for a knife, and he wondered for whom she was making something so nice.

He did not know any of these people, but they all knew him, first by a reputation gained a few years before when he'd eluded every single warrior in their band, like the shadow of an eagle they said. Later he became a benefactor of sorts when he brought them horses, fine ones of sturdy build with a long, fast stride. No one spoke to him now, only nodded in respect. They knew why he was here and graciously pointed him in the direction of the medicine man's lodge.

He didn't need their help. The sweat lodge was obvious to him, a framework of willow poles bound by pairs from tip to base and bent to form arches, a representation of the backbone and tail of the buffalo. Buffalo hides were stretched over the frame and bound by strong cords. A buffalo skull had been placed in front of the lodge facing it.

He paused in the doorway of the lodge, respecting tradition and awaiting the medicine man's invitation to enter. White Buffalo motioned him inside, and Nate readily accepted. He was immediately taken aback by the pungent and spicy aroma emitting from the fire in the center. Tara and Buck lay asleep next to each other on one side of the lodge, and Nate knelt beside them. Although the mask of illness still ravaged their ashen countenances, their sleep seemed more peaceful, their breathing more normal. Nate wondered whether this minute improvement was due to whatever treatment they were receiving or to the fact that they were no longer being jostled over rough trails and had a safe, warm place to rest.

He looked at where White Buffalo was brewing a tea from a collection of tiny white flowers and leaves from the yarrow plant. When it was ready, White Buffalo poured the steaming liquid from a clay pitcher into a gourd that he brought over to Tara and Buck's pallet.

"I'll do it," Nate offered. He took the gourd, moved closer to Tara, and lifted her by the shoulders. Her eyes flickered open, and she slowly sipped the tea, blowing on it between sips to cool it. Her wrinkled nose indicated it wasn't much to her liking.

When it was cooled enough to offer to Buck, Nate lifted him up and put the gourd to his lips. It was tougher to get Buck to drink his share, but Nate managed to get it into him and handed the gourd back to White Buffalo.

"Eagle Shadow, I ask you to join in the sacred sweat lodge ceremony."

Nate nodded his acceptance and humbly expressed his gratitude. *"Nea'ese."* He took his seat where White Buffalo indicated on the opposite side of the lodge from Tara and Buck. White Buffalo seated himself at the back, opposite the entrance to the lodge.

In the center of the lodge was a circular hole about a foot deep and eighteen inches in diameter. A strip of ground between the hole and the entrance had had the sod removed. White Buffalo used the tip of his finger to draw two parallel lines in the pit with the ends connected with a V shape. Then he filled his pipe with tobacco, lit it, extended it to the four cardinal directions, and smoked.

Soon after, he called for the stones to be brought in. His wife entered the lodge with two black stones, two red stones, and one painted half black and half red. These she placed at precise points in the pit and covered with grass. The rest of the stones were brought in, hot from the fire outside, along with a vessel of water that was placed in the pathway leading from the pit to the entrance.

Thus began a long and very ordered, ancient ritual involving prayers, the dripping of water on the sizzling stones, the chanting of songs, always eight in a row, the raising of the outer covering of the lodge, and the lowering of it to begin the cycle again.

Like many other Cheyenne customs, Nate had heard about every detail of the ceremony from his father but had never before experienced it firsthand. Any other time, he would've watched and listened intently, fascinated to see his father's descriptions come to life before him, but with his sick wife and son in full view across the lodge, he was distracted and impatient. The ceremony moved too slowly. He wasn't used to it. It didn't seem to address his immediate worries. He wondered if he'd indeed made a mistake in bringing them here as Lena had warned him. If either Tara or Buck died in this lodge so far from home, he knew his life would be over. He could never shake the memory of this medicine lodge, and the ceremony would only hold horror for him.

But they were here now. There was no turning back. His uncompromised faith was required, even in the strangeness of the situation. He began to watch White Buffalo more, to listen to the words of the songs, and especially to the prayers. The language spoken was Cheyenne, but his mind translated it with no conscious thought. The words spoke directly to his soul. White Buffalo was praying for the sickness to leave and for strength to flow once again through their bodies. He prayed for their life paths not to be disrupted and for divine powers to bear them up and prosper them. The medicine man was so intent, so wholeheartedly devoted to his current task that nothing else even existed at this moment. It was an exercise in concentration and complete faith that was not lost on Nate. While Nate had been afraid for what might happen to Tara and Buck today or tomorrow, White Buffalo was far beyond that. He was praying about their futures and the goodness in store for them.

What had seemed to Nate at first to be a slow and disconnected experience from what Tara and Buck really needed, now seemed instead to be full of hope, the very thing that would restore their health. He closed his eyes and shut out everything but the ceremony. As the sweat rolled from his brow and tears squeezed from the corners of his eyes and slid down his sweaty cheeks, he lost track of how many times the cycle of songs and prayers was repeated. Time stood still, and his mind and heart were fully engulfed in the meaning and intent of the ceremony. All fear was banished. This really *was* why he'd brought them here.

Sometimes he saw Tara awake and watching him through the roiling steam. She couldn't understand what was being said, but through silent communication with Nate's eyes, his peace and serenity were transferred to her. In return, he could see in her eyes that she was comfortable with being here. Being surrounded by a strange language and customs was merely a minor inconvenience. The deeper meaning of what was happening still came through to her powerfully. This wordless communication so bound his heart with hers that he could feel her pulling away from the brink of death and bringing their boy with her.

When at last the outer covering of buffalo hides was raised for the final time and the ceremony was complete, he sat still for a while, transfixed by the intensity of the experience. The cool air softly blowing through the open lodge soothed Tara and Buck, and they rested peacefully.

Nate thanked White Buffalo, knelt beside Tara, and caressed her cheek. "You and Bucky are gonna be just fine," he whispered with a smile. "I'll be back." She nodded, and with his confidence renewed, he felt safe in attending to other business.

Returning to his camp by the river, Nate approached the Appaloosa and scratched behind its ears. "You're the best horse. You got us here with no complaint." The horse nudged him as if he understood. "You ready for another ride? Not so long this time." He saddled the horse, mounted up, and began to retrace his path from the previous day in search of his mysterious follower.

He took his time guiding the Appaloosa through the brush beside the riverbank as they followed the Sun River westward. He was surprised at how unfamiliar the country looked to him. This stretch of river was where he'd been fighting overwhelming fatigue the day before, carrying Buck and trusting the horse to keep to the riverbank. He saw it now as if for the first time, but he paid particular attention to the unmarred tracks and signs along the way, evidence of his own passing by.

He estimated he'd ridden upstream for at least three miles before he found other tracks mingled with his own. He halted the Appaloosa with a slight pull on the reins and studied the tracks. Here the stranger had stopped to water his horse, and there were a man's tracks mingled with the hoofprints. The horse had entered the water and come back out again. Then they had turned around and begun heading back westward.

Nate dismounted and knelt on one knee in the dust to get a closer look. The tracks belonged to a man wearing boots, no spurs, and riding an unshod horse. Immediately his mind started working, considering any possibilities he could think of. They could have been Elijah Medley's boots, but he wasn't certain. He had noticed Elijah's tracks before when he went looking for him at the ranch but not enough to remember them well. And there were a few unshod horses on the Broken Bow. They were in Elijah's charge, and he sometimes rode one regularly while training it.

Nate climbed back up to the saddle and continued upstream, looking for anything else that might give him a clue. After a few more miles, he decided it was useless. This person was careless in the signs he left behind. He obviously wasn't a bit worried about being followed, or maybe just didn't know any better, and he was headed straight back to wherever he came from.

"What d'ya think, boy?" Nate asked, patting the horse's neck. "Shall we give up on this and go back?"

Since he would be returning home in a few days, he figured he'd ask Elijah about it then and enjoy the stunned look of embarrassment he'd receive from his shy wrangler.

***

Nate stayed in the lodge with Tara and Buck the rest of that day and all night. When early the next day Tara sat up to eat something and drink more of the yarrow tea, and Buck sat in her arms to eat a few bites of broth himself, Nate felt relief wash over him like cool water on a hot summer's day. He hadn't even realized how tense every muscle had been until he felt the tension almost tangibly dissipate. He went to them and took them in his arms. He was in no rush to let go, but little Buck, feeling smothered, soon wriggled free, and Nate laughed in amusement. He squeezed Tara harder and, feeling her hugging him back, there was nothing more he needed for his happiness to be complete.

"A lot of people back home are gonna be happy to see you," he whispered.

"Thank you for bringing us here," she replied. "They've been very good to us. I don't believe anyone here attacked those medicine wagons."

His smile faded. He'd momentarily forgotten the attack, and on purpose. He'd shoved it to the back of his mind to focus on his family's well-being, but he was still mystified. She innocently saw only what happened inside this lodge, but due to past experience, his view was just a little bit wider. It was true that what he'd seen here in the last couple days didn't match up with what he'd witnessed at the sight of the attack. But suspicion still plagued him.

Chapter 7

Nate was grateful for the tepee that the Indians bestowed on him. He erected it at the south end of the encampment, close to the river, and moved Tara and Buck into it. He hunted fresh meat daily. Sometimes the chief's wife or White Buffalo's wife would bring fish they'd caught in their traps in the river. He encouraged Tara and Buck to eat to replace weight they'd lost and get their strength back before taking them home.

At the end of their first week with the Indians, they were up and around for several hours of the day, and Nate thought they may be ready to make the trip back home, slowly, pacing themselves according to how they felt.

Red Feather informed Nate one afternoon, "We will be leaving soon, to go west to find good hunting."

"Then I'll leave too, and take my family home," replied Nate. "We will leave tomorrow morning. We are so grateful for all you've done for us, Red Feather."

The chief exhibited a rare smile. "I am glad you brought them to us. White Buffalo's medicine was good for them."

"Yes, it was."

"Your wife and son are very brave. You will be proud of them always."

Nate was immensely pleased. He had longed to share his pride in his family with the chief, but he had not expected any more than tolerance from him. He always had the feeling that Red Feather wanted more from him, more demonstration of loyalty, more affinity for the band of his ancestors. He sensed a sort of distance between the two of them that his annual gift of horses could not bridge. He had done well by the Broken Bow and the people of Timber Fork, but somehow, it was Chief Red Feather's approval that gave him ultimate satisfaction.

While Tara was lulled to sleep in Nate's arms that night by the lazy, burbling roll of the Sun River and the haunting call of a solitary hoot owl in a riverside spruce tree, Nate lay awake for nearly an hour, staring at the two stars that moved across the smoke hole in the top of the tepee. At this particular moment, he was glad to be right where he was, with Tara and Buck resting peacefully close to him. Home was wherever his family was, even in a tepee by the river with buffalo skins for a bed.

Just for now, he would enjoy this moment, for he knew when morning broke, he would miss the Broken Bow and be eager to get on his way. On the morrow he would be impatient for Mrs. Sinclair, Jared, and Rebecca to see Tara and Buck. They would be so happy and relieved. He would take more concern for how Clay and Elijah were coming along with the work. And then there was Lena. He knew he would think about her all the way home and hope for a good reception from her when she saw Tara and Buck well again.

When he finally drifted off to sleep, he slept very soundly.

***

Nate was awakened by a deep, low, vibrating rumble. It must be a distant thunderstorm approaching, he thought. His heart sank. Oh, how he didn't want anything to delay his trip today. He could see the dawn sky through the hole at the top of the tepee, a clear sky, at least in that particular spot. How peculiar that the sound was steady and the vibrating growing stronger. Suddenly he shot up to a sitting position, waking Tara with his abrupt movement.

"What's the matter?" she asked sleepily. "What's that noise?"

Nate was already outside of the tepee, pulling a shirt down over his head. The rumble had risen to a thundering roar emanating from the north end of the camp. When he looked amongst the tepees for the source, he caught sight of running horses flashing between the tepees, bearing riders clad in blue flannel, a cavalry charge. He burst back into the tepee where Buck was awake and trying to run outside, and Tara was holding him back. "We're under attack!" he shouted above the din as he scooped up Buck in one arm and grabbed his gunbelt with the other. "Come on!"

Tara followed Nate outside and across an open stretch of grass toward the river. The eruption of gunfire close by startled her, and she turned at the sound of shouting and screaming women. Then she saw the soldiers and slowed her pace. "Nate, they're cavalry. They won't hurt us."

He stepped behind her and shoved her along in front of him. "They don't know we're here, Tara. No one is safe in front of charging horses and flying bullets."

Shortly before reaching the river and having descended a bank that afforded some protection, he delivered Buck into Tara's waiting arms and began strapping on his holster. "Go, Tara. Find a safe place to hide, and don't come out. No matter what you hear, don't come out till I come for you."

"All right." Her feet seemed to be planted where she stood. "Nate, please be careful."

"I will." He gave her a push. "Get going. And you hang onto him."

She raced to the river and followed the bank east. Every pop of gunfire pounded in her chest, and she tried to pick up her pace to get away from it. But she was still weak, and Buck was heavy. He started to cry, and she attempted to soothe him but could hardly catch a breath. She hit a patch of soft, wet ground and slipped to her knees. Calling on every weary leg muscle to regain her footing, she decided she'd have to stop. Spying a thicket that looked bushy enough in which to hide, she headed for it and crawled in, ignoring the many twigs relentlessly scratching at her face, neck, and arms.

Once she'd settled into a sitting position, she closed her eyes and tried to take a few deep breaths. But Buck was trying to wriggle away from her.

"Wanna go find Pa!" he wailed.

"Shhh. Not now, Bucky. He'll be back soon." She held onto his writhing body.

Frustrated with his curbed freedom, he began to whine, and Tara patted his back. "We have to be quiet, Bucky, quiet like little mice or they'll find us."

In her shaky whisper, the child sensed the urgency of the situation and obeyed.

Tara sat stiffly, listening to the incessant rattle of gunfire and Indian whoops and trying to block out of her mind the horrifying images of what was going on out there in the encampment. She'd been in the midst of battle before and knew what it looked like. She knew Nate was somewhere in the middle of it and that he may have fired his gun by now. She also knew he wouldn't be shooting at Indians this time. He was defensive and would be incensed by this attack. She was incensed too, but she wanted him out of there. Tears stung her eyes, and she hugged Buck tighter while she turned her head and watched the riverside path she had just taken, watching and hoping for him to come.

***

Arriving back at his own tepee, Nate retrieved his hunting knife and started back out, then stopped. He'd better take the Henry rifle too, he thought. He was used to facing combat well-armed, but the surprise of this attack had flustered him.

Outside again, he quickly checked the location of the battle. The Indians were keeping the cavalry at bay near the northernmost tepees in the camp. Keeping his head down low, he rushed forward to join the front lines. He saw Red Feather crouched beside a tepee and moved up beside him. They spoke no words, but as Red Feather fired on soldiers to their right, Nate took aim for those on their left.

The rapidity of return fire from the Indians drove the soldiers to take cover where they could, but more and more troops kept streaming out of the river bottoms on the left and from a grove of trees on the right. With their numbers continually boosted, the soldiers became more aggressive, and the Indians began to retreat foot by foot.

"Try to make every shot count!" Nate shouted to Red Feather over the deafening roar of gunfire and pounding hooves. "I think they've thrown a couple of companies at us!"

Nate's dread worsened as he saw that they may soon be caught in a crossfire. The chief saw it too. With barely more than a subtle nod to two of his warriors, they responded by slipping unnoticed towards the east and west sides of the camp, gathering other braves along the way.

Red Feather had a mind for battle strategy, and Nate immediately understood the plan. They were trying to place warriors outside of the field of battle, while the others would draw the soldiers into the center of the camp. It was a desperate hope at this point, but the only hope.

Nate elected to follow those headed west toward the river. Braves on the front line covered for him and the others as they scurried along. As they neared the river, he caught sight of a Gatling gun through the trees. He motioned all but two others to continue on without him while he stopped to investigate. The two staying with him crouched low, rifles ready, to cover for him. He'd seen this gun before at the fort when it was new, and he guessed that it hadn't been used in battle yet. If it was used today, it would inflict unholy carnage and death in only minutes.

Only one soldier manned it currently, and he was readying to move it into position closer to the battle. Nate recognized this as the best and only chance he'd have to do something. There was no time to formulate a plan. He trained his rifle sights on the soldier and fired. The bullet hit its mark, and Nate glanced around, making sure no other soldiers were nearby, before moving in for his first close inspection of a Gatling. It looked bigger than he'd expected it to be and was fixed-mounted on an artillery carriage. He must work fast. They wouldn't leave such a thing unmanned for long. Surely more than one person was supposed to be in charge of it. Hopefully that person was a battle casualty too, buying Nate more time.

He studied the build of the gun. Six barrels encased in a bronze cylinder and operated by a hand crank. There must be a separate breech and firing pin system for each barrel, but they were inaccessible to him given the short time he had. He'd need tools to pry off the cylinder casing. On the top was an ammunition hopper that worked by gravity feed. Good enough for now, he decided. He looked around on the ground, picked up a handful of the plentiful riverside pebbles, and dropped them into the hopper, reaching in to shove them down as hard as he could. That would at least jam the barrels temporarily, and with any luck maybe even do permanent damage. Next he looked underneath the gun, thinking he'd find an ejection port for spent shells. Sure enough, there was one. Wouldn't hurt to put a couple of rocks in there too, he thought. Hoping he'd done enough to disable the Gatling, he checked his surroundings, dismissed the two braves guarding him, and made his way back to the main line.

It appeared that he was more needed in the center to try and defend the noncombatants in the camp. He found temporary cover in the open tent flap of a tepee wherein a young mother cowered with her small son. Kneeling down, he tossed his rifle across to her. She took it in both hands, chambered a round, and held it at the ready, while he took aim with his Colt .45 at a soldier who was charging his horse through a nearby tepee. As a couple of the lodgepoles broke and the structure began to fold in on itself under the weight of the horse, Nate fired his gun, and the soldier, his chest shot through, lurched backward off of his rearing horse.

Nate barely had time to cock the trigger again before another soldier rode in behind the first one. Seeing Nate, the soldier raised his gun and fired. The bullet whizzed by Nate's head, but Nate had gotten off his shot a half second sooner, and the soldier's advance was successfully stopped. Nate held his position a few minutes more, wounding another soldier in the process, before looking for someplace for him and the woman and her son to go. His trail of bloody handiwork would soon give away his position, and the buffalo hide tepee afforded less protection than he'd like.

Suddenly the very earth beneath him seemed to shake, and the tepee he was in started collapsing around him. He scurried out from beneath falling lodgepoles and wheeled around, revolver in hand. He found himself eye to eye with a large chestnut mare and her stomping hooves. In the midst of churning dust, he glimpsed a gun barrel being leveled at him. With his own gun already in place, he fired, and the soldier slumped forward in his saddle with a ghastly grunt. As the soldier's arm went limp, his revolver discharged, sending a bullet ricocheting off the ground past Nate.

An arm reached out from underneath the collapsed tepee and groped about for something to hold onto. Nate grabbed it and pulled. Out slid the Cheyenne woman dragging her child behind her.

"*Nepevomohtahehe*?" he shouted. She nodded, indicating they were not hurt, and he pointed her in the direction of the river. "*Aseta'xestse*!"

Carrying her child, she ran westward toward the riverbank while Nate crawled under the wreckage of the collapsed tepee in search of his rifle. Lying on his stomach, pulling himself along with his elbows in the suffocating darkness of the buffalo hide while a battle raged around him was most unnerving, and his hands flew until they clamped down on the rifle. He pulled it out with him, cautiously looking in every direction before standing up and sprinting for cover in a nearby stand of tall oaks.

***

Tara remained alert to every sound as she huddled in the thicket with Buck. Her already wildly beating heart accelerated as she heard gunfire break out close to the riverbank. She wrapped her arms further around Buck's small body and pressed her face against his soft black hair. She cared about nothing at this moment but her responsibility to him, his safety and protection, and her own only because he needed her. In her fear, she determined to keep a clear head to carry out her responsibility. She shut her eyes, gritted her teeth, and forced away every thought that could interfere with her task of keeping Buck safe.

Her eyes flew open at the light sound of footsteps approaching at a dead run. The sight of the Cheyenne woman carrying a young child startled her, and she leaned back as the woman brushed past her thicket, sending the branches bobbing up and down. Following were two soldiers on horseback. They immediately closed the gap between them and the running woman. The blast of a revolver directly in front of her thicket caused every muscle in her body to convulse. She heard no more footsteps from the woman. Buck made no sound, but she could feel him shaking and grasping her waist like he couldn't hold tight enough.

She bit her lip to muffle her sobs. These two men and an unknown number of other soldiers were killers of the defenseless, and she now felt at risk, not from accidental shooting, but deliberate killing before they knew who she was. Major Blaine was going to hear about this, she decided, but first she must see the soldiers' faces to identify them.

There was one horse pacing in front of her thicket. The lacy pattern of twigs and leaves partially obscured her view, but she followed the clip-clop sound of the horse's hooves till he passed by an open space in her view. Her eyes traced up the soldier's legs, from his black boots and yellow-striped dark blue pants to his tanned, cold, and expressionless face peering out under locks of sun-whitened blond hair. A powder burn darkened the cheek beneath his left eye. She glimpsed the sleeve of his jacket which bore a gold chevron topped by a small insignia. She squinted to see the insignia. It was only for a second, but she made out the gold patch. He was a saddler sergeant.

"I say we just wait around here for savages to run this way," he said to his companion further upstream. "We can pick 'em off like turkeys at a turkey shoot."

Tara had seen and heard enough. On the ground next to her lay some smooth river rocks about as big as her fist, which spurred her to recall a simple trick Nate had used in the wilderness when under pursuit. She took a firm hold of one of the rocks, then tilted her head to watch through the veil of leaves till both men were turned away from her and looking up the bank toward the battle. Cupping the rock with one hand, she reached behind her head, and with all the force she could summon from her influenza-weakened muscles, she hurled the stone to her right with a prayer that this would work to buy her a moment in which to escape. The rock landed in some riverside brush with a rustling noise and a thud loud enough to elicit the soldiers' immediate attention.

When she judged that the soldiers had ridden a safe distance away from her spot, she darted out from her hiding place and, hugging Buck close to her with one arm and hiking up her skirts with the other hand, she ran in the opposite direction, her footsteps almost imperceptible in the soft ground by the river. She did not dare look back as she ran southward around a bend in the river, through a cluster of willows, and down an embankment. She tired quickly but would not let herself even slow down. When her way was blocked by a creek branching off eastward from the river, she plunged into it without breaking stride. She pushed forward into waist-deep water, against currents which tugged at her cumbersome dress beneath the surface. Exiting on the opposite side, chilled through and breathless, she climbed the bank and broke into a run through the knee-high grasses of a verdant meadow. She had gone for a leisurely stroll here the previous week with Nate and Buck. The beauty and serenity of the meadow had physically invigorated her then and lifted her spirits. But now it seemed an endless expanse with not one tree to offer cover and protection.

Tara felt her insides quivering with cold, and her teeth chattered uncontrollably. Her heavy, wet skirt slapped against her legs as she ran, nearly tripping her repeatedly. Gasping for breaths, she struggled on with her precious burden. Buck kept asking where they were going, and she attempted to answer him, but her head began to feel light and black spots appeared in her vision. She couldn't blink them away. Then she felt herself falling and heard Buck cry out. She was aware of soft grass against her cheek, small comfort for her tortured body. She drifted away into black silence.

***

Peeking out with one eye from behind the wide, bullet-riddled trunk of an aged oak tree, Nate took aim with his Henry rifle at another blue uniform on a charging blaze-faced horse. He was not accustomed to looking into the faces of enemies attacking en masse. They didn't matter to his own survival. But in the split-second interim between sighting this soldier and squeezing the trigger, something made him look up to the face of his target, into the unemotional, disciplined eyes of one Major Blaine. Now Nate's fury over this whole attack came to a head, now that there was someone to receive the brunt of his anger. He laid his rifle down and rushed headlong into the open and straight for the horse, determined to stop its charge like a brick wall.

Major Blaine saw him at the last moment and tried to brace for the impact. But Nate had already grabbed the horse's rein and jerked it downward. As the horse lost its footing and rolled, Nate leaped and seized the major by the arm. He succeeded in pulling the major free of the falling horse, and he and Blaine landed hard in a heap on the ground. Major Blaine struggled to rise, but Nate was faster. He threw a punch that bloodied the major's nose and knocked him off balance. While he still had the advantage, Nate got in two gut punches, afterwards hissing, "What do you think you're doing, attacking a peaceful camp?"

"This camp is a nest of thieves and killers, Nate!" he answered when he was able to draw breath. "The question is, what are *you* doing here?"

Nate never much liked conversing with the major. He aimed his fist for Major Blaine's jaw, but this time Blaine was ready, blocking the punch with his arm and executing one of his own to Nate's unguarded stomach. Nate fell back on the ground with a grunt, but when Blaine pounced on him, he was met with a well-placed foot in the abdomen. With the major off of him, Nate regained his footing. He was distracted by a horse falling next to him, a dust-covered bay with an arrow protruding from its flank. As its rider slid out from beneath the horse and searched the ground for his dropped gun, he didn't even see who was grabbing him and lifting him to his feet. Effectively restrained by Nate's iron grip, he could put up little fight.

Major Blaine started for him, but Nate drew his gun and pressed it to the temple of the young private, halting Blaine mid-step. "Call a retreat, Major."

"You're crazy," Major Blaine growled. "We'll retreat when our objective is accomplished."

"You'll retreat now! Do it!"

"I'm warning you, Nate, you're making a big mistake. You release him now, and I won't bring you up on charges."

Nate cocked the trigger. The struggling private stopped moving, closed his eyes, and swallowed hard.

Major Blaine drew in a breath and backed up a couple steps, pointing a finger at Nate. "Don't think you'll get away with this, Hunter." He took the reins of his waiting horse and mounted. "Retreat!" he called to his troops. He said it once more before he was heard amid the tumult. The command was repeated by lower officers, and the gunfire began to lessen as soldiers heard the command and turned their horses to ride out of the camp. The whole lot of them headed north towards a rendezvous point, trailing clouds of dust and dodging a steady stream of Cheyenne bullets and arrows.

Nate waited till Major Blaine had galloped away and disappeared among the retreating masses before releasing his captive, who scurried to climb atop the horse of a passing soldier who slowed down for him.

When the last of the troops had cleared out and the pounding hooves of their mounts had grown faint, a strange, terrible silence rose to Nate's ears. His eyes surveyed a devastated encampment full of trampled tepees, the still bodies of warriors, small children crying and wandering aimlessly, and a lone old man standing in the midst of it all in a pitiful daze. There were five tepees left standing, and from one emerged a limping woman, screaming for help and pointing inside. Nate angrily wondered what objective of Major Blaine's had not been accomplished.

Amid the destruction which begged for his immediate attention, Nate's first thought was for Tara and Buck. He couldn't reach them fast enough. He retrieved his rifle and headed straight for the river. He soon located the thicket where they'd concealed themselves and followed Tara's footprints from there. He heard a whimper somewhere close by and stopped to listen. It came again, a small cry, and he hurried towards a cottonwood tree directly in front of him. When he saw the young boy with the mass of dark hair, his heart nearly stopped. "Buck?" he said as he broke into a run.

The child jumped to his feet and fled, but Nate quickly caught up to him. It was not Buck. Nate picked him up and attempted to calm him. He could see past the boy, to the body of a woman lying near the water's edge, and a lump rose in his throat. He hugged the motherless boy who so closely resembled Buck in size and build that he still trembled as he had the moment he saw him. The boy recognized Nate and held him tightly around the neck while Nate carried him back to the camp and found a woman to care for him till his father was found.

Nate resumed his search which took him across the creek to the meadow where a herd of Indian ponies, including his own Appaloosa, had settled back to grazing after the chaos. He finally spotted Tara lying curled up on the ground and shivering. Buck lay underneath her, his head shielded by her hands. When Nate knelt down and picked her up by the shoulders, she fell crying into his arms.

"Thank goodness you're all right, Nate."

"And you too. I was getting worried."

"I didn't know where I should go," she cried. "I kept running and running. This was as far as I could get. I guess I passed out."

"You're all right, and so is Bucky. That's the important thing."

She wiped her eyes with the back of her dirt-streaked hands and asked, "How bad is it?"

Nate's eyes glanced down at Buck, still clutching his mother's dress like he would never let go. Tara followed his gaze, and she understood. Their son's innocent eyes would now behold destruction and grief that he could not understand and they could not explain.

But no use in putting off the inevitable, Tara thought. She struggled to her feet, with Nate's help, and summoned her courage. "We have to stay now and help these people, Nate."

"You're hardly in a condition to help anyone," he replied. He said it more to himself because he knew she would try. But he determined to watch her and see to it that she didn't overwork herself.

***

Over the next two days, Nate and Tara attended burial ceremonies where blanket-wrapped bodies were suspended on scaffolds and the souls of the dead sent on their way with songs and prayers and baskets of food. They helped doctor the wounded, assisted in the cleanup of the encampment, and stood in amazement at how quickly the place took shape again, until no sign of the attack remained. That's what came of having a home that could be erected or taken down within thirty minutes, Nate remarked, not without some regret.

Tara's strength was flagging, and Nate was afraid she'd take sick again. She would not voluntarily stop working, so Nate had to make her stop, finally convincing her that the sooner she recovered, the sooner they could go home.

During all of this time, he never indicated any of his thoughts. He moved easily among the people and talked with them comfortably. The worry that nagged him, every moment of every day, he kept to himself. Only Tara he confided in as they sat by the river looking across at the butte that had caught his attention the morning after he had first arrived.

"I've wondered the whole time we've been here, Tara, if some of these braves, even ones I fought alongside just two days ago, attacked those medicine wagons and killed those teamsters."

"Such a horrible crime as you described to me then, surely these people didn't take any part in that."

"The cavalry believes they did. They must know something I don't."

"Do you think it's possible the killers are here?"

Nate thought long and hard. "I'm not sure. But I dare not accuse them without knowing more."

They sat in silence, watching the river meander east, until Nate broke the calm. "I've fought them before, you know, some of these same warriors."

"Yes, I know," she replied, remembering with heaviness of heart the bloody scene at Mount Defiance five years before. She'd been a captive then, nothing more than a bartering item in an argument that didn't involve her. How the politics had changed since then.

"They have forgiven me," Nate went on, "and I them. But if I ever find out..." His voice trailed off. "I will talk to Red Feather about it."

"I gave no such order," Red Feather resolutely replied to Nate's straightforward question. "If I attack, they will know it is me. No one will have to ask, 'Who does this?'"

Nate trusted the chief implicitly. If any warrior in his camp was responsible for the clandestine attack on the wagons, they had gone behind Red Feather's back.

"You understand that I had to ask," said Nate.

"Why don't the soldiers ask me, just like you did? I would have told them. But they never ask. They just come and kill our people and think they are finished." He paused. "It is not finished."

Nate didn't ask him to elaborate on that remark. But he thought it best to leave for home as soon as Tara felt able again.

Chapter 8

"I promise, I feel better now than before the attack," Tara said to Nate after a week had passed, "and so does Bucky. We can make the trip home just fine."

Resting his chin on his hand, Nate looked her up and down thoughtfully. "All right," he said finally. "We'll leave tomorrow."

She smiled, and there was a new spring in her step as she walked to the river to draw water with a canteen. Someone was approaching on horseback on the path beside the river, and she stopped to see who it was. When Ward Taylor appeared, she was surprised and excited to see a familiar face from home, albeit with an uncharacteristic two-day growth of beard. He saw her at the same moment and broke into a smile.

"Oh, Tara, it's so good to see you looking well," he said as he dismounted and moved closer to give her a hug. "You just don't know. I didn't know what news I'd find out when I got here. How's Buck?"

"As rambunctious as ever. Let me get Nate."

Nate's pleasure at seeing Ward was immediately tempered by worry. "Is something wrong back home?"

"No, no, everything is fine. That's not why I'm here."

Greatly relieved, Nate started in on the usual teasing. "So are you here on another diplomatic mission?"

"I wish. We need to talk."

Nate's smile faded, and he nodded. "All right."

Tara excused herself to fix supper for Buck. Ward led his horse to the edge of the water for a drink, and Nate followed him.

"What happened here during the cavalry attack?" asked Ward. "What did you do?"

Nate explained everything, reliving the event from the moment he realized it was happening till the soldiers retreated.

As Ward listened, the lines of concern etched on his forehead seemed to grow deeper. He did not look forward to delivering his message. "I came here to tell you not to come home. The cavalry's issued a warrant for your arrest on charges of high treason."

Nate somehow knew this was coming, but it was still a difficult pill to swallow.

"That damn Blaine," he muttered.

"They've put up a reward," continued Ward.

Nate raised his eyebrows. "How much is it?"

"Three hundred dollars."

"Is that all?" He was determined to find some humor somewhere in this situation.

"The cavalry's set up a presence in Timber Fork," Ward went on, "they say to protect the settlers, and maybe that's part of it, but I think it's also to get you."

"That sounds like their typical waste of manpower. Are you sure it's really for me though?"

"The new commander, a Lieutenant-Colonel McHenry, called in every single one of your ranch hands, one at a time, and threatened them if they saw you and didn't turn you in. Don't worry, they're all still loyal to you, to a man."

"Lieutenant-Colonel McHenry?" This was turning very suspicious to Nate. "I've heard the name, but I've never even met him."

"Well, he seems pretty interested in you. He believes that you're down here rallying support among the Cheyenne nation for a major offensive against him. He knows you've given the Indians horses before, and he suspects weapons as well."

Nate was stunned into silence for a moment. Ward's news had suddenly turned alarming. "Who would tell him that?" he breathed in disbelief. "I mean, I know Blaine's an idiot, but he wouldn't do that."

"They wouldn't tell me. Some kind of military secret I guess," said Ward in disgust. "Look, I studied the law when I was in Minnesota. Maybe I could help."

Nate shook his head. "The cavalry makes their own laws. At least at Fort Mason they do. You know, I think they post the dregs of society to that place? It must be some kind of punishment or something."

They were both quiet for a long time as Nate mulled over the gravity of this news and what it was going to mean for him. He looked around him, at the clear waters of the Sun slipping past them, at the tall grasses across the river that rippled in the summer breeze, at the butte whose uneven granite face was cloaked in patterns of light and shadow as the sun dipped slowly in the west. He had felt appreciation for this place in the past couple of weeks. But now it all looked and felt differently, now that he knew he wasn't leaving it, never to see it again. It had taken on a somber aura that hadn't been there only moments before. The same wilderness that had often been his ally was now closing in and felt like prison walls, and an unknown obstacle now blocked his route to freedom. "This is really gonna cost me, Ward."

Ward didn't even know how to reply. He was afraid that anything he might say would make it worse.

"Will you take Tara and Buck home?" Nate asked barely above a whisper.

"Yes, of course."

"I'll go tell her."

***

She listened to the whole story with lips pursed in anger, until he told her he was sending her back with Ward the next day.

"Nate, no! I will not hear of it."

"Didn't you hear what he told me? I can't go back."

"Then none of us will, until we can go together." Even as she spoke the words, she knew it was an impossibility. Her mind was a tangled mass of confusion. She put a hand to her temple to try to ease the headache that was forming.

He took her by the arm and led her aside, out of Buck's hearing. "There's no other way. I have to stay here, and you and Buck have to go home. Your mother's going to need you more now. I don't know how long I'll have to be here."

Tears flooded her eyes, and she grabbed him and hugged tightly. "I will not let them do this to you. I will get to the bottom of this."

He shook his head. "No, I'll not put this on you. You have enough with the ranch, and seeing to your mother." He caressed her cheek and looked directly into her eyes. "I'll take care of this. Somehow I will."

They shared their supper with Ward, and the time passed mostly in silence, until Nate reluctantly ventured, "Has Lena forgiven me, Ward?"

Ward sadly shook his head. "I think not yet."

"What'd she say when you were gonna come down here to talk to me?"

Ward hesitated a moment. "Nothing."

"Come on, Ward, what'd she say?"

"She was...well, she was angry about you fighting off the soldiers."

Nate set down his plate. He was suddenly not hungry.

"I know she was worried about Tara and Buck," Ward continued. "I believe when she sees them all recovered, it'll help change things. Just give her time, Nate. She'll come around."

"What about you? What do you think about what I did?"

"Were I you, I would have done as you did in bringing your family here. I wish I would've, for Laura."

"I don't mean that. I mean about fighting off the soldiers."

Ward looked away from him, reluctant to answer. "I don't know, Nate."

"Ward, look at me." He waited for Ward to do so. "Red Feather didn't give the order for that attack on the medicine wagons."

Ward thought it over for a while and decided, with some reservation, to believe Nate. "All right."

"You tell Lena that too. If I'm wrong, she can hate me forever. But I'm not."

His confidence buoyed up Ward. "I will tell her."

***

The night had grown dark and still with a cool breeze when all in the encampment were asleep. Only Nate and Tara lay wide awake, guessing at how many hours were left till daybreak would see them bidding farewell for an indefinite time. With blankets in hand, they slipped noiselessly from the tepee and sneaked to the riverbank. They found a level patch of grass on which to lay their blankets and lie gazing at the myriad stars gracing the heavens. Somewhere far downstream, a chorus of coyotes sang their song to the sky, their initial falsetto yips lengthening into eerie howls. Then, from much further downriver, came shrill yelps and howls in answer. Nate and Tara lay in silence listening, as if to speak would break the sacred reverence of nature's concert. After a while, the howls subsided as the coyotes left the river to travel elsewhere.

Nate checked the positions of the pointer stars in the Big Dipper in their counterclockwise swing around the North Star. "It's almost midnight. Goodness, look how bright Antares is tonight."

"That big one just to the left? That's not Antares. It's Arcturus."

"No, it's not."

"Yes, it most certainly is."

"It most certainly is not."

"I guess I know my stars as well as you."

"I guess you don't. That's Ursa Major," he said, pointing, "and just to the south of it is...Arcturus." He laughed sheepishly.

Tara smiled. "You taught me too well. And now you've lost all control of me."

He feigned a serious look. "Did I have control of you at one time?"

"As a matter of fact, yes. Years ago when you first came to the Broken Bow. You pretended not to understand English and spoke only Cheyenne to me and made Lena translate for you. You succeeded in getting me to avoid you altogether."

"Oh, yeah," laughed Nate. "I remember that now. Then one day you heard me speaking English to your father in the store. You gave me such a glare. I could feel it going right through me. You didn't take jokes very well."

"I took jokes well. It's just that yours weren't funny."

He propped himself up on one elbow and looked down at her with a teasing smile. "Oh, I'll ignore that, Mrs. Hunter, seeing as how you married me anyway, and it certainly wasn't for my money."

She held up her index finger. "It was potential. That's what I was looking for. Papa always said potential was important."

He noticed her waxing pensive at the memory of her father, and he quickly attempted to divert her thoughts. "I bet you don't remember the first time you ever saw me."

"Ah, but I do. You hated me."

"Oh, no. Not the *first* time."

"Very soon after," she laughed.

"I saw you riding that black horse you used to have."

"Molly."

"Yes, you were going up to the house to see your uncle. There was a corral in front of you—"

"And instead of going around it, I jumped Molly over the fences," she finished for him.

"You do remember."

"No, I don't. I just remember you talking about it on the way here, when I was sick on the travois."

His eyes widened in surprise. "I didn't know you were listening."

"Oh, I heard every word. I had never heard you talk so long before without stopping. I didn't want to miss it."

His smile melted away, and for a moment, the memory of the fear he had felt during their trip to the Indian camp returned. In a few hours, he'd be sending her and Buck away with Ward their only protector. He had traded his tepee for a horse for her and Buck to ride and an extra rifle for her to carry back. He'd inspected the weapon and found it to be in good condition, and he was confident she knew how to use it. But still, every hour of the next couple of days would take them farther away from him, and the fear he felt about that was almost as intense as that he had felt on the way to the camp.

"We've never been apart for a long time since we've been married," said Tara.

"Shhh, let's not talk about it tonight," he whispered as he leaned in close, brushed his thumb lightly across her lip, and stroked his fingers up through her thick, silky locks.

She slid her arms around his neck and pulled him closer. "I won't be able to say anything if you kiss me."

"I'm going to." He brushed his lips across her cheek till he met her lips, where he lingered for a breathless moment before kissing her hard and long. He followed with more kisses and tighter embraces, letting go only long enough to undo her petticoats and slide them off of her. She started to shiver in the night chill, and he quickly pulled the blankets over them and enveloped her in his arms again.

He made impassioned love to her. Accompanied only by the sound of the river and the gentle rustling of leaves on either side, it was as it used to be, when the wilderness first brought them together. The last four years seemed but a brief moment right now, and though neither spoke their thoughts, they both were keenly aware that they were seizing a moment now that would have to bridge a distance between them for a long time. He was glad it was a new moon so that the darkness could conceal from her the pain in his eyes. But though she didn't see it, she felt it in every movement he made, every whisper in her ear. She felt it in the tense muscles of his work-toughened shoulders as her fingers nimbly glided across them. Their unspoken yearning added both an urgency and a sadness to their lovemaking.

When again they talked, they carefully skirted any mention of the morrow and whispered only of a future when the current problems were past, when after an ordinary day of work on the Broken Bow, they might spend an evening by Elkhorn Creek, by their house, and revisit these same stars that glittered above them now.

Their talking and lovemaking continued on through the night, till at last, an hour before dawn, weary and spent, they fell asleep in each other's arms.

***

It seemed that only a minute later, the rising sun was boring through the trees, spilling orange light over the embankment and across the rippling waters with unchecked speed. One by one the stars blinked out as the veil of darkness mercilessly lifted, and the world seemed to widen as land shapes and trees took form. The spell was utterly broken when shouts from Ward sounded, calling for Nate and Tara as he looked for them. They flew from their blankets and dressed in a hurry.

As they neared the camp carrying their folded blankets and Ward saw them and hailed them, he discreetly avoided making any comments as to where they'd been and announced his intention to leave as soon as possible. Following a quick breakfast and with provisions packed on the bareback Indian pony, Nate gave Buck a hug and admonished him to be the man of the house and care for his mother before gingerly lifting him and setting him on the horse. Then Tara stood in front of Nate, bravely trying to give him the smile she knew he needed to see.

"I would wear a clean dress for today and brush my hair, but you didn't pack me a dress or a brush."

He meekly bowed his head and smiled. "You know I can't be counted on for such things." But then his gaze met hers, steady and intent. "You look beautiful anyway, as much as ever."

"Thank you."

Ward moved closer to shake hands with Nate. "Don't worry. I'll look in on the Broken Bow from time to time and make sure everything's going okay."

Nate's confidence in Tara's business abilities had long been unbounded. He smiled broadly at Ward. "Thanks so much, Ward. That's mighty big of you. And I'll have Tara check on the Split Timber and make sure everything's going okay there."

Ward returned to his horse smiling, and Nate directed his attention back to Tara. "Clay and Elijah will be your best men for running things." He paused. "You think you can handle all those ranch hands by yourself?"

"Don't you worry about those ranch hands. You just keep yourself safe."

Nate nodded. "I could maybe ride with you for a little while."

"No," she quickly answered. "At what point would you turn back, one hour, three hours? It would just make it harder for me."

"Yes," he agreed. "I love you."

"I love you too."

He handed her the rifle he'd acquired in trade, a Spencer .52 rimfire carbine that he highly suspected had been taken off of a cavalry soldier at one time. But it was lightweight enough for her to handle, and he'd made her load it in front of him to be sure she knew how.

After a final kiss and hug, he watched her mount, then too soon, she and Buck were riding away from him. He waved at them and watched them for as long as he could. He tried to swallow the lump in his throat. It felt like a piece of his heart was being ripped out of his chest. He felt emptiness and loneliness closing in on all sides. Inside, he cursed Major Blaine, Lieutenant-Colonel McHenry, and anyone else who could possibly be responsible for this crushing turn of events. He turned back toward the scattered group of tepees. He didn't want to be here, but he must now find something to do, at least some feeble attempt to distract himself.

Chapter 9

Tara and Buck's return to the Broken Bow was met with jubilation from the cowboys as they returned from their work a few at a time. They were disappointed but not surprised that Nate had not come with her, for they knew something was up. Once Tara and Buck's things had been unpacked and the Indian pony turned over to Elijah for saddle-training and, hopefully, a future as a cow horse, Tara thanked Ward for his help and asked him to stop at her mother's on his way home to the Split Timber. She asked him to take the message that she would be in town early the next day. For now, she felt she must speak to the hands first. They had run things flawlessly in her and Nate's absence, not to mention shown their loyalty under scrutiny from the cavalry, though they knew nothing for certain about what had happened in the Cheyenne camp. She owed it to them to speak to them first.

"It is good to see all of you again," she said to the men who, at Clay Tatum's bidding, had gathered in front of the porch. "I thank you for your thoughts and prayers in mine and Buck's behalf."

"You are welcome, ma'am," said one man.

"We're just glad they worked," said another.

Elijah glanced around at the others. "We were all just relieved to see y'all show up today, Mrs. Hunter."

"Thank you," replied Tara. "And I know I speak for Mr. Hunter as well when I tell you that we are ever so grateful for the splendid way you ran things in our absence." She paused, studying each of their faces in turn. They each peered out from under the brim of a hat, squinting against the setting sun, a couple of them chewing tobacco, a habit she detested. But not one cast his eyes toward the ground in the manner of one who wasn't sure what to look at. They all watched her, thoroughly interested in whatever she was going to say, and she determined they'd be on her side of whatever storm could arise. She felt it worthwhile to press on with her planned explanation.

"The Indians were very good to us. No one could have cared for Buck and me better than they did. I saw or heard nothing that would indicate they deserved the surprise attack by two companies of cavalry." She shut her eyes, envisioning the scene again and trying to will it away. "It was horrible," she said softly, "just horrible." She opened her eyes, but they were marked by sadness. "So Mr. Hunter fought to defend the Cheyenne, and he forced the commanding officer to call a retreat. We have since learned that the cavalry believes Mr. Hunter is trying to rally the Cheyenne to attack them, and that he has provided them with weapons to that end. For this they want to charge him with high treason. You may rest assured that he has never even considered any such thing, and does not do so now.

"I know that you each have been interviewed by cavalry in recent days. I apologize for that. The Indians were planning to move from the encampment where the attack happened. Likely Mr. Hunter will go with them. So if you have any more encounters with cavalry, you can truthfully answer that you don't know of his whereabouts."

"It wouldn't matter if we did know, ma'am," one man quickly replied. He paused to spit tobacco juice, and Tara cringed. "They ain't gettin' any information from us." Most of the others vigorously nodded in agreement.

Another man added, "Yeah, they come here all shined up in their uniforms. They looked impressive, sure, but we don't know them. We know Mr. Hunter. He works with us every day. He's one of us."

Tara smiled gratefully. Cowboys were not always a dependable lot, and they had gone through several on the Broken Bow. But Nate had carefully picked these. He had collected a pretty good bunch this time, she decided. She dismissed them, but asked Clay to stay behind.

She invited him to sit on the end of a long bench on the porch, and she sat on the other end. His straight brown hair hung almost to his shoulders, and his weather-tanned skin appeared nearly the same color as his hair, the effect being broken only by his gray eyes. Tara thought him rather plain, and she always wondered what women found so attractive about him. She initiated some small talk about the state of affairs on the ranch, and he dutifully filled her in on details.

"I'll have your month's pay ready tomorrow," she assured him. "I wanted to ask you, I know that you are in town often."

He rushed to defend himself. "Only when work's done for the day, Mrs. Hunter."

"No, Mr. Tatum, that's not a concern to me. You go into town as often as you like. I wondered what people there might be saying about Mr. Hunter and the cavalry's interest in him."

Clay grinned a little uneasily. "Well, truthfully, I don't hear much about that when I'm there."

She smiled politely. "I understand. But have you not been in the store at all?" Ever since her father had first opened his store a decade before and begun drawing his customers into deep conversations about politics and economics, the store had always been the most likely place for news to be spread, even more so than the saloon or the church, though Clay managed to find time to visit both.

He thought for a moment and slowly nodded. "Yep. On a couple occasions."

"And you've not heard any mention of Mr. Hunter there?"

"Maybe some. But you know, I wouldn't expect to hear nothin' but good there, ma'am. I think maybe Mrs. Sinclair would tear into anybody that said otherwise."

"She may at that," laughed Tara. She quickly became serious again. "Are you sure there's not more you can tell me, Mr. Tatum?"

Although she phrased it as a question, Clay perceived it more as a strong suggestion to be upfront with her. He gave in. "Actually I have heard wind of various things, ugly rumors I'm sure, 'bout Mr. Hunter defending the killers of cavalry teamsters." He glanced at her out of the corner of his eye and rushed to soften the news. "Oh, he made a rash decision, I'm sure, caught up in the moment, you know. It can happen to anybody."

"Look at me, Mr. Tatum." She stared him down. "It was no rash decision, and he wasn't caught up in the moment. The cavalry made a grave error. Mr. Hunter believes the killers of the cavalry teamsters are not in that camp."

Clay looked out at the range where tall, golden light-bathed grasses met with a horizon on fire with a sinking sun. He thought a moment and nodded. "Like as not, he'd know better than anybody."

Tara wished for more certainty from him, but she decided against pressing him further. She must be satisfied with the knowledge that Clay didn't usually pay any mind to rumors, as evidenced by his complete disregard for people's speculation about his many trips to town and whatever he did while there. She hoped for him to be loyal to his boss, and she felt pretty sure that he would be, but he was, first and foremost, a ranch hand, and one generally uninterested in weightier matters.

She rose from the bench. "Well, thank you, Mr. Tatum. Good night."

He briefly lifted his hat. "Night, ma'am."

***

The following day, Tara hitched up the wagon, lifted Buck onto the seat, and climbed aboard next to him for the trip into Timber Fork. She'd made the three-mile trip so many times over the years, never failing to gaze in wonder at Mount Defiance by whose foothills the town was situated. It always looked different, in different seasons, at different times of day, and in changing light. Even the shape of it changed as the clouds that frequently hovered above the summit repositioned themselves. She always caught Nate looking at it too, when he was along, no doubt remembering with mixed feelings the two years he'd spent living in the mountains.

As they rolled onto Main Street, she received many welcoming smiles and waves from passersby on the street. News traveled like the wind in town, and most had already heard that she was recovered and was coming in to see her mother this day. Several people inquired after Nate, and she answered briefly, with as many words as a passing wagon would allow.

The dusty street and wooden buildings with false fronts looked as they always did, busy from sunup to sundown with people filing in and out, some carrying boxes and packages. All that had changed over the years was that now there were more buildings and more people, and Main Street was longer than it once was. The lumber mill, one of the oldest businesses in town, was a booming success as always. This was progress to many, a disheartening development to others. It usually held an air of excitement for Tara, but today for the first time, it generated a deep and empty sadness in her. This was the first time for her to come to town since her father's passing, and the loneliness she felt in the midst of people was nearly overwhelming. She tried to imagine Nate beside her on the wagon. What would he say to her now to lift her spirits? It was no good. Nate was in a far different place than this. No imagining could help her now. She must carry on and be strong, especially for Buck. She took one hand from the reins and put it around Buck and hugged him close.

She saw two soldiers from a distance, riding side by side, the only evidence of the cavalry presence that Ward said was here. She had determined previously that if she ever ran into Major Blaine, she was going to have some words with him, and they would not be pleasant ones.

She paid no attention to how far up the street they had come, but her team that had made this trip many times knew to stop in front of the store. The sudden stopping of the wagon jolted her from her reverie, and she looked up to see the front of the whitewashed building that was the Sinclair store. She was surprised to see it closed. Why, on a busy day like today, hadn't her mother and Jared opened the store, she wondered.

Her thoughts were interrupted when the door burst open and Tara's petite mother, Margaret Sinclair, Jared and Rebecca, and her sister Rachel, a stunning sixteen-year-old with bouncing blond curls, ran out smiling and with arms open wide. Someone lifted Buck down from the wagon, and the others all vied to be the first to help Tara down. She felt better already. The group moved in a single mass back into the store and on into the dining room of the living quarters.

Seated around the varnished oak dining table with tea and pieces of Rebecca's apple pie in front of them, the conversation ranged broadly, with Tara telling about the strange tea she'd had in the Cheyenne medicine lodge. She hadn't thought to inquire about how it was made, and she wished she had, for future reference. Maybe Nate would remember, she said.

The Sinclairs, along with the rest of Timber Fork, were relieved that the last of the influenza cases had cleared up while Tara and Buck were gone. People were not afraid to venture out, do business, and visit again.

Margaret relayed her encounters with soldiers in the store. She didn't want to do business with them but knew she must, with a cheerful attitude. At least it was a good thing, she said, that they usually paid upfront with gold.

Jared waited for his mother to finish her story, then he looked at Tara with a twinkle in his eye. "I think it's time we got to the real business at hand." Everyone looked at him questioningly. He stepped over to the buffet, opened a drawer, and drew out an envelope. "Papa's will," he said, holding it up. "He entrusted it to me, and I have gone over it, but I waited for Tara to be here to read it to you all."

Tara regarded him with new admiration. He had stepped up as the patriarch of the family, and he seemed to have suddenly grown ten years older. She hadn't expected a lot of him, but he had matured without her ever noticing. Leadership just might wear well on him after all, she thought.

Jared unfolded the paper and began, "'Know all men by these presents, that I, Edward James Sinclair of Timber Fork, Territory of Montana, being of sound mind and memory, but conscious of the uncertainty of life, do make, publish, and declare this instrument to be my last will and testament in manner following, hereby revoking any and all wills and codicils by me at any time heretofore made. I direct my executor, Jared Edward Sinclair, to oversee the dispersion of my earthly estate as follows.

'To my eldest daughter, Mrs. Tara Sinclair Hunter, and son-in-law Nathaniel Hunter, I leave in its entirety the property known as the Broken Bow, with the mortgage rescinded immediately upon my death.'"

Tara's eyes widened in astonishment. It had never occurred to her to expect such a gesture from her father. She noticed everyone smiling at her, and she didn't know what to say, or who to say it to. She wanted to say it to her father more than anything. Why must these things always be revealed after a person was gone, she wondered. How she longed to throw her arms around her father and thank him profusely, and then tell Nate. Her eyes clouded with tears, and she reached for a handkerchief.

She heard Jared's voice first. "You deserve it, sister."

His kindness threatened to turn her tears into a flood. "But, Mother, you'll need the money," she managed to say.

"Nonsense," Margaret quickly replied. "We are set plenty well here with the store."

While Tara blotted her eyes, Jared continued reading. Edward had directed that ownership of the store and all its chattels be transferred to Jared's name, and that Jared was also responsible for the support of his mother. Rachel was to receive a substantial sum of money to be put in trust for when she married or turned twenty-one, whichever came first.

As Jared folded the paper and replaced it in the envelope, it became obvious he was fairly brimming with more news. "I guess this is as good a time as any to announce my plans. You are looking at one of the new proprietors of the First Bank of Timber Fork."

Everyone around the table looked at each other in surprise, except for Rebecca who seemed to know what this was about.

"Ward and I have been talking. We didn't want to tell anyone until our plans were firm, but we are opening a bank. Timber Fork needs one, and we wanted to be the first at it. While Ward will still keep his ranch going, we both agree he'll probably be better at banking than ranching."

Tara and her mother looked at each other, amused, and nodded in agreement.

"Ward has applied to the territorial legislature for the charter. We're both putting up equal funds to build the building on Main Street. I have some investors lined up in Chicago, among our relatives, and he has some in St. Paul."

"It sounds like you've thought this out very well," said Margaret. "Papa would be so proud."

***

Tara's spirits were sufficiently lifted by the end of this meeting. She stood up. "I need to make some purchases, but I see the store is closed today."

Jared laughed. "For you it is open. Take what you need. I'll cover it." He picked up Buck. "And I bet Bucky has been too long without candy."

"Have I ever, Uncle Jared," replied Buck in his best grown-up-sounding voice.

"Well, we will have to fix that right away."

Once Tara had loaded up the flour, sugar, beans, and cornmeal she needed for herself, and enough extra to restock the bunkhouse kitchen, she returned to carefully study the contents of the glass case where the selection of guns for sale was housed. She chose a .22-caliber four-barrel Sharps derringer with an ivory grip and handled it to see if it comfortably fit her.

"Tara," began Margaret with an air of disapproval, "that kind of gun usually belongs to gamblers and...well...the unsavory sort of women."

"If I have to kill an intruder, you'll be glad I have it, Mother," Tara replied matter-of-factly.

Margaret drew in a breath and put a hand over her heart but kept her silence. But when she saw the amount of ammunition Tara was piling on the counter to go with the derringer and the carbine she'd brought back from the Indian camp, she exclaimed, "Good gracious, there's enough here to fight off a whole regiment, or tribe. Take your pick."

"Nate says to never come to a fight unprepared," Tara answered with a smile.

Margaret shook her head as she began bagging the ammunition.

***

That evening after Buck was tucked in bed, Tara sat in the quiet, with only the light of a solitary candle, and staring at the boxes of ammunition stacked on the table. She recalled her mother's expression at seeing all the ammunition and rolled her eyes at her own silliness. She didn't know why she'd bought so much ammunition either. The false sense of security it had provided earlier had not lasted. She figured she wouldn't be very effective with the derringer anyway unless she was at close range and had time to take careful aim. She dumped the boxes along with the gun into the top drawer of her bureau in the bedroom and went to bed.

In the days following, she grew used to being alone at home with Buck. Her occasional trips to town were more for her mother's sake than her own. Home felt comfortable and safe again, just lonely in the evenings. She often read to Buck at bedtime, but she knew it wasn't the same as when Nate told him stories. Buck missed his father terribly but proved to be a brave boy and did Tara proud.

Clay kept Tara informed of all work on the ranch, but she deferred many decisions to him and remained confident in his ability.

She often saw soldiers in town in small numbers. They appeared to be an insignificant presence, yet they seemed to be aware of all the comings and goings in Timber Fork, and she did see evidence of their passing by the Broken Bow just outside the boundaries.

One particularly hot summer evening after it was dark and Buck was asleep, she felt drawn outside. She pinned up her hair to cool her neck and slipped out the back door in the lean-to in search of a refreshing breeze. A few feet from the door and close to the outside wall of the house was a dark, long lump on the ground. She couldn't remember anything having been placed there. Curious, she stepped closer and strained to see what it was. Suddenly the lump moved and took the form of a person standing up. She hollered and clutched her throat as she stepped backwards. She nearly tripped in her effort to reach for the door.

"Ma'am, please," came a soft Southern voice through the darkness. "Don't be afraid. It's just me."

She recognized Elijah, but her pounding heart and trembling body were far from being calmed.

"I'm sorry, Mrs. Hunter. I am so sorry. Confound it all, I guess I should've told you."

"Told me what?" she hissed. "What are you doing here?"

"I've been sleeping here at night, to keep an eye out for you and Buck."

"Keep an eye..." She swallowed hard, trying to collect herself. "What for?"

"Well, I—I..." He was somewhat at a loss for words. "Well, ma'am, I didn't feel right stayin' at the bunkhouse." He shifted on his feet uneasily. "I do know a little about the history of this ranch, things that happened here before. I just think you need somebody to look out for you, that's all."

"How long have you been sleeping here?"

He hesitated, nervously rubbing his chin. "Ever since the night you got back," he mumbled.

Tara was speechless.

"I really am sorry, Mrs. Hunter," he said again. "I sure didn't mean to startle you."

In a petrified daze, she stammered, "I—I suppose I should thank you." She turned quickly and hurried back into the house.

Sitting in her rocking chair and still breathing hard, she started thinking. He'd been there the very night she'd sat at the table with the newly purchased ammunition, and every night since, just on the other side of her bedroom wall. She shuddered. How many nights had it been? She couldn't remember. It took a good while for her to calm down and relax. When her presence of mind had fully returned, the whole thing turned rather amusing. Elijah had lived on the Broken Bow since Buck was born. He had helped to build the bunkhouse and the stables. She wasn't at all afraid of him, only when he scared her in the dark. She, in fact, trusted him as a protector, and she now developed a concern for his welfare.

She headed back outside. He had lain back down but rose immediately when she approached. "Mr. Medley, I was quite taken by surprise, but I'm all right now. I really am grateful for your concern. And I can't bear to think of you sleeping out here in the elements. You may put your bedroll here in the lean-to."

"All right then, if you don't mind."

She watched him pick up his bedroll and blankets and lay them out in the lean-to. "Feel free to set up here on your own each night. That's if you want. You don't have to. You are not to come inside the house for any reason." She indicated the door leading into the house. "This door is to remain closed and locked at all times."

"Well, now, what if there's any danger and you need fast assistance?"

She looked at the door and back at him. "You'll have to break down the door." With that she went back inside and locked the door.

***

Ever since her return from the Indian camp, Tara had every intention of traveling to Fort Mason and single-handedly straightening out this problem they had with Nate—whoever she had to speak to, whatever it took, using any method or influence at her disposal. Every day in the midst of her chores, paperwork, and caring for Buck, she thought about it and planned it. But the summer heat and lingering effects from the influenza left her weak and tired much of the time, and she was forced to take frequent breaks. She couldn't handle another journey just yet. Little by little, she gained strength and energy, and the everyday tasks seemed less overwhelming. She milked the cow, scrubbed laundry early in the mornings before the heat of the day set in, and worked to rescue the neglected vegetable garden so there'd be food to preserve for the next winter.

But then the sickness came. Every day she was gripped with nausea. She grew pale and thin. She asked Elijah to take care of her own horse, something she had always done herself. Elijah was worried, but she wouldn't speak to him about it.

Finally he confronted her on the porch. "Let me go into town and bring back the doctor."

"Absolutely not. It'd be a waste of his time."

He was growing perturbed with her stubbornness. "Mrs. Hunter, you are not well. You nearly died not long ago. And I will no longer stand by while you refuse offers of help. I am going for the doctor."

"That will not be necessary," she snapped. Instantly she felt guilty for speaking with that tone of voice. Nothing was his fault. He was only trying to be helpful. She had not wanted him to be the first to know, but she couldn't keep it hidden much longer. Her expression softened. "I'm going to have a baby."

He stared at her for a moment, then the tense muscles of his face relaxed. He was relieved to know there was a logical explanation, but then a new concern surfaced that agitated him. "He should be here."

"He would be if he knew about it. He can't take that chance, Mr. Medley."

Elijah nodded. "Listen, if you need anything, I mean anything at all, please let me know."

"Thank you. I do appreciate that. But I do have family in town, you know."

"Yes, of course." He reluctantly turned to leave. He wasn't completely satisfied to leave the situation in this manner, but he accepted it as he knew he must.

Chapter 10

Nate was surprised at the complete acceptance he'd found among the Indians. As he traveled south and east with them miles upon miles over many days in search of good hunting and grazing for the horses, it seemed every person in the band wanted to be a friend. The chief's wife, a short, gray-haired woman with an easy smile, had taken him in as if one of her family. She used hides from kills he had made to sew together a new tepee for him, and she put herself and her daughters in charge of erecting it and taking it down at every encampment. She became his favorite person to tease. He'd always tell her the tepee was not in the right place. Could she please move it two feet to the left? She was on to his tricks by now and would jovially slap his arm. She could slap pretty hard too. He told her he wanted to be there to see whenever she slapped her husband the same way.

He enjoyed his occasional fireside conversations with White Buffalo, the medicine man, whom he found to be one of the wisest in the band. He couldn't forget the powerful prayers he'd heard in the sweat lodge ceremony, and he desired to get to know the earthly man who had such a connection with heavenly forces.

There were young boys who begged him to teach them to throw a knife and hit a target dead-on, and their giggling teenage sisters who crafted beadwork items to give to him. He usually traded those to the chief's wife for whatever she was cooking that was different from the wild game he usually lived on.

He watched the people dance around the evening fires to the pounding rhythms of buffalo hide drums. They tried to get him to join in, but he'd never danced before, and he didn't see any need to start now. He would often divert their attention by pulling out the harmonica that was always in his pocket and playing everything he knew, from cowboy tunes to church hymns. Some of the older ones dismissed his music as white man's folly; the younger ones were intrigued by this curiosity and enjoyed the sound.

His daily associations all served to dull the constant ache of moving ever further away from his family. He contemplated countless plans to address his problems with the cavalry, but there was a hitch in every one. He knew if he entered Fort Mason peacefully to talk it over with those in charge, he'd be jailed with no question and no recourse. There could be no bargaining unless he remained free. What he needed first was information, and a one-on-one meeting with someone who had authority, but how to get it and from whom was a difficult matter.

One day they crossed the great Missouri River. As Nate swam his horse across, he recalled that the last time he'd crossed it was in a wagon when he was fourteen years old, moving with his parents and Lena to Montana. He never expected to be crossing it back again in the company of Indians.

They were in country now that looked different from home. Mountains had become rolling grasslands dotted with stands of cottonwoods and cut with shallow streams. The sky broadened, and he never thought he'd see so far. He began to understand firsthand why the Indians could not willingly give up their open spaces to encroaching white men who built houses and put up fences and laid railroad tracks. But he also found it incongruous that he should be here taking note of such things when he had built a house, put up fences, and driven cattle to those railroad tracks himself. It all depended on where you were born and who your parents were, he told himself.

They entered a large, green valley rich with game, firewood, and fish-laden streams. It was bounded by hills that protected from wind and provided a good vantage point for braves to stand guard against intruders. They were met there by other bands of Cheyenne, some already there, others who arrived later. The valley was covered with their tepees. In a short time, it became a great, organized community.

When Red Feather and some other chiefs and respected council members met in Red Feather's tepee, Nate sensed that something was up and that Red Feather had known all along they'd be coming here. But he was surprised when Red Feather came to get him to join the council session already in progress.

Nate entered the tepee to find an impressive array of Cheyenne leaders decked in their finest beaded buckskin clothing and feathered headbands that denoted each one's importance among the people. They sat cross-legged around the outer perimeter with a small fire in their midst. He was struck by the apparent importance of this occasion—a meeting of the proudest of the proud, the most influential figures among several bands.

They indicated a space reserved for him to sit down. He felt humbled and honored to accept, but he kept his reaction guarded till he knew what this was all about. He was very soon to find out. He listened as they spoke in their native tongue of the attack on Red Feather's camp and the losses suffered. They talked about when and where to strike back at the white men, and Nate's stomach began to churn. This was a meeting to discuss waging war.

Nate could not believe what he was hearing, and he felt wrong to be here. He remained quiet, certain that in such a gathering, it was not his place to say anything. Why had Red Feather brought him here, he wondered. Why did the chief want to let him in on this information? Had he expected Nate to be a party to this ominous scheme?

He nonchalantly studied the face of each brave who spoke, trying to determine which ones were adamant, which ones were more easily persuaded. From the corner of his eye, he noticed there was one brave who was constantly watching him. If Nate caught his eye, he would look away, but Nate knew he was being sized up and studied by this brave, and it made him leery. His thoughts ground to a halt when Red Feather held up a hand and addressed him directly.

"What does Eagle Shadow think of this?"

All talking subsided, and he found every eye resting on him. He refused to feel intimidated. They had asked for his opinion. "I will not go along with any plan to attack the whites. My family, my home, are among the whites."

"Your family and home are safe," one chief quickly assured him. "They come under our protection."

"I do not only fear for my family. I fear for other whites, and the Cheyenne alike. War will not take away your problems. It would only make them worse."

One of the braves smiled. "You are known among us for speaking against war many moons ago."

Nate raised his eyebrows, surprised that he was known very well at all.

"Yes, we remember," the brave continued. "But if you were one of us—"

"He is one of us," another brave sharply replied. It was the brave who had been watching Nate so closely since his arrival in the tepee.

Nate's gaze immediately shifted to the brave and held. He saw before him a sinewy, battle-toughened warrior possibly close to fifty years of age. Hung about his neck was a leather strand strung with the claw of a bear. Nate appreciated the show of support from this unlikely source but wondered at his motivation.

"Gray Wolf speaks too quickly. What I mean to say," the first brave continued, "is that if you were one of us who lost someone in the attack, you would want revenge too."

Nate thought about it and admitted, "That's probably true. But there are more of them than you. You might win a fight, here and there, but you won't win a war."

"We won't win if we don't try," said Gray Wolf. "But everyone here is ready to try."

This stirred up most of the group, with the majority speaking in favor of war, drowning out those who favored more talking. Voices rose; threats were made; order was being lost, and the heated debate showed no signs of dying down.

Nate's shout rose above the others. "Take it to the Council of Forty-Four!" At last they quieted down and eyed him, and he repeated his advice. Throwing away all caution now, he heard himself saying, "If they agree to it, I will too." In the highest ruling body of the Northern Cheyenne nation, all forty-four chiefs would have to agree, and Nate was certain that wouldn't happen. Although many of the chiefs had risen through the ranks of the military societies, they were generally a peaceful body and usually favored entering into peace treaties.

But this council knew what he was thinking, and the brave who had previously smiled at him now calmly replied. "We don't need to take this to the Council. We can decide this ourselves."

Gray Wolf responded, "Yes, we strike at the soldiers' fort. That is where they will all be."

"Fort Mason?" Nate asked, astounded. He shook his head and whispered to himself. "Oh, this is madness."

As they started talking over the stratagem for such an attack, Nate interrupted. "Have you ever been to Fort Mason?"

"No, but you have," said Gray Wolf. "You can help us."

Nate glared them each in the eye in turn. "It's a walled garrison manned by three hundred well-armed and well-trained soldiers. Some are good with heavy artillery, and they have several cannon. They're especially trained for Indian-fighting, and they are posted to Fort Mason knowing that that's what they'll be doing. To attack the fort is worse than futile. *It's suicide!* Don't throw away the lives of your warriors and make their children fatherless, not for this." He rose to leave. "That's all the help you'll get from me."

"Eagle Shadow!" It was Red Feather's voice that halted Nate in the doorway. "We know what you will not do. What *would* you do?"

Every one of the council was watching Nate expectantly. Red Feather had cast the burden onto him, and the others backed up Red Feather. If Nate couldn't agree with them, they were going to require him to suggest a worthy alternative. "I would do whatever I had to, to find those who killed the cavalry teamsters and destroyed the medicine and hand-deliver them to the fort myself." He glanced at Red Feather, confident that he had answered his challenge and was throwing back one of his own. "That is what I would do."

***

Nate sat outside his tepee, absently whittling at a stick. He constantly looked towards the tepee where the meeting was still going on. At last the council began filing out, and he stopped whittling and took a deep breath. When Red Feather approached, Nate stood to meet him.

"Your words were very strong," the chief said. "There will be no war."

Nate closed his eyes in relief, then he focused on the chief's first words. "They decided against it because of me? They are great leaders. What made them listen to me?"

Red Feather narrowed his eyes and gave a hint of a smile. He seemed surprised that Nate truly did not understand. "You do not even know who you are among the people, Eagle Shadow. You do not know the respect you have gained from all of the Northern Cheyenne nation." He saw that Nate was taken aback, and he put a hand on his shoulder. "I will tell you. In your life, we have seen you rise from the ashes of defeat, like an eagle rising to the sun, to become the strongest of warriors. But it was not your strength that marked you among us, no. It was your heart. When the soldiers came, you fought beside us. And when you forced the soldiers to leave, you saved many of our people. Word of your bravery and loyalty has passed among all of the people, and they listen to you now. When you speak, it is with the voice of the heart. You have shown that you are not afraid to use your strength, but you also know when to lay it down and speak with wisdom. There is not one chief on that council, or warrior among our people, who would not give his life to protect you."

Nate could not even reply. Red Feather left him alone, and he sat down to think and take in this news. He found it hauntingly ironic that the defining moment of the battle, the one that had sealed his fate with the cavalry, should be the same moment that had elevated his status among the Indians. But more than anything, he bore a burden now that had not been there minutes before. He did not feel worthy of such esteem from his people, and he certainly could not abide the thought of any of them taking a bullet for him someday.

The following day Red Feather's band was already breaking camp, and Nate felt disappointed. He'd thought this valley was a place he could peacefully settle into for a while. But as he began to gather his things, the chief brought Gray Wolf to Nate's tepee and introduced him formally.

"We have word that the soldiers look for you among us," said Red Feather. "You move to another band now, and you will be hidden from them. Go with Gray Wolf."

"All right," Nate answered with a nod. He was saddened to leave the familiar faces that represented the only semblance of home he knew currently. But he knew the chief's advice was sound and he should take it. He bid farewell quickly. That was easier. Red Feather would tell the others goodbye for him.

Later as he sat atop the Appaloosa and moved out of camp, Gray Wolf rode up beside him, and Nate got his first chance to talk with this curious brave. "Why were you staring at me in the council meeting yesterday?"

Gray Wolf beheld him with penetrating eyes. "I have heard stories of you around our fires since you lived in the mountains and escaped our braves."

"I doubt many of them were true."

Gray Wolf smiled. "Maybe not, but I have wanted to know you for a long time, Eagle Shadow."

"Oh? How long?"

Gray Wolf switched his eyes to the trail ahead. "A long time," was all he would say.

A memory several weeks old was resurrected, and Nate glanced over at Gray Wolf's person. He rode an unshod horse all right, but wore moccasins, not boots. He did wear a white man's type of shirt with his buckskin pants and a red bandana such as a cowboy would wear tied around his head. He carried a rather nice Winchester .44 rifle with polished brass receiver frame.

"You've spent some time among the white men?" Nate ventured.

"Yes. I speak your language very well."

"But I take it you didn't enjoy your time there. Am I right?"

"Yes. I was just a boy when I left the people for a time. Some white men took me and put me in a school. They made me learn about white men's books, white men's religion, and great leaders of white men. I was punished for speaking my own language. They thought they were helping me. But it does not help a boy to take away his freedom. When I became a man, I came back to the people. I will not leave again."

"Why did you go among the whites in the first place?"

Gray Wolf shook his head. "It is not important."

"It must've been at the time," Nate pressed.

He took a moment to reply. "Sometime I will tell you. But I did think it was good that I lived with them for so long."

"Why is that?"

"It is good to know your enemies, to understand their thoughts. It gives a man fire and purpose in his fight against them."

His words were chilling to Nate, but he couldn't quite figure Gray Wolf out. This brave had spent significant time amidst two cultures, yet unlike Nate, he embraced one while disparaging the other.

"Where are we going?" Nate asked next.

"Our hunting grounds are far to the south of here. You will like it."

Nate doubted he would like it much. It only meant he was traveling further away from home. But he did feel that he was among friends, and he felt safe from the cavalry.

The chief and others of Gray Wolf's band readily took in Nate as one of their own. As in Red Feather's band, there were those who wanted to be in charge of his tepee, even argued over it. With his hunting prowess, he often provided meat for himself as well as other families. One was a young widow and her son who was just a couple of years older than Buck. The boy liked to spend time with Nate and try to copy him as he whittled shapes out of wood. He was fascinated with Nate's harmonica and practiced it often while his proud mother looked on.

But it was Gray Wolf with whom Nate spent the most time. Gray Wolf was a fascinating enigma. He seemed principled and very sure of himself. He had a fiery personality yet ample self-control. He had an unwavering belief in the superiority of his people over the whites, but calmness ruled his demeanor.

"Red Feather seemed like he picked this band for me to travel with," Nate said to him one day. "Do you know him well?"

"Very well," Gray Wolf replied. "I grew up in his band."

"Really?" Nate smiled. "I wouldn't have guessed that. How did you end up here?"

"I married into this band."

"Ah, so where is your wife?"

"She died."

"I'm sorry. How did it happen?"

"It was an illness brought here by white men," he answered with an air of disgust. "Small pox they called it."

"Oh, yes." Nate shook his head. "A very bad disease."

"You ask a lot of questions."

"I guess I do. I don't mean to offend you."

"No, no, it is fine. I will ask some now."

Nate hesitated, then nodded. "All right, go ahead."

"Why do you like living among the whites so much?"

Nate was surprised at the pointed question and that he should have to explain what seemed obvious to him. "My mother was white. It is where I have always lived. Surely you know that one is comfortable among a people he grew up with."

Gray Wolf vehemently shook his head. "They are selfish, greedy, and stubborn."

"They are not all that way. Your view is very narrow." Nate was slightly annoyed. "I have seen the same traits in some Cheyenne. I was shot by one of them once."

Gray Wolf smiled. "I have angered you. You have strong feeling. I like that. It is a shame to waste it on the whites."

"That is exactly what they would say about your strong feeling."

"Yes," he said with a nod, "because they are stubborn."

"Oh, who is being stubborn?" Nate laughed. "Why do you dress in part as a white man?"

"It is comfortable."

"And you stay with what is comfortable. Do you not see what you are saying?"

"My shirt does not try to kill me or take what is mine. Do *you* not see?"

There was no arguing with Gray Wolf. Nate decided he'd just have to respect their differences and not question them.

But Gray Wolf wouldn't let the subject alone. Over the following weeks, he asked Nate often about his years growing up, what he'd been taught about the Cheyenne and how he'd accepted it. Nate was guarded with his answers, and he couldn't help but suspect that Gray Wolf wanted something from him.

One evening as he sat by the fire whittling sticks with the boy, he talked with the young widow, Shining Sky. "Do the people all like Gray Wolf?"

"He is liked well enough. But some of them don't talk to him much."

"Why is that?"

"I think they are afraid of trouble he will cause with the whites."

"Does he plan to cause any trouble?"

"I don't know. I have not seen him talk to anyone as much as to you." She watched her son and Nate stay busy with their woodworking. "Does your son make things with wood?"

Nate smiled. "I haven't let him use a knife yet."

"Are you missing him a lot?"

"Very much." He looked up at the gathering dusk where the evening bird calls were quieting down and the land was preparing for sleep. "He would be going to bed about now. He doesn't like to go to bed. He is afraid he will miss something."

Shining Sky laughed. "The same with River Otter."

"I often tell Buck stories at bedtime. He likes that."

"Do you make up the stories?"

"Sometimes. Mostly I tell about things that have happened to me, or that I heard about."

"Would you tell one sometime to River Otter?"

"Maybe, if he would like."

Nate tried it one evening, but his story lacked the spark it had when he told it to Buck. He liked River Otter, but being around him caused the hurt in his heart to grow. He was eager to tell Buck about all the experiences he was having, but how long would it be, he wondered. Even Tara would not know where he was now. He never felt more lost to all that was familiar.

***

"Did you know that Shining Sky is the daughter of a Council of Forty-Four chief?" asked Gray Wolf as he and Nate rode together one day a good ways from camp.

Nate looked up in surprise. "No."

"He has been dead for many winters. But there are many who remember him and honor her because of him."

Nate marveled that such honor had not been apparent to him. The people were subtle in their recognition of importance. In his own eyes now, she seemed hardly more than a forgotten princess.

"Her son River Otter looks up to you," Gray Wolf went on.

"He just misses his father, that's all," replied Nate.

"He never knew his father. He was killed in a buffalo hunt before the boy was born."

Oddly, Nate felt almost relieved and didn't attempt to hide it. "I thought you were going to tell me he died in a fight with soldiers."

"There are many ways to die. But it is an honor to die in battle."

"For you maybe. I think of it as an unfortunate necessity."

They stopped beside a stream and dismounted while the horses drank.

"I was disappointed that you talked the council out of war that day," said Gray Wolf. "Now, because the people listen to you, a wrong will go unpunished."

Nate had had time to think it out, and he knew what Gray Wolf wanted from him. "You want a person of influence to side with you against the soldiers and to lead everyone else to fight with you. That is just what the soldiers already suspect me of doing. But they are wrong, and so are you."

"Perhaps they have not yet angered you enough, Eagle Shadow."

"Perhaps not. I have been very angered by Cheyenne in the past though." He watched Gray Wolf for some sort of reaction, but there was none. He sensed that Gray Wolf purposely saw to it to mask any reaction. Nate shook his head. "I am not like you."

"You are more like me than you know. You will always defend what is precious to you."

"Yes, I will defend. But I will not try to start trouble." Disgusted, he turned away from Gray Wolf and picked up the reins of the Appaloosa. "I am sure that you have been in many battles and found honor in it. And I know that you have killed white men."

"So have you!" Gray Wolf fired back.

His accusation echoed in Nate's ears, and he whipped around. "And I am paying for it!"

"Maybe for a while. But you will see your wife again. I will not see mine."

Nate mounted the Appaloosa. "You have wasted your time trying to make friends with me. You don't need a friend. You need an ally. And I don't need either one."

"No, I have not wasted my time, Eagle Shadow. I am your friend. And I will not speak of this again if it bothers you."

Once again, Nate was bewildered. He still didn't have a handle on Gray Wolf.

Chapter 11

As the crisp autumn air gradually replaced the stifling heat of the summer and earlier sunsets heightened the brilliance of leaves changing color, Tara's condition miraculously revived. Food tasted better again, and she ate plenty of it. She returned to riding and caring for her horse and oversaw the fall roundup herself, helping to choose out the steers ready for market. Her slender frame accentuated her four-month pregnancy, and she had already felt the first stirrings of the child inside her. Everything seemed to be progressing so fast now. Her ardor for straightening out the terrible misunderstanding about Nate and bringing him home intensified. Now was the time to make her move and visit Fort Mason.

She warily realized she'd be traveling the same road where the cavalry teamsters had been killed. She needed a man who was good with a gun to accompany her as a protector, which of course, meant that she needed another woman to go as well. To that end, she visited the Split Timber and explained her plans to Lena.

"You will come with me, won't you?" Tara asked when she'd finished her explanation. "We will just be about three days."

"I—I don't know, Tara. Sarah needs me—"

"You don't have to speak to the commander with me. You don't even have to come inside the fort if you don't want to."

The cold, unfeeling look in Lena's eyes was the same she'd had for months. Nothing could move her. No one could reach her.

"Lena, he's your brother," Tara pleaded. "He would do *anything* for you."

Despite Tara and Ward both watching her expectantly, Lena appeared to feel no pressure. "Please don't take this as a personal insult, Tara. I don't mean it to be. But I'm sure you can find someone else to go with you."

Tara was greatly let down, but she refused to fritter away any more time on this. "All right, that's fine." She immediately left.

Ward stared at Lena when Tara had gone, his disapproval evident. He had endured this behavior for too long. He felt as if he lived alone. "Nate said he doesn't believe the attackers of the wagons are in that camp." He'd said it countless times already. "Do you believe him?"

"I believe that *he* believes it," replied Lena. "For myself, I don't know."

"Then trust in someone who does know more and who is your kin." He'd fought off impatience long enough. His voice became louder. "You know what? It doesn't matter. It makes no difference whatsoever where the attackers are. All that matters right now is that your brother's in trouble, and I don't think you realize the seriousness of the situation. If Nate's convicted of treason, he'll hang. His wife will be a widow. His children will be fatherless. You were made fatherless yourself. Is that what you want for his children?"

"No, of course not!" cried Lena. "I would never want that."

She clapped a hand over her mouth and rushed for the back door. It slammed behind her, and Ward was left standing alone in the quiet house, contemplating whether he should go to her and what he should say. There was nothing more to say. He'd said everything he could think of over the last few months. He was hurting too.

As he started to ascend the stairs, he heard a noise and stopped to listen. It was the sound of Lena's weeping coming from the direction of Laura's grave. In just moments, Ward was beside her at the graveside. She fell against him, pouring out her heart in great sobs. Tears stung his eyes, and he held her tightly.

"I miss my little girl," she cried. "Life goes on for everyone else, but not me."

"I remember telling Nate that you were stronger than me." He pulled away from her and held her face in his hands. "I do still believe that. And we will bear this together."

"I do want Nate to be able to come home again, really I do."

He hugged her again. "I know you do."

***

Rebecca accepted Tara's invitation to go to Fort Mason. That left the matter of who the protector should be, and there wasn't much of a choice. She wouldn't ask Ward if Lena wasn't coming. Obviously Lena shouldn't be left at home alone. Ward had been pretty wrapped up in getting the bank going anyway. And Jared? He was busy with the bank too, but Tara smiled to herself. Bank or no bank, Jared looked more natural with a pencil behind his ear than with a gun on his hip. She didn't feel comfortable asking most of the ranch hands. She communicated to them through Clay and had little contact with them. And Clay was too indifferent. That left Elijah. She had tried to avoid the thought, but he was quite mindful of her security. Every night she would hear him setting up his pallet in the lean-to. He dutifully left for work each morning before she and Buck got up. *More faithful than a dog,* she thought.

"Would you be willing to accompany myself and the younger Mrs. Sinclair on a trip to Fort Mason, for our protection?" she asked him when he came in from his work.

"Why yes, ma'am, it'd be a pleasure—I mean, yes, I will."

"Thank you. We'll leave at first light tomorrow."

"Does this have to do with Mr. Hunter?"

"Yes, it does."

He nodded. "All right. I'll be ready."

***

Elijah's poke was packed in only five minutes. He wished they could leave right then. She was his boss, but he hoped she might also consider him a friend. He'd had so few. He lay awake in his bedroll that night contemplating his previously aimless existence and the fate which brought him here. Did life hold a predetermined plan for everyone? Was he supposed to have ended up here, or was it all just happenstance? None of his reading had ever answered that question for him.

He had started out with an idyllic early childhood in Georgia, until at the age of six, he lost both of his parents to the yellow fever. His poverty-stricken maiden aunt dropped him off at the Catholic orphanage in Savannah and never came back. There the nuns were fastidious about teaching good morals and behavior, and Elijah was obedient and cooperative. But what he was most grateful for was that the nuns had taught him to read, thus providing solace to his lonely life. His world was populated with the characters about whom he read—the swashbuckling adventure of *The Count of Monte Cristo,* the humorous stubbornness of Don Quixote's fantasized fight with the windmills. He thrilled at the resourcefulness of Robinson Crusoe, and became delectably lost in the authentic detail of *Moby-Dick,* which very nearly tempted him to run away to the Port of Savannah seeking a life on the sea. His attention turned to the West with the tawdry "blood and thunder" novels about Kit Carson, outlawed by the nuns but traded secretly among the boys in the orphanage.

When he finally did run away at fifteen, never looking back as he barely escaped the outbreak of the war, the books from the orphanage school library couldn't go with him, but the stories did. He thought of Paul Revere's famous ride to Lexington as he made his way west riding for the Pony Express. A knee injury from an accident with a falling horse ended his mail courier days after two months, but it had been long enough to instill in him a strong rapport with horses. Upon full recovery and with the Pony Express having met its demise, he found a job on a ranch in west Texas. The only previous experience he'd had with cows was milking them at the orphanage, but he was a quick learner, and punching cows and wrangling horses came easily to him. So began a long line of cattle drover jobs on several ranches, most recently in Denver, before he wandered into Montana Territory, wondering what the country looked like there.

Adulthood had mellowed his literary tastes, and he rode into Montana with a mind tempered by Whittier's simple poems of country life and the sensual imagery of Keats. And he had long contemplated William Cowper's thoughts on the difference between knowledge and wisdom. Knowledge came from others' thoughts; wisdom came from within. Knowledge was encumbering unless one knew how to refine it into wisdom. He consistently measured the pride of knowledge against the humility of wisdom, desiring his own character to possess more of the latter.

He never knew what was missing in his life until he came to work on the Broken Bow and it was thrown in his face. Seeing Tara's business savvy and intelligence and her collection of poetry books, he'd always thought she and Nate were somewhat mismatched.

The first inkling he'd had that they were not was spurred by an incident he witnessed in the bunkhouse one day when Nate gave a teenaged ranch hand a black eye and sent him packing for stealing yearling calves and claiming they'd been lost to wolves. Elijah believed the young hand to be innocent, and the next day when Nate had simmered down, Elijah nonchalantly drifted into a conversation with him and began to relate the Welsh legend of Gelert the hound whose owner killed him because he mistakenly thought the dog had mauled a baby. He'd barely started the story when Nate walked him over to a corral and showed him the calves that had been returned unharmed by the fired hand. And then Nate demonstrated his familiarity with the legend by adding, "And if I'd been Prince Llewellyn, I wouldn't have been so rash. I would have searched for the baby first."

Elijah didn't realize his jaw had dropped so far till Nate laughed and then told him about his schoolteacher mother. Elijah smiled too, but Nate's ever-so-subtle message about not challenging him came through clearly, and Elijah never tried it again.

***

As Tara rode on the wagon seat beside Elijah the next morning with Buck in between them, they each were thinking far different thoughts as they pulled up in front of the Sinclair store in Timber Fork. Elijah was eager for the friendly conversation that the trip would afford; Tara cared only for the planned conversation with this Lieutenant-Colonel McHenry who held Nate's fate in his hands. She kissed Buck goodbye while Jared set Rebecca's carpetbag inside the wagon. Although Tara didn't like to leave Buck, knowing that her little family would all be scattered miles away from each other, she was comforted to know that he was in the safest of hands. His grandmother spoiled him, and he would have fun "playing store." Rebecca and Rachel loved being aunts. In fact, Rebecca would probably have preferred to stay at home with Buck than to go anywhere, but she was always agreeable to Tara, and Tara was profuse with her gratitude.

***

"You should be sitting down, Mrs. Hunter," said Elijah on the first evening of their trip.

"I've been sitting all day," she replied without looking at him. "This feels rather good." No one had wanted her to ride a horse on this long trip, but she didn't see where the wagon provided any more comfort. So now she stood up to eat her meal of bacon, beans, and biscuits at their campsite in a creek-side stand of oaks. "Becca, shall we take a walk beside the creek?"

"I would love that," Rebecca concurred.

"You girls be careful now," Elijah warned. "I'm supposed to be lookin' out for you, you know."

Rebecca's ready laugh carried back to him as they ventured away from camp. "You shall hear our screams if you are needed."

They strolled through the oaks, idly poked in the creek with sticks, and tossed pebbles into the water, always staying within earshot of Elijah as he insisted. They only came back when the dark and the chill required it and settled themselves close to the small, flickering campfire.

As stars began to appear, Tara couldn't help but wistfully notice them, and she began to point out constellations as they blinked into view in the clear, moonless sky—Draco the dragon wrapping himself around Ursa Minor, and Queen Cassiopeia reigning from the midst of the Milky Way and flanked by Perseus and the Northern Cross.

"I don't think I've ever known a woman who knew more about the stars, Mrs. Hunter," marveled Elijah.

"Nate taught me everything, and I've never forgotten it."

He had never heard her refer to Nate by first name in front of him before, and she didn't seem to have noticed this time. "He knows the Latin names of the stars?" he asked.

"His mother was a schooltea—"

"Oh, that's right." Hoping to draw her mind off Nate and back to the current moment, he added wood to the fire. It crackled and flamed up, causing many stars to quietly shy away from view.

A lone wolf's howl floated on the evening breeze from far away, and Tara and Rebecca both started at the sound.

"It's just a wolf," said Elijah. "They won't come near the fire. Are you nervous?"

"No," said Tara. She was bothered that he addressed mostly her. "What about you, Becca? Are you nervous?"

"A little. I know we're not far from where the Indians attacked the medicine wagons."

Elijah immediately rushed to dispel any fear that statement might cause. "I expect the Indians all know you, Mrs. Hunter, isn't that right?"

"It depends on which Indians they are, Mr. Medley," she replied, slightly annoyed. "I don't know the whole tribe." She turned to Rebecca and smiled. "I expect if I just mentioned the name *Netse Mahtasuma,* we'd be fine. That means

Eagle Shadow."

"It's too bad I didn't bring a book I could read out loud to us," said Elijah. He suddenly remembered something and reached into his pants pocket. "I do have this poem I copied a long time ago. I carry it with me sometimes." He withdrew a yellowed, worn paper, unfolded it, and held it up to the light of the fire.

"Read it to us," said Rebecca.

"All right." His voice reflected some insecurity as he began, the hesitation of one who wasn't used to reading to others.

"'This book is all that's left me now—
Tears will unbidden start,—
With faltering lip and throbbing brow
I press it to my heart.
For many generations past
Here is our family tree;
My mother's hands this Bible clasped,
She, dying, gave it me.'"

With the women reverently listening, he gained more confidence now.

"'Ah! Well do I remember those
Whose names these records bear;
Who round the hearthstone used to close,
After the evening prayer,
And speak of what these pages said
In tones my heart would thrill!
Though they are with the silent dead,
Here are they living still!'"

His voice settled into a smooth, lulling rhythm as he focused wholly on the words that had always touched his more quiet, private nature.

"'My father read this holy book
To brothers, sisters, dear;
How calm was my poor mother's look,
Who loved God's word to hear!
Her angel face,—I see it yet!
What thronging memories come!
Again that little group is met
Within the walls of home!

"'Thou truest friend man ever knew,
Thy constancy I've tried;
When all were false, I found thee true,
My counselor and guide.
The mines of earth no treasures give
That could this volume buy;
In teaching me the way to live,
It taught me how to die.'"

Silence followed for a moment, then Rebecca softly commented, "Those are beautiful words."

Elijah nodded as he folded the paper and put it back in his pocket, then he looked to see how Tara had received it. She was watching him through narrowed eyes.

"McGuffey's Fifth Eclectic Reader." She smiled. "You copied that from a school book." She wondered why a tanned, rugged cow puncher and horse wrangler would have such a thing in his pocket. Curiosity got the best of her. "Where are you from, Mr. Medley?"

"I've told you, I was up from Denver."

"You were up from Denver three years ago. Where did you grow up? Maybe Richmond, Charleston?"

He smiled and rubbed his chin, as he always did when put on the spot. "You're not far wrong. Savannah."

"I knew I was close." Tara counted it a small victory to wheedle something out of him about his background. "You're a long ways from home."

Elijah gazed into the soft orange flames, thinking of something which he would not say. "No. I'm home now."

"Well, that was perfect for a bedtime reading, and I'm ready for sleep now," said Rebecca, trying to stifle a yawn. She retired to her bedroll underneath the wagon and wrapped herself in blankets like a cocoon.

Rebecca always went to bed early, but Tara wasn't tired enough just yet, and she remained by the fire, thinking of her meeting the next day, trying to guess how it would turn out. She'd done some checking on this Lieutenant-Colonel David Gunning McHenry by having friends talk to cavalry soldiers in Timber Fork. She knew she was dealing with a highly decorated West Point graduate who had friends in high places. How such a man had drawn Fort Mason as a post was a mystery she hadn't been able to solve, and she'd learned little else that would benefit her, but she'd guessed that a respectful, direct approach would be the best course to take.

She pulled her shawl closer around her and gave a shiver, as much from nervousness as cold. Instantly Elijah was laying a blanket around her shoulders. "You don't have to do everything for me," she objected.

"Yes, ma'am, I do. You're—I mean, you're..." His eyes darted down to her abdomen, covered with a loose checkered blouse.

"I'm fine."

He let out a breath, glanced over at Rebecca who was already fast asleep, and squatted in front of Tara. "Look, Mrs. Hunter, it's probably obvious I have powerful strong feelings for you." He rubbed his chin again. He'd never felt so awkward. He was about to bare his soul to her, and he was calling her Mrs. Hunter.

"What are you trying to say, Mr. Medley?" Her words came as a clear indication that she wasn't going to listen for long.

"Well, Mr. Hunter lives sort of a dangerous life. I mean, with all this business with the Indians and criminal charges from the cavalry and whatnot. He's involved in dangerous things. I don't mean to cause you any unnecessary pain, but there's a chance he won't make it home, and I think you know that. If something happens to him, I know it'd be a difficult time for you. I just want you to know I'd be there for you. I'd take care of you. I'd take care of your children...I'd marry you."

Tara tried to hide the fact that she was stunned by his confession. There were so many other things on her mind. How was it that he could be thinking of that? She didn't want to have this conversation. She stood and mumbled something about turning in for the night. But her steps toward the wagon were slow. The thought nagged at her that she must address this now. He was right. Perhaps Nate wouldn't make it home again. What would she do then? She would have two children to raise. She would have to carry on somehow, and how could she do it alone? She knew of no one more loyal, or willing, than Elijah.

She felt the baby move inside her, just a soft flutter, but a palpable reminder of the night of conception. How different were her feelings that night from this one. There was no comparison. Elijah would never be able to make her laugh like Nate did. No matter how many years passed, she would never enjoy looking at the stars with Elijah. Nate and Elijah both protected her like a precious jewel, but Nate had handed her a gun and watched her load it herself. Elijah would never have done that. He didn't want to recognize her strength.

She turned back around and approached the fire again. He was watching her expectantly. "Mr. Medley, you're a fine man, and you'll make some woman a very fine husband someday." She could see his face changing.

"But?" he asked.

"But if anything ever happened to Nate, I could never love anyone else, ever."

"I know you wouldn't love me at first. But maybe after some time had passed—"

"Mr. Medley, I'm carrying my husband's child, and I'm going to Fort Mason to plead on his behalf. You're getting a little ahead of yourself, aren't you?"

"Yes, ma'am, you're right. I'm sorry."

Her mood toward him softened. "You know that wouldn't make you happy.

And you deserve to be happy. Don't make this harder for yourself, or me."

He smiled half-heartedly. "He's a lucky man."

"Thank you. You must realize, Nate and I have a history together. We've endured things you know nothing of."

"Ah, yes. I've seen his scars." He momentarily forgot what had just transpired and was engulfed with the sudden remembrance of an old curiosity. It was a particularly hot, late spring day on the Broken Bow when Nate and the cowboys, taking a break from the scorching heat of branding calves, shed their shirts and raucously flung themselves into Elkhorn Creek to cool off. Nate's scarred shoulder and abdomen had surprised Elijah, and he asked Nate about them. Nate replied that he'd been shot on occasion, as casually as if he was relating what he ate for breakfast, and that was the end of it. Elijah later asked Clay about it, who said he thought it had something to do with Indians, but if Nate wasn't inclined to mention it, he wasn't inclined to wonder about it.

Now was Elijah's chance to know, and he asked her, "Who is he, anyway? I mean, just who is he to the Indians? What's happened with him?"

She hung back like a timid bird, trying to decide if it was prudent to respond. Then she came closer and sat down next to him. This was going to take a while he guessed. Speaking in subtle tones so as not to wake Rebecca, she told a story, a story so intriguing, so surprising to him, and sometimes so violent that he couldn't say a word but just listen. He heard details for the first time of the destruction of a ranching operation larger than what the Broken Bow was now, of Nate as a fugitive surviving many close calls, how he had come to gain favor with a Cheyenne chief, and most surprising of all in light of current circumstances, how the cavalry had once heavily relied on his influence with that chief.

The origin of the two scars came vividly to light. With her descriptions, the faces at the other end of the guns materialized in his mind's eye—the distrustful, malicious drifter who later died with Nate's knife in his chest, and the renegade Cheyenne brave with the heinous contempt for Nate. He, too, paid with a lifetime sentence of banishment from his people.

Elijah shook his head in amazement and whispered, "I had no idea." He turned and looked at the smooth, delicately curved features of her face in the flickering firelight, knowing for certain that a moment such as this would never occur again. "Could I kiss you, just this one time? I swear it will never happen again. No one will ever know, and I would live on it for the rest of my life." The words were out; he could not call them back. Her eyes turned to his, and he held his breath. There was no surprise in her look, no anger, just deep contemplation. Then she stood and backed away to the very edge of the circle of firelight, breaking the spell, and he closed his eyes in defeat.

"You are wrong," she said. "*We* would know. And knowing that it would never happen again would make you want more this time. You are above that, Mr.

Medley. Don't ever ask me that again."

"I'm sorry, Mrs. Hunter. I guess I just lost my head for a minute."

She moved completely out of the firelight then and walked to her bed under the wagon. Long after she had gone, he remained by the fire thinking. He had gravely misread Nate. He had pictured him as a poor, insignificant ranch hand who just happened to luck out by marrying into ownership of a large ranch. He had worked with Nate nearly every day for over three years, but all he'd known of him was just an outer shell. He had been measuring himself against what he'd perceived as a much lesser man.

In telling his story, Tara had unwittingly told him hers as well. She had faced down situations more dangerous than Elijah had been in before. She had saved Nate's life more than once. She had killed, and without hesitation.

He'd had what he now knew to be a very narrow view of Tara and Nate's relationship. That view had now been dynamited wide open. The Hunters may have had some commonality in their knowledge of literature, but their relationship had nothing whatsoever to do with literature. Nor did it concern distant constellations, or even operating a ranching empire. They had stood on the brink of hell together. They had suffered the ravages of the frontier together, and now they were of one mind, of one heart, and the iron connection of their souls could not be broken, least of all by undetermined miles and months of separation, but not even by the finality of death. Elijah was, as always, a lonely outsider. In one fell swoop, she'd broken his heart into a thousand pieces and left him devoid of hope.

He suddenly stopped his thoughts midstream. What exactly had he been hoping for anyway, he asked himself. For her to be a widow? In three years of working for the best boss he ever had, had he really stooped to this level of selfishness? He didn't hate Nate; he was just jealous of what he had. King David of the Old Testament came to mind, an oft-taught lesson at the orphanage. He'd had a man killed so he could marry his wife. David had started out a good man, till his obsession had taken him down a dangerous path. It scared Elijah to his very core to think that he may have such a streak in him. He thought again about knowledge and wisdom, those two traits that seemed to mirror each other, but one only made up a small part of the other. She had just given him knowledge, but did he have the capacity and self-mastery to distill it into wisdom? This time he honestly wasn't sure, and the question haunted him.

Chapter 12

The arrival of autumn, the Moon of Falling Leaves, brought a heaviness to Nate's heart. A whole summer had passed, and he had not held his wife in his arms. He had not seen his son play his boisterous outdoor games, had not led a horse by the bridle while Buck sat on top laughing, his tiny hands clinging to the saddle horn. Buck had probably even grown some by now. Would his son look much different when he saw him again?

He had missed the fall roundup; the shipment of horses he'd planned for the Indians had been forgotten altogether. Were the hands still loyal, he wondered. Were Clay and Elijah still holding things together?

With the Indians and his trusted horse, he had made his way further across the territory, crossing the Yellowstone River, and later the Tongue River. Every moment of every day he had kept his eyes and ears open for at least some remote clue to help him find the attackers of the medicine wagons. Although the people in this band trusted him and talked freely with him, nothing had surfaced that could move him any closer to his goal. It was as if those responsible had made themselves invisible. And it was leverage he desperately needed. He knew he couldn't approach the cavalry without solid proof, or even better, the perpetrators themselves with which to bargain.

He figured that Tara would've tried to do whatever she could. If she had been successful, he was sure that word could've reached him. The Cheyenne nation had a grapevine of communication. They had their ways of knowing where soldiers were looking for him, and bands communicated with each other through messengers, and if within distance, through smoke signals and drum signals. They had often informed him of cavalry activity. But hidden among the people and with their sworn protection, he was virtually untouchable.

He and the Appaloosa had just returned from a successful hunt one day, dusty and tired, when he knelt beside the stream near the encampment. Cupping his left hand, careful always to keep his right hand free to draw his gun, he repeatedly drew water to his dry lips and drank his fill. Muted moccasin steps sounded behind him, and a long shadow was cast over him. He didn't even look up. He'd long since come to recognize the stealthy gait and the shape of the shadow.

"I saw you fall off your horse today," he teased Gray Wolf. "You thought nobody saw?"

Gray Wolf smiled. "That horse does not have sure feet. He broke his stride when he stepped on a slippery rock."

"Come on, you could think of a better story than that."

"I do not have your gift for stories."

Nate hardly heard Gray Wolf's last words. He was gazing longingly out across the stream, his momentary good humor forgotten.

"Where is your mind now?" questioned Gray Wolf.

"This spot right here looks very much like a place on Elkhorn Creek back home. I have rested beside it many times. There are many beautiful places on the Broken Bow." He looked up at Gray Wolf. "You should see it sometime."

Gray Wolf set down his rifle and sat in the grass. "Why do you want to live there, where your father died?"

"It is good land," Nate answered defensively. "I will not let what happened drive me away from it. My heart will not be slave to some murderous Indians."

"You have a strong heart. I admire such strong feeling."

Nate cast him a suspicious glance. These innuendos of Gray Wolf's came almost daily. "My strong feeling is not for your use. I will never do what you are wanting me to do. I will not side with you against the white man."

Gray Wolf remained aloof. "You are just like your grandfather. He was so stubborn about his innocence."

"Because he *was* innocent. Everyone knows that now." Although they had never spoken of it, Nate wasn't a bit surprised that Gray Wolf should have known his grandfather, having grown up in the same band. But he was just a little curious. "You were there, when he was banished?"

"I remember that day. I was a boy, not much older than your father. Your grandfather left angry. He and his wife and son traveled for weeks without stopping. They wanted to get far away. They tried to stay away from the white people, so they wouldn't settle down. They were always moving because that's what they were used to. But it was a lonely life for them, and they died while their son was still young."

Gradually as Gray Wolf talked, Nate's stomach began to twist, and his throat tightened. He sensed that Gray Wolf had found him at the stream on purpose to tell him something.

"That son grew up fine on his own," Gray Wolf went on. "He married a schoolteacher in Missouri and had a son. Three years later they had a daughter."

Nate dared not look at Gray Wolf as he listened to the brave recount things about his family that he had never told him before. He kept his eyes on the stream, but he was unaware of its flow. A sickening dread, one which was unfamiliar, was snaking through his whole body. All time seemed to have halted. "Stop. Don't say anymore." The words were lost. Gray Wolf's voice kept going as purposefully as he had ever heard him speak.

"The schoolteacher's family didn't want her anymore. The children were shunned by other children. They moved to the Platte River after that. They worked on a farm there for many winters. Later they moved to Montana, where they stayed."

It wasn't just the invasion of his cherished privacy that bothered Nate. That was the very least of his concerns at this moment. Gray Wolf was relentlessly boring his way into an area of Nate's life where he wasn't welcome. Nate chanced a look at him and found Gray Wolf already watching him intently and waiting for their eyes to meet. "How do you know so much about me?" Nate breathlessly asked.

"You and me, Eagle Shadow, we share the same blood."

"I have no blood relatives among the people. And I share *nothing* with you."

"I am the younger brother of your grandfather who was banished from the people."

"I was not told about any brother of my grandfather."

"I'm not surprised. My brother and your father turned their backs on our people and forgot about us like we were *supposed* to forget about them."

"No! My father never forgot about his people!"

"You asked me on the day we first talked, why did I go to live among the whites? I followed after my brother on the day he was banished. Even though he was much older than me, our hearts had always been close. I did not want to lose him forever. I followed him for many sleeps, to a land I'd never seen. When he finally discovered me, he sent me away. He said it was his punishment, not mine, and that I should stay with our mother and our people. He was right, but I was sad and angry. I did not want to come home again. So I stayed away, but I always listened for news of my brother, and later, your father. I followed after them when they moved but never came close enough for them to know. Finally, I became sick of the whites and missed my home. So I came back."

Nate did not know what to say. If it had been someone else, anyone else, he wouldn't have minded the news. Perhaps he would even have welcomed it. But he had long perceived Gray Wolf as trouble waiting to happen.

"All right, so you are my kin," said Nate finally. "I accept that. But I don't think you will ever see the Broken Bow." He arose and started to walk away.

"I *have* seen your Broken Bow."

Nate stopped dead in his tracks, a new horror building within him. There was only one time Gray Wolf could have been to the Broken Bow, that terrible night six years earlier when Nate and Lena had narrowly escaped an Indian attack that took the lives of their parents and Tara's aunt and uncle. He wheeled around and headed straight for Gray Wolf, who stood up, taking a defensive stance.

"You were there that night?" asked Nate.

Gray Wolf met his stern gaze resolutely. "Yes."

Nate knew it was impossible that Gray Wolf would have played a passive role in that carnage. He would only have been at the center of action, directly involved, fighting with an unchecked fervor that made Nate shudder. "What did you do?"

"I did what I felt I had to do."

"What did you do?" Nate reiterated, louder this time.

"I saw your father die that night."

"Did you kill him?"

"No, I did not."

"Who did?"

"I don't know. He was not killed on purpose. It was an act of war. But it cut a hole in my heart so deep that I swore revenge. I know he would've come back to our people if he had not been fooled by the whites into thinking he belonged with them."

"No, he would not!"

"I don't believe that!" snapped Gray Wolf. "I lived among the whites. I know how they will try to make us be like them, to *civilize* us." He nearly spat out the word. "They succeeded with your father. And by doing so, they killed him as surely as if they shot the arrow themselves. I would not leave the Broken Bow that night till I paid them back."

The horror in Nate was defining itself now. It was taking the form of the brave standing before him. He knew that whatever Gray Wolf said next would stab him like a knife, but he did not flinch. Now he would finally understand the ambiguity that had veiled Gray Wolf's inner core for these months Nate had known him.

"I and another brave with me broke into the house."

Nate's fists clenched. He had been there. He had seen Gray Wolf. Suddenly he was there again, huddling close to the outside wall of the Sinclairs' home on the Broken Bow, watching helplessly as two braves, only dark, silhouetted forms in his view, disappeared around the side of the house. The gut-wrenching sound of breaking glass followed. The house was breached. He could clearly hear it again now. Time had not dimmed the memory.

"I only meant to count coup on them and leave," Gray Wolf was saying, "but the man, Sinclair, shot my friend. He aimed for me next. I did not give him the chance to fire his gun."

"So you killed the Sinclairs," rasped Nate. When Gray Wolf wouldn't answer, Nate was infuriated all the more. He remembered Tara telling him that her aunt and uncle had been stabbed multiple times. Gray Wolf hadn't even been merciful enough to use one bullet apiece. "Go ahead and say it, you coward! You murdered Boss and Mrs. Sinclair."

"Maybe I was wrong," Gray Wolf conceded. "Maybe I shouldn't have, but I blamed them for turning what was left of my family against our people, because if it wasn't for them, your father would be alive today, and you and I might've been friends."

Nate threw the first punch, and it caught Gray Wolf unawares. The brave sprawled on the grassy bank, but it took only an instant for him to grasp the situation and scramble to his feet. He wasn't fast enough, and Nate's other fist smashed into his stomach.

"How could you have *ever* dared to speak to me of friendship?" Nate swooped over Gray Wolf like an enraged animal. They locked arms, and Nate wrestled him to the ground.

By now, Gray Wolf had prepared his mind for the fight and was ready to hold his own. His left leg swung across and caught Nate's legs. Having lost the control of his legs, Nate tried to use his arms to hold himself off the ground. Gray Wolf easily rolled him on his back, but then Nate grabbed Gray Wolf around the neck and squeezed.

Gray Wolf, choking and gasping for air, used both hands to break away from Nate's iron grip. He was still coughing when Nate threw a punch that landed him face down in the stream. Emerging from the stream dripping wet, Gray Wolf drew upon his reserves of anger and plunged himself fully into the fight. His fists flew like lightning. He held back nothing. But Nate knew every move before Gray Wolf made it and defended perfectly which raised Gray Wolf's ire more.

The barrage of fists continued, and the fight moved up the bank. Then Gray Wolf forced Nate back down the bank. Nate's reflexes slowed, and more of the brave's punches hit their target. One well-executed punch to the jaw sent Nate reeling. As he struggled to rise from his hands and feet, a kick to the stomach cut short his efforts.

This time he didn't try to get up, and Gray Wolf stopped attacking him. As he reached up and caught the blood about to drip from his nose, he drew in deep breaths, each one emphasizing the soreness in his ribs. When he'd caught his breath enough to speak, he looked up at Gray Wolf. "What do you think you have to prove by besting me?"

Gray Wolf appeared disgusted, even insulted by the comment. "I didn't best you. You quit trying."

The brave walked away, but Nate was too overcome by his confused thoughts to get up. He lifted himself to a sitting position and contemplated. He had indeed stopped trying, but why? Surely his thirst for revenge for such a despicable act as Gray Wolf had committed could not have been satisfied by a few swift punches. He had launched into this fight with the fury of one who meant to kill, but his anger had been tempered by distracting memories of his summer-long association with Gray Wolf, of the very subtle sense of hovering protection he'd felt from him. This warrior with the vague demeanor had personally informed him of the whereabouts of cavalry scouts in search of him. They had hunted together, sat by the fire talking together. As he thought of all this now, he was incensed all over again. How dare Gray Wolf behave so decently toward him when he had so much repugnance to hide.

But at the foremost of his mind now, what to do about what he'd learned. Gray Wolf should be turned over to authorities for punishment. Nate rubbed his eyes in exasperation. There was not one authority in all the territory he could count on in this matter. In the eyes of the only law that existed, Nate was a bigger threat than

Gray Wolf, and his own words worthless in the face of the cavalry's sources.

No, it should've been taken care of now, this day. He had just given up his chance to mete out the justice that had been a fleeting dream for years. Never once in his life had he yielded a fight, and today he had yielded one to a murderer—a murderer who was his kin. The shame oozed over him like a thick, sticky mire as he realized this small factor of the relationship had weakened his resolve.

***

The following morning, the Indians found Nate's tepee empty, the doorway flapping neglected in the wind. Nate and the Appaloosa were nowhere to be found. Gray Wolf, Shining Sky, River Otter, and the others stood wondering. He had vanished as imperceptibly as a shadow and left no clues.

Chapter 13

Tara had not expected Lieutenant-Colonel David Gunning McHenry to be such an imposing character, in spite of his impressive credentials. His size and distinctive look undoubtedly matched his reputation. But Tara reminded herself that she, too, had an honorable reputation, and truth on her side, and she proceeded with her customary unfettered confidence to explain the matter to him.

He listened throughout her explanation with his chin resting on one hand, something akin to amusement in his eyes, and she immediately knew this wouldn't be as simple as she'd hoped. When she finished, he leaned back in his chair and clasped his hands over his belt.

"I've actually been expecting a visit from you. I'll even go so far as to say I've looked forward to this little chat with you."

His condescending manner annoyed her, and she struggled to maintain a pleasant voice. "In what way?"

"Just curious, I suppose," he said with a shrug. "Curious to see how far you'd go to grovel."

The flame of her anger sufficiently fanned, she glared at him. "I am not groveling, nor will I. I came here with the intention of explaining circumstances of which you clearly were not aware."

He leaned forward now, for the first time seeming to take the conversation seriously. "Mrs. Hunter, you cannot possibly think I have blindly issued a warrant for your husband's arrest based on one incident. We have so much more evidence against him—"

"You have no evidence whatsoever. You have faulty testimony from an unreliable source."

"I have implicit trust in my sources, *and* I have the benefit of not having my judgment clouded by the need to protect a family member."

"Who are these inestimable sources of yours? Who has given you such information?"

"I'm afraid I'm not at liberty to discuss that with you. You see, this is a federal matter."

She rolled her eyes at his attempt to intimidate. "Come on, I know they're cavalry, and low-ranking at that. You tell me who they are, and I will prove them wrong."

"Even if I could, I don't know that I would tell you anything." He shot a contemptuous glance at her abdomen. "We've been after him for months now, and it's obvious to me that you've seen him in that time, and possibly know where he is."

Tara returned a scornful glance of her own. "I do not know where he is."

"Well, let me help you then. We know that he is no longer with the bunch he was with on the Sun River. He's long since left them behind. But he *is* hiding deep among the Cheyenne nation, and they guard his whereabouts like there's no tomorrow. Does that logically make him sound like an innocent victim of circumstances? I think not."

Tara was too stunned to respond. It was the first she'd heard of Nate not being with Red Feather's band. He must be much farther away than she'd imagined, and the thought disheartened her. He had effectively disappeared among the Cheyenne and now suddenly seemed ever more unreachable to her, to little Buck—and to their unborn child.

"You really don't know where he is, do you?" said Colonel McHenry. He shook his head with feigned empathy. "And now he's left you in this condition to fend for yourself and do his bidding. I do feel for you, Mrs. Hunter."

Tara immediately reined in her thoughts and focused on the moment. "Yes, I'm sure you'll lose plenty of sleep over it. And speaking of fending for myself, I would also like to collect moneys owed on the beef contract while I'm here."

The colonel's hands came down hard on the desk. "Oh, yes, *that's* something I wanted to talk to you about. Thank you for reminding me. I'm canceling that contract as of today. You will, of course, be paid for any purchases already made. Beyond that, it is null and void. I am very sorry to have to do this."

"You can't do that! That's a legally binding contract, and it's not up for negotiation for two more years."

"Oh, but I can, Mrs. Hunter. I have no obligation, nor would it even be prudent for me to honor a contract with someone engaged in treasonous activities." He held up a hand to halt whatever objection she'd make. "I know, I know, 'innocent until proven guilty.' But everything about his actions indicates that he is guilty of what we suspect him of. He is displaying every appearance of criminal behavior. And yes, I know about your family's influence, but it won't get you far around here. You're not going to hoodwink me."

Moments later as she clutched the few dollars that had been handed to her, she stormed from the office and right past Elijah waiting outside. "Paid me off and invited me to leave!" she raged. "Yes, *invited* me to leave. Can you believe that?" She walked so fast that Elijah had to take a couple running steps to keep up with her, but she stopped short when Julie appeared in her path. Tara hadn't realized where she was until she looked up and saw the small school where Julie taught the soldiers' children.

"Tara!" Julie's face lit up. "What are you doing… I didn't know you were expecting a baby. When is it going to be?"

"Don't speak to me unless you or your spineless husband has anything *important* to say. Oh, and remind me again. What did he do to be promoted to major?"

Julie stared at her, speechless.

"Exactly," Tara snapped, "nothing!" She continued on her way, leaving Julie too baffled to even be insulted.

Elijah felt some obligation to smooth the situation over, but he could do no more than shrug his shoulders and shake his head at Julie before chasing after the woman he was supposed to be protecting. He caught up to her as she was arriving at their wagon parked in front of the general store.

"Hoodwink," he heard her mumble to herself. "A colonel tells me I'm not going to hoodwink him. The nerve!"

"Oh, how dare he speak to you that way, ma'am," said Elijah.

"Never mind, Mr. Medley," she replied as she climbed aboard and gathered up the reins. "I considered it an open invitation, to hoodwink said colonel. We're going home now. Find Mrs. Sinclair and catch up to me." She gave the horses a slap of the reins, and the wagon lurched into motion with a creak.

Elijah stood for a moment trying to figure out what she was talking about, then with a start, he realized that their transportation was leaving, and he ran to find Rebecca.

Their trip home was accompanied by a far different mood than the trip to the fort. Tara's austere silence threw cold water on many attempts at conversation by Elijah and Rebecca. They chalked it up to her condition and let her be. When Tara directed Elijah to stop the wagon first at the Split Timber, he obeyed without question.

This time Lena ran from the house to meet Tara. There was an obvious change in her, for the better. "Tara, how did it go?"

"Not well at all, but it does my heart so good to see you happier."

"I should've gone with you."

"No, there was nothing you could've done."

Lena's brows furrowed in concern. "Is there anything I can do for you now?"

"Just talk to Nate the first chance you get, whenever that may be. It'll mean so much to him."

"I will do that, and may it be soon." She looked past Tara at Rebecca and Elijah. "Won't you all come in?"

"We won't be staying," Tara quickly replied. "I would just like some private words with you and Ward."

"Of course. Come inside. Ward is in the house."

Rebecca and Elijah looked at each other questioningly but didn't try to speculate.

***

Although the prospect of the trip had excited him, Elijah found that he was glad to be back, just not around the other cowboys. He tried to occupy himself training one of his newest charges, a sleek sorrel two-year-old gelding with three white socks, but his mind gave him no peace. He replayed his conversations with Tara over and over, until finally, his conscience gnawing at him relentlessly, he put up the horse in the stable and headed for the house. She answered his knock and stepped outside to see what he wanted. He subconsciously backed down two porch steps. Once again, as before, she was his boss.

"What is it, Mr. Medley?"

He was glad to see she was no longer distracted and perturbed. Her eyes were wholly focused on him. He swallowed hard. It was the right time to say his piece. "I came to apologize for my behavior on the trip, Mrs. Hunter. It was unacceptable. I got caught up in the moment there, and I'm plenty ashamed of myself. I was raised as a Southern gentleman, and I know better. You have every right to fire me." He looked down at the steps and smiled. "I'm sure Mr. Hunter would go along with it when you explained it to him." He heard no reply, and he looked up to see what her reaction would be. She was watching him intently, carefully mulling over his words.

"I will give you a letter of recommendation if you choose to leave," she said finally, "but—and you can correct me if I'm wrong—I suspect the Broken Bow is the best job you've ever had, isn't it?"

"Yeah, it is, ma'am, by far."

"Then I ask you to stay, if you would."

Confused, he slowly replied, "But you said on the trip—"

"Not for the reason you think. I need you here, Mr. Medley. I can't run this ranch by myself, and I don't know how reliable Mr. Tatum is."

"Oh, Clay does a fine job, ma'am. There's none better."

Although no one was within their hearing, she lowered her voice. "I don't know if I can trust him. I don't know how loyal he is to Mr. Hunter."

Elijah understood and nodded. "I don't know either. He never says anything."

"I need a good man around here who can handle the work and train the horses. I know that you're hurting, and truly, I am terribly sorry, but I desperately need you to put away any personal feelings for me and do your job."

"You're right," he agreed. "I've been selfish. I owe you my best work, at least until Mr. Hunter is back for good and can replace me. After that, I think it best I move on."

She cast her eyes down for a moment and softly answered. "All right. We will be sad to lose you, but I understand." It saddened her to think of him returning to his aimless, drifting ways when he had so much potential. But she also knew as well as anyone that the heart was a difficult thing to control. How she wished his feelings could have found a different path to follow. "Where will you go?"

He forced a smile. "Wherever my horse takes me."

"I will wish you well when you go. Thank you for staying on till then. I do appreciate your work."

She went back inside, and he stood rubbing his chin. She was all business. That was good, he decided. Just as she should be. This was his own problem to deal with.

***

She discovered him setting up his bedroll in the lean-to that evening and stood in the doorway to the house, eyebrows raised questioningly. "I didn't think you were going to sleep here anymore."

He offered that familiar, shy smile. "I said I was a Southern gentleman, ma'am. Regardless of what you or me or anybody else said, it is still my duty to keep watch for you and Buck."

Tara returned the smile. "You are a credit to your parents, Mr. Medley."

"I don't have any parents. They both died when I was very young. But thank you."

"Oh, I'm sorry. I thought because of the poem you read on the trip... Well, you are a credit to whoever raised you." She closed and locked the door.

She went into Buck's room and sat for a long time watching him sleep. "Where is your pa?" she whispered. Hot tears began to flow down her cheeks. She wiped her eyes with the back of her hand and squinted through the darkness. She was pretty sure Buck had grown in the last few months. She must remember to measure him the next morning. She stroked his black hair, bent to kiss him, and walked to her own room. She lay wide awake on her side of the double bed, never in the middle, and wondered yet again how far away he was and how he was faring. Did he have shelter? A comfortable place to sleep? Enough food to eat? Were the Indians being good to him?

What would he think of how she was running the ranch? He'd surely be upset about the beef contract. She rubbed her temples in frustration when she recalled how he'd asked her before they parted if she could handle the ranch hands. She hadn't counted on having to deal with one falling in love with her. She'd noticed Elijah's admiring eye before, but she hadn't expected him to be so bold about his feelings. Although he'd apologized and she was sure he wouldn't mention it again, she knew the memory of the incident would always be there, hanging in the air between them whenever they spoke. Perhaps she should've just let him leave like he'd suggested, she thought. And if the frontier was populated with top-notch wranglers all looking for a job, she'd have done just that. But it wasn't, and she had had to reveal to Elijah her desperate side.

And where was Clay Tatum? Once she'd returned from her trip and he'd reported the work of the last three days, he'd gone into town again. She was pretty sure he hadn't come back yet. What was he doing there? Did he spend *all* of his time visiting women? Nate had seen him drunk on a couple of occasions, but he was always sober for work. She reminded herself that Clay wasn't acting any differently than when Nate was here. Only *she* was acting differently, generating all sorts of suspicious thoughts. She smiled to herself and closed her eyes.

***

Elijah lay in the dark, looking at the door that separated him from all he dreamed of having. She was always so gracious. Why did she have to be so? The very traits that drew him to her were the same ones that magnified his pain a hundredfold.

He wondered just what he'd do if Nate showed up at the Broken Bow on the morrow. There was cavalry nearby, in town. He imagined the whole scene—himself approaching whoever was in charge. *"Sir, I have some information that you might want..." "I want a guarantee that you won't tell where you got the information..."* He could be in and out in five minutes. And he would be within the law. It would all be so easy, so swift and painless. Or maybe not. He knew if he somehow botched it, Nate would hunt him down wherever he was. The last three years of working together on the Broken Bow wouldn't make a scrap of difference. Nate would leave him dead or wishing he was. There'd be no place he could hide.

A tinge of guilt crept over him. How could he do such a thing anyway, and then keep it from her for a lifetime? *She* trusted him. It was Clay whom she distrusted. Could her instincts possibly be wrong? There it was again—knowledge versus wisdom. He feared he was losing control, failing the test.

Chapter 14

The tent flap of Gray Wolf's tepee lay wide open, like a morning yawn, allowing the sunrise light to penetrate. Suddenly Nate's figure darkened the doorway. The sight of him stopped Gray Wolf's chewing in the middle of a bite of jerky. Nate's tousled hair hung limp in eyes ringed with dark circles. His arms dangled loose at his sides, his right arm slightly behind him.

"Where have you been for three days?" Gray Wolf demanded with the air of a father disappointed in his offspring. There was no reply, and Gray Wolf resumed chewing as he looked Nate up and down. "You look like you haven't eaten or slept since you left." Just at the moment when he noticed that Nate's holster was empty, Nate's right arm came out from behind him and leveled the barrel of his Colt .45 right at Gray Wolf's forehead.

Nate spoke slowly and deliberately. "Did you attack those medicine wagons?"

"Why does it matter to you so much?"

"I owe revenge to whoever did, in the name of my sister's daughter and my wife's father....and her aunt and uncle."

"But I am *your* family."

"And I'm prepared to send you to hell right now."

"Your standing among our people has risen greatly, Eagle Shadow. But if you kill a Cheyenne, you can be banished. You know that better than anyone."

Nate shook his head. "Not when I explain what happened. The people know I won't kill unless I'm justified. And you know *that* better than anyone." His thumb pulled back the hammer of the gun till it clicked, and he steadied his aim. "Before I shoot, I'll ask you one more time. Did you attack those medicine wagons?"

Gray Wolf's eyes bore deep into Nate's. "No, I did not. I have no reason to attack wagons carrying medicine to sick people. That is not my way."

Nate held the gun steady while he carefully studied Gray Wolf's eyes, face, and posture. Gray Wolf never averted his eyes; his hands remained still and relaxed; he had spoken evenly with no hint of indecision. Everything about him told Nate that he was telling the truth.

The tension in the air was thick, and time passed slowly till Nate uncocked the hammer and holstered his gun. "Whose way is it? Was it warriors from Red Feather's band?"

"I don't know. I do not ask questions. It does not matter to me." Unfazed by what had just happened, he indicated a seat by the fire. "Come. Sit by the fire and have something to eat."

Nate shook his head. "I will never share a fire with you again."

Nate left again the same day. He preferred solitude, but no matter how far he rode, he could find no peace. For three days after learning of Gray Wolf's crime, he had indeed gone largely without food or sleep, endured physical and mental torture, the depth of which was known only to him, till finally, beaten down by his condition, he felt ready to pull the trigger on Gray Wolf. What's more, he believed he'd found the long-sought attacker of the wagons. Gray Wolf's assertion of innocence and Nate's conviction that he'd told the truth had derailed Nate's plan suddenly and unexpectedly. He'd wanted it to be Gray Wolf. His search would be over, and he'd be fully justified in whatever he did to him.

A day later he sat in his camp by a stream, the late afternoon sun to his back, whittling idly at a stick of oak wood. This time he wasn't sure he'd return to the Indians at all. Then almost simultaneously, he wondered what Red Feather was doing now. The same sun was about to set on the chief's camp, wherever that was. Red Feather must've known about Gray Wolf, but Nate couldn't blame the chief for not telling him anything. It wasn't his place.

He stopped whittling and looked around. He sensed a human presence in this natural atmosphere. From a bluff somewhere upstream came a faint sound, carried on the breeze toward him, that did not match these surroundings, the sound of metal on metal. Many years of ranch work had trained his ear, and in his mind's eye, he could see a horse shaking its head, the metal bit in its mouth rattling the rings that attached the reins to the bridle. He dropped the wood, grabbed the rifle he kept within arm's reach, and scrambled up the bank behind his camp.

There was little foliage for cover, and he bent low as he quickly made his way northward. He dropped to one knee behind a bush and listened. He barely made out a whispered voice. There were two of them, he deduced, heading south on foot along the stream below him, directly toward his camp. He continued northward, in intermittent sprints, till he knew he and his trackers had passed each other. He saw their two horses from a distance, their reins tied to a low-hanging limb, McClellan saddles on their backs. Cavalry mounts, Nate thought to himself, no surprise there. He headed back down the bank to the stream and started south, following his trackers' route to his camp. He was now in between the trackers and their horses, separating them from their means of escape. He smiled to himself. Was this really the best the cavalry had to send after him?

He soon saw the two men nosing about his camp, clad in the blue uniform shirts and buckskin pants of cavalry scouts. The signature sound of a Henry .44 rifle lever being cranked startled the men, and they rushed to aim their carbines towards the sound, but they were too late. Nate had the drop on them. "Wing those guns into the water."

"You're crazy," said one man. "There's two of us and only one of you."

"But I have two guns on me," replied Nate, "same as you two put together." He raised the rifle, putting the sights level with his eye. "But I only need one. And I can chamber another round in the time it takes you to think about reachin' for your piece."

Each man in turn pitched his weapon into the creek, two splashes breaking the stillness.

Nate lowered his rifle but kept it pointed in their direction. "What are you doing here?"

"Lookin' for you," growled the tougher-looking one with a mustache and beard.

Nate moved closer. "Well, you found me. What are you supposed to do now?"

"Take you back alive to face judgment."

"Well, I admire your dedication, but I think I won't go. Actually I have been wanting to talk to cavalry myself, but you're not high up enough. So here's what you'll do. You go back to Fort Mason and send me Major Joshua Blaine."

Both scouts smiled, and one gave an audible chuckle. "An officer's not gonna meet with you, mister."

"That one will." There was a long silence as Nate and the scouts eyed each other. "Go on now," said Nate. "No, wait just a minute. Chuck your pants off."

"What?" they exclaimed in unison.

"You heard me. Get 'em off now."

"What for?" asked the bearded one.

"I'm gonna make sure you go straight to the fort without stoppin' off anywhere first."

They stared at the barrel of his rifle and decided he wasn't going to lower it anytime soon. Slowly at first, then picking up speed as they went, they removed their boots, unhooked their suspenders, slid the pants down their legs, and stepped out one foot at a time.

"Where do you want 'em?" asked the younger one, avoiding eye contact.

"Right there on the ground is fine. You can put your boots back on."

A moment later, they stood in their boots and long underwear, arms folded, trying to maintain what dignity they could, and Nate had to hold his breath to stifle his laughter. He needed to get them out of his camp before he busted up altogether. "Be on your way then. And remember, send Major Blaine to me."

The bearded one looked plenty disgusted, but the younger one earnestly inquired, "How's he supposed to find you?"

"You just send him down to these parts. I'll find him."

Quite awkwardly the two scouts started back upstream towards their horses. Nate watched and listened till he heard them galloping away, then he waded into the stream after the carbines.

Normally Nate would have thought it wise to move his camp, but he decided to stay put for the night, partially because he didn't expect the two almost naked men to return, but also because he desired to prove to no one in particular that he had the audacity to do so.

"Don't think for a minute that I don't know what you're thinkin'" he said to the Appaloosa with a smile. "You wanna go back to the Indians." He resumed his whittling but watched the horse out of the corner of his eye. The Appaloosa always liked to be spoken to, and it amused Nate how the horse would stay nearby to await conversation. "Yep, you miss that little paint mare, don't ya?"

He spent the first restful night in days, and in the morning, he broke camp and packed his provisions on the Appaloosa. He was going back to the Indians. He'd rather have their protection he decided. The cavalry may very well have better trackers to send after him. In fact, the two he'd encountered would probably be better the next time out. As for Gray Wolf, Nate figured he'd just have to tolerate him for the time being. His anger had lost its sharp edge now. In the days since learning the truth about Gray Wolf, the emotional inner wound the brave had caused was less inflamed and starting to scar over. Nate knew Gray Wolf would be an annoying thorn in his side, but he mustn't let events of the past compromise his current situation.

He left the carbines; the scouts may come back for them sometime. Their pants he took with him. He was sure some young braves would want them.

"All right, you win. We'll go back," he told the horse, who nickered in return. He rubbed the horse's velvety muzzle. "That foal the paint mare is carrying, it's yours, isn't it? Didn't I tell you to stay away from those girls?" The Appaloosa nudged him so hard it almost knocked him over. "You're just mad 'cause you can't hide anything from me," he laughed.

He followed the same route towards the Indian camp that he'd taken away from it, and the same route the scouts had partially followed to find him. He was in rolling hill country now, a land of yellow and brown autumn grasses that moved as one in undulating waves. The effect was occasionally broken by bluffs, their eroded, rocky cliffs jutting off to nowhere, and creek bottoms that fed the thirsty roots of low trees and undergrowth. It was much different than home and required a different set of skills to foil trackers. With fewer trees to provide cover and softer ground that exposed tracks, one needed to maintain a safe distance and have a fast horse. He was grateful to have the latter, but he feared his ability to accomplish the former might be challenged by his sense of daring and curiosity, as it was in the case of the two scouts.

It was late morning when he noticed buzzards circling directly ahead. Vigilance took over his senses, and he slowed the Appaloosa to a cautious pace and kept a hand near his rifle sheath. Somehow, something told him what he would find before his eyes saw it. One buzzard on the ground took flight as he approached, and he winced at the sight which drew the birds' attention. A dead body lay crumpled amongst the tall grasses. Nate recognized the blue shirt and the beard. His eyes scanned a little further ahead, and he found the other one. The two scouts had obviously been killed only hours after their encounter with Nate, their horses stolen. He clenched his teeth in anger as he took in the details. The first one had been shot in the back, the second one in the chest as he turned to face their attacker. Nate couldn't imagine who would've been cruel enough to do such a thing. The scouts had been unarmed. He wondered if the outcome would've been different if he'd let them keep their guns.

He rode around the vicinity looking for clues. Only horses' hoofprints were visible. They led north, but they were nearly a day old. The killer had surely put a lot of distance behind him by now. Nate guessed that the men had been killed for their horses. Cavalry horses were good stock.

Nate had no means to bury them; the best he could do was to gather up enough rocks to pile over them. As he completed that laborious task, he wiped the sweat from his brow and mounted the Appaloosa. He continued his journey with great discouragement. Major Blaine would receive no message now. No one would be coming to meet with him. The small hope he'd harbored since the night before was dashed.

His arrival back in the Indian encampment, though welcomed by all, did little to boost his spirits. Shining Sky and River Otter seemed especially glad to see him. He waited till the others had drifted back to their normal activity before he asked Shining Sky, "Did Gray Wolf go anywhere while I was gone?"

"No, he has been here the whole time," she replied. "Why do you ask?"

"I just wondered." He didn't even need to ask the question. He was beginning to understand Gray Wolf now. Gray Wolf did not kill indiscriminately with no clear reason. He was a man of battle. He attacked with calculating precision when compelled by his principles. He faced only those enemies who at least had an opportunity to defend themselves. Gray Wolf was a brutally tough fighter, but he fought with what he perceived as stainless Cheyenne honor. Nate found it difficult to accept Gray Wolf's version of honor, but at least it was becoming easier to predict what he would *not* do, and perhaps, Nate thought, the ever-present, unspoken threat that Gray Wolf presented now seemed a little less haphazard.

***

Nate had returned just in time. Later in the day, the rumble of plodding hooves and the lowing of slow-moving cattle caused a commotion in the camp. The small herd was passing right next to the camp, and the two cowboys accompanying them seemed unaware that the Indians would feel threatened. Gray Wolf was urging other warriors to prepare for a confrontation when Nate stepped forward to intercept the cowboys. He held up an arm to indicate he meant this to be a peaceful encounter.

"Come over here and let's talk," Nate directed.

Both cowboys, an old-timer and a much younger one, dismounted and approached him.

"Mister, you're passing too close to this camp without even a nod to the Indians," warned Nate. "They don't know what your intentions are."

"Just passin' through, that's all," replied the old one in a scratchy voice, his grizzled mustache seeming to move more than his mouth.

"There's been trouble in these parts lately. You need to be careful." Nate glanced over their herd of roughly a couple dozen, now milling about, searching out tufts of grass for munching. "Isn't it a little late in the season to be trailing cattle?"

"That's why we're movin' so fast. I'm Charlie Wilson. This here's my son Adam."

Nate nodded toward each man and asked, "Where you headed?"

"Goin' up to Montana a little ways. We had us a little ranching venture south of here a piece. Didn't know we was on Indian land. They chased us out, and we decided we'd sell these cattle to a ranch up in Montana that'll prob'ly want 'em."

Adam spoke for the first time. "You speak good English for an Injun."

"I've spent some time amongst your kind," said Nate.

"I judge you have."

"He ain't an Injun, you idiot," said Charlie. "He's a halfbreed."

Nate had heard such insults often enough and held his peace. He knew the best way to get a cowboy back was to offend his cattle. "These are some mighty scrawny-lookin' beasts you have here."

Charlie's mustache fluttered as he snickered. "Son, you don't know your cattle flesh. Nate Hunter up at the Broken Bow will appreciate these fine animals."

Nate took care to hide any reaction from them. He was going to enjoy himself now. "Nate Hunter don't know good cattle from prairie dogs."

Now both cowboys laughed and shook their heads, and Adam muttered something to his father about wasting their time here.

"I reckon he knows cattle a sight more'n' a halfbreed does," replied Charlie.

Nate appreciated the roundabout compliment. "I'll give you eight dollars a head for them."

"Didn't you hear us?" said Adam. "We're not sellin' 'em to you."

"Why not? You said you're trying to sell 'em, didn't you?"

"Hey, what'd you say your name was?" asked Charlie.

"I didn't say. Name's Nate Hunter."

Adam looked Nate up and down. "From the Broken Bow?"

"The same."

"You're foolin' us," replied Adam. "Nate Hunter's no halfbreed."

"Oh? You've seen him before?"

"Nope."

"Well, now you have."

The two cowboys looked at each other, and Charlie's mustache quivered again with a chuckle. "Now that weren't nice."

"Neither were you."

Adam seemed to have suddenly developed some respect. "Sorry about that. No offense."

"None taken."

Adam glanced around at the tepees. "So what are you doin' here?"

Nate was absorbed with the cattle, his eyes going over their weight and build. "Just visiting," he absently replied. "These are good cattle. Ten dollars a head. That's my final offer."

"All righty," agreed Charlie. He waited expectantly for a moment. "Be nice if we could collect money now and leave 'em right here."

"Can't do it," answered Nate. "My wife will pay you at the Broken Bow. You better be on your way then."

They shook hands; the cowboys gave a wave to the Indians gathered around and mounted their horses.

"Don't try to swindle my wife," Nate called after them. "She'll see right through you." He watched the herd pass by, pleased with his future acquisition. As he turned to walk back towards the camp, Gray Wolf blocked his path.

"Why did you tell them your name?" Gray Wolf asked with a scowl. "Now they will be able to tell others you are here."

"I can take care of myself. I don't need any advice from you." He brushed past the brave with no more care than if it was a post in his way. Identifying himself to the cowboys was a chance he was willing to take. He harbored a desperate hope that the cowboys would follow through on their plans, reach the Broken Bow while the weather still held, and tell Tara where they'd seen him.

***

It was now the Moon When the Rivers Begin to Freeze, and the land was preparing for sleep. The arc of the sun lowered in the southern sky. Dusk came earlier and bathed the grasses in amber shadows. Day after day wedges of Canadian geese covered the sky, honking and winging their way southward as if fleeing an oncoming behemoth. Then gradually the wedges thinned out; the honking ceased; and a lonely quiet settled on the land.

The Indian ponies' coats thickened, and the Indians were on the move again, heading for their wintering place. Nate helped them with hunting and brought back more game than anyone for the women of the band to make jerky and warm clothing and blankets. He gave most of his kills to Shining Sky whose need was greatest. She felt complimented, and her gratitude was abundant.

River Otter had grown very attached to Nate. He wanted to hear every detail of how every hunt went, and Nate usually obliged him. The boy spent his days playing out the stories Nate told him. He copied Nate's every mannerism; he wanted to be just like him.

Nate's amusement at the boy was tempered by thoughts of Buck. He wished that Buck could be the first to hear the stories, the first to copy him.

"Will you please take me hunting the next time?" River Otter begged. "I am old enough now."

His simple question pained Nate deep inside. He had not taken his own son hunting yet, and he would not take River Otter hunting before Buck. "I think you're still a little young yet to go hunting."

"It's all right," Shining Sky quickly interjected. "I know he'll be safe with you."

"I'm not his father!" erupted Nate to her great surprise. "And I won't always be here. He needs to know that...and so do you."

She was stunned into silence for a long moment. He refused to look at her, and finally, she took River Otter by the hand and led him away.

Later, as darkness gathered, she timidly approached his fire. When he did not object, she sat down across from him and watched him whittle a piece of wood. "You do not share our practice of having more than one wife?"

"No." His strokes with the knife became more forceful. But he could not blame Shining Sky for her ignorance. Her young life had been so sheltered, her experience so limited. He figured the two cowboys were quite probably the only white men she'd ever seen. "What about Gray Wolf? He needs a wife."

"I will not marry Gray Wolf," she replied. "I believe you will kill him one day, and I do not want to lose another husband."

Nate stopped whittling. Although it wasn't noticeable to her, she had utterly shocked him with that statement. Everyone in the band was aware of the sudden cooling of his and Gray Wolf's friendship, but he hadn't known until now that they expected it to lead to Nate taking revenge. He realized he had still not decided definitively what he was going to do about Gray Wolf. He spent every day in a quandary, choosing to avoid the brave and busy himself with anything that would keep him away for a time. But he must make up his mind once and for all. The stark savagery of Gray Wolf's past would always be there. Death would not erase it. In fact, Nate realized, Gray Wolf's death would not even give him the satisfaction he once thought it would. He had lain awake at nights, mulling over every conversation he could remember having with Gray Wolf, looking for even the slightest indication of remorse. The only words that came close were those Gray Wolf had spoken when he told Nate the news, *Maybe it was wrong. Maybe I shouldn't have.* Nate hung all of his hopes on those words.

He was done with it, he decided. The past was the past, and that's where it would have to stay. To allow anything to distract him from current concerns could prove dangerous. "No, I'm not going to kill him," he answered with confidence. "Not today, not any day."

When she had gone back to her tepee, he sat wondering why in the world he had even mentioned to her to marry Gray Wolf. The brave was at least twice her age. But deep inside, he knew all along what it was. He just didn't care who she married or what she did. Or any of the people for that matter. They were good to him, and he genuinely appreciated it. He was even proud to be one of them and treasured the honor and respect they had developed for him, but this was not home. River Otter's admiration and Shining Sky's attention had only served to heighten his homesickness.

How he wished he had joined the cowboys and gone home. He didn't care about cavalry anymore. He would've just dealt with situations as they arose. Nothing would've kept him from reaching home and staying there however long it was possible. But now it was too late in the season. He would have to winter here and go in the spring.

***

The Indians entered a narrow canyon and set up a winter camp. Cold winds whistled above them, but the camp was safely sheltered. The days shortened; even shorter were the hours the sun shone into the canyon. There was abundant water and firewood, but the place felt confining to Nate. The canyon walls threatened to become his prison walls. Every night when everyone else was asleep, he would come out of his tepee, climb a steep, rocky path to a high vantage point near the canyon rim, and sit gazing at the stars. Arcturus set; Sirius rose. Andromeda dominated the sky above as she followed winged Pegasus. Leonid meteors shot across the heavens like arrows every few seconds. Looking at something so far away was strangely comforting to Nate, for he knew Tara could see the same sky. It was his one connection to home.

There came a night when no stars shone down on his secluded spot, when thick clouds descended, enclosing the canyon in a spherical canopy, blocking any escape and stealing his piece of the sky. He sat in his spot anyway, alone in his thoughts, as large snowflakes glided down around him and silently came to rest on his hair and buffalo robe. He pictured in his mind the little cedar home on the Broken Bow with its nearby bunkhouse, stable, and Clay's log cabin chinked with mud. Surely they'd have prepared by now for the relentless, harsh weather ahead. He thought of Lena entering her first winter without Laura, and he could see the tiny grave beneath the pine tree outside Lena's back door slowly being covered with snow.

His imagination strained to be able to hear Tara and Buck's laughter. The memory was fleeting, and the voices faded into the darkness. Suddenly he couldn't remember the childlike details of Buck's face. He couldn't remember the feel of

Tara's body beside him, her bare skin against his. His heart began to pound. He closed his eyes and tried harder to remember, but tears welled in his eyes instead and slid down his cold cheeks. He was grateful for a place to sit where the people could not see him. He pulled his knees to his chest and buried his face in the buffalo robe, trying again to remember.

Chapter 15

Ward Taylor exited the quartermaster's office at Fort Mason, clutching his copy of the new beef contract. He had only been at the fort for an hour and a half, but he was eager to be on his way back home. He had already sent his ranch hands on ahead. He had his horse untied from the hitching post and was just about to mount when he heard Lieutenant-Colonel McHenry's voice behind him.

"Mr. Taylor, a moment please."

Ward closed his eyes and muttered a curse, then put on his best innocent and pleasant expression and turned around. "Sir?"

"Those cattle in that corral." The colonel turned and pointed to the corral he meant, filled with fifty head of beef cattle. "You brought those here today?"

"Yes, sir, our best."

McHenry waited a moment, apparently giving Ward a chance to explain the obvious. When no explanation was forthcoming, he prompted, "The brands, Mr. Taylor."

"What about them?"

McHenry grew impatient quickly. "They're all Broken Bow brands. Why?"

"Is there a problem with that?"

"There certainly is. We signed to receive Split Timber cattle, not Broken Bow cattle."

Ward stood straighter, feigning insulted pride. "You did receive Split Timber cattle, Colonel. Those cattle belonged to me, and I just sold them to you.

"Then why, pray tell, are they wearing Broken Bow brands, Mr. Taylor?"

"Well, I hardly think such a thing should concern you, but the embarrassing truth is, I have found myself in a spot lately with diseased cattle and such—"

"Diseased cattle," the colonel repeated skeptically.

"Yes, sir. I've been making purchases from the Broken Bow to boost my herd. I sold some of them to you, at a small profit to myself, of course."

"You don't say. Tell me, did Mrs. Hunter have anything to do with this?"

"Of course. Our ranches have always been on friendly terms. She made the offer to help me out. She's very generous that way. I would've branded them over with Split Timber brands if I thought it was important to you, but honestly, I just didn't see the point in it."

Colonel McHenry jerked his head high and glared at Ward. "Mr. Taylor, I don't know what kind of fool you take me for, but this is completely unacceptable. I'm canceling that contract this moment."

"No, sir, you can't do that." He started to unfold the paper. "The only provision for canceling is if I cannot provide you with the adequate amount of beef. It does not stipulate anywhere that the cattle must be born on the Split Timber." He pretended an amused smile. "In fact, I don't think I've ever heard of a contract with such a stipulation, Colonel."

"I see. I suppose you think the two of you have thought this out right well. You can tell Mrs. Hunter—" A sudden commotion near the stables drew his attention. There was shouting, a horse's whinny, and a crowd starting to gather. He attempted to finish his thought but was continually distracted.

"Goodness, it looks like somebody's getting into a fight," said Ward. His plan for keeping the colonel's attention diverted worked, and McHenry hurried away to see to just one of many situations a busy commander dealt with daily.

"I will tell Mrs. Hunter," assured Ward when the colonel was too far away to hear. He seized the opportunity to take his leave.

***

Tara had just started to fix supper for her and Buck when she heard the lowing of moving cattle and recognized the sound as an approaching herd. It struck her as unusual; she couldn't imagine what the cowboys were doing driving cattle now. Drying her hands on her apron and donning a coat, she hurried outside to the porch and watched the road to the eastern border of the ranch. The sky was gray; a light snow fell, throwing a white-dotted haze on the road.

As the herd moved closer, the individual forms of the cows took shape, and she knew this outfit came from elsewhere. She folded her arms and waited in the cold for their approach. When they arrived, it made her a bit nervous when the cows began pawing around the yard by the house. Who were these thoughtless cowboys who had no more respect than to bring their cattle so close to the house, she wondered.

The old-timer with the gray mustache dismounted and stepped up to the porch. He tipped his hat to Tara and extended his right hand. "Ma'am, name's Charlie Wilson. This here's my son Adam."

She shook hands with Charlie and with Adam when he reached the porch. "I'm Mrs. Hunter. I gather you've come a long way?"

"Yes, ma'am, and got here none too soon I'd say. We shut down our ranching operation down yonder this fall. We got some prime cattle here to sell to you."

"How did you know to bring them here?" she questioned.

"Why, I've heard a lot about the Broken Bow. It didn't take us long at all to figure out where to bring 'em to."

She was quietly pleased to hear that the Broken Bow's reputation continued to spread.

"We saw your husband down close to the Powder River amongst a little group of Cheyenne."

Tara's heart skipped a beat, and her breath caught for a moment. *The Powder*

River, hundreds of miles southeast across the territory. "Tell me, how did he look?"

Charlie shrugged. "Fine, I guess, 'ceptin' I didn't know he was a…"

"A what?" She knew full well what he meant, but she'd make him say it anyway and embarrass himself. It might affect the bargaining for the cattle in her favor.

"A…a…" Charlie realized he'd opened himself up, and he looked away from her, smiling awkwardly. "Well, I didn't know he had 'filiation with Indians."

"Is there a problem with that?"

"Oh, no, ma'am. None at all."

Adam leaned in close to his father, making a rather pitiful effort to be discreet. "So that really *was* him."

"Shut up!" Charlie quickly transformed his irritation with Adam into a gracious smile for Tara. "We were askin' fifteen dollars a head for these cattle. But he drives a hard bargain. He wouldn't offer but twelve."

Tara raised her eyebrows as she scrutinized the cattle. "They must've deteriorated since you left him. I'll give you ten. That's my final offer."

"That was your only offer," said Adam.

Charlie elbowed him in the ribs and announced, "We'll take it."

Clay and Elijah had arrived at the house by now, to Tara's relief. "Mr. Tatum and Mr. Medley, I'd be grateful if you'd get these cattle out of the yard. Check them over and see that they're healthy. I'm planning to buy them. Then you can put these men up for the night in the bunkhouse."

"Sure thing," replied Clay. He looked at Elijah. "We'll put 'em in the far corral. I'll go get our horses."

"Uh, ma'am," Charlie began, somewhat nervously. "We're not expected anywheres. I wonder if you might have any jobs for me and the boy. You prob'ly noticed, he's so stupid he lets the wind blow his nose, but he's a hard worker like me."

"Not this time of year. But check back in the spring. I suppose you'll winter somewhere around Timber Fork?"

"I reckon so." He took a long look at her, his curiosity bursting at the seams. "He's a strange one, your husband, visitin' around the country when he's got a wife at home with child."

Tara figured if they were going to be spending time in the vicinity, she'd best fill them in before anyone else did. "Well, to summarize, he was visiting the Indians when the situation turned ugly, so the cavalry wants to hang him for treason…even though they buy beef from us."

"Oooh, doggy." Charlie laughed and shook his head. "Don't that sound just like a guv'ment-caused situation. Well, I'm sure there's more to it than that, but that's good enough for me."

"You men are welcome to join the hands in the bunkhouse for dinner and a bed for the night. If my foreman says the cattle are in good shape, I'll have your money ready for you in the morning." She turned back towards the door, eager to get inside the warm house. Then as an afterthought, she added, "Oh, and you may run into cavalry hereabouts. I hope you won't speak to them about my husband. I'm afraid I'd have to send Broken Bow men to sell your cattle back to you."

"No, ma'am," said Charlie. "Amongst cowmen I've never heard a bad word 'bout Mr. Hunter."

Tara smiled her gratitude. Adam didn't have much personality, but she decided she liked Charlie well enough. She hoped they'd return in the spring. They were experienced at driving cattle long distances, and it would be less hiring she'd have to worry about. They might even be good at price haggling with buyers and sellers less discerning than she.

***

Major Blaine sat in Lieutenant-Colonel McHenry's office. No spit and polish this time. It had been an impromptu summons from an aggravated colonel.

"What do you know of Ward Taylor, Major?" began Colonel McHenry.

Major Blaine shrugged. "He's a fine man, upstanding character, comes from Minnesota I believe. Why?"

"I entered into a beef contract with him."

"That's good. I don't think you'll have any problem with him."

"I already have a problem. He's selling us cattle he bought from the Broken Bow."

"Why is that a problem?"

McHenry was blatantly irritated that the major was blind to a situation that was plain to him. "I purposely canceled the Broken Bow contract because of the situation with Nate Hunter. And now Mrs. Hunter has connived with Ward. I thought that their ranches probably competed with each other."

Blaine stared at him, then hesitatingly spoke. "You didn't know that Ward's wife is Nate Hunter's sister?"

McHenry's jaw dropped. "You are kidding me."

Major Blaine averted his eyes, certain that if he looked again at the colonel, he'd burst into laughter.

Colonel McHenry closed his eyes and rubbed his temple. "Blast it! I also opened a government account at Ward's bank."

"Oh, yes, the new bank he owns with Jared Sinclair," Major Blaine blurted out without thinking. "That's Mrs. Hunter's brother."

Colonel McHenry's eyes flew open, and his fist came down hard on the desk. "For heaven's sake, is the whole damn town of Timber Fork related?" He threw his hands in the air in frustration. "Go on, Major, I don't need you anymore."

Blaine held his laughter in check all the way back across the grounds to his quarters, until he entered the room where Julie was serving supper. Then he sat down and laughed until tears formed in his eyes. Julie's impatience to know the joke could hardly be contained. "Poor Ol' Gun," he managed to say.

When he finally got out the story to her, she smiled, but obviously did not find the same level of humor in it that he did. "Josh, Tara is going to have a baby and doesn't even know where Nate is." She dished a heaping spoonful of mashed potatoes onto his plate. "And I guess she's running the ranch all by herself. She went to Ward to preserve their income. Where is your sense of compassion?"

His smile faded as he picked up his knife and fork and began cutting meat. "Yes, I feel sorry for her. But I know what happened in that Indian camp during that attack."

Julie shook her head, bewildered, as she reached over to cut Mark's meat. "Something's not right about that. I just know he wouldn't take sides against the cavalry. He's never done *anything* like that."

"What proof do you need, Julie? I told you, there were killers in that camp, and he defended them."

"There must be an explanation."

"Well, he didn't take the time to give me any when he was threatening one of my men."

"But just because of that, Colonel McHenry thinks he's giving weapons to the Indians and preparing them for war against us?"

"I never told McHenry any such thing. He obviously has other sources. He won't tell me anything."

"Well, I've tried to talk to the other officers' wives—"

"You've talked to the wives about it?" he snapped.

"Oh, excuse me, Major Blaine, would I have done any better to talk to the officers themselves?"

"It isn't your place to talk to anyone at all about it."

"I care about Tara. She's my oldest friend."

"She insulted me to you."

"She was desperate. I understand that. You *must* find out from Colonel McHenry what is really going on."

"It's not my place. He is not obligated to tell me anything if he doesn't see fit."

"Well, Nate won't care who's in whose place, and I'm guessing he'll get to the bottom of this before you do. And then he'll come looking for you."

His eyes widened. "Julie, are you being disloyal to me?"

"Of course not, dear. You know me, always the loyal soldier's wife." She stopped eating and cast her eyes downward, a heavy sadness descending on her. "But I will never be able to face Tara again."

He held up his tin cup, and she quickly set down her fork, lifted the water pitcher, and filled the cup. "I am sorry about it all, for your sake," he said. "But the proper thing for him to do would be to turn himself in and face the accusations. If he is innocent, then I'm sure that could be proven."

"Do you really think so?" she asked skeptically.

"Of course, I do."

His words were little consolation to her. Being surrounded by so much order and equally as much secrecy felt suffocating. She wished they could break away from it. But after four years, she was fully trained. Duty always came first.

***

Tara sat in her rocking chair in front of the fireplace with Buck asleep against her shoulder, a quilt wrapped around both of them. The sun had long since set, but the snow came down heavily now and lightened the atmosphere considerably. She wondered if there was much snow where he was and what the surroundings looked like. She glanced through the parlor window at the blowing whiteness. What view did he see from his tepee? Had he moved from where the Wilsons had seen him near the Powder River? What were the people like? What did he do every day, and who did he talk to? She had been so tempted to plead for more details from the Wilsons, but she knew she was fortunate to get what she did out of them.

She'd maintained a faint hope that he'd be home for the winter, but that wouldn't be happening now. She and Buck faced months of snow and ice and cold without him. Then the baby would come, just as winter would start to subside. She must be brave so that when he returned, he would find all well. The sense of responsibility that weighed on her would keep her going with her chin up.

They were set well for food. Shelves in the lean-to were lined with jars filled with the bounty from the garden. The small apple orchard near Elkhorn Creek, planted years before by her Aunt Charlotte, had produced well this year. The cowboys had shaken the trees for her, dislodging the apples, and she had given them all that they wanted and loaded the rest into the root cellar. They had also chopped and stacked a couple cords of wood for her, and she could make trips into town on clear days as needed.

She heard the back door open and Elijah stamping snow from his boots. He settled down quickly, and it was quiet again, but she was annoyed. Why did he have to sleep there every night? Who would come to endanger her and Buck in a storm like this? He was too used to sleeping there, she thought. Surely the floor must make a hard bed, night after night. Well, if he didn't have any more sense than to go back to the bunkhouse, that was his problem.

She laid her head against the back of the rocker, closed her eyes, and tried to imagine what it would be like with Nate in the house again, asleep in the bedroom, no one in the lean-to, his Henry rifle on its hooks over the door, his holster on another hook beside the door. *That* would make her feel more secure than anything. It was a good thought to fall asleep on.

Chapter 16

Long months of quiet, cold isolation had passed. The people had looked on soberly while Nate saddled the Appaloosa and packed all the provisions he could carry. They had tried to talk him into waiting a little longer, but he kindly refused. His mind had been distracted for a long time, and finally, in the Coyote Moon, he felt he must be on the move.

Now at last, as night began to settle in, he was within five miles of home, and he wasn't about to stop. He was grateful for a full moon to light his way. The two-week-long journey had been difficult. He had lost some weight over the winter. His horse was tired and slowing his pace, but he remained undeterred. He had ridden through blizzards to get here. He'd had a dangerously close encounter with a winter-starved wildcat that he killed, but he'd pressed on with an uncommon stamina that originated somewhere deep within him.

As he drew ever closer to the warm hearth and welcome that lay just ahead, he suddenly became nervous. He'd been immersed in another world for so long. With the exception of meeting the cavalry scouts and the cowboys, he had not spoken in English since bidding an agonizing farewell to Tara beside the Sun River early the previous summer. He had not sat on a chair, eaten at a table, or slept in a real bed. He had not seen a solid building, driven a wagon, or even seen anything with wheels on it. He had listened to Cheyenne drumbeats and songs till they were seared into his memory like a cattle brand.

He stopped short, his stomach tied up in knots. There it was—his house, cutting a dark shape out of the moonlight, surrounded by patches of snow that shone pale blue amidst a sea of brown earth. There was no light inside. They would already be asleep by now. He headed first for the stable to put up his horse. Once inside the house, he didn't want to come out again tonight.

The Appaloosa remembered his stall and plodded straight into it. Nate jovially slapped his flank. "Bet you don't remember how to work cattle that well. You've been lazy for so long." The horse threw his head high and gave a nicker. "And sassy too."

With his horse settled, it was time for the big entry. He saw tracks close to the back door of the house. Unless Tara had taken to wearing men's boots, there was someone else inside the house. Stealthy as a shadow, he pulled his gun, slipped inside the door, and watched the figure asleep on the floor. He sank to one knee and put the gun to the man's temple. Instantly Elijah awoke and started with a gasp. When he saw Nate, he rubbed his eyes and looked again.

Nate was equally surprised for a wordless moment before taking command of the situation. "What the hell are you doing in my house?"

"I come here every night to keep watch for Mrs. Hunter. She gave her permission.

It's just for protection. That's all, I promise."

"A fine job you do. I could've killed you." He holstered his gun, stood, and waited, but Elijah didn't move. "Well, I'm here now so you don't need to anymore."

"Yes, sir." Elijah hurriedly arose and began rolling up his bedroll. He was conscious of Nate watching his every move. But his anxiety from the sudden rousting was soon replaced by irritation with Nate. "Well, somebody needs to stay with her now that…" He stopped himself just in time.

Nate's eyes bore down on him. "Now that what?"

Elijah shook his head. "Like you said, sir, you're here now."

His impatience getting the better of him, Nate turned and leaned into the door to the house. He was surprised when it did not give way, and he jiggled the doorknob. He was locked out of his own house. He thought he heard a snicker from Elijah and whipped around, but Elijah was fast. He had already erased any trace of amusement from his face and was busily tying a rope around his bedroll.

Nate waited while Elijah seemed to purposely take his time putting on his boots and gathering up his bedroll and gunbelt. The very second the door closed behind Elijah, Nate turned and knocked on the door to the house. In only a moment came the sweetest sound he was sure he'd ever heard, the soft whisper on the other side of the door.

"Mr. Medley?"

His face close to the door, he whispered back. "The coward deserted his post."

There was an audible gasp. The door flew open, and their arms locked around each other. Immediately his hand went to her bulging abdomen. He tried to back up, but she had him around the neck. "Wh—what is this?"

"Shhh, Bucky's asleep." She pulled him, nearly stumbling, the few steps to their bedroom, closed the door, and pushed him to sit on the bed. All at once she was on his lap, crying and kissing him, on his cheeks, on his lips, while he tried to talk.

"Tara, I didn't know. I'm so sorry. I didn't know."

"Of course, you didn't know. It's all right."

"No, it's not all right. I should've been here. I would've come back, Tara, if I had to tie up and pistol-whip a hundred soldiers, I—I don't know. I would've found a way. Sweetheart, I'm so sorry. Gosh, why didn't I guess? I could've guessed that there was a chance. All those months, I never even once thought—"

"Stop talking." She was laughing through her tears. "Just stop talking for a minute, please."

She moved to the dresser and fumbled in the dark for a match, struck it, and lit a lantern. "Let me look at you." As the flame flickered to life and cast its soft orange glow across the room, it revealed his eye-catching smile, the memory of which she'd had to live off of for so long. She could hardly believe he was really there.

"When is it going to be?" he asked.

"Probably just a week or so. In the meantime, it looks like I need to feed you well."

"Well, that really is why I came back."

She laughed as she returned to the bed and started unbuckling and removing his gunbelt.

He relished the sound of her laugh, the feel of her hands around his waist, everything about being home, except for one thing. "Elijah is attracted to you."

"Don't be angry with him. He doesn't mean any harm."

"Well, he's got his blasted nerve, waiting like a cougar to pounce the minute I'm dead." He paused. "But the funniest part is, he's the only one of the hands I completely trust to look out for you."

"He does do that. But he's not you." Her face near his, she whispered in his ear, "And he never will be."

His cocky smile returned. "I know that."

"I have a surprise for you."

His shoulders slumped. "How many surprises can a man take in one night?"

"Lena's here."

"She's here? Really?" he asked loud enough so that Tara clapped a hand over his mouth.

"Shhh. She and Sarah are sleeping in Buck's room. She and Becca and Rachel have been taking turns staying with me for the last week."

Nate jumped to his feet and headed for the door, but Tara grabbed his arm. "Let her sleep. You can talk to her in the morning. I want you to myself tonight."

He sat back down on the bed, suddenly feeling worried. "Will she talk to me?"

"Yes, she will. How long can you stay?"

"As long as I can if they don't find out."

"I tried to talk to the cavalry."

"I knew you would. I can guess how that went."

"Whatever you do, don't try to go in and talk to Colonel McHenry yourself, without some kind of assurances first. He's getting bad advice from somewhere. I couldn't find out anything."

"Well, if he wouldn't listen to you, it's a cinch he won't listen to me."

She sensed he felt hopeless about the subject, a feeling aggravated by his fatigue after the long trip. "You get some rest now," she said as she slid his jacket off of his shoulders and down his arms.

He lay on the bed and closed his eyes. "It's so good to be home," he whispered just before dozing off.

She blew out the lantern and lay down beside him, even though she knew she wouldn't fall asleep for a long time, if at all. Everything was right about the world for now. She blocked her mind from thinking about anything past tomorrow. She reached for his hand and slid hers into it. He clasped hers in return. Even in his sleep, he was aware of her next to him.

***

Nate was seated at the table long before sunup, a habit formed early in a life of ranch work. He'd missed family meals at this table. He'd made the table and two flanking benches himself. It was an amateur effort; benches were easier to make than chairs. His eyes scanned about the house. Everything was the same. The top-heavy lamp still sat on the marble-topped table by the window, still in one piece. Jerome Sinclair stilled stared out from the parlor wall, only now the picture served as a vivid reminder that Nate knew who his killer was.

Tara cooked pancakes and sausage as he watched the closed door to Buck's room and waited. Finally, he could stand it no longer. "Does anybody do anything around here but sleep?" he shouted.

Almost immediately the door was flung wide open, and Buck tore threw it and raced to Nate. "Pa, you're back! Where you been, Pa?" He sprung into Nate's lap and grabbed him about the neck.

Laughing, Nate squeezed him tightly. "I was a long ways away. But I couldn't wait to see you, my little bear killer."

He saw movement out of the corner of his eye, above Buck's tousled head, and switched his eyes back to the door to Buck's room. Lena appeared in her nightgown and robe, carrying Sarah who was still rubbing sleep from her eyes. Setting Buck down on the bench, he arose and went to her, throwing his arms around her and Sarah. When he felt her free arm grasping him tightly, the last knot in his stomach disappeared, and sheer gladness took its place.

"Gosh, it's good to see you, Lena."

"You too. What a surprise! Welcome home. Did you get all the way here without any cavalry trouble?"

"Yes, I did. You know those soldiers. They can't take cold and discomfort. Why, they're all sittin' by a warm fire with hot coffee, waitin' for conditions to be just right to do any work."

Lena laughed while she helped Tara carry the plates of steaming food to the table.

It was the best breakfast Nate had had in months, and he devoured two plates of it. Even better was the pleasant conversation with family. He swore he'd never take that for granted again. But he could tell that, behind her smiles, there was something on Lena's mind. She was unsure about him, but not wanting to spoil this occasion for Tara. Nate would have none of it. Time with her was too precious to him to waste it on unspoken worries. He pushed his empty plate aside and leaned both elbows on the table.

"I'm here now, Lena. For how long, I don't know. But make use of it while you can. Ask me anything you want to know, and I will tell you the truth. Go ahead. Let's get this over with."

"All right." She looked deep into his eyes across the table from her. "Tell me to my face that you didn't do the things they're accusing you of."

Without hesitation, he began, "When the cavalry attacked, I sent Tara and Buck running, but I returned to the fight. I fired on soldiers, and I killed some."

Lena cast her eyes downward in disappointment, but he pressed on undaunted.

"I found Blaine, and I forced him to withdraw his troops by threatening a private. It was a merciless rout, Lena. The Indians didn't stand a chance without what I did."

"And you're sure there were no killers among the Indians?"

"Yes, I'm sure. I'm sorry that I was not able to find out who attacked the cavalry wagons, but I have no doubt that they were not with any Indians I was with."

She paused a moment, then nodded. "All right."

"The Indians look up to me greatly now because of what I did. They listen to me; they protect me. But even though their loyalty to me is strong, I swear to you, on my life, Lena, I did not do those things I'm accused of."

"Why is the cavalry saying—"

"I have no idea. Likely the story of the attack got much bigger in the retelling. Maybe it's someone who hates me, someone who wants to get ahead. I don't know. But I tell you, I have not one reason to give the Indians weapons or lead them to attack the whites." He leaned closer to her to emphasize his point. "Lena, I talked them *out* of a war."

Lena's eyes widened.

"Yes, that's right. I was in a meeting where many chiefs were planning revenge, and *I stopped it*. Those chiefs listened to *me*."

Tara and Lena looked at each other soberly, then back at Nate.

"Forgive me for questioning you," said Lena.

"No, it's all right. You question me all you want if it puts your mind at ease. I miss my sister. I don't just mean being away for the last months. I miss the sister I used to know, and I'm so sorry about Laura."

"I know. There's no hard feelings." The smile she gave him was sincere. "I must be on my way home now."

"So soon?" asked Nate, disappointed. "We just had breakfast."

Lena glanced at Tara and Buck and smiled. "I think there's others you'd prefer to spend time with."

She returned to the bedroom and reappeared a short time later, herself and Sarah dressed and her overnight bag in hand.

"Tell Ward I said hello," said Nate.

Lena dropped the bag and clapped a hand to her mouth. "Oh, I forgot. Ward's not home now. He joined the cavalry. I wasn't supposed to say anything."

Nate's jaw dropped, and he stared blankly ahead. Quiet settled on the room. He looked over at Tara, but she was turned away, studying something outside the window. A muffled sound from Lena drew his attention back to her. Her eyes were squinted shut, her face turning red. Finally, she could stifle it no longer, and she burst into uncontrolled peals of laughter.

"If only..." Lena began, struggling for composure, "if only you could see the look on your face." She wiped a tear from her eye.

Tara was laughing now too. Buck didn't understand the joke, but he watched Nate and giggled as well.

Nate glared at Lena. "Go ahead. Have a laugh at my expense." She had fooled him in more than one way. They had always enjoyed teasing each other. The sister he used to know was back after all. He smiled as she picked up her bag and Sarah and headed for the door. "I knew you were kidding all along."

She shook her head. "No, you didn't." She ran through the door and slammed it before he could reply.

He turned to Tara, attempting one last-ditch effort to save face. "I did know she was kidding."

"No, you didn't," she laughed.

"No, you didn't, Pa," shouted Buck.

Nate stood and ruffled Buck's hair. "Well, I see there's no battles to be won here. I'm going out to see the ranch hands."

He exited through the back door, then halted. Elijah's boot prints were still in the damp ground from the night before. He suddenly remembered the mysterious follower from his trip to the Indian camp the previous year, the one with the boots and unshod horse. But these were not the same tracks. Elijah's boots had narrower heels which sunk deeper into the track than the ones he'd seen. It was so long ago now, the matter didn't press on him as much. He afforded it no more thought as he continued his walk to the bunkhouse.

He paused outside the door to the bunkhouse. Elijah would have informed the others by now of his arrival. He knew he faced several minutes of good-natured ribbing when he entered. He took a deep breath, steeled himself, and opened the door. There were the nine cowboys seated at the long table eating their breakfast. They wasted no time starting in on him.

"Well, look what the wind blew in."

"There he is, the missing papa."

"I bet you were more surprised than she was last night."

"I was at that," Nate admitted, smiling.

"I'da given anything to seen your face when you got home last night."

"Hell, I'da given a month's pay to see that."

"I bet you ain't never been caught off guard once in your life till last night."

"Yeah, leave it to Mrs. Hunter to be the one to do it."

Clay smiled. "Good to see you again, sir."

"Shore is," said another. "We're tired of lookin' at each other, and we miss yer harmonica at the barn dances."

"That part don't matter," a man said in reply. "No use havin' dances. Every time we try to spark a town girl, she says she belongs to Clay. I wish he'd hurry up and get married or somethin'."

"Sit down and have some breakfast," Clay urged.

A plate was shoved in front of Nate, and he didn't object.

"I remember how you like your coffee," said Clay, pouring a cupful, "black as night and thick as Platte River mud."

"Only because you can't make it any other way," replied Nate.

As they ate and visited, Nate realized how much he'd missed this too, the camaraderie that had always existed between Broken Bow cowboys.

"I'd be terribly negligent if I didn't thank you boys for all the hard work you've put in all this time for the ranch, and my family." He glanced at Elijah at the other end of the table. Elijah wasn't saying much, but his manner was amiable like everyone else's. Nate found it impossible to determine what his thoughts were. "So I understand," he continued, "that all's well with the ranch. I guess we sell to the Split Timber now." His comment was met with knowing smiles.

"Yeah, it works out better all the way around," said one man. "Much less time-consumin' to drive the dogies to the Split Timber than Fort Mason."

"I am grateful for your loyalty as well," said Nate. "I know the cavalry's put the pressure on you, and, well, you've been more loyal than I have any right to expect from you."

"Aw, they ain't much," drawled a tobacco-chewing cowboy. "We seen cavalry around from time to time. Whenever they see a Broken Bow man, they straighten up and look real threatenin'-like." He imitated the posture. "It's kinda funny actually."

The others laughed in agreement.

"We heard you were down near the Powder River," said Elijah.

Nate nodded. "I was. And I still came across Fort Mason cavalry, even that far away."

The men turned serious. "Now that's plumb persistent," said one.

It was quiet for a moment, then the tobacco chewer spoke up. "I wouldn't worry 'bout it none. I bet they're all still lookin' for ya down at the Powder."

"I hope so," replied Nate.

The following days saw Nate jumping full-bore into the ranch work alongside the hands. He rode fence lines, checked on how well the cattle had wintered, and rounded up strays. Afternoons and evenings were spent with his family. He gave Buck horseback rides, marveled at how much Buck had grown and learned, and how much more involved their conversations could be now. He even thought to let Buck hold a knife and try to do some whittling.

He found Tara's derringer in the top drawer of the bureau and tested the feel of it, taking practice aim at a distant object outside the window. He pronounced it sufficient for knocking something down that was in the way. Then he saw her cache of bullets. "Goodness, are you starting a sideline ammo business?" he queried in amusement.

On Sunday afternoon, Tara's mother, Jared and Rebecca, and Rachel came for dinner, the only day they could all come at once and leave no one to run the store. Nate was glad for the chance to offer his profuse thanks to all of them for the gift of the Broken Bow in Edward's will. "I'm indebted to you for everything," he said to them over dinner.

"For nothing," Jared replied with a smile. "Papa was pleased with the good showing the Broken Bow has made. He had every confidence in you and felt that you had earned that gift."

"Then I trust I'll be viewed in good standing if I ever have to make a loan from your bank," Nate teased. "On second thought, I'd probably send Tara to do it anyway."

"I'm afraid Jared is more wise to my ways than Fort Mason is," added Tara, drawing laughing nods of agreement from everyone.

Nate especially enjoyed the visit, for he could only see Tara's family, or Lena, if they came to the Broken Bow. He knew it wouldn't be safe to go into town or even leave the ranch and let himself be seen.

During evenings in front of the fireplace, Tara wanted to know everything about the time he spent with the Indians, who he talked to, who his friends were, so she could form a picture in her mind of what his life was like during those long months. He related his humorous exchanges with Chief Red Feather's wife and his fireside conversations with the medicine man White Buffalo. He told all about the demure Shining Sky, and River Otter's antics. He carefully skirted Gray Wolf's name and any mention of his time around the brave, a difficult thing since Gray Wolf had been such a pervasive presence during the past months. But he hoped she would never find out about him. He didn't see any point in upsetting her with something that was now a distant matter.

***

Tara's pains began in the night. Knowing Nate's keen perception of everything around him, even in his sleep, she lay perfectly still. It would still be many hours before the baby came. She was able to doze off between pains, but hardly an hour had passed before strong contractions gripped her and made rest impossible. It was progressing far more quickly than it had with Buck. Her breathing awakened Nate.

"Is it time?" he asked.

"Yes."

Wide awake in an instant, he flew from the bed and lit the lamp. Then he paced the room in a quandary. "I'm going into town for your mother," he said at last.

"You can't go into town," she objected. "You might be seen."

"Not at this hour," he replied nervously.

She gritted her teeth against a pain. "Would you stop walking back and forth?"

"I can be in and out of town in a heartbeat. Nobody'll know." He was putting on his first boot when she moaned.

"No, please don't leave me alone, please."

He was paralyzed for a moment. Of all the situations he'd been in, needing to be in two places at one time was one he'd never come up against. *This could have been planned much better ahead of time, he thought.* "I'll send Elijah for your mother," he decided.

"No, you won't."

"Tara, he'd love to go." He was pleading now. "How else do I get your mother here?"

She struggled for a breath. "It's too late. She wouldn't get here in time."

He saw her spreading her legs. His face turned white, and he felt lightheaded. "Tara, I can't do this," he breathed. "I can't."

"Oh, for pity's sake," she lashed out between breaths. "You've never been afraid of anything in your life. Now pull yourself together right now!"

Sufficiently reprimanded, he closed his eyes and breathed deeply. "Okay, all right. I'm fine now. What do I do?"

"Just talk to me."

He approached her side of the bed and sat down with his arm around her. "All right, what do I say?"

"Anything. Just talk to me."

"Okay," he nodded. He thought quickly. "I shot three buffalo in one day once. One of them right through the heart. I mean right—"

"Not that!"

"Okay, all right, I'll think of something else." Amid her worsening agony, he fought to clear his mind. He'd been able to do it before when in the throes of suffering himself, but this presented a far more difficult challenge—how to lift his thoughts above his acute awareness of her pain. He closed his eyes and held her sweat-laden face tightly against his shoulder. His breathing calmed, and he relaxed his trembling hands and twisted insides. "There was a canyon," he began, his face close to her ear, "a narrow, secluded canyon where we spent the whole winter. Wind and blizzards whistled above us, but where we were, not much moved. Just snow falling down, and cold, so cold. But as much as I wanted to just sit by a blazing fire, I couldn't. I had to be by myself because that's the only way I felt closer to you. There was a spot near the canyon rim, a rock ledge that jutted out. There was brush all around it. You couldn't really see it from the camp."

She uttered a gasp and grabbed him around the neck, very nearly unnerving him, and he struggled to maintain his focus.

"I went there every night after everyone was asleep. For some odd reason, it always seemed important to me that no one ever knew that I did that. I would sit for, I don't know, maybe an hour some nights, and watch the stars. If it was clouded over, I'd sit there anyway and picture where every star was supposed to be."

She leaned forward to push, pulling him with her, her fingernails dug into the back of his neck. He swallowed hard, bit his lip, and continued with his story.

"On snowy nights, the canyon was so light, like dusk even though it was late at night. I could easily make out the drawings on the tepees at the bottom. It reminded me of the winter we spent in the Lewis and Clark range, in that trapper's cabin. I remembered it like it was y-yesterday. So quiet. I really liked l-listening to the qu-quiet." He cleared his throat. He was losing his train of thought.

She had stopped breathing. Intense fear seized him. With both arms, he grasped her in her sweat-dampened nightgown and gave her a shake.

"What are you doing?" she gasped.

He looked into her face. She was only bearing down; she hadn't stopped breathing at all. He felt lightheaded again. He had said he couldn't do this, and he was right. He wished for a bowl of cold water to plunge his face into.

Then he noticed something he hadn't before. She had not uttered one scream, no shouts or wails. She wasn't even crying. She was grappling with her labor the same way he had dealt with pain before. Her concentration was unbroken. She was strong beyond his belief, a Hunter through and through.

He got his second wind now. Perhaps he could finish this thing after all. "Well, it wasn't always so quiet. There was a wolf that would sit on the next ledge over from me and howl. I know he knew I was there, but he didn't seem worried about it. I wouldn't move a muscle, just listen to him. Right there, in that place, on those nights, it was the loneliest sound I'd ever heard."

She fell back against the pillow, panting heavily, and in the next moment, a baby's cry sounded as the first light of dawn filtered through the eastern window. Nate excitedly grabbed the child and held him aloft, laughing and tears streaming at the same time. "Our son, Tara, look at him! Just look at him!"

He used his hunting knife to cut the cord and was soon placing the blanket-wrapped boy in her waiting arms.

They smiled down at the small, round face topped with short, velvety dark hair. "Oh, he's beautiful," sighed Tara. "Your pa did just fine, didn't he? Yes, he did."

"I didn't do anything," said Nate, still in awe.

She looked up at him. "Yes, you did. You took me to where you were. All those months when I wondered where you were and what you were doing, you made me see it, just like I was there."

Buck came bounding into the room and climbed onto the bed.

"See your little brother?" Tara tilted the bundle to show him.

"Finally, someone to play with!" exclaimed Buck.

***

Nate entered the bunkhouse, once again at breakfast time, and the men all gave him the once-over.

"You look like a dogie sat on you," drawled one.

"Just about." Nate smiled. "It's a boy."

The men broke into whoops and cheers.

"And Tara and the baby are fine," continued Nate, "but I'm exhausted."

Clay produced a bottle of whiskey and began setting shot glasses on the table. "Well, here, you need this."

Clay poured, and Nate raised his glass for a toast. "To my son, Jackson Lee Hunter."

"To Jackson," they all repeated before they drank.

"You just turn those boys over to us," one hand suggested. "We'll have both of 'em trailin' cattle by this fall."

"No doubt you would," replied Nate. How he liked being here, sharing his big news among friends. But the offhand reference to the next fall drove home a stark reality—that his future was shrouded in a cloud of uncertainty. These days of bliss couldn't last. With a sudden pang, he wondered how much longer he would have.

Chapter 17

April came in a rush. Melting snows turned gentle Elkhorn Creek into a raging torrent, and seasonal showers greened up dormant grasses. Some of the more hardy species of wildflowers poked up through the damp earth. Whenever clear skies prevailed, branding fires blazed on the Broken Bow. Charlie and Adam Wilson returned, looking for work, and Nate hired them. They were hard workers and got along well with everyone else.

Nate had been home for a month, and he counted every day as a privilege. He kept Buck busy stoking the fires and heating the branding irons while he and the cowboys rode into the herd, cut out and roped the calves, threw them down, and tied their legs together. Then, bawling lustily and with their hips still sizzling from the imprint of the Broken Bow brand, the B shielded on the left by a broken half circle, they were released to find their way back to their mothers.

After each day's work was done, Nate would help Buck practice tossing a lasso. Buck was becoming proficient at roping tree stumps, fallen branches, and boulders and did Nate proud. And every evening there was a bedtime story. Nate insisted on holding the baby during the story and enjoyed seeing Jackson's eyes fixed on his face as if trying to memorize its every detail. Nate told every story he'd saved up for Buck, and Tara listened in as well, smiling throughout. They especially loved the one about the cavalry scouts who had to ride off without their pants.

Tara's family had all been to the Broken Bow to see the baby, as well as Lena and Ward. But when Lena burst into the house one day during the noon meal without even knocking first, Nate and Tara knew something was wrong and set down their forks.

"There're soldiers coming here for you," she announced breathlessly.

Nate stood. He'd expected this day ever since he'd arrived. "How far away?"

"Maybe thirty minutes, no more. I was in the store. They were already there, stocking up on supplies. Jared gave me a look and nodded towards them. He couldn't get away to talk to me without raising their suspicion, but I overheard them. They said they had good information this time, and they knew they had you. They were still in the store when I left. I ran the horse all the way here to tell you."

Nate looked over at Jackson, asleep in the cradle near the fireplace, and silent rage began to build. *They had good information this time.* The phrase rang in his ears as he headed for the door, seething.

Tara stood and grasped Buck's shoulders. "You stay in the house and look after Jack." She rushed past Lena and through the open door after Nate. He was already way ahead of her, headed straight for the bunkhouse. She gathered up her skirt and raced after him. She caught up to him near the old oak with the rope swing but said nothing as she followed him the rest of the way to the bunkhouse. She was pretty sure what was on his mind and eager to see what came of it.

He pushed open the door with a single pound of his fist and, without breaking stride, walked the length of the table where the cowboys sat eating, to the far end where Elijah sat. He clamped down one hand on Elijah's neck and the other on his left shoulder and handily dragged him backwards off the bench. Elijah landed in a heap on the floor and scrambled to gain his footing, but before he could, Nate's fist in his jaw sent him reeling across the floor and against one of the bunks.

"You at least waited long enough for me to be with my new son," Nate hissed. "And I suppose you thought you were doing me a favor."

Elijah made an attempt to respond but didn't get a chance. Nate grabbed his collar and stood him upright, then planted another fist into his stomach. Elijah coughed but recovered enough to guard against the next blows and start fighting back.

The other cowboys backed out of the way, eyeing Elijah with suspicion, and Tara turned her face away from the sight, devastated that it had come to this.

Another powerful hit knocked Elijah against the wall with a thud. Satisfied that he'd disabled the wrangler enough for the moment, Nate backed off but remained ready to resume the fight in an instant. "Been talkin' to the cavalry, have ya?"

"What? No!" replied Elijah incredulously.

Nate's fists clenched. "Damn you! I've trusted you with everything I have. Don't you lie to me!"

"Mr. Hunter, I swear to you on my life, I've never talked to the cavalry about you." He struggled to catch a breath. "I've never even left the ranch since you been here." He gave a glance around at the others. "None of us have."

The room was dead silent. Tara stepped forward and studied Elijah's eyes. He wouldn't dare meet her gaze, but she saw what she needed anyway. "I believe he's telling the truth, Nate."

Nate turned and looked at each of the cowboys in turn. Lastly his eyes fell on the one who went into town the most. "Clay?"

"No, sir." Clay's resolute answer came with no hesitation. "I've purposely stayed on the ranch since you been here."

Elijah couldn't hide his disgust. "I thought you were the one that didn't like to be rash. You like to find out everything before you accuse somebody."

Nate grabbed his collar and held him fast against the wall, and Elijah stiffened.

"You don't need to fight me. I'm done with it," Elijah conceded.

Nate beheld him for an uncomfortably long time then finally loosened his grip. "I'm sorry."

The words were hollow, and Elijah knew it, but he nodded.

"Get my horse ready," Nate directed.

The cowboys looked at each other questioningly.

"What's going on, sir?" asked Clay.

Nate was already leaving the bunkhouse as quickly as he'd arrived, and Tara answered for him. "There are soldiers on the way here from town."

There were muttered curses, expressions of disapproval, and Tara carefully but furtively noted each man's response.

Then Charlie Wilson stepped forward, donning his hat. "Coupla you boys come with me to innercep' those blue boys. We'll play stupid and see if we can't stall 'em awhile."

Immediately some of the men followed him.

"Thank you," said Tara, and she left to follow Nate back to the house. They met Lena on the way.

"I'm going back a different way," said Lena. "I can't let the soldiers see that I came here."

"Yes, you go ahead now," replied Nate. He hugged her tightly. "Thank you for the warning."

"You take care, and good luck." She mounted her horse and kicked him into a gallop northward.

Tara helped Nate hurriedly throw together some provisions, fill a water canteen, and roll up blankets. Elijah had the Appaloosa saddled and ready in front of the porch when they came out with the gear. As Elijah held the reins, Nate readied the saddlebags and tied on the blanket roll.

Nate was unsure what to say to Elijah under the circumstances. "Don't let the work slack up while I'm gone."

"No, sir. Mr. Hunter?" Elijah waited till Nate looked at him. "You can trust me."

"I know you didn't talk to the cavalry, Elijah," Nate impatiently replied.

"I don't mean about that." He glanced towards Tara. "I wouldn't do you wrong, sir."

Nate's busy hands were stilled, and he looked at Elijah. "Thank you." He stood facing him. "I do truly appreciate that. You don't know how much."

Elijah did know how much. He'd imagined himself in Nate's shoes a million times, and he knew exactly how much, and that was the linchpin upon which he'd made his decision. He had faced down his demons before Nate had ever come home. A fierce battle had raged within him, but wisdom had conquered. His honor was preserved, and he felt stronger for it, if not happier.

When all was ready and Tara came down the porch steps holding the baby and leading Buck by the hand to say their goodbyes, Elijah quietly melted away into the background.

Nate struggled to remain upbeat as he knelt down and hugged Buck and then stood in front of Tara and looked down at Jackson. He stroked the baby's fuzzy head and bent to kiss him on the forehead. "Don't let Jack forget about me," he said with a smile.

"I won't." She smiled too, but it was laced with sadness. "You better go. They'll probably be riding in any minute."

"I hate leaving you here when the soldiers come."

"We will be fine, I promise. The best thing you can do for us is not be caught."

There was a quick kiss, and Nate mounted the Appaloosa. The feisty horse was raring to go, and Nate fought the reins. "Bring horses for the Indians in late May when the work slows down some. Meet me at the Dearborn River, where it joins the Missouri. I'll make sure I'm there." He started to leave but stopped again. "And bring Buck. There may be a boy for him to meet."

"All right, I will."

He gave the horse the reins and galloped away towards the south with Tara and Buck waving after him.

All too soon it was quiet again. The ranch hands were not around; Lena had left, and now Nate. Tara was surrounded by quiet and loneliness, a feeling she knew would once again be a constant companion. She switched her eyes from the direction Nate had taken to the road which led to town. No sign of soldiers yet, but time must be short. She guessed that the cowboys wouldn't be able to hold them off for long. She hurried back inside the house and laid Jackson in the cradle. He immediately began to cry, and she set Buck to rocking the cradle while she inspected the house for signs of Nate's presence. The bed was made, but there was a shirt lying on it. She stuffed it into a drawer and returned to the kitchen. She collected the three plates and cups from the table and set them in the dishpan. Buck's cradle-rocking wasn't working; the baby was crying to be held. She started to go to him, then looked at the dishpan once more. On second thought, she grabbed one plate and cup, gave them a cursory swipe with a dish towel, and thrust them into the cupboard.

Faraway movement outside the kitchen window caught her eye, and she looked out at the road that led to town. Sure enough, galloping horses were in view, kicking up a cloud of dust as they quickly approached.

Jackson was screaming now, and Tara's anxiety intensified. She went to the cradle, scooped him into her arms, and rewrapped him in the blanket he'd kicked off. Then, holding him close with her left arm, she rushed back into the bedroom and opened the drawer where the derringer lay. She closed her right hand over it and returned to the front room, holding the derringer behind her, hidden by the folds of her dress.

The baby's cries subsided, replaced by soft whimpers, and she could hear the soldiers arriving at the door, their boots on the porch sounding to her like an army advancing on her home. Her heart pounded, and she bit her lip to still the trembling. The expected knock came as a vehement banging. "Open the door, Buck. And then come and stand beside me."

Buck unlatched the door, and the moment he did, a soldier burst inside, knocking the boy down and leading in four men behind him. Buck ran to stand beside Tara, clutching her skirt with one hand.

Tara watched, horrified, as soldiers entered both bedrooms, and their leader, a tall, mustached lieutenant whose searching eyes were not used to missing a thing, looked about the main room.

"What do you think you're doing?" she demanded. "I didn't say you could come in here."

"Official business, ma'am," replied the lieutenant. "We don't need your permission." He glanced at the hook beside the door where Nate's gun would hang, then walked around, looking at the fireplace mantle, the table, and finally, the dishpan. The other soldiers were back in the main room now.

"No sign of him here," said one.

"Go look in the stable and that other building out there," said the lieutenant. "And I think I saw the door to a root cellar out back." Two soldiers left through the open door.

"Mr. Hunter is not here," Tara insisted. "What do you want with him anyway?"

The lieutenant stopped in front of her and beheld her through stern eyes that had not the least regard for her or the children. "Your husband, Mrs. Hunter, on top of everything else, is now charged with killing two cavalry scouts near the Powder River last fall."

Tara's eyes widened. "He didn't do that."

"Hangin's too good for his kind of vermin."

His scratchy voice was as irritating to Tara as the words he spoke. "You should know about vermin, you, the basest of men."

"Ooh, a little sharp-tongued fireball, ain't ya? Doesn't really matter though. We *will* find him." He looked down at Buck, seeming to notice him for the first time. Then he squatted down and looked him in the eye, certain that such a young child would be useful in breaking down the obvious, secret barriers in place here. "Where's your pa?"

Buck jerked his chin high and answered in a loud and clear voice. "He ain't here."

"*Isn't*, Buck," Tara corrected.

"He isn't here neither."

The lieutenant's eyes widened slightly. Put off by the insolence of the child and Tara's failure to do anything about it, he stood and addressed her again.

"Harboring a fugitive, that's serious, you know."

"As you can see, I'm not harboring a fugitive, but I do have a gun in my hand, specifically for intruders invading my home." The click was audible as she cocked the hammer behind her.

He backed up a step but kept a cautious eye on her while he addressed the others. "Looks like we just missed him, boys. That's all right. He can't have gone far. We'll trail him."

The soldiers all met up in front of the porch. Tara peeked out of the front window to watch. After some short, indiscernible conversation while they looked at the recent tracks in the dirt, they mounted their horses and set off galloping southward, the direction Nate had taken.

After they were gone, Tara put away the derringer, calmly assured Buck that all was well, and settled down in the rocking chair to nurse the baby. She didn't give a scrap of attention to the soldiers' intention to trail Nate. Nate was in his element throwing off trackers. It didn't matter if they sent the whole regiment after him. They were sadly outmatched.

***

Nate kept the Appaloosa at a steady gallop, grateful that his cowboys had apparently bought him a little time to get ahead of the soldiers. He raced through range country, his direction set for a lake to the south. Nearly ten miles later, he was within sight of it, a placid body of blue-green water lined by rushes and fed from the north by Elkhorn Creek. He needed to rest the Appaloosa for a while, and this would be the place to do it. His past experience evading trackers did not involve having a horse, and while the horse was handy for giving him speed in the chase, it required a new set of tactics.

He guided the Appaloosa down a stony embankment, through a thinly growing patch of rushes, and into the water. He turned the horse to follow along the lake's edge. The Appaloosa was knee-deep, and each step stirred up clouds of brown silt that would settle long before any soldiers arrived.

He had gone only a short ways when he spied a small beach along the shoreline, an expanse of smooth, trackless, damp soil. He could just picture Buck grabbing a stick and drawing in the dirt, as if on a clean slate, a message of some sort. The boy would be irresistibly drawn to such a spot, much the same way Nate was now. But Nate's interest ran deeper, connected to a memory being dredged up of another shore, a dusty riverside bank. There was something he wanted to know, and there was perhaps a slim chance that this clean slate of a shore may yield a message for him and confirm a suspicion that had just now come to light.

"Are you thinkin' what I'm thinkin', boy?"

He rode closer and halted the Appaloosa just before the horse would've stepped out on land, then he dismounted with a splash at the water's edge and looked around, considering every visible resource and coming up with a plan. He began gathering rocks of varying sizes and chose an obvious spot to build a cairn. He took care to keep most of the beach unmarred, keeping his own footprints behind the cairn. Moments later it was done, and he stood looking proudly at his simple creation. It needed a little something more, he decided. He picked up a piece of quartz with a sharp edge and set to work scratching a figure into the smooth sandstone which would rest on top of the cairn. He smiled at the finished product. With any luck, the soldiers would stop to investigate this find and possibly suspect that it was some secret message to the Indians. All they would really be looking at was a pile of rocks with the Broken Bow brand scratched on the top stone. No matter. It only needed to be enough to get at least one or two of them off of their horses, if even for a moment.

He remounted the Appaloosa and continued his ride through the shallows around the edge of the lake. He guessed that once the soldiers figured out that he was disguising his trail in the water, they'd probably split up, each group going a different direction around the lake and watching for signs of where he came out of the water. So he could potentially make it about halfway around the lake before having to strike out for other parts. But it was too predictable, he decided. They'd probably be onto his idea from the beginning. He would exit the water sooner, after the soldiers had split up and when the group going the opposite direction from him would be far enough away so that a rendezvous would delay the entire group.

He carefully judged his distance and tried to anticipate where they'd make the decision to split up, then he rode a good ways further. He chose a particularly rocky, pebble-strewn area to leave the water. He guided the Appaloosa over the smooth stones and away from tall grasses that could become mashed under a horse's hooves.

Back on gently rolling rangeland, he picked up speed, quickly making up for time lost at the lake. He knew this country well. He was familiar with every grassy rise, every brush-studded ravine, and every grove of trees and how to use each to his advantage. He was crossing a shallow creek when he heard the distant report of a rifle. That would be one group of soldiers signaling to the others that they had picked up his trail. The sound told him that the soldiers were further behind him than he expected, but he also knew that those who had given the signal would not wait for the others to catch up.

He held up the back of his hand at arm's length to the sun. Lining up the sun on top of his hand, he counted the distance in fingers to the horizon, one finger for every fifteen minutes. There was about an hour and a half of daylight left. He turned the Appaloosa to the left and headed for a bluff a couple miles to the east. There was just enough light left to make a wide circle back towards the lake. He rode with utter confidence. In this terrain, his trail would be tough to follow, and they wouldn't be expecting him to return to the lake.

In dusky, golden light, as shadows of the day were fading, he cautiously approached the smooth, little shore where he'd left his cairn. His hopes heightened when he saw new tracks in the damp earth in front of the cairn. The soldiers had indeed stopped, and at least two had dismounted. Sorely impatient to satisfy his nagging suspicion, he left the Appaloosa further up the bank and moved closer on foot. Standing to the side of the new footprints, he beheld them in stunned disbelief. The track the boots made was identical to those of the mysterious rider who had shadowed him and Tara to Chief Red Feather's camp the year before. He remembered the rounded toe and the wide, flat heel. He doubted that the follower was among these soldiers. Many of these tracks included a faint mark in the dirt just behind the heel, indicating they wore spurs, and there were no unshod horses among this group. But there was no doubt that the boots were standard military issue.

With this discovery, his questions only deepened. Why would a lone rider attached to cavalry have followed him back then? Had he been set up, even before the attack on Red Feather's camp? He recalled Major Blaine's anger at his refusal to help track down the attackers of the medicine wagons. For just a moment, he wondered, then he shut his eyes and shook his head. "No," he said aloud, "he could *not* have ordered that. That's not at *all* like Blaine."

There was nothing more he could do here. He must be on his way. He mounted his horse and kicked into a gallop for the bluff on the eastern horizon, now rose-colored in the hazy twilight. An hour later, in the dark, he set up camp on top of the bluff with the soldiers' campfire visible in the valley below. He built his own small fire far back from the edge of the bluff, hidden from the soldiers' view.

Following a few short hours of sleep, he sat in the grass against a boulder near the edge of the bluff, intermittently dozing and watching the soldiers' fire. Sometime before daybreak, the fire started blinking, indicating soldiers moving back and forth in front of it. That was his signal to be off.

He stood and stretched. "It's time for me to ride hard and fast." He gave a casual right-hand salute in the direction of the soldiers. "Goodbye, sirs. Don't exhaust yourselves."

He struck camp in just minutes, mounted up, and set a breakneck pace for the Sun River where he hoped to find Red Feather.

***

Three days later, Nate rode into Chief Red Feather's camp, some distance beyond the Sun River. He was met with a welcoming smile from the chief as he dismounted. He was back reluctantly in the world he'd left behind two months before, but glad to see Red Feather. "*Haaahe*," he said with a smile. "*E pe va'e*."

The chief returned the greeting, then looked Nate and his horse up and down.

"You have traveled fast, Eagle Shadow?"

Nate nodded. "I left home in a hurry four days ago with soldiers on my trail."

They began walking towards Red Feather's tepee, with Nate leading the Appaloosa.

"I lost them sometime yesterday," continued Nate. "I think they were out of provisions. They didn't expect to come this far. Don't worry. There were only a few of them, not enough to put up a fight against you."

"No one fears the soldiers when you are here. The people will be happy to see you."

"Just the same, I'll move to another band soon."

Red Feather stopped walking and looked at Nate with a sort of fatherly concern. "Perhaps you will see Gray Wolf again?" Nate couldn't look him in the eye, and Red Feather perceived why. "You know that he is your kin, Eagle Shadow."

"I feel no kinship to him."

"You must try. Gray Wolf has waited long to know you and count you as his family."

Nate resumed walking. "Then he shouldn't have done what he did."

"I have known him all of his life. There is much good in him. Much good. Do not let the past ruin the future as well."

"My future lies at the Broken Bow, whenever I can return there." He smiled proudly. "I have a new son."

"A new son?" The chief grasped Nate's shoulder. "That is good news. I am happy for you. Come. Let us tell the people. We will celebrate tonight."

Chapter 18

Ol' Gun was unhappy again. Major Blaine could always tell by the way he rubbed his temple, displaying the impatience of one who wanted everyone to know what he was thinking without his having to take the time to explain it.

"That rat slipped through our fingers *again*," he grumbled.

"Rat?" Major Blaine dreaded having to ask. "What rat do you mean, sir?"

"That friend of yours, Nate Hunter."

"Oh, him. He's not really my friend, sir. Mostly his wife and my wife—"

"No, of course not. He's only your friend when it suits your purposes. Heaven help you, Mr. Blaine. Stop trying to say what you think I want to hear."

"Sorry, sir. He frustrates me too."

"Frustrates?" Colonel McHenry's half-hearted chuckle at the major's choice of words quickly transformed into a scowl. "An understatement if I ever heard one. We were this close." He held his thumb and index finger an inch apart and shook them to emphasize his point. "*This close*, I tell you, and he still slipped by like butter off a hot biscuit. How does he do that?"

"I'm sure I don't know, sir." Major Blaine knew the colonel was unaware of Nate's past eluding the best trackers among both the Indians and the cavalry, but he decided not to bring it up now. He wasn't particularly eager to see another of Ol' Gun's rants. "But it's been a long time since we heard he was trying to rally the Indians against us, and there's not been one attack."

"Maybe not en masse, but I'm tellin' you, he killed those two scouts. And there's been more attacks on ranchers down in Nebraska, on that land that used to be protected by treaty. I'm sending you down there with a contingent, Major. I want you to demand the surrender of those Indians, bring in their ringleaders, and set up a presence to discourage any more of this behavior."

"Will do, sir. This sounds like an extended campaign. My wife has accompanied me before on such trips."

"Yes, I'm sure she will enjoy the change. The school is not in session now. You can handpick your men. I think I can give you whatever you ask for. As for this Hunter rogue, maybe I'll start personally overseeing that situation myself."

Major Blaine was astonished at such an unconventional suggestion. He wondered why the colonel would attach such importance to the matter. He decided to venture asking the question that had dogged him since Julie first alluded to it. "Do you trust your sources, sir?"

There was a surprisingly lengthy pause. "I don't know."

It was the first crack Major Blaine had ever seen in the colonel's rough and confident exterior. "Perhaps there's something I could do to help?"

Colonel McHenry placed his elbows on the desk and clasped his hands. "I'm going to speak plainly, Josh. Let's dispense with formalities just for now. Call me David."

The request seemed about as unnatural as snow in July to Major Blaine, but he held his reaction in check.

"Good leaders surround themselves with good men, Josh. I called you here today to give me some input."

"All right, Ol' G—uh, David. I'll do my best."

"My friend U.S. Grant, brilliant tactician. He said to me the last time I saw him, 'David, my failures have been errors of judgment, not of intent.'" He stood and walked to a cabinet behind his desk, from which he produced a pair of shot glasses and a bottle of whiskey. He set the glasses down, uncorked the whiskey, and filled both glasses. "Have a drink. I want to talk to you about something."

***

Spring roundup was finished, and Tara wasted no time in preparing for her journey to the Dearborn River to bring the horses Nate had promised to the Indians. She directed Clay and Elijah to separate out a couple dozen head of the finest, such as the Indians were used to receiving from them.

When the task was completed, the two men stood at the foot of the porch steps waiting for her to look over their choices. She looked pleased as she made her way from the corral to the house.

"Excellent choices," she pronounced as she passed them on her way up the steps. "They will surely meet with Mr. Hunter's approval. Tell the Wilsons to come along. I think that will be enough help for this trip. Be ready to leave at first light tomorrow."

Elijah turned to leave, and Tara started for the front door.

"Uh, ma'am." It was Clay's voice that stopped them both. "I'm not planning to go on this trip."

"You're not? Do you have some prior commitment?" She couldn't imagine what plans he could have that would take precedence over this trip.

"No, not really, just..."

He was becoming increasingly uncomfortable and clearly preferred not to say his reasons. Tara was instantly suspicious. "Why not, Mr. Tatum?"

"I—I got plenty to do around here and—well, I'm not too keen on helping the Indians right now."

She was watching him intently, unconcerned that her penetrating gaze was causing awkwardness for him. She well remembered that when several ranch hands went to intercept the soldiers the day Nate left, Clay had not gone with them. "Mr. Hunter specifically asked that I bring horses to the Dearborn River. Now of course, you don't have to come if you'd rather not, but I feel like I'm missing something here, and I want you to be honest with me. Is there anything you've been hiding?"

Clay was taken aback by her accusatory tone. "No, ma'am."

"Speak your mind, Mr. Tatum. Now's your chance. I will find out if you don't tell me."

"Well, all right, since you put it that way. I know I don't state them often, but I got my own principles, Mrs. Hunter. You ask too much of me. You expect me to overlook the problems we'd cause by helping the Indians right now." He shot a contemptuous glance in Elijah's direction. "Just like you expect me to overlook the improprieties going on here at the house in Mr. Hunter's absence."

It was dead quiet as the words came to settle on stunned ears. Elijah's first instinct was to come to Tara's defense and plant a fist in Clay's jaw, but as he saw her slowly, purposefully, descending the steps, her eyes fixed like bayonets, he sensed that in this particular case, he didn't need to.

"You have one hour to pack your things, report back here to draw your wages, and get off the Broken Bow, Mr. Tatum. Furthermore, there has *never* been any impropriety in this house, and if you *ever* speak one word on the contrary to anyone, or malign me in any way, I'll see to it you don't get a job anywhere in the Territory, even so much as cleaning pig sties. Do I make myself clear?"

"Very clear, Mrs. Hunter." Thoroughly disgusted, he gave her a last sharp look before turning to head for his cabin.

When he was out of earshot, Tara turned to the shocked Elijah. "See to it he gets off the Broken Bow, Mr. Medley. That's your first official duty as the new foreman. Congratulations."

"Thank you," he managed to stammer about the time she was entering the house and slamming the door behind her. He watched Clay's back. "What's that your Yank President Lincoln said?" he whispered. "'Tis better to be silent and be thought a fool, than to speak and remove all doubt."

He smiled to himself over this fortuitous turn of events, simultaneously making a mental note. Not only would he never marry her, he would also never cross her.

Chapter 19

As he approached the confluence of the Dearborn and Missouri Rivers in mid-May in the company of Red Feather's band, Nate looked forward with anticipation to the arrival of Tara with the horses. The meeting would still be one to two weeks away, but he'd urged Red Feather to move the band in plenty of time to be ready for them. It was easy to do. The Indians were eager to see their new acquisitions. A general lightheartedness pervaded the people. Horses such as they'd seen from the Broken Bow before were of tremendous worth to them. It meant an increase in power and mobility, superiority over enemies, and gave them a pride unmatched among several bands.

Nate cared only to see his family, to see Buck run and play, and hold Jack, who surely had grown enough to be barely recognizable from the tiny bundle he'd left behind. Homeless again upon his return to the people, Nate stayed now in Red Feather's tepee as a special guest of his family. The chief's last two daughters had married in Nate's absence and owned their own tepees in the same band. He opted to stay with Red Feather for as long as he could. There had been no word of scouts searching for him, or cavalry activity of any kind. Nate was glad; he liked it better in this band. He had come to overlook the markings on the chief's tepee that may or may not have stood for the erstwhile attack on the Broken Bow. He had even added one of his own, when no one was looking, with some buffalo tallow paint he'd procured, and no one in the family had ever noticed. How they'd missed his painstaking rendering of his exploits in the battle on the Sun River he'd never understand, but the whole thing was an insult.

They set up camp in a small, secluded meadow along the Missouri, a prime place to stay for a while, thought Nate. The Dearborn, muddy with spring run-off, joined the clear waters of the Missouri at a visible line in the middle of the river. Gray rocky cliffs and crags studded with pine trees surrounded their camp. Buffalo had been spotted in the vicinity, and all the braves were excited at the prospect of successful hunting excursions.

They were not to remain alone here for long. In the late morning on the second day, as Nate cleaned his rifle, he heard shouts from across the camp. He'd barely grabbed his revolver when his vigilance relaxed. They were joyous shouts of recognition. More Cheyenne had arrived. Nate shared in the enthusiasm; this meant bigger hunting groups, bigger celebrations around the evening fires. Then he saw who it was, Gray Wolf's band, and he backed away and returned to cleaning his rifle.

Red Feather had already left for a hunt, and his wife had followed with other women to clean the fresh kills. Nate's rifle was ready; his saddle lay on the ground at his feet; and he was bridling the Appaloosa when suddenly, Gray Wolf and three other braves Nate knew from that band appeared in his way.

Nate glared at the brave he'd hoped he'd never have to see again. "What're you doing this side of the Missouri?"

"Following the buffalo, same as you."

Nate didn't believe him for a minute. Gray Wolf was never that plain and simple. "I doubt it."

"We left the winter canyon two moons ago. We were not far from here. I also heard that you were here."

"That's what I thought."

"Don't go hunting today." Gray Wolf indicated his friends who accompanied him. "We have something to tell you."

Nate wanted to leave immediately and not even give Gray Wolf time to state his purposes. But if they'd come this far to find him, he knew he'd best listen. He was sure he wouldn't like whatever they'd say, but all the more reason for him to know about it. He dropped the bridle where he stood and, without a word, walked back inside Red Feather's empty tepee. The four braves followed closely and seated themselves around the smoldering remnants of the morning fire.

"Are Shining Sky and River Otter here?" asked Nate.

"Yes, all of us came. We do come for hunting, as I said. It is a special time when many Cheyenne join together."

At least that was good news to Nate. Buck could finally meet River Otter. "So what do you come to tell me?"

"We are prepared to avenge you."

Nate closed his eyes. "Please, don't try to do any favors for me. I don't need your help."

"A contingent of soldiers left the fort two sleeps ago on a long journey to the south. They are led by your enemy, the major."

Nate's eyes flew open. "Blaine?"

"They will pass within a day's journey from here. There are women with them. They will travel slowly." Gray Wolf sneered as he looked at his companions. "White women cannot travel like Cheyenne women."

"How do you know this information?"

"From someone in the fort."

Nate sat frozen for a long moment, silently reeling from this revelation. "Who could you possibly know inside the fort?"

"Someone loyal."

Nate studied the faces of each brave, but they didn't give away anything. "What are you going to do?"

Gray Wolf's expression suddenly altered into an unyielding, malicious glare that sent chills down Nate's spine. "They cross Cheyenne land with no fear. Such disrespect deserves to be punished."

Nate swallowed hard.

"Join with us, Eagle Shadow. We will stop them before they set one foot in the great river. We will stain the ground with their blood."

"Are you mad? Why would you think I would take part in that?"

"Because you are my family. I have no other left."

"And as your family, I beg you not to do this thing."

"Eagle Shadow, you have returned to our people because you are not welcome among the whites. They make the world smaller for you with their laws and their false accusations. Do you not want to pay them back, even now?"

"Not that way!"

"What way then? I know. You want to talk to them, but they will not listen to you. They want to hold you under their foot and break your will as they want to do to us. I answer them with hate. Hate keeps us alive."

"It won't keep you alive for long."

"Where is your pride? How can you not thirst for their blood?"

"Killing them will get us both in trouble like we've never seen before." His voice rose. "And speaking of blood, they should've had yours a long time ago!"

Gray Wolf's eyes blazed. "The whites have poisoned you, Eagle Shadow. I am disappointed in you. For so long I wanted to believe in you. I used to have dreams of the day we'd meet."

"Blast your dreams! You've come a very long way for nothing."

"You have not been able to convince all of the people of your ways. These three braves agree with me and will fight with me against those who cross our land."

"That's because they are the only ones you could get. They are weak and will follow any wind that blows."

"You shame your people with your words." Gray Wolf stood and signaled to the others. "We will go."

Nate stood also and blocked the doorway. "I will not let you attack those soldiers."

Gray Wolf reacted calmly; he had planned for this. He motioned to the other three braves, and they immediately moved towards Nate.

Nate clenched a fist and thrust it at the first brave to reach him. It caught the brave in the stomach, but before he could throw another punch, the other two grabbed his arms and began forcing him downward. The first brave rose and returned the punch to Nate's unguarded stomach. He went down quickly but flipped himself over and kicked and struggled with all his might. Gray Wolf's muscular arms clamped down on his legs, and with the other three holding his arms and body, he knew he wasn't going anywhere.

Gray Wolf pulled lengths of rope from his belt, handed one to another brave and used one to tie Nate's ankles. The others used the other rope to tie Nate's hands behind his back.

"You had those already, you filthy son of a…" The ropes tightened, pulling his arms into an unnatural position and sending jabs of pain up through his shoulders. He grimaced and tried again to wrench free of their grips, to no avail. "Who do you know inside the fort?" he growled. They all ignored him. "Tell me! Is it anyone I know?"

Leaving him bound and helpless on the ground, they began filing out of the tepee. Just before he left, Gray Wolf pulled Nate's hunting knife out of its sheath and took it with him.

"Do I know them?" Nate shouted after them. "Tell me!"

They were gone. He kicked his restrained feet against the ground in anger and swore Gray Wolf would pay for this. Breathing hard from the fight, he laid his head on the blanket beneath him. No one would be paying for anything while he lay here filled with rage. He rolled onto his side, ignoring the pain it caused in his right arm, bent his knees, and fought to clear his mind, a nearly impossible task. Gray Wolf's cold, hardened expression and his repulsive words invaded his thoughts. How someone of such callousness, bereft of a conscience, could share one drop of blood with Nate was beyond his comprehension.

Nate took deep, slow breaths and relaxed his muscles. The pain lessened, and he could think better. It was so quiet with the camp mostly deserted. He could yell. There would be someone to come untie him, a few women, maybe some small children. They would have a good laugh for certain. He rolled his eyes. It was an affront; he was in no mood for laughing children.

His mind switched to the soldiers leaving Fort Mason on a slow, steady trek southward. Gray Wolf said there were women along. That meant Julie Blaine was with them. He'd known her for as long as he'd known Tara—innocent, good-hearted Julie. And her young son. If Gray Wolf was prepared to attack with a force only four strong, he'd make every move count. He'd be confident in the abilities of the other three braves, even in the face of highly vigilant soldiers. He'd know the lay of the land the soldiers would pass through and find a place to lie in wait, then he'd use every seasoned skill he possessed to inflict grave damage and do it with the utmost surprise. And he wouldn't lose one man. Julie and the others were riding directly into an ambush.

The thought horrified Nate. He couldn't let this happen to Julie. He looked around at the interior of the tepee. All the knives, arrows, and spears were gone, taken to the hunt. There was not one useful tool lying about to cut himself free. There were bowls, baskets, cooking utensils, some rawhide bags and clothing, blankets and furs, and the smoldering embers in the center, some flaring up into an occasional glow.

He didn't like the idea that came to him, but it was worth a try. He writhed and scooted himself closer to the firepit, then positioned his heels to face the coals. In one swift motion, he kicked his legs, sending hot coals tumbling across the ground away from the pit. One glowing piece of wood rolled to the left of the pit by itself. Feeling somewhat like a fish taken from its watery home, he flipped over and rolled and scooted his way over to the smoking wood. Then he turned himself around and positioned his wrists over it. Slowly he lowered his wrists, unsure of exactly where the ember was. A sudden, burning pang of heat stung his left wrist, and he yanked it away. He held his bound wrists up while reconsidering this tactic.

The inside of the tepee was turning smoky. He twisted his head around and was startled to see a tiny flame emanating from a stray ember and licking the bottom of one of the lodgepoles. He leaned backward and tried to blow on it, but he was too far away. The flame was already reaching the buffalo hide covering. Seized with new urgency, Nate turned back around, moved his wrists slightly to the left, and lowered them again. He tilted his hands up as far as he could, exposing mostly the rope to the hot coal. He gritted his teeth and steeled himself against the sharp, searing pains as he held the rope against the ember. He raised his wrists for momentary relief and pulled against the rope. After a few more times of raising and lowering his wrists, he felt the rope start to give way. His groans of pain turned to a guttural cry of relief when he felt the last strand of rope snap, and he at last brought his arms around in front of him.

All one side of the tepee was on fire now, and the crackling flames were eating their way towards the smoke hole at the top. A loud crack warned of the imminent collapse of the first lodgepole. Nate's eyes began to sting, and he coughed from the smoke, but his hands flew as he untied the rope around his ankles, then, rolling onto his stomach and keeping his face to the ground, he slithered to the doorway and out into some fresh air. He took a deep, gasping breath and continued farther along the ground. He stopped abruptly. There, under his nose, lay his hunting knife where Gray Wolf had discarded it as he left the tepee. Nate let out a moan of frustration. He could've rolled out of the tepee and used his own knife to free himself.

He sheathed the knife, scrambled to his feet, and ran as the lodgepole collapsed inward. The other poles followed in succession, dragging down the covering into a mangled, blazing heap. Dark smoke curled skyward, and large ashes floated on the breeze. Nate was briefly aware of some Indian women and children gathering to watch the burning tepee, pacing helplessly, hands over mouths. He bridled the Appaloosa and put the reins in his teeth, then he gripped the horn of the saddle in one hand and his rifle with the other and ran to escape the intense heat, the Appaloosa following at a trot. Close to the river, he dropped the reins, set down his belongings, and half stumbled his way to the bank where he fell to his knees and plunged his reddened, swollen wrists into the water. Relief was instantaneous, but so was his cognizance of the time lost. He returned to his horse and hefted the saddle to its back. With the straps buckled and his rifle in its sheath on the side of the saddle, he mounted and kicked into a gallop northeastward.

He gave a cursory glance back at the burning tepee, a total loss. He was glad he wouldn't be there when the chief returned from the hunt and first laid eyes on the damage, but there would be hell to pay when they met up again. He hoped by that time Red Feather would have gotten over it. *Small chance*, he thought. At least those infernal markings on the tepee wouldn't annoy him anymore, for now.

Ignoring the pain in his wrists, he contemplated his options as he rode. Gray Wolf had gotten a good head start on him, plus the brave would likely be expecting Nate to be freed and follow after him at some point, so he'd be moving fast. Then Nate wondered what he'd do when he caught up to them. There were four of them. They could just as easily overpower him again. It'd be better to skirt around the Indians, ride ahead, and warn the soldiers, he decided.

"It's all up to us," he told the Appaloosa. "Well, up to you, I should say. You're the one doing the running."

The Appaloosa, used to doing fast runs lately, handily kept up the pace Nate asked of him. As they loosely followed the Missouri River, it was easy to trace the route Gray Wolf's group had taken. The same path had been used by buffalo and other animals and by Indians hunting them. Nate slowed down often to let the horse rest and drink water. He was certain they were gaining on the Indians.

It was well after midday when he first spotted the braves watering their horses and collecting water for themselves in bags about a quarter mile ahead. Nate guessed that this would be where they would leave the river and head north to intercept the contingent. He looked out at the river. It was a good fording place—smooth banks for rolling wagons, calm water. This would be where the soldiers and their supply wagons would cross.

Nate tugged at the reins and pointed the horse north. As he rode, he took note of every speck of landscape—stands of cottonwoods, rolling hills, bluffs from which one could see for miles, numerous places conducive to an ambush.

He had come a few miles from the river when he topped a bluff and used it as a vantage point. His eyes scanned the countryside near and far and immediately picked up the object foreign to this natural landscape, a dark line of horses and wagons moving out of the northwest. As he watched them draw closer, they took on individual shapes. This was the prey that Gray Wolf hunted, four wagons and possibly up to a dozen riders. Gray Wolf was outnumbered, but he could still wreak unholy havoc given the right location from which to spring an attack. Nate searched for that spot and found it roughly a half mile ahead of the contingent, a place where the trail they followed temporarily disappeared from his view behind a tree-covered rise. He needed to make it to that spot ahead of the contingent and Gray Wolf, and it was a long shot. He studied the valley before him, making a mental map of all the physical features, planning his route to get him there fast and without being seen.

He estimated he had no more than fifteen minutes. He guided the Appaloosa down from the bluff and into the course he'd mapped out, then kicked into a gallop. He slowed periodically to look and listen for signs of Gray Wolf's group. There never were any, and that heightened Nate's dread. He knew Gray Wolf and his warriors were out there, somewhere. They were keeping well-hidden and quiet, but Nate could feel the air crackling with the growing threat. It was a race against time, and against a warrior who knew the land and the ways of his prey and was as determined to strike with deadly terror as Nate was to stop him.

Soon he heard the creak and rattle of the wagons. The distance was closing quickly. He saw his destination just ahead and rushed headlong for it. Breathless with anticipation, he left the Appaloosa tied to some brush tall enough to hide the horse. "I'll take it from here. Wish me luck."

With rifle in hand, he darted noiselessly up the rise amongst the trees. Still no sign of Gray Wolf, but they surely must be there now, just on the other side of the rise from him, poised, ready and waiting. He was certain of it. He must act quickly.

But in his rush to get here, he hadn't thought about how to handle this. Soldiers weren't about to listen to him, not about anything. And that was exactly what Gray Wolf had said. Nate was struck with the irony.

The line of wagons and riders was approaching his position now, close enough that he could see the soldiers' eyes as they scanned the surroundings watching for anything unusual. He slipped behind a tree, holding the rifle upright. The sound of the iron-rimmed wheels grinding on axles, the clink of the trace chains, and the accompanying chorus of stepping hooves grew closer. The advance riders were beneath him now. He recognized one as Major Blaine. He thought fast.

"Julie Blaine!" he shouted above the din. "Get out of there now! You're riding into an ambush!"

The whole procession jerked to a confused stop, everyone looking around them, rifle levers cranking one after another. Through a gap in some branches, he saw Julie appear in the opening of the canvas of the second wagon. He stepped into her view. In the split second that their eyes met, he knew she'd heard his warning and believed him. She disappeared inside the wagon and emerged almost immediately from the back with her son under one arm. She jumped to the ground and half dragged and half pushed the boy towards the slope that led to Nate's position.

A rifle blast sounded, and the bullet ricocheted off of a tree a few feet away from Nate. He jumped back behind his tree as Julie screamed. Through the branches, he saw two soldiers grabbing ahold of her arms and stopping her and Mark's ascent. More gunshots rang out, and bullets grazed tree trunks and the ground around Nate. He was appalled. They thought he was the major threat, and this wasn't helping Julie at all.

"Listen to me! There's an ambush just ahead!"

His last words were drowned out, for the number of gunshots suddenly doubled. The air was split with deafening cracks in rapid succession, more than what he expected from cavalry. But he soon realized that no more shots were being aimed at him. The action had been shifted to the east of his position. Gray Wolf had attacked, probably earlier than he wanted to, before Nate's warning could be heeded.

Nate watched, horrified, as the soldiers beneath him took a beating in front of him. One slammed against a wagon canvas, shot through the head, then he slid slowly downward, leaving a deep red stain on the canvas. Another took an arrow to the chest and hit the ground dead. Amidst the gunfire and blood-curdling Indian war whoops, Nate felt frustrated and helpless. There was a hill between him and the attackers, a barrier he couldn't cross without leaving Julie behind. He couldn't see Major Blaine anymore and guessed he must be fighting up ahead, out of Nate's sight. Julie still struggled to get away from the soldiers intent on protecting her.

"Let her come up here!" he called down. "She'll be safe here!"

Instead they began to shove her and Mark behind the nearest wagon for cover. They were almost there when the soldier on her right whipped around, his knee and shoulder torn by bullets. He crumpled to the ground. Immediately the one on her left fell wounded as well, clutching his abdomen. Nate chambered a round and nimbly stepped and slid down the steep, rocky incline towards her. The attacker came into his view now from the right below him. The brave snatched Julie from behind and drew his knife. *"Eneoestse!"* Nate shouted, his rifle sights trained on the brave's head. The Indian stopped on his command, and Julie enveloped her pale, terrified son in both arms, shaking and crying.

Gray Wolf emerged from the trees. "Take them captive," he commanded. He looked up at Nate, as if awaiting his permission. In the midst of the chaos he created, his expression seemed calm. He understood this was someone Nate would kill for, and he was allowing Nate a say in the matter.

"All right, take them," said Nate. "But *do not* touch one hair of their heads. They will be in my charge."

Gray Wolf gave a subtle nod, and they were off with Julie and Mark in tow.

"Don't be afraid, Julie," Nate called after them. "You and Mark will be fine."

They were already out of his sight around the bend. Nate turned and climbed the hill and ran back down the other side to his horse. The gunfire lessened as he did so, and he heard the Indians' horses galloping away. He rode around the hill to where the attack had begun and looked down on the trail. Soldiers were busy tending the wounded and calming fidgety horses. A young and skittish private looked around nervously, his finger firm on his rifle trigger. Nate eased the Appaloosa backward out of his view.

Nate looked at every soldier in sight, at least twice. Major Blaine wasn't there. He heard more gunshots in the distance, in the direction the Indians had taken. The major had chased after the Indians, he figured, to retrieve his wife and son. He dug his heels into his horse's sides and started after them at a run.

There were no more gunshots. The air grew quiet. Nate had put a good distance between himself and the site of the attack, and the Indians were now far ahead of him. Major Blaine must be ahead of him too. He wondered what he'd do when he found the man. The major would be agitated over his family, and Nate was likely the last person he'd want to see. Nate pressed forward. He'd figure it all out as he went, he decided.

Another half mile and he saw a riderless, blaze-faced bay horse trot up from a ravine, stirrups swinging at its sides. He turned the Appaloosa and leaned back as the horse descended the steep sides of the ravine. He picked his way through brush and rocks, a taut dread rushing through him. Suddenly there in his path lay Major Blaine on his side, silent and still, a smooth strip of dirt behind him where he'd slid down from the lip of the ravine. Nate looked on for a breathless moment, then dismounted and stood over him. The blue flannel of the major's uniform was darkened and soaked with blood from two bullet holes, in his shoulder and right of his abdomen.

Nate shook his head. "Oh, how dare you get yourself killed." He thought he saw the major's chest rise and fall, ever the slightest bit. Quickly he knelt and pressed two fingers against Blaine's neck. He was still alive. Filled with new hope now, Nate stood and tried to collect his thoughts. He remounted and went after the major's horse, got hold of the reins, and led him back down into the ravine. He glanced back in the direction from which he'd come. There would surely be soldiers coming along soon, looking for their missing officer. He must hurry. There was no time to lose.

Chapter 20

What Tara proudly proclaimed as the finest herd of horses ever assembled on the Broken Bow had reached the banks of the Sun River after a day and a half of skirting the Lewis and Clark range. Tara drove the chuckwagon while Jack rode on her lap or in a basket inside the wagon. Buck sat beside her and eagerly jumped at the turns she gave him to try his hand on the reins. The whole trip was an adventure to him. He was filled with boundless energy all day and slept soundly at night. Tara felt the bouncing motion of the wagon every night in her sleep, but it was worth it to her to meet up with Nate again. She often found herself pushing against the floorboards with her feet, as if to make the wagon go faster.

"We'll cross in the morning," Elijah announced, "maybe make the Dearborn the next day."

Buck climbed down to the ground using the wheel of the wagon and ran to find his own horse to ride bareback while Tara prepared to cook supper for Buck and the men. Elijah was the first to notice the approaching soldiers, two of them on horseback. He ran after Buck and hurried to lift him into the wagon before they arrived.

"Get inside the wagon, Mrs. Hunter."

Her chin jerked high, and she stared right through him. He instantly realized his mistake. "Uh, please, ma'am? If you would?"

She hesitated, as if still unsure if she should trust him around soldiers, and he prayed for her to move faster. Finally, she gathered up her skirt and climbed back inside, and he spoke to her through the canvas. "Please keep the boys quiet and don't be seen, ma'am. I'll handle this."

The soldiers slowed their horses as they rode into camp, carefully taking note of the horses, wagon, and the three men of the outfit. "Which one o' you's the boss?" asked the one with a mustache and beard and brown curls flipping out from beneath his hat.

Elijah stepped forward. "I am. Is there a problem, gentlemen?"

"That all depends. We're on the lookout for a renegade, and we're supposed to report any suspicious Indian activity. You seen any Indians hereabouts?"

"Nope. Not a one."

The other soldier, who had a scarred lip and missing front tooth, squinted at Elijah. "I recognize you. You work for the Broken Bow."

"Not anymore I don't," Elijah replied smoothly. "I'm with the Split Timber now. Take my advice, gentlemen. Never, *ever* work for a woman."

The soldiers looked at each other and burst into laughter. "Found out the hard way, did ya?" It was the long-haired one, and he seemed to loosen up more now.

"Where you headed with these ponies?"

"Down Wyoming way. There's a little startup operation that wants to buy them...Butterfly Ranch."

"Butterfly Ranch," echoed the scarred one, wrinkling his nose. "Sounds like it belongs to another woman."

"Well, I'm not gonna work for her if it is. I'm just droppin' off these horses and gettin' outta there fast as I can."

The soldiers chuckled again. "You'd best hang on tight to your scalps. You may run into some hostiles in these parts."

"We're packing enough iron, but thanks for the advice. We'll be on the lookout."

The soldiers bid a hasty farewell and galloped away, and Elijah and the Wilsons breathed a collective sigh of relief.

Tara emerged from the wagon and raised her eyebrows at Elijah. "Butterfly Ranch?"

He motioned for her to follow him and walked her over to the herd. He pointed to the hip of the closest horse whose brand caught her eye. "I branded them all again just before we left."

The original brand was plainly visible, a B shielded on the left by a broken half circle, but immediately to the left of it was a fresh brand on which Elijah had simply turned the branding iron upside down. The result clearly formed a butterfly figure.

Tara's jaw dropped open, then gradually, she broke into a smile that became a laugh. "You'd better be glad those men didn't know anything about brands, Mr. Medley."

"Well, that's what I was countin' on, ma'am. Lucky for us."

"Mr. Hunter will definitely hear about this. And I'm sure he won't object to the raise I'm giving you."

His smile remained long after she'd returned to the cooking. Actually he didn't mind so much working for a woman.

Chapter 21

Nate guided the sure-footed Appaloosa over rough terrain to the remote, well-hidden rock overhang he'd chosen as a stopping place. It was in view of the Missouri and would do for a temporary shelter. He led the bay horse by the reins with Major Blaine slumped over the saddle. His occasional moans had subsided, and Nate desperately hoped and prayed he could keep the man alive.

He dismounted and pulled Blaine off of the horse, breaking his fall as best he could, but the major grimaced in pain.

Major Blaine rolled onto his side and struggled for a breath. "Are you trying to kill me?"

"No. Somebody else already tried to do that."

Nate gathered up dried grass for tinder, and larger kindling that he stacked nearby. He unsheathed his hunting knife and drew a quartz stone from his pocket. Holding them over the tinder, he struck the quartz against the back side of the knife till he created a spark. Quickly he nursed and tended the tiny flame and added kindling, a little at a time. Soon he had a fire he figured would burn for a while without help.

"Where's my family?" rasped the major, his eyes closed. "Have you seen them?"

"They're just fine." Nate set his canteen next to Blaine. "I'll be back very soon. You hang on till I get here. Your wife and son will be worried about you. Just keep thinking about them, okay?"

Blaine opened his eyes and looked at Nate like he intended to rip out his jugular. Nate was encouraged; if Blaine was angry, he'd fight harder for his life.

He tied the bay in the bushes some distance away, just on the outside chance that the major got up enough strength to attempt an escape, then he mounted the Appaloosa and began retracing his trail back to the other soldiers.

As he neared the ravine where he'd found Blaine, he could hear brush rustling and a solitary horse's hooves. He dismounted, dropped to the ground, and used his elbows to pull himself to the edge of the gully. A soldier on horseback appeared almost beneath him. The man, bearing the gold chevrons of a sergeant's insignia, studied the ground for signs. He passed Nate's position, and Nate scooted along the ground to stay even with him. When he turned his horse to climb out of the gully, Nate crouched behind a bush and kept watch through the sparse leaves. As the horse passed right by him, Nate sprang into the air, clamped his arms around the soldier's waist, and pulled him from his mount. They landed in a heap as the horse whinnied and sidestepped away from them. The startled soldier struggled to rise, but Nate regained his footing first, pulled his Colt revolver, and held it to the man's temple.

"I don't intend to hurt you," said Nate. "I just need something from you."

The soldier grabbed hold of Nate's arm that was locked around his neck. "I… can't…breathe," he gasped.

Nate loosened his hold slightly. "You got medical supplies in those wagons?"

The soldier managed a nod.

"You listen to me, Sergeant, and don't ask questions. I need you to get some things for me. I need needles, suture, bandages, some laudanum, and a couple bottles of whiskey…and some food. Will you do it for me?"

"That depends. Who's hurt?"

"I said no questions."

"Is it an Indian?"

"No." Nate rather admired the sergeant's nerve. He released him and kept the gun pointed at the man's chest as they faced each other. "What's your name, Sergeant?"

"Sergeant Travis Van Deen." He rubbed his neck and took a couple deep breaths. He seemed to recover quickly and looked Nate up and down.

Nate studied the high-cheek-boned face of this brown-eyed, dark-haired sergeant who appeared to be close to his own age, and suddenly felt uneasy that the man was studying him as well.

"Do you know who I am?" asked Nate, careful to hide any discomfort.

"Yes."

"If you'll get me the things I need and not turn me in, then whenever you get a chance to get over to the Broken Bow, I'll pay you more money than the reward."

"I don't know if I can trust you. The three hundred dollar reward, that's a sure thing."

"Yeah, it'll buy you a nicer coffin."

Sergeant Van Deen seemed unaware and unconcerned about the gun barrel still less than a foot from his chest. "And if I do turn you in?"

"If you turn me in, know this. I know where Major Blaine is. Nobody else does, and I'm not telling. He's badly in need of medical help. If he doesn't get it, he's a dead man. You understand?"

Van Deen's expression changed at the mention of the man he'd just been looking for. "Yeah, I'll do it."

"Get going. I'll wait right here."

Sergeant Van Deen galloped away, and Nate waited by his horse, gun in hand but confident in the sergeant's reliability. Van Deen did indeed return, unusually quickly, bearing a bulging cloth sack in his hand. He vaulted from his horse and handed the sack over to Nate.

Nate checked the contents and began tying it to his saddle.

"Is Major Blaine gonna be okay?" asked the worried sergeant.

"I don't know. Don't try to follow me."

"Hey, you can't tell me what to do, mister."

"*Don't* follow me." Nate suddenly felt the need to ease Van Deen's concern. "I'll do the best I can for Blaine. You have my word."

"All right," answered the sergeant with a nod.

Nate never expected him to comply so easily. *For once, an agreeable attitude from someone in the cavalry,* he thought. "You the next in command of this outfit?"

"Yeah."

"Tell the others Blaine's going after his family and wants the rest of you to return to the fort."

"The major wouldn't do it like that."

Nate gathered his reins and mounted. "Then you think of something better."

"What about the major's family? Everybody's in a panic."

"No need to be. They're safe."

"You really gonna pay me more than three hundred dollars?"

"Yes."

Van Deen was amazed at such a generous offer. "Why?"

"It's worth it to me." He left with no further explanation.

A short time later, Nate rode into the camp under the rock to find Major Blaine, pale and sweaty, rocking back and forth in pain. He administered a couple of drops of laudanum to him at once.

"Please get me back to my outfit," begged Blaine. "They can help me."

Nate made no reply; he was too preoccupied with the dreaded task at hand. He took one of the bottles of whiskey and held it out to Blaine. "Here, drink this."

The major was only too eager for some hope of relief to notice anything else that Nate was doing. Nate sat cross-legged, knife in hand, and went to work on the cloth bag that had held the supplies. He cut it at the top and began unraveling it around and around into one long strip. Then, concealing most of it in his hand, he knelt near the major's head and attempted to distract him. "So, you were headed south, right?"

"None of your blame business."

"Were you movin' for good or just temporary?"

"I told you—"

Quick as a flash, Nate thrust his arm out, grabbed the major's hands, and pulled them up over his head. Amidst Blaine's loud objections, he wound some of the cloth strip several times around his wrists, looped it through to hold it, then tied it to a nearby exposed root. He cut off the unused strip, tied Blaine's feet next, and anchored them to a jagged piece of rock in the overhang. *Just like tying down a steer,* he mused.

Major Blaine continued to object with every ounce of strength he could muster.

"Nate, no, don't do this. You don't know how. You're gonna kill me."

Nate was ripping open his jacket and shirt.

"Please, listen to me, don't do this."

Nate struggled to shut out Blaine's pleas and focus wholly on what he needed to do. There was a hole in the bloody, soaked shirt over the abdomen. There was cloth inside the wound which would have to come out. He'd seen his father do this before, but it was a very long time ago. He tried to remember how it looked. His heart raced, and beads of sweat formed over his upper lip. There was no time for faintheartedness now. He grabbed the whiskey bottle and took a long swig.

Steeling his nerves, he passed his knife through the flames of the campfire on his right while pouring whiskey over the wound on his left. The major yelled when the sting hit him, and Nate looked around nervously, hoping Van Deen and his bunch had not tried to follow him.

When the knife was hot, he picked up a small, dead branch from the kindling pile and broke off a piece of it. This he shoved crossways into Blaine's mouth. Blaine hollered and bit down when the knife touched him, his face contorted in pain, but Nate kept a steady hand on the handle with his right hand while reaching into the wound with the thumb and index finger of his left hand. The major had passed out by the time he drew out the first bullet and the tiny piece of cloth with it. He held the cloth over the hole in the shirt he'd ripped away; the piece was complete. He went to work on the shoulder wound next and extracted that bullet more easily. Next he fumbled with the needle and suture till he had closed the wounds, shaking his head all the while at his unskilled efforts.

When he was finished, he sat back, holding his bloody hands away from his body, and tried to calm his nerves. He fervently hoped there were no injuries to Blaine's internal organs. He had no idea what to do if there were.

The major started coming around as Nate poured water over his hands and wiped them down with a cloth. Encouraged, Nate moved closer. "I did the best I could," he said, "but you're gonna have bad scars, I'm afraid."

"So are you when I get done with you," growled Major Blaine.

Nate raised his eyebrows. "Well, I'm glad you're planning to recover so you can do that." He handed the whiskey to the major.

Later as Nate sat idly poking at the fire with a stick in the growing darkness, he watched Major Blaine doze off into a fitful sleep. He guessed that he wouldn't sleep much better himself. He thought about Julie and her son facing the coming night in an Indian camp, waiting, expecting someone to come for them. He felt cruel to have allowed her capture, but he'd been away from her for so long that he strangely felt the need to talk with her and see where she stood in all this. In the moment he'd surrendered her to Gray Wolf, the hope had risen within him that if he got her away from soldiers, maybe there was some information she could give him, something she could do to help his situation, anything. She used to be a reasonable person. Maybe, just maybe, she would take his side, that is, if she forgave him for letting her be captured.

He had no worries for her safety. Gray Wolf's plan to ambush the soldiers had come as no surprise at all to him. But just as he understood the hate and violence he could expect from Gray Wolf, he also understood the brave's vision of the rules of war. Gray Wolf was honor-bound by the nod he'd given to him, and Nate could count on it as sure as the sun would rise. This seeming contradiction in Gray Wolf's character made complete sense to Nate. The complexities of the brave's mind were not something Nate particularly wanted to understand, but there were times when it was definitely helpful.

***

At the first light of day, Major Blaine opened his eyes to find Nate already awake and watching him. As he fought through the cobwebs of his mind, feverish and hazy with laudanum, he issued a moan of desperation. "Julie! Where's Julie?"

"She's fine," Nate assured him. "She's not here now, but she and Mark are fine. You don't need to worry."

More fully awake now, and remembering more clearly the night before, the major painfully pulled himself to a sitting position and leaned against the rock wall. He struggled to catch his breath from the effort.

"Here, you need to eat something," said Nate, tossing him a hardtack he'd found in the sack from Van Deen and passing a canteen of water to him. He watched Blaine bite into the hardtack. "I've eaten better than that in a starving Indian camp, but you're probably used to it." The major slowly rejuvenated as he ate and drank, and Nate prepared himself for more important matters. He finally had the elusive Major Blaine where he wanted him.

Blaine looked over at his horse. "I've gotta get back to my outfit."

"Not so fast."

"What, am I your prisoner?"

"What do you think?"

Major Blaine stared hard at him, his first real good look in ages at the man who caused a decorated lieutenant-colonel so much grief. "I think you're not the Nate I used to know."

"I believe I have you to thank for that." Nate narrowed his eyes. "I never figured you to be a loyal friend. I doubt you know the meaning of the word. With you it's always duty, isn't it? Always doing your job, never asking questions, afraid you might find out somethin' that doesn't fit with your rules."

"Nate, I swear I didn't know you'd be charged with a hangin' offense. That wasn't at all how it started out."

"Oh? Got a little out of your control, did it? I bet that needled at ya."

"I don't have to listen to this." Major Blaine attempted to rise but fell back against the rock from the exertion.

"Oh, but you do. Believe me, it wasn't out of the goodness of my heart that I cut two bullets out of you yesterday. We're gonna talk. What's gotten into McHenry anyway?"

Blaine rubbed his eyes and took a couple deep breaths that appeared to hurt. "That Indian land that the ranchers been moving onto, his son was one of them. He was killed by Indians. They smoked him right out of his cabin, 'bout a year and a half ago. He was found with *seven* arrows in him. Turns out that's why Ol' Gun—that's what we call him—asked to be posted to Fort Mason."

"For revenge," said Nate. "That explains a lot. Who's been feeding lies about me to him?"

"You remember Beartooth?"

Every muscle in Nate's body stiffened at the sound of the name. He blankly stared at the major, not sure if he'd heard him right, but knowing he had. Beartooth—the first Cheyenne Nate had ever seen besides his father. The epitome of treachery, the brave had turned on him even as he tried to bring peace to their people. He still carried the scar on his abdomen, a daily reminder. Beartooth had been Red Feather's friend, but the chief, recognizing the threat to their people, had banished him without mercy. Beartooth held Nate fully responsible. For at least a couple years following, Nate had watched his back, till finally, he figured the brave was either long gone or dead. Now with one brief sentence from Blaine, he'd discovered that Beartooth was neither. He answered in a whisper. "Yeah, I remember him."

"He's been working secretly for the cavalry as a scout."

Silence followed while Nate let it sink in. "How on earth did that happen?"

"He came and started talking to Ol' Gun a while back. Gained his trust by bringing him Cheyenne scalps he said he'd taken. Believe me, Nate, I didn't know about any of this till just a couple weeks ago when Ol' Gun and I sat down to have a drink. I would've warned him if I knew, you know I would've. Only he and a couple others Beartooth worked with knew he was a scout. Ol' Gun purposely kept it that way."

"Couple others he worked with? The ones that were found dead? The ones I've been accused of killing?"

Now it was Blaine's turn to be in shock. "Oh, no. Beartooth turned on 'em, didn't he?"

"More than likely, knowing I'd be blamed."

Major Blaine reached for the nearby bottle of whiskey. Nate grabbed it first and moved it out of his reach.

"If you want whiskey for breakfast, you have to answer some questions first." He had so many questions he hardly knew where to begin. But he decided to just keep to a few important ones. "When did Beartooth first come to McHenry?"

"What does it matter?"

"I need to know."

"Last summer, probably about the time you first went down to the Sun River."

"And he identified warriors in Red Feather's band as attacking those medicine wagons?"

Major Blaine cast his eyes downward. "He named Red Feather himself as the leader."

Things began to fall into place for Nate now. The mysterious follower in cavalry boots who had trailed him and Tara to Red Feather's encampment now had a discernible face. Moreover, this renegade Indian whom Nate remembered as a top-notch tracker had been stalking him ever since. He remembered Lena's words, *They had good information this time*. He had punched Elijah, unaware of the more real, invisible threat that had lurked close by all the time. And that wasn't all.

"You and I were both blinded, Nate," Blaine was saying.

"Well, I'm not so blind I can't see the facts. Those medicine wagons weren't attacked by Red Feather's band, and it wasn't retaliation for the treaty being broken. That attack was the work of only one man, Beartooth. He's probably waited four years for a chance to get revenge on the Indians. When the treaty was broken, he saw his chance. He used arrows and not guns during that attack, knowing the Indians would be blamed."

Major Blaine was turning a deathly pale, and it had nothing to do with his recent injuries. He couldn't breathe. He couldn't speak. He just stared glassy-eyed, and Nate knew why.

"That's right. You attacked a peaceful camp on the Sun River that day. There were women and two children killed in that attack."

"I didn't know." Blaine held his aching head in his hands and spoke in a horrified whisper. "I swear I didn't know. How could I have done such a thing?"

Nate kept silent a long time, feeling the sadness of the Sun River tragedy all over again, and allowing Blaine to wallow in the guilt.

Finally Blaine looked up, eyeing Nate suspiciously. "What were you doing mixed up with those Indians who ambushed my men yesterday? And how is it that you showed up only *seconds* before the ambush?"

"The Indians tied me up, hands and feet, so I wouldn't warn you."

The major shook his head skeptically. "You're lying."

Nate swung his arm around and slapped Blaine's cheek with the back of his hand, stunning the major speechless. Then he pushed up the sleeves of his shirt to reveal the burn scars on his wrists. "You call me a liar and you better have something to back it up with besides your arrogance."

Major Blaine rubbed his cheek but kept his peace. He couldn't argue with the fresh scars he'd just seen.

"The fact is," said Nate, "your colonel should've investigated before sending you on that rout last summer."

"Damn it, Nate! Didn't I beg *you* to help me investigate? Didn't you stand right there in my office and refuse to track the attacker?"

"An attacker who now works for McHenry! He's a lieutenant-colonel. He's fought in a war. He commands a fort. He knows better! He gave an order based on nothin', and you all followed it like sheep. He let his personal feelings get in the way, and I know firsthand that's a dangerous mistake. Your colonel failed you. And he failed the Indians. Don't you see that?"

Blaine calmed down. "I think he was starting to suspect Beartooth wasn't being straight with him. After he talked to me and I filled him in on what Beartooth was like, he wants to bring him in, when he can be found."

Nate stood and paced in front of the fire. "Well, that'll be the hard part, won't it?"

"I know you think so little of me," sighed Blaine.

"I won't argue with that."

"I can't say as I blame you at this point. So why are you even helping me?"

Nate moved closer, squatted in front of the major, and fixed a piercing gaze on him. "Your wife and son are being held by the Cheyenne as we speak. You're looking at the only person who can get them released peaceably. And I'm damn well not gonna do that unless you help me clear my name."

"You son of a bitch, how can you treat them like pawns? For the love of all that is decent, Nate, you have a family yourself."

"Yes! And I want to be with them again."

"And so you let the Indians take my family."

"They were about to be killed. I *gave* them to the Indians with an agreement that their lives be spared. Now let's see if you can come through for her."

"Why, you sorry—"

"Your men did a lousy job protecting her. Oh, they tried all right. But it's lucky I was there."

"And I expect you want me to thank you."

"I don't give a damn what you expect. I need you to clear my name, and you need me to get your family back. Are you ready to deal or not?"

Major Blaine rubbed his forehead in frustration. "Nate, nothing can change the fact that you fired on members of the Seventh Cavalry." He suddenly remembered something. "And you jammed that Gatling gun, didn't you?"

"You bet I jammed it. Counting coup, that's what the Indians call it."

"You ruined a very expensive, brand-new gun."

"You shouldn't spend so much money on such cheap equipment. Now listen. You tell that no-account lieutenant-colonel that I am Cheyenne. You tell him that my people were under attack, and I fought in their defense and in the defense of my family. That's not treason. And furthermore, you tell him that the fact that I fired on soldiers, then turned around and saved the life of his major ought to prove it."

"I swear if anything happens to Julie and Mark, I'll kill you."

"Nothing will happen to them."

Blaine thought for a long while. "Can you *guarantee* their safety?"

"Absolutely. I knew Julie long before you did. She never meant any harm to anybody."

"All right then, I'll do it. Are you coming with me?"

"No, uh-uh, you bring your people to me, under a white flag of truce. I'll be at the Dearborn where it meets the Missouri. Arrange for a meeting there and guarantee me immunity. I'll go there today and make sure Julie stays safe."

"I'll see what I can do."

Nate returned to the fire, picked up a hardtack, and took a big bite. "You know, I was just thinking, I would've liked to have cut bullets out of a lieutenant-colonel, but a major will do fine. You're a high-ranking officer at that excuse for a fort. You can do a lot more than you're lettin' on."

"I said I'll see what I can do. There's such things as protocol."

"Oh, yeah, that's right, protocol." He swallowed and wiped his mouth with the back of his hand. "That may be fine for you, but not everyone is playing by your rules."

He picked up the whiskey bottle and handed it to Blaine, then started gathering up his things.

The major watched him in surprise. "You're leaving me here?"

"You'll be fine. You got food and water. When you're able to ride, go back to the fort. I think Sergeant Van Deen is already headed there."

Major Blaine raised his eyebrows. "How do you know him?"

"We exchanged a few pleasantries." He tightened the girth on the Appaloosa's saddle and strapped it into place. "He's a good man. I like him."

"You would," replied Major Blaine, rolling his eyes. "He's just like you. He's not opposed to bending a rule here and there."

Nate mounted up. "Oh, no, no, Major, mm-mm. '*Breaking* the rules' is the term you mean. We're not opposed to breaking the rules." He kicked his heels into the horse's sides. "See you at the Dearborn."

Chapter 22

Nate entered Shining Sky's tepee to find her and Julie sitting across from each other, Julie holding her son tightly against her.

Julie's eyes grew big when she saw him, and she clapped a hand to her mouth, struggling to hold her emotion in check. "Nate, we've been waiting for you. Can you get us out of here?"

Nate looked over at Shining Sky. She understood she was expected to leave them in private, and she seemed immensely relieved to do so.

"No one here speaks any English," Julie continued. "Please, Nate. You've got to get us out of here. I'm not staying here another night." Her voice started to break. "Where is my husband? Why isn't he here?"

He sat across from her. "I left him in a camp a little ways from where the ambush was. He took two bullets yesterday. He'll recover."

She gasped and buried her face in Mark's hair. "How can you be sure?" she cried.

"He threatened to kill me. That's probably a good sign."

She looked up at him, tears streaming. "Is someone helping him?"

"I helped him. I got the bullets out. And he's not a very grateful sort."

Offended, she sat up a little straighter. Mark looked up at her. His small, gray eyes were full of tears also. She hugged him close and pleaded in a whisper. "I must go to him. Can you get us out of here?"

"Julie." There was so much he wanted to say, but he hardly knew how. And she was in no frame of mind to talk about anything. "You and Mark are not captives. I told him that you were, so he would help me clear my name."

She glared at him with the fury of a wildcat. "What are you trying to do?"

"Whatever I can to get both of us out of here. The major is going to talk to Colonel McHenry, and then he will be coming back here. I'm asking you to stay here until then."

"Stay here? Are you mad? These people tried to kill us yesterday! You get me a horse right now!" She stood, took Mark by the hand, and exited the tepee with Nate following closely behind.

"Don't try to go back by yourself, Julie."

She stopped and faced him. "You said that we were not captive. Is that right?"

"Yes, but I promised your husband you'd be safe. I'm responsible for you, and I'm staying here until they come. With you here, I know for sure that they will come and negotiate with me. Please, it's just for a few days. You and Mark will be completely safe here, I promise."

"Only because it serves your purpose."

"No…no. I would never let anything happen to you, Julie, even if Blaine failed. You and Tara have been friends your whole lives. I'm asking you to do this for her, and me. I just wanna go home to Tara, that's all."

She softened at the mention of Tara's name. After looking thoughtfully at her surroundings and down at Mark, she replied, "I would like to help. But if it appears that I'm being held here against my will, you'll have to answer for that. If they know I stay voluntarily, amongst the enemy, well, my husband is an officer, Nate. How will that look?"

"Neither way is good, I know. I'll abide by whatever you decide. This tepee belongs to Shining Sky. She is very nice. You will get along well with her." Something behind him distracted her, and her face paled. He followed her alarmed gaze and saw Gray Wolf.

"He was there yesterday," she breathed.

Nate forgot all about Julie. He headed straight for Gray Wolf, and the brave took a determined stance, expecting a face-off.

"Beartooth?" Nate narrowed his eyes and shook his head. "Beartooth was who you talked to in the fort?"

"I said that it was someone loyal."

"Don't give me that, you scum! You knew what he did! You *knew* he tried to kill me!"

"And I am glad he did not succeed. I know that he disagreed with Red Feather those five winters ago. He believed the treaty would not work. And you can see now, he was right. And he was right when he told me about the soldiers coming this way from the fort."

"Did he tell you he attacked the medicine wagons? And then laid the blame on Red Feather? Or that he's been following me and telling the cavalry all the lies about me? Everything he has done has been to hurt our people and see me hang." He thought he saw a flicker of surprise in Gray Wolf's eyes, but it did not last.

"I have known him longer than you. I do not believe he would hurt our people."

"No, and you don't believe my father was happy living where he was. You don't believe that I would never join your side against the whites. You don't believe anything you don't want to."

"I did what I did to the soldiers for you and—"

"You thought you were doing me a favor?" His voice rose, and a sparse crowd gathered to watch, from a distance. "Beartooth was banished because he shot me and left me for dead. Why didn't you fight *him* when you had the chance?"

"Because I chose those who have caused the *most* harm to our people. Those soldiers were going to demand the surrender of Cheyenne braves. I stopped them."

"And have now threatened any chance for peace because of it." He pointed towards the people standing nearby, among whom was Shining Sky and her son. "You have now endangered the lives of these people and their chiefs. There are soldiers coming here to negotiate with me, and now I will have to convince them that these people are innocent and the attackers acted alone."

Gray Wolf sharpened his glare. "You're bringing soldiers here?"

"Yes, and you won't be tying me up inside a tepee this time."

"I see now that it will take more than tying you to silence you."

Nate pointed a finger in his face. "Don't you threaten me. If you knew how many times I've had to talk myself out of killing you—"

"Why don't you try?"

He'd barely spoken the last word when Nate's fist slammed into his chin, splitting the skin and causing blood to ooze. A barrage of punches followed, but Gray Wolf's reaction was lightning fast. He blocked every one and returned one that bruised the cheekbone under Nate's left eye. Blinded for a moment, Nate ducked more oncoming blows before ramming head first into Gray Wolf's stomach, causing him to lose his balance and fall on his back. Nate landed on top of him and grabbed him by the neck. But Gray Wolf remembered Nate's chokehold from the first time they fought, and he was ready this time. He caught Nate's hands and threw him onto his back.

There was a moment when Nate's hands were free, but he did not seize the chance to defend himself. Gray Wolf handily pulled his knife and held the blade against Nate's neck, just hard enough to smart. Nate looked into his opponent's eyes with no fear, and with a detached indifference that disgusted Gray Wolf to his core.

"You're right. You have nothing to fear," said Gray Wolf. "I would never kill you." He sheathed his knife and stood over Nate. "Why do you start fights with me that you won't finish? I know that you have never shown weakness to anyone, yet you show it to me. Why will you not decide about me?" He beheld Nate with disdain. "I don't think you know why."

He started to walk away, and Nate struggled to his knees and sat back on his ankles. He knew all of the answers to Gray Wolf's questions but had never been able to bring himself to say them. He watched Gray Wolf's back moving further away and opened his mouth, but no words would come. He was acutely aware of being watched by Julie, Shining Sky, and a few others. Torn between pride and the inner burgeoning need to be honest with Gray Wolf, he looked towards him again. Gray Wolf would soon be beyond earshot. The urgency became overwhelming; if he didn't say it now, he never would. He swallowed hard. "I'm trying to find some good in you," he called out, as loud as his fight-wearied voice would allow. Gray Wolf stopped and turned around, and Nate looked down at the ground. He could only do this if he didn't look Gray Wolf in the eye. "Something redeemable about you, something that would make amends." The feelings that were welling up in him were strange and unfamiliar. He had quelled them for so long. "I'm looking for a reason to forgive…" His voice caught. It didn't matter; he was finished. But Gray Wolf was coming back. Nate stood to face him. He wouldn't let Gray Wolf look down on him again.

"Maybe you're not looking hard enough," Gray Wolf sternly replied.

"Or maybe it's just that there's nothing to find." His voice grew pensive. "I would've taken you with me to the Split Timber. I would've let you meet my sister."

"And I would still go."

Nate shook his head. "No. She's had enough pain. She doesn't need any more."

There was a tense pause while Gray Wolf studied him thoughtfully. "You said I believe what I want to believe. Well, so do you."

With that, Gray Wolf was gone again. Nate turned, and his eyes caught Julie's. She had seen everything, and even though she didn't understand it, she was suspicious. He didn't care; she wasn't part of this.

That night as he lay awake under the stars outside the tepee where Julie and Mark slept, Gray Wolf's final words to him that day repeated themselves in his mind. They had pricked him like a pin initially, but gradually, as he continued to unpeel the many layers of Gray Wolf's character, he had come to understand. Gray Wolf's efforts to gain an ally and friend in Nate and to protect him had never been intended to compensate for the past because he didn't think compensation was needed. The brave's past actions meant little to him; they were acts of war, fairly executed in his eyes. His efforts to win Nate over stood independently and were sincere by his own definition.

No, thought Nate, it wasn't good enough. It would never be good enough. He could never overlook the past as Gray Wolf did. He just wanted to get away from here. How fast could Blaine get here, he wondered. Would such a meeting even accomplish anything, or was he digging a deeper hole for himself? He would find out soon cnough. There was nothing to do but wait.

Chapter 23

Lying on his stomach with his head in the crook of his arm, Nate opened his eyes to see moccasins, shining amber in the early morning light, about two feet away from his nose. He recognized the beaded decoration on top of the feet and the fringe around the ankles and knew whose legs stood in them. He closed his eyes, hoping it was a dream and they'd be gone when he reopened them, but no such luck. It was time to answer for himself. He rose to his feet. With his shirt untucked and feeling groggy and disheveled, he felt quite unprepared to face Chief Red Feather and attempt to explain anything. He waited for Red Feather to speak first.

"Is there a good reason why you burned down my tepee?"

"It was an accident. You know I would never burn down your tepee on purpose."

"I have never known anyone who burned a tepee by accident, as you say."

"Gray Wolf tied me up in your tepee. It's his fault."

"Was Gray Wolf there when it burned?"

"Well, no, but—"

"Then it is not his fault. You were there. You burned down the tepee."

Nate opened his mouth to reply but realized he had no more excuses that would make sense to Red Feather. Then he saw the twinkle in the chief's eye and the corner of his mouth turning up in a smile.

"My wife is making another tepee, and my daughter is making one for you."

Nate's eyes widened, and he wondered to what he owed this generosity.

"It is a gift," Red Feather continued, "so you can stay out of my tepee. Next time you want to burn a tepee, you can burn your own."

As Red Feather turned to walk away, Nate stood taken aback by the exchange. "I'll—I'll do that," he stammered, then he smiled widely. *That went rather well,* he thought.

***

Two days following saw a giddy excitement arising at the north end of the encampment and moving through the camp in a wave. Nate was one of the first to hear the growing plodding sound of a horse herd. It meant only one thing to him. His family had arrived, and even earlier than expected. He ran all the way through the encampment from his new tepee in the east section, followed closely by Julie and Mark. He and Tara spotted each other at the same time and shouted greetings. She handed down Jack to his waiting arms, climbed down herself, then turned to help Buck, except he had already jumped to the ground on his own.

Buck wrapped himself around Nate's legs, almost unsteadying him, as Nate kissed Tara over the baby.

Tara pulled back and lightly caressed his bruised cheekbone with her thumb. "What happened to your eye?"

"Oh, nothin'," he replied, laughing. He grabbed her and kissed her again.

She looked past him and saw Julie for the first time. Her mouth dropped open. "Julie! What in the world are you doing here?"

Julie stood looking at the two of them, saddened that she couldn't share in their excitement. "We were attacked. My husband was shot, and I was brought here by Indians."

Tara covered her mouth with her hand. "Oh, Julie."

"Nate says he's okay," she continued with a displeased glance toward Nate, "but I wait here for him to come."

The two women stood for a brief, awkward moment before Tara stepped forward and hugged her. "I'm glad you're okay," she whispered.

Julie looked at the baby and managed her first smile. "You have another boy. What's his name?"

"This is Jackson."

Julie carefully took him from Nate's arms, while Nate's eyes searched over the herd and Elijah and the Wilsons.

"Where's Clay?"

Tara took a deep breath. "I fired him."

"You what?" Nate beheld her, horrified. "You don't mean that. Tell me you don't mean that."

Tara turned away from his penetrating gaze and walked towards the herd, not knowing why except just to have someplace to walk at this uncomfortable moment. "Yes, I did."

He kept pace beside her. "Why? Tara, he was the best foreman. Can you get him back?"

"No, I can't get him back. I don't want to talk about it. Mr. Medley is the foreman now. He'll do fine."

"What do you mean you don't want to talk about it? That was our foreman you fired. He's always been our foreman."

She stopped walking and looked around, confused and desperately hoping to see something that would spur a change of subject. "So where is the chief? Does he want to see these horses?"

Nate closed his eyes and let out a sigh of frustration. Obviously he wasn't going to get any more information out of her at the moment.

***

Tara and Julie sat facing each other in Nate's tepee, hardly knowing how to define what they each felt.

Nate knew when he was in the way. "I'm sure you girls have some catching up to do and, well, I probably don't wanna know how that's going to go. Come on, Buck, I will introduce you to River Otter. Do you want to come too, Mark?"

"No," Julie answered for him. "Mark does not leave my side."

"All right," he conceded. Buck followed him outside.

The women took little notice of his leaving. Julie broke the icy silence first.

"We have done many things together over the years, but I never would've expected us to meet each other in an Indian tepee."

"Nor I," Tara agreed.

"But you are happy to be here. I am among enemies."

"Yes, our lives have taken different paths as of late. But you are still my friend."

"And you are mine."

"Then you must know that Nate could not have done those things the cavalry has accused him of."

"Yes, I know." She looked down at her lap pensively. "I've always known that."

"Then why doesn't the major understand that, Julie?"

"Oh, I tried to explain that. But I'm just a schoolteacher. No one at the fort will listen to me. Most certainly Colonel McHenry wouldn't listen to me."

Tara nodded, remembering her fruitless meeting with Colonel McHenry. "I don't doubt that."

"But they understand now, I think. Josh recently found out something from Colonel McHenry. It seems there's a renegade Indian who has been giving false information to him. The colonel was quick to trust him because he's been looking for ways to get revenge on the Indians for killing his son."

Tara's brows furrowed in concern. "And Nate knows all this?"

"I learned much of it from Nate." There was an air of disappointment in her voice. "I think Josh told Nate more than he even told me."

Tara smiled in an attempt to lighten Julie's mood. "Well, at least that answers some questions we've long had."

"Yes, and so I wait here for Josh and other soldiers to come to negotiate with Nate."

Tara couldn't help but feel extreme hope amidst Julie's hardship. Maybe finally, things were starting to work out in Nate's favor. "I will wait here, too, for them to come. You will not be alone."

"I know that Mark and I are safe with you and Nate here, but the rest of them are killers, Tara."

"Even though I don't know what happened, I do not share your views, Julie.

These are good people who took care of Buck and me and made us well."

"We are on opposite sides of the fence," said Julie gravely.

"But please, let's not let it affect our friendship again. I am very sorry about your husband."

Julie's brave exterior began to crumble, and tears came to her eyes. "I just wish I could be with him." She felt the gap in their friendship closing as she realized her and Tara's common affliction. "You've been apart from Nate so very long. How do you do it?"

"I never doubt that he will be home again. It is difficult, but I have much to keep myself busy. And I look at my children. It's like having a part of him there with me."

Julie looked down at her son who, having grown accustomed to his surroundings, showed no fear and smiled up at her. "Yes, Mark is a consolation. And I know Josh will come for us as fast as he is able."

"This renegade Indian," Tara queried, "do you know his name?"

"Nate called him Beartooth."

Tara's face paled. The name held a terrible dread for her as it had for Nate.

"You know him?" asked Julie.

"I know who he is," she whispered, staring past Julie at the wall of the tepee but her eyes not seeing it.

"Nate says he attacked the medicine wagons last year."

Tara's eyes switched back to Julie. "So it was him. That's why Nate couldn't find the attacker among the Indians." Remembering Julie's edgy discomfort, she smiled. "Although I'd wish for different circumstances, it is good to see you again, Julie."

Julie returned the smile. "It is already better since you got here."

"Come then. I'd like to meet River Otter. I'm sure it would do Mark good to play with children his age." Julie still looked uncertain, and Tara continued, "It will be fine, Julie. Nate has told me about this boy. And we will be close by."

Julie looked into Mark's hopeful eyes and nodded. "All right."

Tara picked up Jack, and Julie led the way towards Shining Sky's tepee. The sun was dipping low in the western sky, and they squinted to see their way. They found Shining Sky outside scraping a hide pegged into the ground with wooden stakes. Nearby River Otter and Buck played with toy bows and arrows while Nate watched. Shining Sky looked up from her work, and her eyes immediately darted to the baby in Tara's arms. With a big, straight-toothed smile, she dropped her tool and rushed to Tara, holding out her arms to take the baby. Tara glanced at Nate, and he nodded his assurance that it was all right.

Soon Shining Sky was lost in her own world of longing, swaying Jack back and forth and singing a lullaby while Julie watched her and the rowdy boys in turn, and marveled at this peaceful picture of everyday life among enemies. The place suddenly felt less strange to her. She had spent so much of her recent life in the fort and accompanied by soldiers outside of it that it had not occurred to her that an Indian camp could be a perfectly acceptable place to be for her closest friend's family. She remembered her last conversation with Tara, at Jared's wedding, wherein she had expressed her desire to let Mark see more of the world outside the fort. Well, now he was, and she decided maybe this wasn't such a bad thing.

"I'll be back," Nate said to Tara. "I'll go see the hands and tell them to stay here a few extra days till we see how it goes with the soldiers."

***

As Nate returned a short time later in the gathering dusk, he was shaking his head in confusion. His talk with Elijah hadn't done much to clear up the situation about Clay Tatum. Elijah had said something about Mrs. Hunter not trusting Clay, then Clay showing disrespect to Mrs. Hunter and wondering what happened at the house. It didn't sound at all like Clay. Then Elijah had rambled on about butterfly brands and thanking Nate for his raise, clearly an effort to divert Nate's attention from his original question. *Why does Clay give a hoot what happens at the house anyway? I just need to get back home and take charge of things.*

The sight before him slammed his thoughts to a halt, and his blood ran cold. Tara was engaged in conversation with Gray Wolf outside of Shining Sky's tepee. Their manner seemed pleasant enough, which angered him all the more. That was how Gray Wolf had first approached him. He picked up his pace, reached them, and stepped in between them. "Stay away from her," he told Gray Wolf, accompanied by a cold, hard stare.

Gray Wolf backed off and left without a word, and Tara beheld Nate in surprise. "What's wrong? He was very polite to me."

"Just stay clear of him. Don't even talk to him."

"Why?"

He did not answer her, and Tara noticed his uneasiness and the way he kept looking in the direction Gray Wolf had gone, the way he paced like he wasn't sure what to do next. "I see your bruised cheekbone, and the cut on his chin," she said. "What's happened between the two of you?"

"He led the attack on the soldiers a few days ago."

She drew in a breath and put a hand over her heart. "No wonder Julie disappeared so quickly."

He was somewhat relieved that he had eased her curiosity. Perhaps she would not ask any more questions. But it was not to be so simple. She was the one person who could always see right through him.

"You've had problems with him before now, haven't you?"

Her words pierced him. He had no idea how to respond.

"He told me his name was Gray Wolf."

Hearing her speak the name cut him deeper.

"When you came home a couple months ago and told me everyone you were with, you never mentioned his name. I would've remembered his name."

"No doubt you would."

Tara waited, but he was not offering any more explanation. "He speaks very good English," she prompted. "Where did he learn it?"

"I don't know. I don't care."

She attempted a half-hearted smile. "I'll tell you exactly what happened with Clay Tatum if you'll tell me about Gray Wolf and why he bothers you so much."

Nate had already forgotten Clay. There was no comparison; she was offering a mouse for a bear. "I couldn't care less about Clay. He probably got what he deserved." He caught Shining Sky's eye several feet behind Tara. She still cradled the sleeping Jack in her arms and didn't seem in a hurry to give him up yet. "Watch the children for a little while?" he asked her. She eagerly nodded, and he turned and started to cross the distance to his own tepee. It wasn't far; he wished it was further, much further.

Tara hesitated and looked back once more toward Buck and Jack. Shining Sky gave her a reassuring nod, and she followed after Nate.

He heard her moving along beside him, and a knot began to develop in his stomach. How little could he get away with telling her, he wondered. Could he avoid telling her at all? They entered his tepee and sat facing each other. It was dim inside. No words were spoken while they allowed their eyes to adjust. The emptiness and the quiet heightened the tension already hanging thick in the air.

He watched the doorway for the longest time, not in expectation of anyone coming, but because he must work himself up to looking into her eyes, for as soon as he did, she would know that something was terribly wrong.

Tara's voice rent the silence first. "It's all right that you don't get along with him, you know."

"I did once," he replied, his eyes still fixed on the doorway.

"But something happened?"

"Yes." There was no turning back now. The two worlds he'd kept separated for so long had crashed together in front of him and would never return to their former places, in ignorance of each other. He had battered himself for too long over this, and the person who meant the most to him must know the reason why. He had to tell Tara what he knew. She could go her whole life and never find out, but she was entitled to know. He turned to her, and his eyes met hers. "I'd give anything to spare you heartbreak."

The sorrow she saw in his eyes stunned her speechless for a moment and struck fear in her heart. "What do you mean?" she whispered breathlessly.

He knew his next words would be a crushing blow, but he was certain now. To keep it from her would be wrong. She needed to know. "It was Gray Wolf who killed your aunt and uncle during the massacre."

The sting of the news paralyzed her, starting at the top of her head where she began to feel dizzy, then continuing to her pounding heart, nauseous stomach, and numb legs. When she remembered to breathe, she asked, "Are you sure of it?"

"Yes, I'm sure. He told me himself."

She blinked several times and swallowed hard. "You've—you've known all this time and you haven't turned him in?" She struggled to maintain composure. "You haven't done anything about it?"

"What could I have done?"

Anger washed over her now like a river. "You could have killed him and ripped him to pieces like he did my aunt and uncle."

"Believe me, I've imagined it countless times."

"Then why didn't you?" she almost screamed.

He looked down, ashamed to admit his relation. "He's kin to me. He's my grandfather's brother."

She paused for only a moment. "I don't care what he is. He is a heartless killer." She shook her head. "He murdered my family." Her eyes switched suddenly to the doorway. "And our children are out there. I must get them."

He caught her by the shoulders as she arose. "Our children are safer here than anywhere else. At least eight chiefs in three bands of the Northern Cheyenne nation have sworn to protect me and my family. Gray Wolf himself has warned me away from cavalry scouts several times. As much as we might hate him, Tara, I do know that he would protect me, and the boys…and you."

"That doesn't make up for what he did," she insisted, her eyebrows knit together. "Have you actually forgiven him?"

"No," he was quick to reply. "I have not. I don't know if I'll ever forgive him, but I've accepted it." He saw tears forming in her eyes, and his voice softened. "Tara, if it hadn't been him it would've been somebody else. They still would've died that night. How I wish it had been somebody else. But we've always known there was somebody out there who killed your aunt and uncle, somebody who shot my father to death. I know this is hard right now, but life will go on just the same."

"Except that now I have a face to match my nightmares. And I will not rest until he rots in the grave!" She scrambled to her feet and moved towards him, her face reddening with anger. "Hand me your gun. I'll do it right now."

He saw a look of burning hate in her eyes such as he'd never seen before, and it terrified him. She was a stranger. He felt an urgent, desperate need to pull her back from an unseen destroying force which held her bound. He thought quickly and did something completely opposite from his instinct. He pulled his gun and held it out to her handle first. "You want him dead? You go kill him, and here's my gun to do it."

His unexpected action slowed her impetus.

"But you'll have to live with yourself," he continued, "and it won't change the past." His voice grew strained with sadness and regret. "But it will change you. You won't be the same woman that I know and love."

She fought to bring herself back under control. She knew he was right, but she didn't care. Her family's killer was in this camp, nearby; she had spoken to him unawares, and it disgusted her. How could she possibly erase him from her thoughts, now or ever? How could Nate's feeling of kinship outweigh such a horrific past? To accept it as Nate did seemed incomprehensible, but she realized that at this moment there was nothing else to be done. She had never experienced powerlessness such as this. It overwhelmed her, and her tears flowed freely now and turned into great sobs. He reached for her. She tried to pull away but found her very strength sapped.

"Let me hold you," he pleaded. "I know you don't believe me, but I know what you feel."

"You know nothing of what I feel," she cried.

"Yes, I do, Tara." He continued to pull her to him, gently countering her resistance, until she fell helpless and spent against his shoulder.

"How can you be so calm about him?" she asked between sobs.

"Because I've already been through all the feelings you're having now. For months I've had to be around him. It was not a camp as big as this. There was no place to get away from him unless I left. I hated it too, but there was nothing that could've made it better. All I could think about was being with you again." As soon as the last words escaped his mouth, he felt her tense up. She was trying to pull away from him again, and inside, he cursed Gray Wolf for this wedge he'd driven between them.

This time he restrained her, his need to protect her from anything that would cause her pain prevailing over any other concern. His lips found hers and pressed against them, but she was not responding as she always had. "I swear I never wanted you to meet him," he whispered in her ear.

"Well, I did, and I am *not* just going to forget—"

"Shhh." He put a finger to her lips. "You can be sure that he's on a dangerous path already. He's gonna get what's coming to him. He won't need our help."

Her tears ran down over his fingers as he caressed her cheek. "I wish I could be sure of that," she whispered.

"Forget him, Tara. I have missed you so. I made Red Feather move a whole camp here because I could not wait to see you."

"I am so tired of this whole situation. You've been away so long you don't even know what's happening at the ranch anymore. And now I find out you've been around this killer all this time."

"But he is not the one responsible for keeping us apart. He never was. There is another."

Tara closed her eyes and nodded. "Beartooth."

"Yes."

A moment of contemplative quiet followed as Tara's thoughts shifted to this new underlying threat, one more pointed and immediate. Her uncertainty about the future heightened. She desperately needed solace here and now, where it was to be found, yet she still wasn't ready to accept it. But he was still holding her, caressing her. She wanted to get away, to think, to make sense of her chaotic feelings. He let go of her to remove his holster and jacket. There was a fleeting moment in which she could still grab the gun, but she let it pass, knowing she no longer possessed the will to kill a person. She felt her dress being slid off of her shoulder, and her resolve intensified. As he firmly eased her down onto her back underneath him, her hand caught the front of his shoulder and resisted, but in one effortless motion, he closed his hand on hers, moved it aside, and held it down. She lay powerless and unable to move, a captive to his unfamiliar aggression.

"Please don't," she begged through tears.

"Tara, I don't know what's going to happen when the soldiers come. The Indians are nervous about soldiers coming here. I don't know what I've gotten us into. And I don't know where Beartooth is. All I know is what's right here, right now. Don't turn me away." His lips traced down the smooth curve of her neck, then returned to her face. He swept the tousled strands of hair away from her eyes, cupped her cheek in his hand, and kissed her again, long and hard.

This time she kissed him back, for in his strong touch, she sensed a hidden weakness, a subtle, creeping dread of what the future held. He was worried, and desperate to seize any finite moment he could. Her hand slid up under his sweat-dampened shirt and brushed across the scar on his abdomen. She had touched it countless times without thought, but this time it sent a shudder through her. The encampment was safe, as he said, but danger still lurked out there somewhere beyond. The uncertainty set her heart to pounding and created an urgent need to comfort him. He felt her shudder and, with a hand against the small of her back, pulled her into him until he felt her beating heart against his. She grasped him in return, and he was assured that everything was all right with the world, for now.

The camp gradually grew quiet and settled itself for sleep. Soon the only sounds were the rolling river, the rustle of trees bending in a soft wind, the melodic chirp of a cricket very close to the tepee, and another one further away, near the river. Inside the tepee, the fire died down, and the coals dimmed with an occasional pop. They found their comfort in each other and in the quiet, and fear was banished for a few quick, stolen minutes.

Later, as Tara slept, Nate arose and went to Shining Sky's tepee where he found Buck and Jack asleep. Neither awoke as he carried them, one in each arm, back to his own tepee and settled them under blankets. He was wide awake and thought he would sit outside for a while. He pulled a blanket over Tara's shoulders and was surprised when she reached up and took hold of his arm.

"Stay by me," she whispered.

So he lay by her and watched her drift off to sleep again. Having all of his family around him, hearing their breathing—this was better than being outside. The soldiers were drawing closer. He could feel it. He shoved aside thoughts of Beartooth, Gray Wolf, and the injured Blaine. He would deal with each in turn.

Chapter 24

Tara and Nate stood soberly watching as the line of mounted soldiers moved into their view. They were cautiously relieved to see the white flag of truce, but the number of soldiers who had come was unexpected and a little unnerving. More and more kept riding around the bend of the river, single file, and forming a line across the northern end of the encampment. When the whole line had stopped, it appeared to be an entire company.

All in the camp had come out to watch, and the warriors moved to the front, guns and bows ready, all eyes holding on the white flag aloft. Only Julie, standing near Tara and with her arms around Mark's shoulders, was quietly bursting with joy at the sight.

"Have Shining Sky take the boys to the far end of the camp," Nate said to Tara, never taking his eyes off of the soldiers, "in case this doesn't go well."

Tara hurried off to accomplish the errand and returned shortly. Elijah moved up beside them. The Wilsons had been camped upriver for the last three days, but Elijah was curious and had stayed close by.

Tara leaned in close to Nate. "See that big man near the middle of the line? That's Lieutenant-Colonel McHenry."

"Well, well, the commander himself. I wasn't expecting this honor."

"Wait here," said Julie, "until I've talked to them first." She took Mark by the hand and walked toward the soldiers. Almost immediately Major Blaine emerged from the company and jogged towards her, obviously slowed by pain but unable to restrain himself. She and Mark broke into a run, and they met in the midst of the open space in a hug.

After a few private words, Julie pulled away, walked towards Colonel McHenry, and stood in front of him. "I and my son are fine, Colonel," she said, loud enough for all to hear. "I want it to be known that we were *not* captives. Nate Hunter himself assured me that we were free to leave at anytime. I chose to stay because I felt that we were safer here than if we traveled across open country by ourselves."

With a nod from McHenry, she and Mark walked the rest of the way to the soldiers, disappeared somewhere behind them, and Blaine returned to his position on horseback next to the colonel.

Nate mounted the Appaloosa and started forward at a walk across the thirty or so yards of open ground. He felt better knowing that he was backed up by at least as many Indians as there were soldiers. He arrived in front of McHenry and halted the Appaloosa.

Unable to mask his curiosity, McHenry looked him up and down. "Nate Hunter."

"Colonel?" answered Nate with a nod.

"We finally meet."

"Yes, I assume Major Blaine delivered the message I asked him to."

"He did indeed. Apparently a mistake has been made, although I am not sure to what extent. From my point of view, I'm looking at your word against Beartooth's, and I don't even know you, Mr. Hunter.

"Well, this is your opportunity to change that. I have spent the better part of a year trying to find out who attacked the medicine wagons. You didn't spend even half as long before you made up your mind who was to blame."

McHenry sat up a little straighter. "I don't need a man who runs with Indians and dodges the cavalry to tell me my business."

"Unless that man dodged cavalry because he knew there was no chance they'd listen to him. Obviously the word of someone who got you to attack the Indians on the Sun River was stronger than mine would've been."

"Let us not forget, Mr. Hunter, that the tables were turned last week when Major Blaine's contingent, that included his *family*, was attacked by Indians. And you didn't exactly boost your integrity with me when you showed up at that attack. You obviously knew about it beforehand."

"And it would've been worse had I not interrupted it."

"So I've heard," Colonel McHenry conceded. "I am prepared to admit an honest mistake, and to listen to you now." His expression grew stern. "But not without a price."

"What's that?"

"I want the ringleaders of the attack on Major Blaine's contingent."

"I don't know who they are. I was tied up."

"Who tied you up?"

Nate shook his head. "You're not gonna use me that way. This is not a fair trade."

"They're not your friends. They tied you up."

"Yes, but that's all they did. You'll hang them."

"After a trial, of course."

"There was only one ringleader."

"Very well. Give me his name, and tell me if he's with this group here. We'll handle it from this point. I wouldn't expect you to bring him out under false pretenses."

"I will give you his name, *and* I will bring him out to you myself, no pretenses, by force if necessary—and this is a solemn promise—*if* you will bring forward the ringleaders of that unprovoked attack on Red Feather's camp and let them face Cheyenne justice. Or, would you be one of them?"

Colonel McHenry bristled. "If for nothing else, I can arrest you for obstruction of justice."

"Why are you so bent on arresting me, when you know there's someone else responsible for all this? You don't even need my word *or* my integrity. Major Blaine can tell you everything you need to know."

"Don't worry. Beartooth will be brought to justice."

"Oh, he will, but I doubt you'll be the one to do it. Good luck trying to apprehend him and get him into your court."

A nearby commotion drew their attention. Nate looked to see two soldiers attempting to wrestle Elijah to the ground while he fought them every inch of the way.

"You lied to us," said the one with the scarred lip and missing tooth. "You said you wasn't with the Broken Bow anymore."

"Take your hands off him!" Nate demanded. "He has *no* part in this." He looked to McHenry. "He has nothing to do with this. Let him go!"

McHenry nodded to the two soldiers, looking very much tired of the whole situation. "Let him go, for pete's sakes." The soldiers reluctantly released Elijah, and McHenry turned back to Nate. "I will not negotiate further. It's your call. You gonna give me that ringleader or not?"

Nate didn't have to think about it, but he waited, and he studied McHenry's eyes. They were the eyes of a proud man who would never admit a mistake without qualifying it, who would continually look for ways to gain the upper hand. This had become a battle of wills, and Nate had nothing in his arsenal to fight it. He almost preferred a gunfight. "No deal," he growled. Leaving McHenry cursing under his breath, he whipped the Appaloosa around and galloped back to Tara. The warriors nearby closed in and filled in the gap in front of Nate, their fingers on the triggers.

"What happened?" she asked when Nate had vaulted to the ground.

"He wants the ringleader of the attack on Blaine."

"So you're going to tell him, right?"

"No, I'm not."

"What?" she asked, incredulous. She shook her head in disbelief, and her eyes blazed. "Even now you're not going to report him, even now when they *handed* you a chance."

"We share the same blood, and I don't want his on my hands. You don't have to worry. Julie knows who led the attack." His disgust was evident. "No doubt she'll fill them in."

Tara closed her eyes and struggled to calm herself. When she opened them, she glanced around at the braves standing guard between them and the soldiers, and her eyes fell on Gray Wolf, the one directly in front of Nate. Without a word, she grabbed the Appaloosa's reins from Nate and climbed into the saddle. She kicked the horse's flanks, and the braves parted for her to pass through.

Elijah and Nate stood side by side, watching her approach the line of soldiers. "What's she doin'?" asked Elijah.

With a fleeting look at Gray Wolf, Nate replied, "I don't know."

Tara halted the Appaloosa well short of the soldiers and called out, "Major Blaine, a word in private please."

The major rode forward and met her on the open ground. "Before you say anything, Mrs. Hunter, it's obvious to the colonel what's going on here. You're here. Your wrangler's here. You've given the Indians horses again."

"The horses are part of an old agreement, and you knew about it. They do not come to bear on anything currently."

"What did you want to say?"

She lowered her voice. "I assume it is still military policy not to shoot at unarmed women and children in battle?"

"Of course."

"Then you'd better clean out your own ranks. At the Sun River, I saw an Indian woman shot in the back, on purpose, as she was running away and carrying a small child. I was hiding behind a bush with my own child. The man didn't know I was there."

"Well, I'm sorry to hear it, but what good does that do us now? That was a year ago. I'm sure you wouldn't be able to identify—"

"A blond-haired saddler sergeant with a powder burn under his left eye." She saw his jaw drop and knew she had struck a nerve.

"I see," he whispered.

"I *strongly* suggest that you work with my husband, or so help me, I *will* bring down the entire high command of Fort Mason over this."

Blaine made a poor effort at a polite smile. "Will that be all, Mrs. Hunter?

"Isn't that enough?"

The remains of his smile faded, and he turned and rode back to McHenry while she rode back to Nate.

"What is it?" the colonel asked.

"She witnessed the murder of an Indian woman by one of our men on the Sun River."

"She can't say who it is, can she?"

"She accurately described Sergeant Rawlings of B Company."

"Oh, good grief." Colonel McHenry rolled his eyes and shifted uneasily in the saddle. "Is he still at Fort Mason?"

"Yes."

McHenry thought for a long while. "What do you think about all this?"

"Her word is irreproachable," replied Blaine. "She could bury us over this. Are you wanting me to advise you, Colonel?"

"I am, Major," replied McHenry in his most impatient growl.

"Well, in the interest of sparing any further embarrassment to the cavalry, I say you should let Hunter off and call a truce with Red Feather."

"All right. See to it that Sergeant Rawlings gets immediately transferred to the furthest post on the most remote piece of dirt you can find, and I don't want to know where."

"Yes, sir."

Colonel McHenry looked across at Tara and thought aloud. "Why didn't she tell me that a long time ago when she had the chance?" He knew why. She'd kept it up her sleeve on purpose in case she really needed it. He gave in and chuckled. He had now been hoodwinked twice by the venerable Mrs. Hunter. "My hat's off to the lady." He tipped his hat to her, and she nodded in return. "Should I pass her my saber as well?"

"I don't think that'll be necessary—"

"It was a joke, Mr. Blaine."

Major Blaine paused. "Yes, sir, I knew that."

McHenry looked over at him and found him smiling. He glared at the major until his gaze was returned, then he spoke gruffly. "Well, what are you waiting for? Call him back."

When Nate again stopped his horse in front of him, McHenry hid all signs of his injured pride. "We've decided we can get the ringleader without your help. But we do need to find out more from you about Beartooth and determine if the case is strong enough to bring charges against him. I want you to come to the fort right away for a formal deposition."

"I will not enter the fort," replied Nate.

"Mr. Hunter, I know that if anything happens to you, I will have the entire Northern Cheyenne nation at my doorstep, and I don't want that. I am done with this. I give you my word, my troops will stand down when you enter the fort."

"Then I bring a contingent of Cheyenne with me, and I will not disarm."

"I just said my troops would stand down. I can't have them do that if armed Cheyenne enter the fort."

"I have to trust you, you'll have to trust me. With all due respect, Colonel, there's a lot more of you than us. I'm the one at a disadvantage here."

McHenry fought to keep his frustration in check. "Major, do you vouch for Mr. Hunter?"

"Absolutely, one hundred percent. The troops will stand down, but they will be battle-ready and at your command, Colonel."

Nate closed his eyes to keep from rolling them. *Typical. Always trying to impress the boss.*

"Very well," said McHenry. "Be it known, this does not, in any way, affect my dealings with those Cheyenne who've been attacking ranchers in Nebraska. You'd be advised to let your friends know I'm coming for them with hellfire if they don't surrender."

Nate nodded. He knew he'd gotten as much conciliation as he was going to get from McHenry.

Nate rode back to Tara and assured the Indians they could relax their stance. He sought out Red Feather right away.

"You may come into my tepee," said Red Feather, "as long as I am here to watch you."

Nate smiled. The chief would never let him hear the end of it, he guessed.

"I wish I could've done more to protect the people, now and in the future," said Nate as they were seated.

"It is more than any one man can do," replied the chief. "You have done much already."

"But the cavalry is not going to do right by that broken treaty. They want those braves that have been causing trouble there to surrender."

"I am guessing that you do not want us to fight for what is ours. Is that right?"

"Yes. I am so sorry."

"It is easy for you to say. It is not your land. You will not lose anything."

"If the people fight, you will lose even more—more land, more braves." It pained him to say it, but he looked the chief dead in the eye. "You *cannot* win."

"You urged us not to fight before, when our people were attacked, and we listened. Now you speak the same words again. Is that what your father taught you, to give in?"

"No, and maybe he would disagree with me. I do not claim to live up to all my father taught me. But I'm not asking you to give in. I'm telling you that if the chiefs show more peaceful control over the people and rein in those rogue attacks, you stand a better chance of having the whites listen to you. They will never listen at the point of arrows. My task is to be an emissary. What kind of emissary would I be if I was not truthful with you?"

"No one among us questions your honesty. But you are not a chief. I will tell your words to others, and they will decide what to do. Your mind can be at peace knowing you spoke the truth."

"My mind will not be at peace unless I know all is well with you."

"I do not know what will happen, but if we die fighting, we die with honor."

Nate was suddenly reminded of Gray Wolf, who had also spoken of dying with honor in battle. So had his own father, who gave up a chance to escape and save his own life because of honor. But he was proud of his father, and now equally proud of the close association he'd developed with Red Feather. He wanted the Cheyenne to fight back, but the mediating position in which he always found himself prevented him from saying it. But he figured Red Feather could see right through him anyway. There wasn't much he could hide from the discerning chief.

Red Feather offered a knowing smile. "You go home to your family, your land, where you belong. Your time here with us is finished."

Nate returned the smile as he arose and shook hands with the chief.

"May Heammawihio go with you and protect you," said Red Feather.

"And you."

Nate's steps next led him to the tepee of Gray Wolf. The brave invited him to sit down, but he declined. He didn't intend to stay long. He looked around at the inside of the tepee while trying to think of how to start. "My wife doesn't know I'm here."

Gray Wolf ignored the comment as he continued to whittle away at a pipe he'd barely begun. Nate watched him, more hopeful than angry this time, waiting for some kind of sign, anything to tell him there was something inside Gray Wolf that needed to come out. There was nothing. It wasn't going to happen, Nate decided, not now. Probably never.

"I'm leaving tomorrow," said Nate. "I will be going back to the Broken Bow soon."

Gray Wolf stopped whittling and looked up soberly. "That's what you have always wanted."

"Yes. You should know, there will be no danger here in this camp from the soldiers. They will let the Indians off, and they will let me off, but they will find out about you, and they're going to want to hang you. I've done all that I can do."

"I don't blame you for not helping me—"

"I *am* helping you, by giving you a chance to do something about it now. I will not protect you from what you've brought on yourself, but neither will I help the cavalry find you....if you weren't here in the morning."

Their eyes locked, and Gray Wolf nodded. "Thank you."

Nate quickly ducked out of the tepee.

***

The cavalry had already pulled out by the time Nate and Tara stood beside the Dearborn to say goodbye once again. "It won't be long now till I'm home," said Nate.

"I know."

She seemed distant, and it bothered him. She had been so ever since he'd refused to give up Gray Wolf. Then a crazy thought out of nowhere loomed and distressed him. "Has Elijah ever laid a finger on you?"

"I should say not! Don't you think I would seriously disable him if he did?"

He raised his eyebrows and smiled. "My mistake."

"I should come with you to the fort."

He knew she spoke out of duty. Her concern wasn't genuine. "No, there's nothing you could do."

"You're right, I couldn't. You're walking into a fort of three hundred men with twelve Cheyenne."

"We couldn't win a battle, but we could probably take out two for every one of us."

"That's not funny."

"The cavalry's not stupid, Tara. It's mostly for show, to help them remember who I have backing me up. Beartooth is who'll be looking for me."

She put a hand on his chest. "Take care of yourself. Buck and Jack need their pa at home."

"I will." He lowered his eyes. She didn't say *she* needed him at home.

He gave her a kiss goodbye and walked her to the wagon. Once he'd handed Buck and Jack up to her and she was settled, he waved and watched as she slapped the reins on the horses and the wagon lurched into motion, jiggling pots and pans in the back. As it moved away, the emptiness in him grew. This was a different parting than he'd experienced before, a sharper pain. Something was unfinished, and he hated leaving it that way. He looked down at the ground and idly rubbed his neck. Then he raised his head and opened his mouth to call to her but changed his mind. He turned towards the river, but his insides felt jumbled. Nervousness, even dread, crept over him as he heard the sound of the wagon grow distant. He looked back at the wagon, took a couple of unthinking steps in that direction, and stayed focused on it till it was tiny, then disappeared behind trees.

He considered riding after her, but the fear that she wouldn't want him to bound him where he was. What would he say to her anyway, he wondered. With a pang, he wished he'd sacrificed Gray Wolf. It wouldn't have hurt as much as this. He turned and walked quickly towards his own tepee to make ready to leave himself. He just needed to get this cavalry business over with and get home again so he could fix things.

***

Tara stared straight ahead, her eyes clouding with tears. She tried to blink them away and attempt a smile for Buck. A part of her wanted to turn around and see Nate one more time, maybe offer a final wave, but she could not bring herself to do it. All she could think about was the day before. He had betrayed her. She never would've expected it.

***

Elijah rode on ahead. With no horses to herd, there was more time to think. He sensed there was something bothering Tara. He didn't even need to be near her to know that. He would never ask her, and he knew she wouldn't say. He was keenly aware that his time on the Broken Bow was nearing an end. He had said he would leave when Nate returned home for good, and he needed to stick to it. He liked to think she might miss him when he left. Maybe that's why she was pensive. He knew that wasn't the case, but still, it was a halfway pleasant thought.

Chapter 25

Nate kicked out the flames of the campfire, gathered his effects, and threw a leg over the Appaloosa, then sat gazing at the fortress in the distance while the braves mounted their horses. Surrounded by some of the proudest and most skilled warriors among the Cheyenne, Nate was glad to have them along. It had been easier than tracking a skunk to gather a small band to accompany him. As soon as the word was out that Eagle Shadow wanted to enter the fort with an armed guard in a symbolic show of strength, it was only a matter of choosing which ones he wanted out of the many willing to go. The task for Nate had been to weed out the impetuous, trigger-happy ones in favor of the even-tempered braves.

The sendoff had been grand, akin to leaving for a big buffalo hunt. Everyone turned out to bid farewell, especially to Nate whom they knew wouldn't be coming back. Only Gray Wolf was missing. No one knew where he had gone.

From the wooded rise, Nate looked across the open expanse to their destination. Although he and the braves had given McHenry and his men a few hours head start, they'd avoided traveling the same trail and had arrived here ahead of the soldiers. Here they had waited for a day, and watched the night before as the soldiers entered the fort. He figured by now, notice had been given that he was coming and they'd be ready.

He signaled his companions, and they nudged their horses at a walk. A short time later as they approached the big log gates, they could hear scrambling and orders being shouted inside. The gates were opened, and the group entered without breaking stride. Inside, soldiers at attention lined their path on either side.

"At ease!" came a shouted command.

The soldiers all stood at ease, their right hands holding the barrels of their carbines which rested on the ground by their feet. Nate looked into the faces of many of them as he passed. They were clearly puzzled as to what was happening, and some looked downright annoyed. This wasn't what they'd signed up for, to watch helplessly as Cheyenne warriors in full, colorful regalia and possessing weapons of various sorts passed by in front of them unimpeded.

Nate's eyes scanned beyond the lines of soldiers, at men at their stations on the interior walls, men outside the doors of buildings where their work had been interrupted. Every eye in the place was on him, and the quiet was deafening. He glimpsed Julie outside her cabin door, and she nodded in his direction.

The further he rode into the stockade, the more surrounded and powerless he felt, but he was aware that his renown counted for something and had gotten him this far, so he kept his chin high and cast only his eyes downward as he watched for any sign of trouble. He listened for the slightest noise, the swish of a rifle being raised, the cocking of a hammer, anything that would require a split-second reaction. Every brave with him would hear it too, and react lightning fast. But only the muted sound of horses' hooves on dirt broke the silence as the party proceeded to the commander's quarters.

He dismounted in front of the door and held up a hand to the others. *"Noxa'e."* They stayed on their horses. When he entered the front office, he was greeted by the orderly of the day who immediately opened the door to the inner office and informed him that Colonel McHenry was waiting. Inside he found both McHenry and Major Blaine, who stood to shake hands with him.

"Have a seat," said McHenry.

Nate leaned his rifle against the wall and sat in a chair facing the colonel's desk.

"How was your trip here?" inquired the colonel as he gathered some papers in front of him and set them aside.

"Oh, very enjoyable. Saw three herds of moose along the way."

"How interesting."

Either the colonel wasn't aware that moose didn't travel in herds or he just plain wasn't listening. Either way, Nate deduced, small talk wasn't his strong point. Out of the corner of his eye, he caught Blaine trying to suppress a smile.

The orderly entered, sat down at a smaller desk next to McHenry's, and set out his paper, quill pen, and inkwell.

"This is my orderly," explained McHenry. "He will be taking down your statement."

"Blast it," muttered the orderly. "My ink is almost gone. I'm sorry, sir. I'll be right back."

He disappeared and left the three of them in an awkward silence. McHenry impatiently twiddled his thumbs but didn't attempt any more small talk. Blaine looked down at the floor, and Nate watched both of them.

Finally the orderly clattered back in with more apologies and settled himself again at the desk. "I'm ready, sir."

McHenry began his dictation. "This is a deposition of Mr. Nathaniel Hunter to be used in a federal trial of the Indian scout Beartooth." He glanced at some notes in front of him. "When did you first meet Beartooth?"

Nate reached back in his memory, further than he thought he'd need to for this occasion. "I was eighteen. He came to our home. I didn't know any other Indians at that time."

"Was he alone?"

"No. He was very much a part of the Cheyenne then, and a close friend of Chief Red Feather's." He summarized his past dealings with Beartooth, and the brave's actions that had led to his banishment from the Cheyenne.

"That corroborates precisely with what Major Blaine has told me. So I do believe you are telling the truth."

"Why wouldn't I?" These military types always boggled Nate. *He should've questioned the moose comment.*

"So clearly Beartooth had it in for you and the Indians. But what proof have you that he attacked the medicine wagons?"

"Nothing that I can show you. I just know him and what he would do. That attack had his name written all over it. I'd have known it sooner if I'd known he was involved with the fort."

McHenry broke eye contact in a moment of discomfort, but Nate's eyes pierced him all the more.

"And he followed me all the way to the Sun River last summer. He could easily have caught up to me, but he didn't. He wanted to make sure I was in that Indian camp before he got you to attack. *All* of this, everything he has done, has been for his own vengeful purposes."

"But now you are using it to deflect attention away from your actions at the Sun River."

"Actually, Colonel, I think you're using the Sun River to deflect attention away from the fact that Beartooth fooled you."

McHenry fumed. He was not accustomed to such brazenness from anyone around him. "But you did not know at the time you threatened that private in front of Major Blaine that the Indians weren't guilty."

"Does that matter so much now?"

McHenry stared hard at him, in a less threatening way this time, more contemplative. He signaled the orderly to stop writing. "This is off the record. Would you really have killed that private?"

Nate thought for a moment. "I don't know. I'm glad I didn't have to make that decision."

McHenry leaned back and clasped his hands over his stomach. "What about the two scouts who were murdered near the Powder River?"

"Well, I'm responsible for the loss of their pants, but that's all." He explained in detail his encounter with the scouts and his discovery of their bodies the next day. "I think if you find my camp by the creek down there, you may still see their guns that I left there. If I'd killed them, don't you think I wouldn't have left anything of theirs lying around?"

"But how can we be absolutely sure you didn't kill those two scouts, if you felt threatened by them?"

At that, Nate burst into uncontrolled laughter, surprising both the colonel and Major Blaine. "Threatened by those two? There were *five* soldiers who tracked me all the way to the Sun River. They never once laid eyes on me, but I can tell you where they camped, when they ate breakfast, what kind of horses they had, how many times they stopped—"

"All right, all right, you made your point." Feeling sufficiently foolish, he opted to put an end to this. "I think we have all we need to bring charges against Beartooth, don't you, Major?"

"Yes, sir. I'd say so."

"Good," said Nate. "So can I go then?"

"In a minute." McHenry straightened up again. "I'm well familiar with your skills at evading trackers, but Major Blaine here informs me that you're equally good at tracking yourself."

"Yes, sir." He knew what was coming.

"Beartooth's not been seen for a while now. Will you help us track him down and bring him in?" He held up a hand to stop any quick reply from Nate. "Now, I'm not ordering you. There'll be no argument if you say no. I'm just asking."

"You don't even have to ask. The very minute I heard Beartooth's name, I knew I'd be meeting up with him. Is there a reward?"

"What do you mean 'reward'?"

"Well, he killed two teamsters, two scouts, instigated an attack on a peaceful camp, and tried to frame me. What's the goin' price for that these days?"

McHenry was at a loss for words. The last thing he wanted to do was to pay Nate for anything. But Nate had him over a barrel in front of Blaine and the orderly. "Two hundred fifty dollars."

Nate was pleased at the number but found it humorously ironic. He himself had been worth more for doing less.

"So, you'll want to be on your way then," said the colonel.

Nate glanced at Major Blaine and the orderly. "I guess that's my signal." He arose and picked up his rifle. As he looked down at the colonel, already busying himself with the papers he'd set aside earlier, something akin to pity welled up in him. "For what it's worth, sir, I am sorry about your son. The rancher who was smoked out?" McHenry looked up in speechless astonishment, and Nate saw a flicker of humanity surface in his eyes. "I'm a rancher myself."

The colonel paused before he responded. "Thank you. I appreciate that." He quickly looked back down at his papers.

***

Nate rode alone on the road to Timber Fork. He'd sent the braves home as soon as they'd exited the fort. He liked the quiet. It afforded him time to focus on his homecoming and what he would say to Tara. He wouldn't look for Beartooth just yet. He rather suspected Beartooth would find him. The brave seemed to have done pretty well at that before.

He thought about the ranch. Soon he'd be able to resume his regular work schedule. He was actually looking forward to that. He could spend evenings with his boys now, watch them grow. He could mingle freely in town, and all this with no worries of soldiers coming for him. He wondered if it would seem strange to be in town now, after so long away. Suddenly Clay Tatum came to mind. Where was he by now? For the first time, Nate had a chance to feel like he'd miss him. But he smiled with the memory of Clay's affinity for town life. Maybe he hadn't gone far.

Storm clouds gathered low in the western sky, and the air chilled slightly. He'd probably be getting wet sometime in the coming night he guessed, but he was too close to home to care.

He pulled up the Appaloosa under a cool creekside stand of oaks and dismounted. It was getting late in the day, but he really didn't want to stop yet. This place would make a good temporary stop. He could water his horse and maybe have a bite to eat himself. It was a spot where travelers between Timber Fork and Fort Mason often stopped because of the handy access to water and firewood, and the remains of a fire were evident in a shallow pit surrounded by rocks. While the Appaloosa grazed, he walked around for a bit, chewing on a blade of grass and looking for anything interesting that someone may have left behind.

It was apparent that someone had been here only the previous night. The ashes in the firepit were cooled but not very old. He marveled at the coincidence. Not that many people traveled through here on a regular basis. There were no wagon tracks. It must've been just one person on horseback. He ventured closer to the creek, keeping an eye to the ground. There were hoofprints that belonged to the Appaloosa, made moments before when the horse had come to drink. Then he saw other hoofprints, at once distinguishable from his own horse's tracks. They belonged to an unshod horse.

His idle curiosity took on a serious note, and the blade of grass slipped from his mouth forgotten. He quickened his pace and studied the ground more intently, now searching for something in particular. There they were, a man's boot prints with a rounded toe and wide, flat heel. Instinctively he pulled his gun and backed up against one of the oaks, shifting his eyes in every direction. His quarry had been in this very spot. Could he still be here, watching Nate from a hiding place? He'd never forget Beartooth's sneaking up on him during a nighttime ambush five years before. No one but Beartooth could have outwitted him that way, and Nate had learned his lesson.

He sidestepped around the perimeter of the campsite, moving quickly between trees, looking and listening all the while. It was only a precaution. He sensed early on that he was alone here. Any hint of Beartooth's presence had faded, but he'd missed him by only hours. The brave was still keeping a close proximity to Nate. Except that this seemed odd. Beartooth wasn't following Nate this time; he'd been in this camp first. Nate searched for more tracks in about the place where a person might ride away from the camp. He had to circle out a ways to find any signs clear enough to read. He finally found one, the track of the unshod horse facing west. A few steps further in that direction and he saw another. He looked up at the western sky where the sunset would be hidden by the growing cloud mass. Why in the world would Beartooth be headed for Timber Fork, where there would be many people, people who would be alarmed and suspicious by the sight of a lone brave?

Gut-wrenching terror suddenly seized him. Beartooth wasn't headed for Timber Fork. He was riding directly to the Broken Bow. He was going for Tara and the children, and he probably knew that Nate wasn't there. In a foggy mental haze, he ran for the Appaloosa, swung up to the saddle, and kicked its flanks hard, sending the horse into a dead run.

Across the thinly wooded, grassy hills and towards the storm he raced, his mind numb with an uncommon fear. She had a derringer and a carbine, and the ranch hands were there. He let out a harried groan. Beartooth would not be put off by such minor hindrances. He slapped the horse's flanks again, a useless action, for he was already going as fast as he could.

"I need your help again, boy," he said, close to the Appaloosa's ear. "Tara needs your help. I know you can make this run." He willed the horse to understand, and he was sure that it worked, for it took small urging to keep him going.

Nate entered the fringes of the storm. The wind kicked up, and he felt raindrops against his face. Reining in his horse occasionally to spare him from being run to death was a challenging exercise in self-control, but he knew he'd be walking if he didn't. He hit the brunt of the storm well after dark. The Appaloosa slowed some. The blackness of the night was thick and suffocating. He could see nothing in front of him, but he trusted the instinct of the Appaloosa to keep the right direction. Great gusts of wind roared by him, and cold rain beat him and stung his face and neck. Lightning flashed and for brief moments provided the only light for passing landmarks. Then they were cloaked in darkness again as the thunder crashed.

He was soaked, but his mouth was dry as cotton from sheer panic. His thoughts tortured him, and helplessness overwhelmed him. He would never make it home in time. He knew he was riding fast only to see the results of Beartooth's rage. "Tara, I'm sorry!" he cried aloud. "I'm so sorry. Just stay safe so I can tell you that. You find a way." His words were lost in the wind. The darkness, the storm—all were taunting him with their massive control over his small fate. He buried his face in the horse's drenched mane. Brightness flickered out of the corner of his eye. He snapped his face upwards, trying to see something before the light went out again, but his tears blurred everything.

Chapter 26

Tara tossed another pitchfork full of straw into her horse's stall. It was good to be home again. She almost wished she'd never left. Busyness and the passage of time had worked before at healing wounds. Maybe they would again. Thunder rumbled in the distance, and she paid little attention. It was the close-by sound of footsteps that suddenly interrupted her thoughts. She whipped around, her heart pounding. She hadn't heard the barn door open. Elijah appeared in the dim lantern light, and she let out a breath.

"You startled me," she said with a smile, "again."

"Sorry, Mrs. Hunter," he chuckled. "Here, let me do that. The weather's gettin' bad out there. Why don't you go on up to the house and see to your guests?"

"All right." She handed him the pitchfork, and they brushed by each other in the doorway to the stall. She looked back at him, already bent over raking straw. "I'm sorry to have gotten you involved with those soldiers."

"Oh, don't worry 'bout that, ma'am. Just adds flavor to the day, that's all."

She stood still, reluctant to drop the subject so quickly. He stopped working and looked up at her.

"I suppose Mr. Tatum was the smart one, not wanting to get mixed up in it," she said.

Elijah clasped his hands over the handle of the pitchfork and rested his chin on it. "No, I think he missed out. I gotta tell ya, you and Mr. Hunter are nothing if not interesting. I don't expect to come across anything so eventful once I leave here."

"I'm glad you see it that way," she laughed, and he followed suit. She studied him thoughtfully a moment. "I do hope you'll find a woman to use that smile on."

"I'll try to do that, ma'am."

She nodded. "Good night."

"'Night."

Outside, the wind blew her skirt around her legs, almost unbalancing her. The rain began as she reached the front door of the house, and she was grateful for the light and warmth of the fireplace inside. Rebecca and Tara's sister Rachel greeted her with a cup of hot tea.

"You won't be able to make it back to town tonight," said Tara as she accepted the tea and took a sip. "Mother will know you decided to stay here."

"Yes, I'd just as soon play with the boys anyway," said Rebecca.

Tara was glad for their company. They had come as soon as they'd heard Tara had arrived home that day, but the time had passed so quickly she wasn't ready for them to leave yet. After a supper of beans, cornbread, and dried apple pie, and a rousing game of Blindman's Buff with Buck, Rebecca and Rachel tucked the boys into bed while Tara added wood to the fire.

The storm intensified. Wind whistled above the chimney, and rain pounded the western-facing window. Every lightning flash startled the women, then they laughed at themselves and marveled that the children could sleep through it. None wanted to admit their discomfort with the storm.

"We can have a girls' party," announced Rachel.

"Oh, yes," replied Rebecca, clapping her hands. "It's been so long since I've been to a girls' party."

"Tara, you go get some hair combs and ribbons," said Rachel. "We'll do each others' hair."

"All right," said Tara, "and you can tell us all your shocking secrets."

"I think she's seeing someone, but she won't tell us anything," teased Rebecca with a nudge against Rachel's shoulder.

A deafening crash of thunder silenced them. It was the loudest yet and seemed to shake the house. It had a faintly different sound, almost like something fragile breaking. The pecularity of the noise baffled them.

"What was that?" asked Rebecca.

None of them spoke, just listened. From the lean-to came a stomping sound and a door slam. Rebecca and Rachel's eyes grew wide.

Tara looked at them most seriously. "Ladies, have no fear. Mr. Medley is here."

Rachel and Rebecca burst into shrill laughter. Tara smiled and shook her head at them. They heard Elijah removing his boots.

"Well, his blankets have to be all wet," laughed Rebecca. "Doesn't that bother him?"

"And he never takes the night off," added Rachel. "He is absolutely undeterred, isn't he?"

"Shhh," Tara urged with a finger to her lips. "He'll hear you."

"I don't think she cares," Rebecca replied.

Rachel collapsed into a chair, laughing harder.

"I'm going to change into my nightgown," said Tara, "and I'll bring out nightgowns for you."

"Thank you," said Rebecca, "on behalf of myself and the insensible Rachel."

"I'll be back," said Tara, looking down at Rachel, "when you've grown up." She paused at her bedroom door. "Don't tell any secrets yet."

She entered her room and shut the door behind her. The room was surprisingly cold and the wind more audible than in the rest of the house. She even thought she could *feel* the wind in here. She groped for a match and lit the lantern on the dresser. Then she saw it. The window by the bed was shattered. A few small pieces of jagged glass still clung to the edge of the frame. Several shards of glass on the bed reflected the lantern light like a broken mirror. The wind changed direction, and a gust of rain blew in, adding instant wetness to the chill.

"Oh, no," she whispered shakily. She started to cross the room, watching for shards of glass on the floor. A shadowy motion caught her eye. She looked up to see a tall, muscular figure move noiselessly from the darkened corner. She gasped and backed up against the dresser, banging into it with a thud. The face that appeared in the lantern light horrified her. Black eyes full of hate stared at her from a scarred face partially obscured by clumped strands of stringy hair. She recognized him immediately. She had been present the day Nate's father had cut his face in a fight. The same face had later threatened her at knifepoint in a tepee. Her heart raced now as it did then, but she trembled far more deeply. She'd ended up in the tepee by her own doing, but this time he'd come, a great distance she guessed, especially for her.

She sidled along the dresser and felt behind her for the drawer that held the loaded derringer. He watched her like a hawk. She couldn't make a sudden move; he was poised to spring any second.

"The soldiers will not hang him." Beartooth's low, distinct voice sent shivers down her spine. "But he will still pay, and he will not like the price."

Her fingers shook so that she couldn't even grasp the drawer handle. A whimper escaped her throat; she swallowed hard.

"You need not fear, yet," he said through gritted teeth. "I will not hurt you, until *he* is there to watch. The soldiers would not give justice, so I will take it myself. I will begin where it will hurt him the most." His right hand went to a sheath at his side and slid out a knife. A lightning flash glinted off of the blade. "Where are the children of Eagle Shadow?"

Tara screamed. Like a lithe cougar, he sprang towards her. She took a quick breath and screamed again. Rebecca and Rachel burst through the door and shrieked as they saw Beartooth grabbing Tara around the waist and clapping a hand over her mouth. A gunshot rang out, Elijah shooting through the lock on the lean-to door. A second later he was there, ramming into Beartooth and throwing him down on the bed.

"Get the children out!" Tara yelled as she fumbled with the drawer handle.

Rachel disappeared from the room, but Rebecca stood paralyzed, hands over her mouth, engulfed in sobs.

Elijah jabbed the barrel of his gun into Beartooth's chest, but Beartooth's knife plunged into Elijah's exposed wrist, wringing a grunt of pain from his throat. The gun dropped to the floor, and blood spurting from his wrist soaked the quilt.

Tara held her derringer in both hands, which did little to steady it, and aimed. He was right in front of her. She couldn't possibly miss. The gunshot ripped through the chaos, the sound magnified by the small room. Beartooth lunged for

Elijah, but the bullet tore off his left earlobe before embedding itself in the opposite wall in a spray of splinters. He winced but hardly slowed down. While he grabbed Elijah with one arm, his other arm swung back and cleanly knocked the derringer out of Tara's hands, sending it across the room where it clinked against glass on the floor.

Elijah sunk an elbow into Beartooth's ribs and freed himself, then turned and attacked with both fists. Beartooth dodged the blows, while Tara shielded her head with her hands and attempted to scoot by them.

As Tara reached Rebecca and began to shove her towards the door, she heard the pace of the scuffle slow down. There was a ripping sound, a gasp, and a choking groan. She turned to see Elijah's eyes fixed on her while he tried to pull Beartooth's knife from his chest. "No, stop it!" she screamed. She beat Beartooth's forearms with her fists but couldn't budge them from the knife. Blood dripped from Elijah's mouth, and his legs started to buckle. He tried to make a sound but only gurgled. She knew he was telling her to run. Her tears blinded her as she turned and ran for the door. Beartooth caught her in the doorway with an iron grip around her waist. She grabbed the doorjamb and hung on for dear life, but it took him only a moment to yank her free. She heard sobs other than her own and knew he had Rebecca locked in his other arm.

He dragged them across the house like sacks. Tara desperately looked for Rachel and the boys but couldn't see them. The front door was wide open; she harbored a faint hope that they had already gone far enough to save themselves. She called on every ounce of strength to fight and kick as she was dragged through the door and down the porch steps into the rain. Their last hope was the ranch hands, if she could yell and make them hear her from the bunkhouse. She could scarcely breathe in his tight grip, but she struggled to take in enough air to make a sound. Suddenly a fist slammed into her left eye, and she landed in a heap on the sodden ground. She fought to keep her senses amidst throbbing pain in her head. Her strength was sapped; she could see only blackness. She felt like she was moving but didn't know how it happened. She tried to dig her fingers into the ground, something she could hold onto, but what she felt was not ground. It was wet animal hide and flexing muscles. Now she was being bounced mercilessly, and the jarring sound of galloping hooves filled her ears. She realized she was lying limp and face down across a horse's withers. The awkward position constricted her chest, and her lungs burned as she gasped for air. She had no control of her neck, and her face pounded horse flesh with every stride, like a rag doll. The pain in her head sharpened. She heard moans and didn't know if they came from herself or Rebecca, or if Rebecca was even still with her. Consciousness began slipping away, and she welcomed it.

Chapter 27

As the rain subsided, a break in the cloud cover revealed a few stars, and those soon faded as a hint of light filtered through from the eastern horizon. Nate had watered and rested the Appaloosa and was ready for the final run to the ranch. He had traveled through the night on no sleep, but he wasn't tired. The anxiety only deepened as he neared his destination, and he tried to steel himself for whatever this day might bring. How does one do that, he wondered. How could he possibly prepare for shock and grief of such magnitude? He shut the thought out of his mind. Better to avoid it and force himself to hope.

He dug his heels into the horse's sides. No more stopping. No more pointless thinking and imagining and torturing himself. He would soon know everything. He needed a clear head. Mile after mile the horse galloped, the rays of a rising sun chasing him till some buildings on the outskirts of Timber Fork appeared ahead. As he drew close, he caught sight of a horse tied to a hitching post in front of the bank. He pulled his reins; the Appaloosa skidded to a stop in front of the hitching post; and Nate was off and grabbing the reins of the other horse from a startled man whom he recognized as a Split Timber ranch hand.

"I need a fresh horse!" Nate exclaimed. "No time to explain."

The man consented before he fully comprehended what was happening, and by then, Nate was already far down the street.

The road to the Broken Bow was dotted with mud puddles, evidence of harrowing weather that matched what Nate had ridden through. Finally he could see his house. A few ranch hands were in the yard along with a wagon. There seemed to be a flurry of activity. He could not see Tara among them.

A couple of cowboys saw him approach and caught hold of his horse's bridle as he pulled back on the reins and vaulted to the ground. Then he saw the pair of feet, with bloody socks, protruding from the back of the wagon.

"What's happened here? Who is that?" All he heard for certain was that Tara and Rebecca were gone. After that he just heard snippets in an incoherent fog.

...Elijah stabbed...

...Rachel saved the children...

...safe in town with the Sinclairs...

...took 'em most the night to get there...

...soaked and cold...

...How can one Indian get away so fast with two women...

...We're leavin' to go after 'im...

The last one snapped his attention back to the present. "No! I go alone!"

"Not a chance, sir. We're with you every step. We'll bring those women back whatever it takes."

Nate pointed a finger in the man's face. "No, you will not! You don't know this Indian like I do. He doesn't care a bit who he kills."

Four cowboys stood facing him now, and they were adamant. "That's why you need help, Mr. Hunter. All us together can take 'im at once."

"That's right," said another. "I'd like to carve 'im up for what he done. The onlyest reason we hadn't left yet is we couldn't see a thing last night. Had no idea which way they went."

Nate sternly looked at each of them in turn. "Listen to me. I appreciate you wanna help, but soon as he figures out there's a bunch of us after him, he'll do somethin' to 'em for sure. This Indian's outsmarted me before. He'll outsmart every one of you."

Nate mounted the horse, and the hands backed out of his way, reluctantly resigning themselves to staying behind.

"I'm sure Jared's already left to find him," said Nate. "I need you men to go find Jared, wherever he is, and *get him home*. We don't need him gettin' killed. You make damn sure he doesn't leave town. I mean, you hold him down if you have to."

His tone sprang them into action. While Charlie Wilson climbed onto the wagon seat and the others went for their horses, Nate pointed his mount northward, towards the mountains. Something told him Beartooth would head in that direction, where he could hide, where he could slow Nate's pace. Through the wet grasses of Broken Bow ground he guided the horse, slowing where grass gave way to dirt to look for signs. He did spot the mud-filled track of the unshod horse. Nate could tell the Indian had traveled quickly upon leaving the house. They had gotten a head start of many miles and many hours. And all those miles and hours would give Nate more time to worry, to be careless, and to take more desperate chances.

He thought of Tara and Rebecca and how terrified they must be. Tara knew this Indian and thus knew what he was capable of. But she would stay strong for Rebecca, who was young, came from a city, and had never experienced anything close to this in her life. Tara would try to escape, but not without Rebecca, and he was sure they both couldn't get away.

The sun was drying the surroundings as he neared the north boundary of the ranch. He topped a rise, stopped, and looked over the vast land. His quarry seemed to be swallowed up in such a place. A wave of hopelessness overcame him. Beartooth would be expecting Nate to follow, but he wasn't going to make it easy.

His eyes settled on an object in the far distance. Its pale bluish color looked slightly out of place in the landscape. He clicked his tongue to urge the horse in that direction. As he descended the rise and crossed a little valley of tall grasses, a lonely breeze blew softly out of the west. There was no other sound. He saw more tracks of the unshod horse, all several hours old. He still wasn't gaining on them.

He lost sight of the object but kept progressing in that general direction. Finally he saw it again much closer. Whatever it was, it hadn't moved. He wondered if it was worth his while to even stop for this. He looked and listened around him. There was no immediate danger. He dismounted, left the horse ground tied, and walked through grasses down a gradual slope. In a spot just ahead, barren of grass, he saw it more clearly, the wrinkled folds of a pale blue dress. He broke into a run.

The sight stopped him abruptly—a limp, curled-up figure; muddy, matted hair; and the blood—an abomination so unspeakable he wondered if his eyes deceived him. In shocked horror, he covered his eyes with both arms and backed up as if pushed by an unseen force. "Please, God, not this," he weakly stammered. "No, no, no." He turned away, dizzy and sick. He tried to run, but his languid legs wouldn't hold him. He stumbled and fell. He couldn't draw a breath. He clutched his stomach as he vomited in the grass. He rose to his knees and sat back on his ankles, shaking all over. "No, no," he kept repeating to himself. His voice grew louder until finally, with the knowledge of what'd he'd seen sinking in, he lifted his head skyward and uttered a prolonged, guttural wail that carried on the wind and pierced the countryside like an arrow. It echoed against ridges and through shallow canyons, to anything living that could hear.

He rolled off of his ankles to a sitting position and pulled his knees tightly to his face. Rocking back and forth, his lament turned into great, heaving sobs that racked his entire body. There was no one around for miles. He was alone with the rocks, trees, and the big sky. No one heard his pain.

Chapter 28

Nate entered the Sinclair store to find that a large crowd of mostly men had gathered. A couple of women and Lena, now several months pregnant, lingered behind the counter, their hands on the shoulders of Margaret and Rachel Sinclair. The room fell dead silent as he entered.

"The boys are okay," said Rachel. She held a blanket around her shoulders, and her hair still bore traces of moisture.

His eyes met hers only briefly, indicating he'd heard her, but his appearance was jarring. He was covered in dirt and sweat; his face was devoid of expression, his eyes vacant as death. "Everybody out."

His quiet demand invited no argument. Everyone bustled towards the door, and the store was emptied in moments, except for the Sinclair women and Lena, and Clay Tatum who remained near the counter, as if he had some right to be there. Nate moved closer to the counter, laid his rifle down, and glared at Clay until he got the message. With a last glance toward the Sinclairs, Clay put on his hat and left the store.

When he heard the door slam shut, Nate looked up at the women, who waited, pale-faced and trembling, for him to speak. "Where's Jared?"

Rachel broke away from the others and rushed through the door leading to the attached house. She quickly returned with Jared, who looked drained but hopeful, until he saw Nate's face. He joined the women behind the counter.

Sliding one hand along the counter, Nate made the long walk down the length of it, around the end, and back towards the waiting family. Margaret and Rachel stood on either side of Jared, their arms linked with his, their fingers clasping him so tightly their knuckles turned white, their lips quivering. When Nate gripped Jared's shoulders with both hands, Jared swallowed hard, and a tear began to slide down his cheek. One of the women muffled a sob.

"Becca's dead. I found her."

"No, not Becca, no!" he wailed.

The women threw their arms around Jared as he started to crumple. As they sat on the floor, their sobs filled the room and gnawed at Nate's already-twisted insides. But his eyes remained dry. He'd passed through hell itself today and exhausted all of his emotions. He didn't even respond when Lena tried to hug him. He was past all feeling.

It was many long minutes later when Jared looked up at Nate again. "What—what did he do to her? Where is she?"

Nate met his gaze but did not answer.

"Where is she?" repeated Jared, his voice cracking. "I'm going to get her. I need to bring her home."

"I buried her where she lay." The stark severity in his voice silenced them all. "You leave her be, Jared. And don't ever ask me about it again."

Margaret Sinclair stood and struggled to get the words out through her sobs. "Is Tara alive?"

"Yes." Of that Nate was certain, even though he'd seen no sign of her. Beartooth would save her alive until Nate was there. Rebecca had gotten in the way and slowed him down. She'd simply been unlucky. But Beartooth would want to see Nate's reaction when he did whatever he was planning to Tara. He was out there somewhere, waiting for Nate.

In this he would not be disappointed, thought Nate. He walked back to the front side of the counter. "I need cartridges for the Colt and the rifle, and provisions for several days."

"I'll get the pr—provisions," sputtered Rachel, helping Jared up. "Come and rest in the house, Jared. We'll take care of you."

Margaret and Rachel left with their arms around Jared, and Lena looked for ammunition and tearfully watched Nate's preparations. He unbuckled his holster, reached for the ammunition she set before him, and slipped a cartridge into every open loop of the belt, then he opened the chamber of the Colt .45 and loaded it. After strapping the holster back on his hip, he opened the magazine of the partially loaded Henry rifle and inserted the balance of the fifteen rounds it would hold. Next he went on a quick look through the store, chose a leather shoulder cartridge belt with over seventy-five loops and filled those with rifle shells. He hung this over his shoulder, then searched the store for other items he could use. He set a sharpening stone on the counter, pulled his hunting knife and drew the blade across the stone several times, stopping to hold it up to the light and check the precision of the cutting edge. When he was satisfied with it, he replaced the knife in its sheath. He found a smaller knife with an ankle sheath, knelt on one knee, pulled up his right pant leg, and buckled it in place. The pant leg fell back over his ankle, completely hiding the knife. He stood to find that Lena had laid a hatchet on the counter, and he tucked it under his belt.

Rachel reappeared with a cloth sack which she set on the counter. As Nate reached for it, a movement out of the corner of his eye caught his attention. He turned to see little Buck standing close by watching him, trying to remain brave despite the confusing, frightening happenings around him. Showing the first stirrings of sympathy since he'd entered the store, Nate squatted in front of the boy and looked him square in his tear-filled eyes. "I'm going to bring back your mother."

The decisiveness in his voice comforted Buck, who held his head a little bit higher. "Yes, Pa."

Lena had moved up beside Buck and reached for his hand, but Nate stood and grabbed her elbow. He scooted her quickly to a far corner of the store, out of earshot of Buck and Rachel.

"If I'm not back in three days, send somebody to look for me. If neither Tara nor I make it back—"

"Don't say that," cried Lena, putting a finger to his lips.

He pulled her hand away. "Promise me you'll take my sons. I'd want them to go to you, not the Sinclairs." New tears coursed her cheeks, but he was unaffected. "Promise me."

"I promise," she weakly whispered.

He picked up the provisions and his rifle and left without another word. Outside, the curious crowd backed out of his way. The man with whom he'd traded horses earlier had brought the Appaloosa to the store, and Nate loaded the provisions on his own saddle, grateful to be reunited with his trusted horse for such an important journey. The Appaloosa's innate understanding of his hold on the reins would be the only ease afforded on this trip. He mounted and kicked into a gallop down the main street with Lena watching after him. She held her chin high, so no one would know how afraid she was.

He looked for Beartooth's trail north of the Broken Bow, leading in the direction of the rugged mountain country. He picked up the trail along Elkhorn Creek. This part might prove easy. He figured Beartooth likely, hopefully, followed the creek all the way to Mount Defiance. Nate knew that country well. He'd lived in it for two years and could still remember every ridge, ditch, creek, even every oddly twisted tree. But Beartooth knew that about Nate. If the brave was leading Nate to that country on purpose, it was because he wanted the satisfaction of outwitting him amidst the familiar.

As the land became steep and rocky, he found places where a horse had kicked rocks as it climbed, and as the creekside brush grew thick, he found plenty of broken twigs, evidence of a rider passing by. There were more of the broken and bent twigs than he would've expected from a seasoned tracker and hunter like Beartooth. His hope heightened with every sign he found as he now believed that Tara herself was purposely brushing against the bushes, leaving every sign she could for him to follow. Grateful that she was coherent and able enough to do that freed up his mind to concentrate on the job at hand.

The deeper into the wilderness he rode, the more vigilant he became. He couldn't allow himself to be in a situation where Beartooth watched him unawares. The trail briefly went through a draw, but Nate rode along the top edge of it. His lack of sleep began to catch up to him now. It took greater effort to remain alert. The sun was dipping low in the sky. Before long he would have to force himself to try to sleep. He must be in possession of all his faculties for a confrontation with Beartooth. How he abhorred the thought of leaving Tara overnight in the clutches of that ruthless killer. He took comfort in the fact that she was strong; she'd faced similar hardship before. She probably didn't know how close he was, but she would know he was coming and bide her time till then.

As the woods darkened, he looked for a place to grab a few hours of sleep. He opted to go up high and chose a spot on a heavily forested ridge. If Beartooth came toward him, he would have to climb up, and Nate would have a better chance of hearing him. He dismounted and forced down some cold biscuits and an apple. Then he opened his canteen and drank some cold water, the only thing that tasted good right now. He dared not build a fire. Beartooth surely was watching for him. He unsaddled the Appaloosa and left him to graze while he took his rifle and climbed into a nearby tree. He didn't doubt that Beartooth could walk up on him as he slept, and he wanted to remain above him if that was the case. Well off the ground and hidden by thick foliage, he found a large branch curved just right for resting. He settled into it, and with his rifle resting across his waist, his finger on the trigger, he waited for sleep.

It would not come easily. Darkness overtook the forest, and the usual sounds abounded—the breeze rustling the leaves, the song of crickets, an occasional nocturnal creature scampering around. He and the Appaloosa were used to them; the sounds alone couldn't affect his sleep. But his tortured mind could. As he stared up through the swaying branches and caught glimpses of stars in between leaves, horrendous thoughts plagued him—memories of what he'd seen that day, anticipation of what might lay in store...and the grinding guilt. If only he'd gone after Beartooth before going to Fort Mason. If only he hadn't assumed Beartooth would come after just him and not his family. It had been five years. Beartooth hadn't seemed to be in a big rush to meet up with him. Nate had mistakenly thought he still had time. He remembered Buck's face, struggling to be brave as Nate prepared to leave that afternoon. And Jack, a child too young to know what was happening around him. Then the shocking thought cut through his insides like a knife. *He waited five years on purpose. He waited till I had more that I could lose.*

This revelation sent Nate's mind reeling in a different direction. He was dealing with more than an angry renegade. The separation from his people had turned Beartooth into a cold, calculating killer. And Tara was with him this night. This endless night in which Nate was sure he would go mad. He wondered how much Tara knew of what had happened to Rebecca, if she had seen it happen. He shook his head, attempting to banish it from his mind.

Hate keeps us alive. It was Gray Wolf's voice he suddenly heard in his head. Nate figured he was sometimes right; it was hate that drove him to do now what he should've done before. He was surprised at just how many things Gray Wolf had been right about.

He shifted his position in the tree to combat the growing numbness in his back and one leg. He didn't realize he'd dozed off till a slight movement of the branch in the breeze jarred him. He looked and listened. The Appaloosa shook his head and mane and took a step in the grass but remained unbothered. Stars still shone through the leaves above him. Probably only minutes had passed as he dozed. His eyes closed again, for a little longer this time. Excruciating hours passed as he drifted in and out of a disturbed sleep.

Shortly before dawn, he sat up, wide awake and holding the rifle ready. Someone was in the woods nearby. Nothing but intuition told him so, but he trusted his intuition at least as much as his own eyes and ears. He stilled every muscle and waited for what seemed like thirty minutes or more. He'd developed extreme patience for situations such as this. To suppress anxiety like he was feeling for Tara was a challenge, but it could make the difference between life and death, hers and his. When the first morning light penetrated the atmosphere and dappled the forest floor, he studied every tree in his vision till he was certain not one of them concealed an immediate danger. Then he nimbly climbed down from the tree. When his feet touched ground, his horse instinctively came to him. He hefted the saddle with one arm and managed to strap it in place while still holding the rifle the whole time.

From this point on, he would not ride the Appaloosa but lead him by the reins instead. The experience he'd gained in the mountains had been on foot, allowing for quicker reactions and more mobility. He proceeded down the eastern slope of the ridge and stopped at the same spot by a creek where he'd filled his canteen the night before. He filled it again, looking as he did at the rocks strewn on the bank. He saw one that had been scooted from its original resting place in the damp soil. With the canteen tied back on the saddle, he bent over the rock and lifted it. A fresh footprint was pressed into the ground underneath. He looked further and found two more rocks concealing footprints underneath. Beartooth had been here that morning, not fifty yards from the tree where Nate had spent the night. The brave was alone, without Tara and without his horse, and he was looking for Nate.

Nate's heart sank. Beartooth probably left his horse wherever Tara was, and the only way she wouldn't use it to escape herself was if she was either tied up or hurt so badly she couldn't move. The mental image of that nearly unnerved him, and he struggled to rein in his thoughts. He must not break his concentration now.

The Appaloosa rubbed his forehead against Nate's shoulder, a sign that he was ready to move on. "All right, let's go, boy," Nate whispered. "We're getting close."

He led the Appaloosa back into thick foliage for cover and picked up his pace. Just ahead, a flock of blackbirds took flight, and he stopped abruptly. He wasn't close enough to have startled the birds himself. Beartooth had permitted a careless moment. Nate dropped to his knees as a gunshot rang through the woods and a bullet ricocheted off of the aspen trunk above his head. He whipped his own rifle against his shoulder and trained the sights on the spot from which the birds had flown. A head of black hair and buckskin-covered shoulders rose above the bushes and moved quickly away. Nate fired, chambered another round lightning fast, and fired again. Beartooth had already disappeared, making no sound. Nate grabbed his horse's reins and gave chase, almost at a run. When he came to the spot where Beartooth had been, he slowed down and watched for signs.

Tracks led across a clearing. Nate skirted the edge of the clearing, keeping to the cover of the woods. At any time Beartooth could turn back and be on the offensive again. Once more Nate spied movement ahead. When he got another clear view of the brave, he fired again. It was another miss. Beartooth fired on him twice more, but his aim wasn't even close. Nate guessed it was just a delay tactic.

Nate stopped trying to fire, although the temptation was strong to dispatch the brave at any opportunity. Beartooth was leading him to Tara. If Nate killed him too soon, he may have a devil of a time finding her, and he was sure now that she needed help. He figured that Beartooth never meant to engage him in a rifle match, and in fact, probably never meant for Nate to come up on him in the woods like this. The brave had been tripped up by his own impatience in wanting to see if Nate was on his trail.

Nate hurried faster, hoping the increased speed of the chase would cause Beartooth to become more reckless and make mistakes. It wasn't working. A couple of hours passed at a consistent stop-and-go pace, but the distance between them increased. At last Nate stopped, a little longer this time, to water his horse and give the situation some thought. They were in a narrow, pine-covered canyon. A creek strewn with granite boulders carved its way down the middle. They had gained considerable altitude during the chase. Mount Defiance loomed just southwest of him, and he knew that the ridge opposite him sloped down to a valley on the other side. Beartooth was leading him up high. He looked northward, where Beartooth had gone, and imagined the lay of the land in that direction as he remembered it. Less than a mile ahead, the canyon veered slightly eastward. Due north was a steep, thinly wooded slope where loose rocks made the way difficult. The top of the slope opened onto a small tableland, then to the west, it dipped back down into a sort of bowl, thickly wooded except for where a pool of water collected in spring and early summer, then dried up by autumn. That was where she was. He was certain of it.

But there was a quicker, less tedious route to get there. If he crossed the creek and climbed over the ridge, it would just be an easy hike on old game trails down a gentle slope till he reached the pond. Beartooth probably knew that but intended to wear him out on the tougher trail.

Nate scratched his horse's neck. "Let Beartooth wear himself out." There may even be a chance that he could beat the brave to the destination. He mounted the Appaloosa, crossed through water that came up to the horse's knees, then guided him up the side of the ridge.

***

Sitting on the ground with his legs crossed, Beartooth snapped off a few small pieces of dried branch and tossed them onto his campfire. Flames leaped up, casting a hot orange glow on the trussed-up, helpless figure curled on the ground beside him. He had just barely returned to his camp to find all was as he had left it. He glanced at her, a taunting smile playing on his lips. "It will still be a long time before he gets here. I lost him hours ago."

Her one good eye widened, but she was not looking at him. He followed her gaze, and his eyes also widened at the unexpected face that appeared through the smoke above the flames. The fire abated, revealing more of the buckskin-clad person with eyes boring down on him, eyes full of anger and purpose, but equally patient. He had seen Beartooth long before Beartooth saw him. But he had come, and he was ready.

Chapter 29

Tara's appearance shocked Nate. He had tried ahead of time to prepare himself for this moment, but his emotions were still rattled. Her left eye was swollen almost shut. Purple bruises covered half of her face, and dried blood from her lower lip coated her chin. Her muddy dress was torn over one shoulder and several places throughout the skirt. Her hands were bound behind her back with a coarse rope, as well as her feet, and she lay curled up on one side facing him. He'd recently been bound in the same fashion and could almost feel the strain on her shoulders and upper arms. He could not help her yet, but he knew there was only one thing she needed at this moment.

He mustered what calmness he could and looked unflinching into her face. "The boys are fine."

She gave a slight nod, and her whole body seemed to relax. Now he turned his full attention to her captor, his first good look at him since his banishment. He could instantly read in Beartooth's face and clothing what the intervening years had brought him. His scarred face had aged more than five years. Dirty, unkempt hair was tied back with a strip of leather. Half of his left ear was gone, a fresh wound crusted over with dried blood. He wore crude-cut buckskin trimmed with tufts of fur, bone, and feathers. His eyes flared with hate; his soul had become deadened to any other emotion. He was an empty shadow of his former self, and a poor representative of his former people, a proud and honorable people who called themselves 'beautiful' by their very name.

Beartooth looked from Nate to Tara and back again. "So your children are boys. You can be sure, when I have finished with you, I will find them and kill them, so they will not look for me when they are grown."

Nate had already stopped listening. In the most subtle way possible, he was taking stock of Beartooth's weapons, how many he had, how accessible they were. After five years of living by his own wits and mostly in isolation, Nate knew the brave would be proficient with whatever he had. He couldn't miss one trick from Beartooth.

The air grew tense as Beartooth began to taunt him, and Nate struggled to ignore him.

"Did you expect to find that other woman alive?"

He's got an old Winchester rifle, probably the same one that shot me. It was on the ground within Beartooth's easy reach.

"She screamed too much. It was easy to kill her."

A revolver on his hip. That was a newer acquisition, and he was probably good with it.

"She begged for mercy."

Tara's eyes were squeezed tightly shut, but tears still freely escaped. Nate's thoughts began to unravel, and he fought to control them. *He's trying to get to me. Ignore him.*

"You couldn't have saved her."

A hunting knife in a sheath on his other hip.

"But you weren't there to try, were you?"

I know there's a tomahawk somewhere. He couldn't see one, but what he'd seen the day before told him there was one. *Two guns, a knife, and a tomahawk.* In the brief moment that his and Tara's eyes caught each other, her eye darted down to Beartooth's lower leg, then back up at Nate. *He's got another knife strapped to his leg, inside his boot.* He was every bit as prepared for a fight as Nate was. Now Nate faced the daunting task of figuring out how to separate Beartooth from each of his weapons.

He noticed that Beartooth had moved to a squatting position, ready to spring. His eyes fell on the well-worn boots, split at the toes, that Beartooth wore.

"D'you get those boots off a dead cavalry teamster?"

"Don't tell me *you* care," laughed Beartooth. "I have more friends in the cavalry than you do."

"I've made more recently. Seems you're not on the payroll anymore, but I am, as soon as I'm done with you, that is."

Beartooth arched his eyebrows. "You think you can kill me? Down on the Sun River, thirteen moons ago, I followed you all the way to Red Feather's camp. You couldn't have even defended yourself. In the morning, I watched you sleeping by a river, close enough for my arrow to pierce your heart."

Nate hid the fact that he was stunned. He suddenly remembered that morning, when he woke up by the river with the feeling of being watched. His mind flashed back to the tracks he followed the same day. They'd gone into the river and back out again. He'd supposed it was to water the horse. But Beartooth had crossed the river at that spot and made his way to the butte, then returned the same way.

"I could easily have killed you," Beartooth was saying. "You're alive now because I *let* you live."

"You wouldn't have killed me then because you wouldn't have enjoyed it," replied Nate. "I'm alive now because of your sick hatred for me."

"And why should I not hate you?" snapped Beartooth. "You turned my people against me and made them listen to you. You were *never* as loyal to the people as I was, but you drove me away from them. For five winters I have lived like an animal. I am dead to all who knew me, but you, you have lived with no guilt for anything. You have your ranch; you have your woman; you have your children." He paused, and his eyes grew distant. "You have Red Feather's friendship. Red Feather was a great chief once. You have fooled him and made him weak. I have nothing. Did you really think I would forget that?"

In one fluid movement, Beartooth leaped up and over the fire. Standing as a wall of stone, Nate met the blow with his rifle held in front of him. He deflected Beartooth off to the side where he landed in a heap on the ground. Nate tossed his rifle aside and pounced on top of Beartooth. He did not even get in one punch before Beartooth threw him off and regained his footing.

As Nate paced in front of him, alert to Beartooth's every muscle twinge, the brave's eyes followed him intently. Beartooth unbuckled his holster and cast it aside, then watched and waited for Nate to accept the challenge. Without hesitation, Nate rid himself of his own holster as well as the shoulder cartridge belt. Knives suited him just fine. Beartooth was now separated from two of his weapons. So was Nate, but at least they were even—two knives and a hatchet, still possibly a tomahawk on Beartooth.

Out of the corner of his eye, Nate saw movement from Tara. She was wriggling and straining against the bonds, but she was held too tightly. She made no sound so as not to break his concentration, but he could feel her distress, and he wanted to finish this. He pulled his knife, and Beartooth did the same.

The hope Tara had felt when she first saw Nate across the fire now disintegrated. Blood would be shed in front of her, for the third time in two days. She knew that her life depended on the outcome of this fight. She'd watched Nate fight before, but her anxiety was no less intense this time. Again she yanked at the bonds. They wouldn't give an inch. She struggled to ignore the pain, clear her mind, and force herself to watch.

Beartooth lunged first, his knife held at an upward angle. Nate blocked his arm, and the brave retreated quickly. Two more lunges followed from Beartooth, two more quick retreats. He was feeling out Nate's readiness and skill. Nate would have none of it. The less Beartooth knew about his skill, the better. He decided on an all-or-nothing approach and launched a relentless attack on the brave. Swiping his knife so fast it was hardly visible, his enemy had no choice but to back away, but Nate stayed after him, determined not to stop till he'd drawn blood. Beartooth raised his arm to block one of Nate's blows, and Nate seized the opportunity to slash the inside of Beartooth's upper arm. Beartooth grimaced but came after Nate all the more aggressively.

Nate stood his ground and parried the blows, except one. Beartooth found an opening, and his knife plunged into the front of Nate's right shoulder, just under the collar bone. Searing pain shot through his shoulder and upper arm and took his breath away. He almost dropped his knife. Beartooth jerked the knife back out again, pulling Nate forward for a stumbling step and drawing a grunt of pain from his throat. He heard Tara crying and felt warm blood soaking through his shirt.

Like a wounded animal, he went after Beartooth again with renewed fury. He knew this injury would weaken him; he must act quickly. He ignored the burning pain that accompanied every move of his arm. He drove for Beartooth's chest, but when the brave effectively guarded himself, he dropped down and cleanly sliced open his leg above the knee. The unexpected move stunned Beartooth, and he staggered backwards and fell. Nate dove on top of him, but Beartooth was ready for him. He caught Nate and threw him to the ground beside him. Nate hit the ground hard and rolled onto his stomach. Just as he did, a penetrating blow to the back of his right shoulder paralyzed him for an instant. He heard a prolonged moan and didn't realize at first that it came from him. Excruciating pain engulfed him. He heard Tara screaming his name as if from a far distance. He didn't know Beartooth's knife was in his shoulder until it was yanked out again.

His back was to the enemy, the worst position to be in. He rolled himself onto his back, holding his knife above him. As he did, Beartooth's bloody knee thrust itself into his stomach, knocking the wind from him. He thrashed with all his might till he could draw a breath. Trapped beneath the enemy, he was keenly aware of the danger he was in.

Beartooth's left hand clamped down over his right wrist. Nate maintained his hold on his knife but couldn't fight the pressure Beartooth exerted on him. Beartooth raised his own knife over Nate, but Nate's left hand caught his wrist and held it away from him. They remained poised in that position for a ceaseless moment, connected in a brute test of strength. But Beartooth was losing blood from his right arm while Nate's left arm was uninjured. Slowly Nate twisted the brave's arm away till he forced Beartooth off of him, then they each raced to beat the other to his feet.

Nate stood first. He took advantage of the brief head start and lunged toward Beartooth, taking backhanded jabs with his knife. On one jab, the brave caught his wrist and forced it down over one of the rocks lining the campfire. As the metal struck stone, the old knife snapped cleanly in two near the hilt. Beartooth backed off, gloating on his coup. Nate looked at the knife stub for one horrified instant, then he dropped it and grabbed a large stick from the fire. Beartooth's eyes widened, and he backed up, but Nate swung the flaming end of the stick, striking it hard against Beartooth's scarred cheek. The brave yelled in pain, but Nate stayed after him, battering him again and again till Beartooth turned and ran for the nearby pond. It was then that Nate saw the tomahawk, tucked into the back of Beartooth's belt.

Racked with burning pain, the brave blindly plunged into the water with Nate close behind. Nate dropped the stick and dove on top of him, attempting to dislodge the tomahawk. He had one chance to try for it before Beartooth knew what was happening. He couldn't grab hold of it fast enough. Beartooth writhed free, and Nate fell backwards into the water. Suddenly Beartooth was on top of him again, holding him underwater by his neck and forcing his chin upwards. Nate lay with his back on the rocky bottom of the pond, only a foot of water over his head, but it was enough to drown him quickly if he couldn't escape Beartooth's iron grip over his neck.

Nate struggled in a flurry of splashes and bubbles. He could see nothing but red-tinted water and didn't know whose blood it was. He heard a distant scream, its sound muffled by his watery trap. He desperately needed a breath; he had merely seconds. Pushing against Beartooth with his left arm, he forced his weakened right arm in between their flailing bodies and closed his hand on the hatchet at his waist. He exerted every ounce of strength he could muster to pull it out, extend his arm, then swing it out of the water and down onto Beartooth's back. He felt the brave's chest vibrate with a grunt of pain, and the hold on his neck loosened. He swallowed a mouthful of water just as he broke free and dragged himself, coughing, onto dry ground.

The hatchet had slipped from his grasp and was somewhere on the bottom of the pond. He wasn't going back in that direction, he decided. But there, on the ground within his reach, was Beartooth's knife where the brave had absently dropped it before falling into the water. Experiencing a small measure of relief at this discovery, he lunged and grabbed it. From the corner of his eye, he saw Beartooth grabbing the stick with which Nate had burned him. Nate rushed to regain his footing and get out of the way, but the wood crashed down on his right ankle with a sudden force that felt like a tree falling on him. He yelled and wanted to grab his ankle, but he knew to expect more blows if he didn't move fast. Once he was back on his feet, Beartooth stopped his advance.

Nate attempted to hide his agonizing condition. Standing up had brought on a wave of dizziness, but he blinked and willed it away. He shifted his weight, favoring his throbbing sprained ankle. His wet clothes clung to him, and he could no longer tell the difference between blood and water dripping down his body. Another coughing spell overtook him; he hadn't been able to catch a sufficient breath since having the wind knocked out of him. Black spots appeared in front of his eyes, and he felt his stance wavering. He was mildly aware of Tara speaking to him, but her words were lost in a fog. The next thing he knew, he was on his knees, clutching his stomach and throwing up water and blood. It felt as if his insides were coming out, but at least there was a momentary relief. He looked up, expecting Beartooth to be upon him, but the brave was faring no better than he was. Beartooth was faltering. Blood was beginning to puddle on the ground at his feet.

Tara's voice came through to Nate now, strong and encouraging. "Nate, you can do this. He is weakening. You'll have no better chance than now. Get him!" She saw Beartooth reaching behind his back. She knew what was there. Nate knew too, and he rushed forward to stop him, knowing he wouldn't reach him in time.

"No!" Nate yelled as the tomahawk sailed end-over-end through the air. At the last possible second, she rolled aside, and the tomahawk hit the ground with a thud, pinning her dress down with it.

Nate changed direction now, jumping over the firepit and landing at Tara's side. He figured Beartooth didn't have anything left to throw, and he would have a few seconds, using Beartooth's knife, to cut the rope from Tara's wrists. Tara held still while he rapidly sliced through the two loops of rope, all the while keeping one eye on the enemy. Just as her hands fell free and she sat up, he stood to meet Beartooth's advance. There was no time to grab the tomahawk first. With Nate positioned in between Beartooth and Tara, and brandishing a knife, Tara seized the chance to sit up and untie her ankles.

Beartooth stood with empty hands, making false starts with Nate matching each one. The brave dodged to the left; Nate dodged to his right. Then the other direction. There was no way around Nate to get at Tara.

Tara had now freed her ankles and yanked the tomahawk from the ground. She sprang forward, reaching the tomahawk behind her as she did, then with a mighty force she swung it around toward her intended target. Beartooth evaded the blow, then answered her offense with one of his own. In the blink of an eye, he drew the knife at his ankle, knocked the tomahawk from her hand, snatched her around the waist, and held her firmly against him with the knife at her throat.

Nate simultaneously discarded the knife and grabbed his own gun from the holster lying at his feet. Beartooth froze as he found himself staring down the barrel of the Colt .45 less than ten feet away.

"You cheated," said Beartooth.

"So did you." He cocked the trigger.

Beartooth's grip on Tara tightened, and the knife pressed harder on her skin. Her lips quivered, and she, too, stared at the gun.

"Your arm is weak," said Beartooth. "You can't shoot straight."

"I wouldn't bet on it." He held his arm steady and squinted down the sights at the brave's head. From the corner of his eye, he saw Tara's lips move. She was mouthing words to him. He switched his gaze to her long enough for her to repeat the words.

"Take the shot," she silently begged, a tear coursing down her dirt-smudged cheek. The fight had vanished from her. She knew her children were safe, and she no longer cared about anything else.

He only had one chance. He studied Beartooth's hands. They were poised, ready to jerk Tara into the line of fire in an instant. He looked into the brave's eyes. They were solidly fixed on Nate's trigger finger, ready to detect the faintest movement and react. Beartooth was completely unfazed by any pain he felt, unaware of any blood loss. The point of his thin blade held steady against her neck, and it was clearly hurting her.

Nate fought to ignore his own pain and the growing weakness in his arm. He must follow through with this now. If he lowered the gun, Beartooth would cut her throat in that instant. He kept his trigger finger dead still, but while Beartooth was watching his finger, it was Nate's eyes that were doing the work. The dizziness and black spots were gone by sheer force of will. He focused on the gun sights till they appeared in sharp relief against the brave's face.

The gunshot was sudden and deafening. The bullet ripped off Beartooth's right ear and grazed his head. He wheeled around and fell, and Tara dashed away, covering her mouth and breaking into sobs. Back beside the firepit, her legs gave out, and she sat in the dirt, gasping for breath between sobs. Her pounding heart seemed nearly audible. She rubbed her good eye with the palm of her hand, to clear away enough tears to see. Nate was jumping on top of Beartooth with the tomahawk in his hand. But only she could see that Beartooth was not unconscious.

"Look out!" she rasped in a failing voice.

In one fluid movement, Beartooth threw Nate down on his back and rolled on top of him. Nate writhed to free himself. Tara's eyes blurred again; Nate was pinned in an odd position. She couldn't tell what he was doing. Beartooth still clutched the knife he had held to her throat. Now he was raising it high above his head for the final stab. She heard it go in, a sickening thrust through flesh and muscle. She became lightheaded and tried to scream, but no sound came out. Then she saw the knife still in Beartooth's hand, and his wide, stunned eyes. The knife slipped from his grasp, and blood poured from his mouth in a steady stream. Nate pushed the brave off of him, and she caught sight of the knife stuck deep in Beartooth's chest, the one Nate had discreetly pulled from the sheath at his ankle.

"This is for Rebecca," growled Nate. "And this..." His left hand brought the tomahawk down squarely onto Beartooth's back. "...is for Elijah."

Tara flinched. She had wondered and hoped against all hope that someone had found Elijah and helped him before it was too late. Now she knew for certain. The shy wrangler was gone.

Within seconds Beartooth breathed his last, and Nate finally relaxed on his back, staring up at the sky and panting heavily. Tara shakily stood up, and with fury now replacing her fear, she picked up one of Beartooth's knives from the ground and started for him.

Nate saw her bending over the brave's head and knew what her intentions were—to do what she had seen done to Rebecca.

"No, stop!" he yelled as he tried to reach for her. "Not you. Don't let him poison you." She stopped but wouldn't drop the knife. He swallowed and gasped for a breath. "If it was anybody else...I'd say go ahead, and I'd help 'em.... But not you. You're better than that."

"No, I'm not," she cried.

"Yes, you are. Think of Buck and Jack."

At the mention of her boys, she dropped the knife, and Nate breathed his relief.

She came to him then, pulled open his jacket, and peeled away the wet, blood-stained shirt to see the wounds. She bit her lip at the severity of the front shoulder wound. Looking up, her eyes scanned the surroundings. "Did you bring the Appaloosa?"

"He's tied in that stand of cottonwoods…past the pond."

"I'll be right back." She located the horse quickly and led him back to Nate, then untied a blanket and brought that and the canteen over to him. He had rolled onto his side and was shivering. "Help me get your shirt off."

He slowly pulled himself to a sitting position and let her peel the wet shirt from his body. Then she wrapped the blanket around him, and he experienced some small relief. He watched her as she took Beartooth's knife, cut a section from the hem of her dress, and started wrapping it around his shoulder, covering both his front and back wounds. He became dizzy and had trouble focusing on her; she kept moving fast, and it bothered him.

"You're not well yourself," he muttered. "Your eye…"

"I will be all right. My eye will heal, but we've got to get you home as soon as possible. Here, drink some water."

"I already drank half the pond."

"Don't try to be clever now." She moved about the campsite, gathering up all of his weapons and packing them on the horse. When she handled the Colt .45, she paused to look at him. "I knew you could make the shot."

"I never wanna have to make such a shot again."

Even with only half of her vision, she could see that his strength was waning. She looked back at the Appaloosa that would have to carry both of them. Beartooth's bay horse was grazing far beyond the campsite, but she quickly closed her eyes to it. She would, under no circumstances, ever go near that horse again.

Nate sensed her thoughts and whispered, "I'll get on first…and take the reins." To reassure her, he attempted to hide his pain and force himself to rise. She helped him mount the horse, then he reached his good arm down and helped her on behind him. The ride ahead would be a long one, and he desperately hoped the horse could find his way home. "Just please get us home, boy…and then I'll let ya rest for a week." He took hold of the saddle horn to steady himself and urged the horse onward.

Back up the game trail away from the pond they rode, then over the ridge Nate had crossed earlier and down the narrow canyon. It was slow going, and every step brought Nate more twisting, jarring agony than the last. Tara held onto him tightly and steadied him the many times he swayed in the saddle or started to fall asleep. She knew she ought to talk to him to keep him awake, but her ordeal so drained her that any words were difficult. Horrifying images were now branded into her memory; she wondered if she would ever be free from their frightening hold. She did not want to return home, where Elijah's last moments had been spent inside her house. She dreaded seeing her mother's home, where a smiling Rebecca would never greet her again. All that kept her sitting on the horse behind Nate was the need to comfort her sons. They would need her more than ever now, and she must also try to get Nate back to them alive.

A sudden jolt smashed her train of thought. The Appaloosa had tripped on a loose rock. She gasped when she saw how close they were to a steep embankment. The horse fought for a foothold and partially recovered, then again succumbed to sliding dirt under his hooves. Nate and Tara both leaned toward the uphill side, but the momentum of the falling horse was too much. The Appaloosa's terrified whinny echoed off the mountainside as he tumbled downward. Tara lost her hold on Nate and cried out as she felt herself falling backwards with nothing to hold onto. She was thrown clear of the horse and slammed against a bush, preventing her further fall down the embankment. Nate hit the ground in front of her. Amidst an avalanche of stones and dirt and flailing hooves, she saw the horse's flanks crash onto Nate's sprained ankle. He yelled in pain, once, then was quiet. She covered her head with both hands as the whinnying Appaloosa rolled past her, the hooves just missing her body.

A moment later, the stones and dirt stopped sliding, and an eerie silence settled on the mountainside, broken only by Tara's soft, breathless weeping. She lay still a little longer, wondering if she was hurt and hadn't discovered it yet. Then she slowly and cautiously rose to her hands and knees and crawled towards Nate, who lay face down with his arms above his head and hanging onto a bush. She saw that his ankle was twisted into a grotesque position, and he was moaning but not moving. When she laid a hand on his back, he moved slightly.

Another sound distracted her, some low, rumbling grunts from the Appaloosa at the bottom of the embankment. She turned to see the horse lying on his side. He raised his head briefly, then put it back down. As she scrambled down the embankment, she could already glimpse the severe injury to the Appaloosa's right front leg. She felt down the leg with both hands and gasped in disbelief. It was broken in several places. She was already numb with grief and didn't know it was possible to be even more so, until now. She had never killed a horse before, had never seen it done. The Appaloosa's pain-racked eyes were watching her as his body writhed, and it tore her heart to pieces. This was going to devastate Nate too. They had never known a more loyal horse.

She closed her eyes tightly and fought off her emotions. To delay wouldn't do her or the horse any favors. She climbed back up to Nate, pulled the Colt from his holster, and held it carefully while she scooted back down the slope. She muffled her sobs while she patted the horse's neck one last time, then she pulled back the hammer with both hands and held it against the Appaloosa's forehead. Her eyes clouded with tears, and her hands shook. She wiped her eyes enough to see where the barrel of the gun pointed. She didn't want to have to fire but one shot. It was in the right place. She pressed it hard with one hand to avoid having it slide out of position, and buried her face in the crook of her other arm. She squeezed the trigger. The earsplitting gunshot startled her as if she hadn't expected it, and she cried out.

Nate was jerked awake by the gunshot and turned to look. Horrified by the sight that met his eyes, he lashed out in anger. "No, not my horse! What did you do that for?"

She chanced a peek at the horse through her fingers, just enough to make sure the deed was done, then she made her way back up the slope. "Nate, he was finished. His leg was shattered. There was nothing to be done."

"My ankle's broken too," he growled. "You gonna shoot me too?"

"Stop it!" she sobbed. "Just stop it!"

He turned away to hide an escaping tear. The Appaloosa had been his closest friend for months. The pain of losing him every bit equaled the physical torture that held his body captive now.

When Tara crested the embankment, she tugged on Nate's good shoulder and his jacket, and with his exertions coupled with hers, he was soon back on level ground. They were both silent as they struggled to catch their breaths.

"We've hit a run of bad luck, haven't we?" said Nate finally.

"Yes, but I'm going to splint your ankle and make you a crutch, and you're going to hike out of these mountains with me."

There was a long pause. "All right," he said at last. "I'll give it a try." He much preferred to be left with his horse, but he would let her help him anyway. It would keep her mind occupied, he figured, and help *her* to get back home.

Chapter 30

As dusk settled on the mountains, Nate and Tara had tediously made their way across miles of wilderness. The ankle splint she had made from a piece of wood tied with a strip cut from his shirt was holding up so far, and he had helped to chop a forked branch from a ground-level bush as he lay next to it. Although a bit short, it was thick and strong enough to serve as a temporary crutch. Promising him she'd send someone back for the saddle, she'd gathered up the food sack, canteen, and rifle and thrown the blanket around his shoulders.

She tried talking to him as she helped him along with her arm around his waist. It was all nervous chatter and, with fatigue setting in, didn't always make sense. He didn't seem to notice.

He could think only of his horse being left behind to rot on some remote mountainside. His fevered mind alternated between cursing the Appaloosa for this predicament and mourning him. It was the Appaloosa who had carried his sick family to the Cheyenne, proved his worth on buffalo hunts and kept him company during long months away from home, provided him with an impressive entrance into the fort, then ran his heart out that stormy night to get Nate home. Thinking on that, Nate turned to cursing himself for not being able to do better for his faithful horse in the end.

They reached a clearing divided down the middle by a narrow stream partially hidden by tall grasses. It was here Nate reached his limit. "I can't go any further," he whispered. "There's a rock overhang just over there."

"There's still daylight left. We can't stop."

"I have to lie down for just a little while." Despite her objections, he stopped by the rock and eased himself to the ground with his blanket.

"Nate, if you go to sleep, you won't wake up again," she warned, her voice breaking.

He opened his eyes. "Yes, I will. I just need to rest a couple hours." She was still skeptical, and he sharpened his gaze at her. "You have my word, I *will* wake up, and I will walk out of these mountains myself."

The grim determination in his voice gave her a small degree of confidence, and she proceeded with gathering kindling and lighting a small fire. He was asleep by the time she was finished, and she lay next to him and tried to sleep herself. But the fire did little to fend off the frightful chill within her. The sounds of a wilderness nighttime, though she'd experienced them before without trepidation, now seemed louder than ever. She felt very close to being alone here. She turned her thoughts to her children. Buck must surely be worried and wondering if he'd see his parents again. How she longed to enfold them in her arms.

She dozed only when she could no longer keep her eyes open. It seemed that only minutes had gone by before she was awake again. Nate had not moved. The fire had dwindled to weak, glowing coals, drawing the darkness of the night ever closer. She wondered if she should try to wake him but decided against it. They couldn't go anywhere anyway, till there was some light.

She didn't have to wait long. He stirred and groaned for the pain so little movement caused.

"We'll go now," he suddenly whispered.

Her heart gave a tiny leap. One small victory. He would get up again, without her urging.

His short rest had made him more clear-headed than she thought. He knew another day would pass before anyone came to look for them, and small chance they had of being found when someone did search. Nate was the best tracker around. A couple of Broken Bow hands were fair hunters and could be somewhat useful. That was about it. It was up to him to get them back soon.

They pressed ahead through darkness. Nate seemed to instinctively know the right direction, and she trusted him to lead. She only held onto him to keep him moving. Their progress was harrowingly slow, but by the time it was fully light, the mountains were beginning to flatten, leading to the valley close to home.

When they stopped to rest and she forced him to eat yet another biscuit, he chewed one dry mouthful and swallowed it. Then he sat still, looking at the ground. "You haven't said anything about what's happened to you in the last couple days."

"I don't want to think about it."

"When did you get the black eye?"

"When he first dragged me from the house that night."

He looked up at her eye, then at her muddy and torn dress. He drew in a breath to speak but had difficulty uttering the words. He closed his eyes and swallowed hard. "Did he…did he…"

"No, he did not. He would've had to kill me first."

He let out a breath of relief. "Thank goodness."

But she was not feeling thankful. She covered her mouth, and her shoulders began to shake. Her own unfinished biscuit fell to the ground forgotten. "I tried to save her, Nate. I tried." She burst into uncontrolled sobs. "I fought as hard as I could."

He reached for her with his good arm, and she fell against his shoulder. "You couldn't have done anything," he said. "I know that." His heart was breaking all over again for her, for the memories inside her that he would never be able to erase. "You cry all you want to now. And then we're gonna have to put this behind us. That's all we can do."

She continued to cry, until she felt his fevered body begin to shiver, a reminder that they must push for home while he had any strength left at all.

By afternoon they were trudging along a little-used road to Timber Fork, marked only by two faint wagon wheel ruts. He still leaned on the crutch with his right shoulder and kept his left arm around her shoulder while she held him around the waist. She had long since run out of words to distract him. She was ready to give out herself. She no longer measured their progress by landmarks but by each small, laborious step. His head hung low, and he moaned with every step now. He little realized his weight against her was increasing as he let up on the crutch with his injured shoulder.

They were so close, yet seemed so far. She fervently wished for a wagon to come by and help them. When she heard the creak of wagon wheels in the distance and a horse's nicker, she was sure it was in her mind. She'd imagined it so hard it seemed real. But she looked up and saw a cloud of dust far up the road in front of her.

"Nate, a wagon!"

He looked up and squinted but had no strength to react.

"You wait here. I'll go on ahead and wave him down."

He willingly dropped the crutch and sat in the grass, more relieved for her than for himself. Her journey was almost over. He had kept his promise to Buck to return his mother to him.

Soon the wagon pulled up beside him, and he saw Ward Taylor jump to the ground beside Tara.

"Don't tell me you're the best tracker they could get," Nate said as Ward helped him up.

"I volunteered," replied Ward.

Nate wondered why Ward didn't seem to be in the mood for the usual teasing. As they helped him into the back of the wagon and he lay down on his back, he thought he heard Tara whisper, "I fear he doesn't know how badly he's injured."

Nate attempted to reply, but the wagon lurched forward, momentarily stealing his breath. The rattling, bouncing wagon was torturous on his weary body. The ride was unnatural, and it took him awhile to realize that the horses were running. As he floated in and out of a painless blackness, he was briefly aware of the wagon coming to a sliding stop, then many hands under his back carrying him up a flight of stairs and laying him on a bed, and lots of indecipherable voices. Where were they coming from? What were they saying? It was all confusing, but he stopped trying to make sense of it. Sleep beckoned.

Chapter 31

Nate's attempts to sleep were continually interrupted by the distant-sounding voices and the hands that poked his shoulder and leg. He tried to tell them to stop, to no avail. Then a shooting pain seized his ankle and wouldn't let go. A yell escaped his throat, but then he slept.

When next he awakened, the room was dark except for a dim lamp by the bed. Thankfully, all the people were gone, and it was quiet. He couldn't remember ever feeling so drained and weak. It took a major effort to turn his head to the side where he saw Tara sitting beside him and smiling down at him.

"Welcome back," she said, placing a cold, wet cloth on his forehead.

He smiled in return. "Your eye is looking better."

"Yes, the swelling's gone down."

"The doctor was here?"

"Yes. He stitched up your wounds and set your ankle."

"I vaguely remember. I don't think I liked it."

"You didn't. You punched him, and he refused to continue until Jared, Ward, and Major Blaine all held you down."

He managed another smile. "Well, I hope he learned his lesson." Moving only his eyes, he looked at his surroundings. "Where are we?"

"We're in Mother's house."

"Is this your old room?"

"Yes."

"Ah," he sighed, "the many nights you must have lain in this bed thinking about me."

"Mm-hmm, right. You just think on that." She stood. "It's almost morning. Buck wanted me to wake him when you woke up. I'll bring the baby too."

The reunion with his sons gave Nate an immediate surge of strength. At last, all of his family together in one room. But it was in the midst of a hug from Buck that, now fully awake, he realized something Tara had said.

"Did you say Major Blaine was here?"

"Yes. He'll come see you again, maybe tomorrow."

"Oh, good grief," he groaned, scooting Buck off of him and rubbing his temple. "He has the worst timing. I bet it's something to do with that Gatling gun."

Tara smiled as she shook her head. "I don't think so."

***

Just as expected, Nate found himself the recipient of a visit from Blaine the following day. He was sitting up in the bed by now, propped up by several pillows, his shoulder in a sling. He didn't hear any of the major's small talk. Something was different, and he was trying to figure out what it was. Then it dawned on him, and he interrupted whatever Blaine was saying.

"I don't think I've ever seen you out of uniform, Major."

"I resigned my commission."

Nate was suddenly taken with a coughing fit, but soon recovered. *"You?"*

"That's right. I found better opportunities elsewhere."

Completely at a loss as to why Blaine could drop such news and not offer an explanation, Nate fumbled for words. "Well, c'mon, I mean...what happened? You weren't happy with the cavalry?"

"I just found better opportunities elsewhere."

Nate stared at him, but he guessed that he wasn't going to get Blaine to admit anything about the cavalry. "So you found better opportunities. Here, of all places?"

"I've accepted the position of the first sheriff of Timber Fork."

Nate covered his face and uttered a frustrated moan. "Oh, of course. That's great. Just what I needed."

Blaine chuckled. "It's not as bad as all that."

"I suppose going after Beartooth like I did is against the law."

"Yes, the proper thing to do would have been to form a posse, deputized by me. But anything before now doesn't apply."

Nate laid his head back on the pillows and beheld Blaine through half-closed eyes. "You didn't come here just to tell me that worthless news. There's something else."

"Yes. You and I haven't been on the best of terms throughout all this."

"Well, that's a nicer way than I would've said it," replied Nate, rolling his eyes.

"I know, I know. I came to try to make amends. I hardly know where to—"

"Why do you always do that when I'm in bed, trapped, and I have to listen to you?"

"I don't always do that." Blaine shifted uneasily in his chair. Even while bedridden, Nate's gaze had a way of piercing him to the soul. "I only remember one time, long time ago," he conceded. "But I bear you no ill will. Julie wanted me to tell you she doesn't either. After all, we're going to be neighbors."

"I don't have to be neighborly."

"Come on, Nate, we have to get past this. Don't let this destroy you. Don't become like Beartooth."

At this, Nate's eyes flew open and flashed with anger. "If I weren't in this bed, I'd punch your teeth out for that."

"I'm sorry. That was..." Blaine held up a hand in surrender and shook his head. "That was the wrong thing to say. Listen, I'll come back when you're feeling better."

Nate had summoned a reservoir of strength and was already halfway out of the bed. "No, let's get this over with now."

"I'm not gonna fight you, Nate. Simmer down." He waited till Nate lay back down. "I made mistakes, and I well know it, some big ones. So did you. I'm trying to fix mine. That's why I left the cavalry."

Nate closed his eyes, reflecting on all the recent losses…and his overwhelming guilt. "I can't fix mine," he whispered.

"Well, don't make another one now. If there's one thing I've always been able to say about you, it's that you've always been fair with people. The reason you didn't go after Beartooth long before now is because he hadn't done anything to you. He'd already paid for what he did to you years ago. You didn't owe him any revenge."

Nate was surprised that Blaine should so precisely pinpoint what was bothering him, and he even began to appreciate the words of understanding. It made it just a little easier to do what he'd told Tara they must do in putting this all behind them. He cast a sidewise glance towards Blaine. "I ain't callin' you Sheriff."

"That's fine. You can call me Josh."

"All right, Josh." Nate liked the sound of that much better. "Let's see if you mean business. The doctor said I could have some whiskey for the pain, but Mrs. Sinclair wouldn't give me any. Will you get me some and sneak it up to me?"

"Sure."

"And tell my ranch hands I want somebody to go into mine and Tara's bedroom and tear up the floor where it's covered with blood and put in new boards. I want it done before Tara goes home."

"All right. I'll do that."

***

Nearly a week later, Nate and Tara were ready to return home to the Broken Bow. Tara's eye was less sensitive, and the black and blue had faded to a pale yellow. Nate was getting around well enough with a crutch.

Tara sat in the wagon in front of the store with Buck and Jack, and Margaret and Rachel went back inside. Only Jared stood in front of Nate beside the wagon.

"I wanted to thank you for going after Beartooth, Nate."

Nate nodded and stood quietly for a moment. He hated leaving the Sinclairs yet, to try to resume their daily doings. "You gonna be okay, Jared?"

"Yeah, I'll make it. Becca would want that, you know."

Nate took heart in his determination. The Sinclairs knew what it was like to live a relatively easy life, but even so, the whole family had always had an uncommon constitution that fitted them for the frontier, and Nate admired them for it.

He awkwardly struggled aboard the wagon and took the reins. Their route took them down the length of the main street, then up to the cemetery on the hill behind the town. It was a quiet spot where weeping willow trees graced straight rows of tombstones. From here, one could see all of Timber Fork and many miles beyond, yet it was shielded from the busyness of the town by its distance and afforded a place for contemplation. Nate and Tara both knew almost everyone buried here, but their destination today was the fresh grave on which no grass yet grew. Elijah Medley's headstone bore nothing more than his name and date of death, for so little had been known about him.

"I need to tell them to put 'Savannah, Georgia' on it," said Tara as she stood beside the grave.

"I don't know of any family that needs to be informed about Elijah," said Nate. "Did he ever mention anyone to you?"

"No. I don't think there was anyone." She fought the lump that tried to form in her throat. "He was only going to stay long enough for us to replace him. I wish I'd let him go sooner."

"He may have saved our boys' lives. I'll always be grateful to him." He had carried a small book from the wagon, and he looked down at it now. "Charlie Wilson brought me his effects. He didn't have much. But this was something of yours he borrowed."

She took the book from him and looked at it. "Tennyson. He borrowed this a long time ago. I forgot he had it." She idly flipped through the pages, and a folded piece of paper fell out into her hand. Opening it, she recognized, in his own handwriting, the poem he'd once read to her. She read through it silently, and her eyes fixed on the last stanza.

> 'The mines of earth no treasures give
> That could this volume buy;
> In teaching me the way to live,
> It taught me how to die.'

"You didn't know how true that was, Mr. Medley," she said as she refolded the paper and placed it back in the book. Nate had already left her side and was limping back to the wagon.

"So, you fired a good foreman," he began as they sat together on the wagon seat, "the next best one is dead, and you killed the best horse I ever had." She cast her eyes downward, till he reached over and tickled her ear. "I'm just teasing you." She wasn't amused, and he gave up trying to make her smile. "So what do we do now?"

"Well, Sheriff Blaine said—"

"Please don't call him that."

"Joshua said that there were several other soldiers wanting to leave the cavalry. They know about horses. Maybe they could apply for the foreman job."

"Oh, that's very funny." He took a swig of whiskey from the bottle he still kept close to him, then caught her smiling at him.

She leaned in close. "I got you back, didn't I?

"Yes, you did." Her smile alone, the first he'd seen in weeks, did wonders for him.

"Well, the best foreman I ever knew is sitting right here on the wagon. And I got you a new horse."

"You did?"

"Yeah, a big sorrel with three white socks and a white blaze on his forehead. Elijah trained him, did a wonderful job. He's all ready for work."

"Well, I wanna go see 'im." He slapped the reins against the horses' flanks, and the wagon rolled on.

As they reached the road to the Broken Bow, Tara took the reins from him and, with no explanation, turned the horses slightly north from their path. It wasn't long before Nate knew where she was taking them, and his mood darkened as they drew near. She halted the wagon and climbed down. He followed her and found a large, sawed-off tree stump on which to sit with his crutch propped up next to him. She laid the baby in a basket in the grass and helped Buck down, who bolted across the field to play. She was obviously planning to stay awhile.

He watched her stroll around the imprint of the old Sinclair mansion house. The burned remains had long since been cleared away, but the foundation pit, now overgrown with grass, was visible, and a keen eye could still pick out charred bits of wood, tiny shards of china, or even a half-buried, intact glass bottle. But he knew as sure as night follows day that, in her mind's eye, she was seeing it as it used to be, when her aunt and uncle lived comfortably in it, enjoyed views of this countryside from tall, paned windows, and even had a maid to clean them. Furnished with velvet draperies, a European tapestry, fine plush furniture, and an organ, it had been a showcase of big-city luxury unequaled anywhere on the frontier, until that night. A night of bloody terror and destruction, and when the day dawned, everything of beauty had been reduced to smoldering wreckage.

Now, by bringing him here, she had forced him to remember too. Without even speaking Gray Wolf's name, she had thrown the brave in his face once again. That wasn't all that bothered him. Unbeknownst to her, he had watched her face at Elijah's grave when she read the poem. He resented the poem and the book and the fact that he knew nothing of what it was all about. She had confirmed at the Indian camp that Elijah had never laid a finger on her, and he believed her without question. But he knew that they had had conversations with each other, and not about ranch work. And now he was jealous of a dead man who over the past year had always been there for her, while he had not.

"I know why you came here," he muttered.

"Do you?"

He was certain she was trifling with him. She had stayed by his side and helped him recover, probably from a sense of duty, lifted his spirits about the new sorrel horse, complimented his ability as a foreman, but now she was ready to state what she really felt, and she had picked an appropriate location to stick the knife in his heart.

"I wanted to come here to see how I'd feel," she said.

Whatever she felt, he was determined to fight for his place in her heart. "Tara, there's something I've wanted to tell you ever since you left the Dearborn."

"Shh, don't say anything."

He held his breath while she approached him and looked him in the eye. "You told me in the Indian camp to just forget Gray Wolf. I can never forget him, Nate. I hate him." She looked away briefly, trying to think of the words to say. "But how much harder it must've been for you to be around him for so long and keep yourself from doing anything to him. I can't imagine that kind of restraint. You were the last person to see my aunt and uncle alive, and I know that weighs heavily on you. But I understand why you didn't turn Gray Wolf in. I still don't like it, and I hope I never have to lay eyes on him again. But I understand, and it's all right. Gray Wolf was never a threat to our family like Beartooth was. If he was, you'd have given him the same you gave Beartooth."

Nate sat speechless for a moment, allowing his tension to dissipate. "You're a good woman," he said finally, struggling to keep his voice even. "I've always asked so much of you. But I hope you know I would enter the gates of hell for you."

"You already have. And I never gave anything that I wasn't willing to give." She moved closer, sat on his lap, and put her arms around him, caressing his cheek and hair. "I do so love you, Nate Hunter," she whispered close to his ear. "And I have always loved only you."

He drew in an astonished breath. Tears filled his eyes, and he could not stop them. He clasped his arms around her and buried his face against her neck. Suddenly nothing else mattered. The past year seemed but a short time. He was home, and she was safe and in his arms. She laid a hand aside of his cheek, turned his face toward hers, and they kissed, again and again. He tried to speak and tell her what this meant but couldn't get any words out. But she embraced him tighter. She knew.

Chapter 32

Nate casually rode into Fort Mason on a sunny, hot August day. The place was, as usual this time of year, abuzz with activity with wagons and riders coming and going in a steady stream. Unlike his entrance with the Cheyenne a couple of months previously that garnered so much cautious attention, this time he created no stir at all. He was just one of the crowd; no one looked twice at him. He found it all amusing. He was the same law-abiding person he'd been then. All that had changed was other people's perception of him.

Colonel McHenry had requested an appointment with him, and he was eager for it. He entered the colonel's office with a slight limp, the only visible evidence of his recent ordeal in the mountains.

"Mr. Hunter?" McHenry began, reaching to shake Nate's hand. "I heard you had some trouble a while back. I'm very sorry. You're healing up fine, I trust?"

"Yes, I am. Thank you." The colonel's concern didn't sound very sincere, but Nate didn't care. In just a couple of minutes, he'd have McHenry under his thumb, giving him whatever he wanted. He took a seat, put on a sufficiently curious expression, and waited. He wouldn't have to wait long; he knew there wouldn't be any small talk.

"I wanted to speak with you about renewing the beef contract with the Broken Bow."

"Oh, I see," replied Nate slowly, seeming a little surprised. "Well, there's no contract to renew. I guess you mean writing a new one."

"Sure, whatever you want to call it," agreed the colonel. He didn't want to spend any more time with Nate than he absolutely had to.

"Actually my wife handles all of the business. She's outside. Let me go and get her to come in." He started to rise.

McHenry hurriedly held up a hand. "No, no, we...uh, would prefer to deal with you." He nervously waited till Nate was settled back down. "You see, Ward Taylor's operation just isn't big enough to supply our needs...especially since the Broken Bow cut off sales to him."

Nate grinned. That had been Tara's doing. *Starve the source and the cavalry will come crawling back.* She'd taken a chance, but it worked. He withdrew a paper from his pocket. "Let me refer to my price list here. You know, I have to have this written down or I can't remember it." It was not a price list. It was a list of instructions written by Tara, who waited back at the ranch, for just this occasion. Knowing the cavalry wouldn't meet with her, she had outlined for Nate every bargaining point, complete with advice on dealing with a colonel who considered it beneath him to negotiate beef contracts. He loved her for it. Refolding the paper, he looked up. "It looks like our prices have gone up a bit since the last contract." He shrugged his shoulders. "That's to be expected, you know. It's happening everywhere these days."

"Of course, I understand. You have more employees now. You have to pay them." He was hating this meeting.

"If the first contract was still in effect, you could've locked in those prices for another year, and then—"

"What's your price, Mr. Hunter?"

Nate smiled. He was in charge of this meeting now.

And a short meeting it was. McHenry agreed to all of the bargaining points with little negotiation, and then called for his orderly of the day to come in and write out the contract. The man entered the office and smiled at Nate.

"You remember me?"

Nate indeed recognized the dark-haired sergeant from the day of the ambush. "Sergeant Van Deen, just the man who wants to see me."

"How is Major Blaine keeping?"

"Oh, Josh is fine. Staying busy."

Although clearly in the dark about this exchange, McHenry smiled politely. They commenced with the writing of the contract and signed it with Van Deen as a witness. Then McHenry stood, unlocked a drawer behind his desk, retrieved the cash box, and unlocked it. "In accordance with the contract, here is your good faith money, one hundred dollars." He began counting out bills.

"What about the reward money for Beartooth?" asked Nate. "Two hundred and fifty dollars."

"Of course." He begrudgingly counted out more bills.

"Colonel, I want you to know I've forgiven you. I'm even warming up to the cavalry. Where else could I get paid for going after the man who was recently paid to come after me?"

McHenry stopped counting and looked up. "Has anyone ever told you how taxing you are, Mr. Hunter?"

"Oh, yes, absolutely." But at least hc got McHenry to return his smile. Nate glanced down at the stack of bills and chanced a peek into the cash box as well. He noticed a couple of bills stamped with the name, First Bank of Timber Fork. "I see you do business with my brother-in-laws' bank."

"Yes, that's a fine institution Ward Taylor runs there."

"I also meant my other brother-in-law, Jared Sinclair."

McHenry recognized Nate's attempt to ruffle him. He ignored it but lost count and had to start over again.

Nate remained quiet this time, but he could see out of the corner of his eye Van Deen eagerly eyeing the money. When he accepted the cash, the most he'd ever held in his hand at once, he immediately handed it to Van Deen.

"Thank you!" exclaimed Van Deen as he grabbed it.

"You're welcome. And thank you, Colonel. Nice doing business with—"

"Just…one…minute. What the hell is going on here?"

"Just a small debt I owed him."

"Small debt! That's three hundred and fifty dollars!"

Nate looked at the money and back at Van Deen. "He's right. That's a lot of money." He pointed his finger in Van Deen's face. "Spend it wisely." Almost to the door with the contract in his hand, he stopped and turned around. "Oh, and I would count it again if I were you, make sure it's...whatever amount he said it was."

McHenry watched him leave and waited till the door was shut. "How I dislike that man."

Van Deen smiled broadly as he flipped through the bills with his thumb. "Not me."

***

Tara was happy to greet Nate when he walked into the house, until she saw his slumped look of defeat. "What's the matter? What happened?"

"I didn't bring back any money," he replied, "just this."

She impatiently grabbed the paper he held out to her, unfolded it, and started to read. The top line and the numbers were all she needed to see. With a wild shriek, she jumped into his arms. Still unsteady on his right leg, he toppled and fell backwards into the marble-topped parlor table, sending the fragile lamp tumbling to the floor where it shattered with a deafening crash. They both sat on the floor in stunned silence, hearts pounding, as they looked over pieces of glass scattered for several feet and the spreading puddle of kerosene on the wine and tan rug, thankful that it had not been lit.

"*You* broke the lamp," Nate said calmly. "I thought Bucky would be the one to do that. And so much for the rug."

Her elated smile returned. "We can buy another lamp, one for every room."

"And some spares for when you break those."

Chapter 33
Missouri River, Montana Territory
Summer, 1873

Nate walked with Chief Red Feather beside the great river for what he expected would be the last time. He'd gotten word from other Indians that, after prolonged fighting in Nebraska, Red Feather had agreed to present himself at an army post there to surrender the fought-over land and negotiate a new treaty, in exchange for avoiding arrest. The chief, with a few braves accompanying him for protection, had traveled north just to visit with Nate one more time. Nate had met him halfway, on the banks of the Missouri.

He would've traveled farther to meet with the wise and honorable chief with whom he'd developed a strong rapport. Red Feather would probably stay with most of his people in Nebraska, and this farewell was important to Nate. So much so that he'd brought five-year-old Buck with him. He wanted the boy to see and remember the chief of his ancestors' band, to have that lasting connection to carry with him over the years and to describe to his little brother Jack. "Watch him, listen to everything he says, and remember it," he'd told Buck on their trip, "even if you don't understand it. Someday you will know why I wanted you to do that."

Now as they walked with the chief beside the same river Nate had crossed with him two years before, on a summer day that looked much like this one, it was Nate who felt he had something to say. "I never really properly thanked you for taking in my family when they were sick, and for all of the help and protection you gave me during my trouble with the soldiers, and now I hardly know how. The time is so short."

"You do not need to speak what I already know. I am sad, for your sake, that Beartooth's heart was bad and caused the trouble." He stopped and beheld Nate with a gleam in his eye. "But if you should ever need the help of the Council of Forty-Four, you will be able to find me."

Nate's eyes widened, and he slowly broke into a smile. "You? You are on the Council of Forty-Four?"

"The fight that I led against the soldiers in Nebraska earned my place on that Council." He resumed walking. "So as I have risen among the people, the soldiers looked for me, to punish me. The same as what happened to you, Eagle Shadow." He favored Nate with a rare smile. "I may need to ask you for your advice."

"And I would gladly give it, but I doubt I could say anything you don't already know."

They came to a fallen tree trunk by the river and sat down on it with Buck in between them. A quiet ensued that lasted for a long while. No one felt inclined to speak. Even Buck sensed the solemnity of the occasion and remained still. The muddy waters flowed serenely by them. The land on either side of the river spread to the horizon under a cloudless blue sky. It was so big, yet not big enough.

"I have chosen a life apart from the people," said Nate at last, "and it's a good life. But I exclude myself from your problems and do not suffer with you. I'm sure you think me unfair."

"I do not," the chief countered. "You are the light for our people in this land. As long as Eagle Shadow and his children dwell in this land, some of the spirit of our people will remain here."

"And you? Do you know where you will go?"

"We will seek a place where we will hunt, dance our sacred dances, keep the stories alive for our children, and where no one will burn our tepees."

Nate grinned sheepishly. Red Feather still could not pass up an opportunity to chide him about that episode.

The chief laid a hand on Buck's knee. "Has your father told you the story of the burning tepee?"

Buck giggled while Nate looked awkwardly in the other direction. It had made a good bedtime story more than once.

"And has he told you about a warrior named Gray Wolf?"

Buck shook his head, and Red Feather rose and gave Nate a piercing gaze. "Tell your children, Eagle Shadow. They share his blood."

"They don't share anything else with him."

"Ah, but I think you are wrong. They share with him a love of his people and a strong loyalty to family. You never had the chance to know those things about him."

It was the one thing on which Nate couldn't see eye to eye with Red Feather. His children also shared blood with those Gray Wolf had killed. But he thought it polite to ask anyway. "What do you know of Gray Wolf now?"

The chief looked at him intently and gave a slight nod, as if he'd been waiting for Nate to ask. "I have been told by other chiefs on the Council that he escaped from an army jail in Nebraska in the last moon. He was seen going northward. He was injured in the escape, but you know that Gray Wolf is strong." He smiled proudly. "I expect they're still looking for him yet."

Why, oh, why, wondered Nate, did he have the uneasy feeling that Gray Wolf was coming to Montana to find him? Why else would he have headed north? There was no other reason that made sense. Somehow Nate just knew. Maybe it was in the blood they unfortunately shared.

"May Heammawihio go with you and protect you," said Red Feather, extending his right hand.

Nate stood, and they grasped each other firmly by the wrists. "And you." He lingered with Buck for a while, watching the chief walk away, regal and proud, on his way to try to reclaim what he could of his old life.

Epilogue

Nate and Buck topped the last rise before riding onto Broken Bow ground. It had been Buck's longest trip on his very own horse, and he'd handled it well and did Nate proud. Now they were both excited for the homecoming that awaited them.

"You go on ahead and see your mother," said Nate. "I'll be along behind you." He smiled as Buck galloped ahead, already an accomplished horseman. Nate wanted to enjoy the anticipation of the reunion just a few minutes longer.

You are the light for our people in this land. The poignancy of the chief's words called for private contemplation. He had come a long way to receive such a compliment from the great chief, but it was a responsibility he was glad to bear. He often spoke to Buck and Jack only in Cheyenne for an entire day, as his own father had done to him since before he could remember. Once when Buck complained to his mother about it, she assured him that it was part of being a Hunter, and he'd best get used to it. He did, and he was catching on to the language pretty quickly now.

Nate thought about the rising generation around Timber Fork and was confident that, given room to grow and rest from Indian wars, they'd turn out just fine. Jared was remarried, to Becca's younger sister Virginia, and their son John Edward had been born nine months later to the day. Ward and Lena had twin daughters, Laura and Lydia. Ward often joked about not having any sons to work the ranch, but judging from the tomboy demeanor developing in all three of his daughters, that wasn't likely to be a problem.

Tara's sister Rachel was now living on a ranch some sixty miles distant, married to their foreman, none other than Clay Tatum. Tara had hit the roof when she'd learned of the relationship that they'd kept a secret for months. Nate thought it was because Clay was not in her social class, and he reminded her of how they themselves got started.

"It's not that," she assured him.

"So, it's all Clay's women then? You don't think he can settle down?"

"No, although that *is* a concern."

He waited for an explanation, and when none was forthcoming, he queried, "What is it then?"

"It's because I once fired Clay, and now I'll have to see him at family gatherings."

Nate laughed so hard he almost spit his coffee. "I can't imagine you losing any sleep over that. You used to try to get me fired, and you see me at family gatherings." That drew a smile from her, and, ever gracious, at the very first opportunity that afforded itself, she had sought Clay out and made her peace with him. For his part,

Clay, thoroughly enamored with her sister, was most obliging.

Jared worried that Clay was only attracted to Rachel's money. Nate had been perfectly willing to go teach his former foreman a thing or two with his fists if that were the case, but Jared insisted he had a better way. He produced a document in which Clay refused all legal access to Rachel's money. When Clay stumbled all over himself in his rush to sign it, Jared, satisfied that Clay had passed the test, ripped the document to shreds and gave his permission for Rachel to marry.

Now the couple was negotiating to buy the ranch on which he worked. Nate waited patiently to see how that would go, because if they got the ranch, he was planning to approach them about forming a conglomerate. He knew Tara and Rachel would agree, and Clay would fall in with whatever the others decided. Of course, this meant the Split Timber would probably have to join up too, to prevent going out of business. If he could get Ward to take himself out of the ranching end and concentrate on his bank, it just might work. The ranches and bank could mutually benefit each other. And it would ensure the future of beef contracts with the cavalry. They would have to buy from the partnership, he mused, or else pick up Fort Mason and move it clean out of the Territory. He might be called a cattle baron. Cattle barons hated that term. But Nate wasn't going to quibble over a couple of words. He'd been called worse. Snapping out of his reverie, he realized he was getting far ahead of himself. *Patience...patience....*

Then there were the Blaines, a class unto themselves. Tara and Julie's friendship withstood all, but Joshua could be a pain. When he'd learned that Nate was going to meet with Red Feather, he remarked about how glad Nate must be that the chief would be long gone, and that would help Nate stay out of trouble. In the past, Nate would've wanted to punch him, but having Blaine in such close proximity for the past year, he was getting used to his dumb statements.

Blaine had offered to deputize Nate to be in charge of cattle rustling activities, so he could legally shoot at the thieves. Nate flatly refused, saying he'd sooner eat buffalo testicles than work under Blaine. Then Nate told the usual crowd gathered in the store about it, and they laughed so hard the sheriff left in embarrassment. He never did anything Josh Blaine suggested, no matter how much sense it made. Indeed, he had found enjoyable ways to aggravate Blaine without ever being outside the law, so the good sheriff never had reason to bother with him. Then again, there was that little incident the summer before in which Nate and several hands had been involved in a shootout that left two pesky cattle rustlers dead on Broken Bow ground. But Nate had made darn sure Josh Blaine never found out about it. The Broken Bow hands were trustworthy. They knew what running a top ranch entailed; Blaine didn't.

Nate was within sight of the house now, and there was Buck leading Tara by the hand as they walked to meet him, with Jack toddling along behind. But it was the child in Tara's arms that Nate was eager to hold. Their daughter Catherine was just a few months old, but he already knew she was going to be just like her mother. She had the bluest eyes he'd ever seen and had been the princess of the family ever since she was born. Nate doted on her like there was no tomorrow. Lena, with her vast experience with daughters, had warned him of the dangers of spoiling her, but Nate never listened. What Catherine wanted, Catherine was going to get.

"Will you be staying a while this time?" asked Tara with a smile.

"Don't get saucy," he laughed, dismounting, taking her into his arms, and kissing her hard.

www.ingramcontent.com/pod-product-compliance
Lightning Source LLC
Chambersburg PA
CBHW030825310726
48980CB00006B/635/J

* 9 7 8 0 9 8 2 1 7 6 6 0 3 *